The Overman

Michael Morton

The Overman

First Edition (2022)

Copyright © Michael Morton

ISBN: 9798365802841

Cover photo Parkside Colliery – provided by kind permission of Geoff Simm

Legal Disclaimer

The book is from start to finish entirely a work of my imagination. Although it refers to the National Coal Board, British Coal, Cronton Colliery, and Parkside Colliery. It's to provide context only. All the characters and their actions in the story are entirely fiction. Any resemblance to real persons, living or dead, is purely coincidental.

Acknowledgements

I received numerous comments and plans from people associated with Parkside. I'd like to thank Geoff Simm, Lee Reynolds, Terry Reynolds, Ken Thompson, Malcolm Chattwood, Mark Worthington, Peter Davies, Dave Brownsword and as always, my wife Irene, an inspiration and support in my writings.

Other books by Michael Morton:

<u>Coal Mining</u>
Shafted
The Undermanager

<u>Aviation</u>
Time To Move On
Flymeawaybabe.com

<u>Romance</u>
Love Is In The Air

<u>Children</u>
Message In A Bottle

Available at:

https://www.amazon.com/author/michaelmorton

Andrew & Janine

Contents

1984

1. A Time of Uncertainty

It was my final year at North Staffordshire Polytechnic. Hopefully passing my exams and getting back to what I loved best. I was a Deputy at Cronton Colliery. I'd been there nine years. Straight from school as a sixteen years old. Cronton was a family pit producing around a quarter of a million tonnes per year. With a workforce of nearly five hundred and sixty men. Known reserves of some twenty-five years were concentrated in three seams. London Delph, Ince Six Feet and Higher Florida. Production was currently from L8's in the London Delph with several faces blocked out already. We'd been the first pit in the country to adopt the retreat method of mining. Operating with one face had occasionally lead to a gap in production. This year being no exception. There were two main developments. The Main South Intake, MSI now back in coal but had been stood for the last fifteen months. The men having been redeployed on outbye work. The Main South Return, MSR, still on drill and fire was only occasionally being worked, again due to the shortage of manpower. This year we were heading for a loss of nearly three million pounds. Culminating last year with us being placed in the Colliery Review Procedure. Morale was low but the ability to take the piss was still at an all-time high.

There were changes at the top of the Coal Board too. A new Chairman had been appointed. He'd been Chairman at British Steel. Some of my colleagues raised concerns at what he'd done there. Closing plants and reducing the workforce. The NUM National Executive had concerns too. Not just with the new Chairman. The major concern was with the Government and their plans for the industry. They conducted two national ballots over the last two years for strike action. One in October 1982 and the other in February 1983. Neither got the necessary percentage in favour to carry the mandate through. This was followed by a vote at the NUM Delegate Conference for an overtime ban in protest to the Coal Board's offer of a five point two per centage pay rise.

The effect of this meant we couldn't carry out weekend work particularly on the outbye belt system. Nor make up any shortfall in the production targets. Already operating with manpower below budget was the reason for little if any progress in the developments. We had a new Manager, Ron Groves. I got on well with him although he could be a moody fucker. His Deputy Bob Stevens had recently left for Bold Colliery working for our ex-Manager. I don't think the relationship was good. Rumour had it he was about to join the Mines

Inspectorate. Although at college I was still required to cover off overtime and carry out our underground safety inspections.

□

I wasn't due to be in work until two o'clock Sunday afternoon. Unusually I'd been given the two ten shift in the Control Room. Checking the roster on Friday confirmed I was taking Shaun Galway off. Shaun was NACODS Branch President. A young lad for his position but very knowledgeable. He'd attended the Colliery Review in July the previous year. A follow up meeting was planned later this month. Something called the National Appeal Hearing. I was keen to get his view on expectations.

I turned into the pits entrance off Foxes Bank Lane. It was a crisp cold afternoon. The trees devoid of their leaves at this time of the year allowed the sun to shine through. Blinding me momentarily I lowered the sun visor. I reflected on the old guy they'd found dead last summer in the undergrowth adjoining the road. He was one of the coal prep lads. Arriving each day on his push bike. The coroner had confirmed he'd had a heart attack coming into work. Leaving the road, the bike had travelled a short distance before crashing to the ground. Completely obscured from the road it was a further two weeks before the alarm had been raised. The guy lived alone in a flat in Ditton.

I followed the road around to the left. Passing the training office and baths. I parked up outside Control. Shaun obviously not expecting to see anyone jumped up from his seat. I waved back. Climbing out of the car I looked across to the recently ploughed farmers field. Something I wouldn't do later in the year after the farmer had spread the cow shit. We never lingered once the farmer had done his bit. I grabbed my snap box and continued forward.
"Fuckin ell Mick. Argument with the missus fella. You're a tad early." I laughed.
"Yeah, she wasn't particularly happy me leavin at this time. Anyway, how's it going?"
"Pretty steady. The lads have reported shunts at pit bottom are full. Last count another twenty chocks to come out first thing tomorrow. Belts will want running last thing. Try to empty number three bunker ready for a start tomorrow."
"Why what's in number one?"
"Only half full."
"Strata bunker?"
"Empty. Make sure you get one of the lads on their rounds to empty the Braithwaite at 45's. Harry's had to change the suction hose. Looking at the

roster you've only got four Deps." I jotted Shaun's comments down as he spoke.

"Someone needs to check the MSI. Build-up of gas in the GB. I think that's it."

"I believe you're all off to the National Appeal Hearing, Hobart House next week?"

"Yeah, gang of us."

"What are our chances?"

"Fuckin ell Mick I think that's obvious." He stopped to reflect how much to say. "The chocks we're salvaging off L6's should be for L9's."

"I thought they were going back down after they'd been refurbished."

"Don't believe it for one minute. Could be done underground whilst we're still coaling on L8's."

"Doesn't sound good then?"

"Doesn't sound good? While you've been living it up at college, Area sent a geologist onto L8's to look at a so-called upthrow fault. Eight fuckin inches in a seam of three metres."

"For fucks sake."

"If you want my opinion, there's the bigger picture. The Government were forced into an embarrassing "U" turn in 1981. She's just been biding time. Coal stocks are running at an all-time high at both the pits and power stations. Anyone with a modicum of sense can see what's coming. Beat the miners and industrial relations would change forever in the UK."

"A national strike! Just can't see it."

"Wait and see young man. Listen Mick if you don't mind could do with getting a way bit early meself. Let's catch up again next week.

☐

The following Sunday I was on a seven till one. We'd just arrived at pit bottom. Having checked the roster earlier I knew Shaun would be taking us off. The cage had just arrived. Afternoon shift disembarked. The lads with me exchanging places. I waited. Shaun was last out.

"How did it go then?"

"Bloody ell Mick how long have you got. Tell you what though. I'd love to see how much it costs to run the place."

"Where you on about?"

"Hobart House no wonder we're losing money. What with our Anderton House and Staffordshire House. Bet every other area has headquarters too. Plus, the number of staff. One of the biggest meetings I'd ever been to. There were eleven guys from the Coal Board, including Director and Deputy Director for the Western Area. Union officials from NACODS, NUM, local and national."

"What about from here?"

"Me, Keith, Frank, Norman, Platty and Roach. You won't know him. He's our President based at Parkside. NUM, Johnny, Brian, and Keith's brother Alan."

"You coming Mick or not?" One of the dayshift Deputies shouted.

"You lads carry on. I'll catch you up. Give us a mo Shaun." I walked across to signal the Winder. Waiting momentarily until the cage disappeared. I walked back to Shaun.

"Who said what?"

"After introductions NUM President gave an overview on the pit and its history. He got in the fact that the Area Director at the time of the national ballots in 1982 and 1983 indicated there were no plans to close any pit in the North Western Area. A few weeks after the 1983 ballot future of Cronton was at risk. Talked about the reserves in the three seams. On the Western side mentioned we had hundred years of reserves. Talked about opening a Cronton No 2 tuther side of fault. Talked about a production gap this year. Mentioned the current unemployment stats nationally and locally. Pit heading for a loss of two to three million this year. Don't think the Coal Board guys were too pleased when we mentioned the lack of investment. Particularly on the outbye belt system."

"Yeah, heard that said last week. We've got something like seventeen belts from coal face to the number one bunker."

"We mentioned that too plus the fact we're running short of budgeted staff numbers. Thirty to be exact. Resulting in not keeping the developments manned up."

"Yeah, must be fourteen or fifteen months since the Main South Intake was last worked."

"Told them that too. Plus, the cost of having plant pool items on stand. L6's chocks, the two Dosco Roaders and Dintheader. Must be costing us an arm and a leg. Just kept coming back with how hard we were all working but the geological conditions hindered progress." I shook my head. Gerry's update did not bode well for the pits future.

"How many times have we heard that excuse."

"Even said if the same attention had been paid to us as it is up at Selby, we'd be in a very different position by now." Shaun laughed at his own comment. "Never heard Cronton compared to Selby."

"What did the NACODS Secretary have to say?"

"Pretty much covered the same points as the NUM. His biggest concern was the Coal Board not following due process. Their failure to follow the Colliery

Review Procedure. Suggested it had lost all credibility. Remember that surface borehole to the south of the workings?"

"Yeah."

"It proved at least six workable seams."

"How would you rate our chances then?"

"Fuckin ell Mick. You're putting me on the spot there lad." I passed Shaun my tin of snuff. "Thanks. It was a good meeting. We couldn't have put the case over to keep us open any better. However, the one thing that worries me was the comment about coal stocks. By the end of last year mentioned there was over sixty million tonnes."

"For fucks sake!"

"Hello Shaun. Hello Shaun Galway. You getting on this rider or what?" One of the Deputies he'd descended the shaft with shouted. He turned and waved his cap lamp towards where they were sat. They waved back. He passed the snuff back.

"I best get gone or it'll be a walk-in."

"Yeah, just one more thing. How long before we find out?"

"End of next month. I'd expect the worst."

□

The news Cronton Colliery was to close came as no surprise. However, it was not something I'd planned for. I was disappointed too. It was a first for me; particularly knowing the amount of reserves still accessible and the panels of coal already developed. I guessed the new Chairman and the rest of the Coal Board knew what they were doing.

"What are we going to do? And we've got our second child on the way." My wife asked after I gave her the news. I was working from home today on my final year project for my degree at North Staffordshire Polytechnic. *Like I've got a fuckin clue!*

"Oh, don't worry it'll be fine. There's plenty of other local pits I could transfer to."

"All this studying and this is what it comes to. It's an absolute disgrace. What's the country coming to? Four and a half million people on the dole. What's the name of the pit just a little further down the M62 motorway?"

"Sutton Manor."

"Yeah, that's the place. It would be good if you could get in there."

"We'll see. At least there's several alternatives. Coal Board have been clear there'd be no compulsory redundancies. Love if you don't mind, I need to get on with this." I offered pointing to the paper work our son, Jamie had started to write on.

"Sorry, I'll get out your hair. I'll see you later. I plan to do a bit of shopping in Old Swan. Anything you need?"

"No, I'm good thanks."

"Come on you sonny Jim, you're coming with me." Before Jamie could offer any resistance, he was whisked up and out of the room.

It was now becoming a reality. One of the lecturer's at the Poly had attended a paper in London given by the Coal Board's Industrial Relations Director, the previous month. The paper was a review of the 1974 Plan for Coal. The market for coal had reduced from that envisaged in 1974. He was suggesting the industry would have to lose three to four million tonnes of old production. They were still talking about modernising the industry. Including new pits, investment in those existing and the latest newest equipment. Particularly around the use of heavy-duty coal faces. By the end of last year, a further seventeen million tonnes of new annual capacity had been created with more on the way. Some five and a half billion pounds of investment. This in turn would see closure of those pits not financially viable. Cronton Colliery was obviously one of them. There would be others I had no doubt. Latest estimates suggested the consumption of UK coal was expected to be one hundred and four million tonnes of which seven million would be exported. Coal stocks too, were running at record levels.

I would need to take this into account when choosing the next pit. Sutton Manor was the closest. There was also Golborne, Parsonage, Bold, Bickershaw and Parkside. If I were going to get on in the industry, the decision I took would need some thought. What I did know from conversation with members of senior management. You had to be prepared to move and that meant anywhere. Something I was not going to mention to the missus just yet. I had enough shit going on now.

Three days later now back at college the Coal Board announced the closure of Cortonwood in South Yorkshire. Not that this meant much to us. We were far too busy preparing for our final year exams. Within hours the Yorkshire NUM had announced strike action.

☐

Friday was always something to look forward to. I'd meet my wife at her parents' house for tea. The usual one-eyed stew was cooked for us. It consisted of bacon ribs, boiled potato, and cabbage. Plus, a jar of homemade pickle onion slices. My mother-in-law always commented that "the ribs had been left to soak overnight." She was never one for grease on her food.

We sat down at the table. Her parents waited on.

"What's the latest at work?" Annie's Dad asked.

"You heard then?"

"Bin on radio Merseyside today. Production stopped as of today."

"Yeah, believe so. Still plenty goin on though."

"Do you ever worry about your job?"

"How do you mean?"

"The future, you and Annie one child and another on the way."

"No. Blimey they'll always want coal. I'll be here till I retire." My last comment caused my wife to add.

"Yeah, Mick reckons there's over three hundred years of coal reserves in the country."

"I hope you're right. Some of the papers reckon you could be in for industrial action. Seem to think Thatcher will be ready this time." Her dad's comment caused me to nod in agreement. The newspaper headlines back in 1981 citing Maggie's first U turn when the possibility of the miners taking strike action loomed.

"Yeah, I remember...Jamie!" Our conversation suddenly interrupted as our son threw his spoon at the wall.

"Looks like he wants more stew!"

Returning to Poly the following week we watched with interest the goings on between the Coal Board and NUM. On the Tuesday there was a meeting between both parties. We later heard the Chairman confirmed to the NUM a further twenty pits were to close. This seemed to ignite the fuse. The Scottish NUM announced a strike from 12th March. We had assumed the strike action would affect us too. Each of us making calls back to our union officials at the pit. I don't think it was something they had considered. However as most of us were in the National Association of Colliery Overmen, Deputies and Shotfirers, NACODS, we were told to continue as we were. Cronton, it seemed had been given a dispensation from the strike, because the closure had been announced before the strike was called. Production had ceased the day after the Cortonwood announcement. We would continue to salvage the chocks off L6's. These were off to another local pit.

The following weekend I was on shift in the control room. Being on earlies I took the chance to go and look for any NUM officials. I made my way to their office. I'd been in many times as I'd been a member of the NUM before becoming an official. I was in luck. My old mentor Tommy Hanley the Cronton Branch President was clearing out some paperwork. Tommy had been our supervisor during my time as a mining craft apprentice. I was hoping to get some clarity on what the fuck was going on. I smiled as I walked in, still hanging from the back wall behind the Secretary's desk was the red USSR flag.

12

Emblazoned in the top left-hand corner was a gold hammer crossed with a gold sickle, beneath which a gold boarded red star.

"Tommy me old mucker. How are you?"

"Fuckin ell Mick la you scared the shit out of me." Tommy hadn't seen me enter the one roomed office. Even with his thick lensed glasses he couldn't see that well.

"Oops sorry." I laughed. "I hope you've not come to nick Johnny's red flag. I heard he got that off Brezhnev?"

"Fuck off Mick, can't you see I'm busy." I don't think Tommy was comfortable being at the pit during a weekend.

"Sorry mate. I'm just trying to understand what is going on. I'm unsure how there can be a national strike if there's been no ballot."

"Don't need one. You not read the NUM Constitution?"

"Nothing in the rules of the Cronton Branch." My comment caused Tommy to shake his head.

"You won't find it in there la. Under Rule 43 a national strike can only be called if the union have a national ballot and a majority of fifty-five per cent vote in favour."

"Exactly my point."

"Fuckin ell Mick can ye keep your fuckin gob shut while I try to answer the fuckin question." That was me told then. "Under Rule 41 official sanction can be given to a strike declared by individual areas."

"I still don't get it. There's no guarantee individual areas will vote for a strike."

"Flying pickets."

"Flying pickets?"

"Yep, the very same. Used to great effect in the '72 strike. You won't remember that. Probably still walking round in your shitty nappies." Tommy grabbed a folder from the drawer. He now seemed more relaxed. Obviously found what he was looking for. "Now Mick do us a favour and fuck off I've got work to do."

By the start of the following week roughly half the pits were still in work. However, by the end of the day there was over one hundred now out. The Lancashire NUM had called for a vote on what action should be taken this was now delayed. A vote had been called for by Nottinghamshire and Derbyshire too.

For fucks sake I thought we were exempt! We'd finished early at the Poly so on the way home I'd decided to pop into work and hand my expense form in. Ahead of me on the pit drive were half a dozen guys. I didn't recognise any of

13

them. They'd all been sat on the side of the road. Seeing me approach had caused them all to stand and block the width of the road. Some big blond fucker, with a matching Mexican moustache, he was the leader stood in the middle. He was holding the wooden shaft of a seven-pound hammer. Bouncing it on the road surface. He held a hand up as I reached the line. Being sat in my car, a Mini put me at a disadvantage. I decided to get out. Blondy was still a big fella though. I was six foot he must have been six and a half.

"Ow do, shagga. Official NUM picket line mister. You're not allowed to cross." Now this could go one of two ways, I was certain not in my favour.
"We're exempt, dispensation I believe." I responded climbing out of the car.
"No exceptions shag. One out all out!"
"And I'm a member of NACODS."
"No exceptions tha'nos."
"I'll think you'll find there is." My last comment caused them all to move closer. I was later to find out that one of my colleagues at this point had turned round and gone home. Something I wasn't planning to do. And there was a question I wanted answering. I'd asked several of my union officials previously and never received a satisfactory answer.
"How come no one called for strike action when they closed us?"
"Does it chuffin matter?"
"Does to me."

One of his mates wearing a denim jacket displaying a number of badges *Coal Not Dole* stepped forward.
"Told this was a waste of fuckin time. Should have gone to that other place up road. Parkgate war it?"
"Parkside ye daft apeth. And no, we wasn't. Delegate said summat bout enough lads got that covered from South Wales. Sutton Manor was place meant to be tha'nos. Which I fuckin well told thee when we passed exit." The lads momentarily seemed unsure of their next step. I'd been forgotten. Watching as a bystander as events unfolded.
"Come on then. What waiting for. Let's fuck off. Place stinks of shit anyway."
"Hey shag is there a pig farm nearby?"
"Yeah, across the way there." I answered. And that was it. The lads moved off to where a couple of cars were parked. Climbing back into the car I drove off to the pit yard.

The next few weeks at Poly I watched as the strike began to spread. It was the main topic of discussion each lunch time with the lads on the HND course. The same group I'd completed my HNC with. The strike was headline news each night and given front page coverage in the tabloids. The news presented each

14

night provided conflicting stories. Nottinghamshire announced the results of a ballot. Seventy-three per cent voted against striking. This was followed by area ballots in the Midlands, the North West, and North East. Of the seventy thousand miners balloted fifty thousand voted against strike action.

South Wales miners had initially been reluctant to join Yorkshire due to a fall out the previous year. Latest reports suggested twenty-nine pits were working normal.

▢

By the end of the month, it was time to return to college. Catching up on the odd lecture and working from home revising for the forthcoming exams. I'd been given the heads up that the Deputy Manager from Parkside would be visiting Cronton on Wednesday. Even though I'd decided to transfer there it was a chance to get a little more detail on the set up. There's was only three of us going to Parkside. Most of the officials were off to Sutton Manor. Still close to home, our ex-Deputy Manager was also there.

He was using Dennis Hales old office to meet with me. Dennis our ex-Undermanager had gone back to one of the Staffordshire pits. The door was open to the office as I entered the passage way. He was on the phone.

"Gaffer can't persuade anymore. Dunna know. I wanna but canna. Yep, mostly Manor and Golborne." He looked up towards me. He was smoking. By the look of the ashtray, it wasn't his first. "Listen I'll have to go. Yeah, one of our new recruits. Think it's Mick Gibson." Again, looking towards me. I nodded, I guessed he was talking to the Manager.

"Ay up Mick." Replacing the handset. He stubbed out what remained of his fag. He held an arm out towards me. He had a friendly face but with a worried look. The acrid smell of cigarette smoke everywhere.

"Mr Keech, good to finally meet you."

"Pleasure's all mine marra. I suppose you heard that?"

"Yeah. Manager, was it?"

"Mr Creed. Plenty new developments starting up need officials. Particularly shotfirers." *That obviously won't include me. I've been acting Overman. Colliery Overman at that!* "Might be worthwhile you coming and avin a looksee theesen?"

"Good idea."

"Leave that with me. I'll get our Personal Manager, Ron Gold, to arrange."

"Sounds like a plan." He sat back down.

"Right let's get down to business. Grab a pew. Believe you're at Stoke Poly?"

"Yeah. Only few more weeks. Finish altogether other than taking my Manager's papers. Currently Acting Colliery Overman. Before that Acting Face Overman."

"When did you became a Dep?"

"1982. April."

"Two years then?" I wasn't sure how to respond. He checked his watch.

"How much do you know about Parkside?"

"Other than it being the newest pit around. Not a great deal."

"That bit's true and still to realises its full potential. Strike doesn't help, hopefully they'll get that sorted soon."

"Working four faces, C15, Crombouke. W6's Wigan Four Foot, L30's and L31's, Lower Florida. C15's our little jewel in the crown." He smiled at his last comment. "One thousand seven hundred men, give or take." *Bloody ell four times what we've got here.* "Tonnage this year half a million." My expression must have conveyed my thoughts. "Don't forget like most places the overtime ban has had a knock-on effect. Previous year we hit eight hundred and fifty thousand." He stopped to extract another fag. "What do you have to do for a cuppa round here?" He looked towards the door.

"I'll go and sort one if you like?"

"Nah dunna worry. I'll be making a move soon. Right where did I get to?" Extracting a lighter from his trouser pocket he lit the fag hanging from the corner of his mouth. Inhaling his expression changed. He looked more relaxed.

"Over the next couple of years plan to bring the numbers down to thousand men producing from two coal faces in the Wigan and Ince Six Feet. The first of which we're about to start developing. W11's. It'll be our first heavy duty face. Both operating we'll be set to break through the million tonnes.

"How's the strike affecting production."

"We're keeping the places ticking over. Particularly L30's and 31's. Florida faces suffer big time with floor lift."

"Any problems with pickets?"

"Originally yeah. Quite a few early days. Bit scary too. Cars taking a hammering and all that." He began laughing. "In fact, one of the Undermanager's had the side panels bashed in either side of his motor. Only just bought it."

"How long do you think it will go on for?"

"Not sure. Been better if he'd gone for a full ballot. Guess though he wouldn't get the full mandate for strike action. I dunna blame the lads though Mick. This lot's made a right fuckin pig's ear of it."

"Government?"

"Nah. Fuckin Coal Board. Goaded them into a fight. We should be working together to ensure the industry survives. I mean look at this place. Put another shaft tuther side of fault coal there last us for years. Good quality too. My

16

biggest concern is how long this goes on for. Canna see it being a short dispute. Then what happens when either side agree to settle? Fuck up if you ask me." I was somewhat surprised by Mr Keech's openness. I liked that. He looked at his watch again. "Right Marra look forward to seeing you at some point. I need to keep going."

"Thanks for coming across."

☐

I'd booked to stay down at the Bowden Hotel on the final week of exams. A short walk from the Poly passed the railway station. Arriving late Sunday night, the lads I was sharing the room with had already gone to bed. It had been a good day. Jamie had given me a card for Father's day. Plus, a Guiness four pack. The late evening news was on. As usual headlines showed a group of miners outside the British Steel Orgreave coking plant in Rotherham, South Yorkshire. They were having little effect. Coppers had the picket line held back as several open top trucks filled to the gunnels with coking coal exited the plant. Footage then switched to what was happening in the Nottinghamshire coalfields. Police cars stationed at the exit points along the M1 motorway. Turning cars and coaches back to whence they'd came. I wondered how long it would go on for. There seemed little appetite from either side to sit down and resolve the dispute. One of the lads on a picket line reckoned some of the cops were from the Met and had little understanding of the local community. I left it at that and went to bed.

The exams today had been in Rock and Soil Mechanics, which I fuckin hated and Geology. The Rock and Soil hadn't gone well. I wasn't in the best of moods returning to the hotel. I decided to go next door for a pint. The place was full of students, obviously having the same idea. The bar however was deadly silent except for the television. It was the six o'clock news covering the day's events at Orgreave. I watched in shock as the police wearing riot gear moved forward. Using their truncheons to hammer against the long rectangular shields. It reminded me of the film Zulu. The warriors advancing on Rorke's Drift. Hard to believe this was Britain in the eighties. It was a beautiful early summer's day. Most of the miners topless making the most of the weather. They were paying little attention towards the police. The miners seemed to be boxed in. There were even police dogs at one end. The scene depicted suggested there was more to come. Then without warning, the miners were as surprised as us, the phalanx of shielded police parted. Charging in at a canter were the mounted helmeted police with truncheons drawn. It resembled something off a medieval battle field. I spotted a police helicopter overhead. No doubt filming events on the ground.

The police on horseback charged a group of miners. They had truncheons drawn, clubbing individuals as they passed alongside. A further group of police with smaller round shields followed in. Grabbing any fallen miners back to behind police lines. Several meat wagons lined up to take those arrested away. The reporter estimated there were five thousand police against some ten thousand pickets.

"For fucks sake." One of the students nearest television shouted. "Only tryin to protect fuckin jobs." A reporter at the scene began to interview one of the police officers. He was still holding a loud hailer. The room became silent again as he spoke.

"We had little choice once they started throwing bottles and bricks at the police lines."

"Fuckin load of shite." Another student shouted. The cameras then turned to a waiting ambulance. A helmetless copper was sat on the step. Dabbing a trickle of blood from his nose.

"Soft cunt. Deserve everything you get." The students couldn't contain their anger each offering a comment.

"Fuckin soldiers some of them cunts."

"Fuckin riot squad. I canna fuckin believe it shag. Fuckin government want smash the NUM once and for all. It's an absolute disgrace. What's fuckin country comin to when a man wants to protect his job."

The camera then shot across to one of the Yorkshire mining villages. The footage showed several bandaged police men.

"Fuckin BBC. Conning us. All bout government wanting public to see it's miners who are at fault. Fuckin shambolic that's what it is. Don't treat folk like that in fuckin Russia!"

"Legalised state violence." Another student shouted.

One journalist on a piece to camera described it as "a defining and ghastly moment, changing forever the conduct of industrial relations and how this country functions as an economy and as a democracy."

□□□□□

2. A New Start

"Big fuckin mistake that Mick. Mark my words, executive will be calling for another vote now!" Norman Thomas told me as I entered the control room. He was the Branch Treasurer for NACODS. He was the only union official now left at Cronton. Shaun Galway, Branch Secretary had transferred to Sutton Manor the previous week. Norman had a gob full of bacca. The juices of which had already begun to run down his chin.

"How do you work that out Norm? We've already voted against strike action last April."

"Mick you don't fuck about tellin membership they have to cross picket line. It's an individual's choice mate." To date I'd tried to keep away from any of the politics of the current dispute. I had heard from NACODS colleagues in Yorkshire they were being paid for staying at home. I was certain that wasn't sending out the right message.

"Suppose we'll have to wait and see."

"Tellin ye Mick that cunt of a Chairman has overstepped the mark this time. One out all out. And they want a stop to the pit closure programme." This was something I certainly couldn't see the logic to. If the pit were exhausted of reserves how the fuck could you justify keeping a pit open. Norman could see I had a problem with his argument. "Take here. We know from our own study there's plenty of coal to go at. Seventy-five years at least. Plus, the five panels of coal we're leaving behind in the London Delph." I nodded. He had a point. "I'll tell you lad. It's a management and Coal Board conspiracy. Backed by this fuckin Government. And they've done it whilst the Secretary and General Secretary are on holiday."

☐

I felt excited and a little anxious as I drove out of Liverpool. That feeling I suspect most people get when starting a new job. Although this wasn't a new job. It was the same job but a different location. Most of the guys I knew had transferred to Sutton Manor Colliery, a little further along the M62 motorway from Cronton Colliery. I'd been there previously to see their system of pump packing, as part of my college work. It hadn't seemed a lot different from Cronton, a "family pit" as we liked to call it. I'd made the decision if I were to progress to the position of Undermanager, I needed to be exposed to something outside my comfort zone. Something bigger, something I hadn't experienced before. Parkside Colliery was only sixteen miles away. I'd been there a couple of weeks before to meet up with the Personal Manager, Don Gold. He'd certainly made an impression on me. Full of energy and personality. Could the man talk? I'd never seen anything like it. For the one sentence I got out he'd uttered another half a dozen. One of those guys you could take too immediately. He was the guy we'd need to report to as soon as we arrived.

Another subject giving me a little concern was the prospect of crossing the picket line. I'd heard Parkside had been heavily picketed for several weeks. That was back in March and April. Now August about half the workforce had returned.

I was momentarily distracted as I drove along the M62. Off to my right various trucks and bucket loaders were operating in the field adjoining the motorway.

Rumour had it the site was for a new Ikea outlet. A Swedish company. There was even talk of a Marks and Spencer. Being late summer the early morning sunshine was already out on full view. I pulled the sun visor fully down and sat further up in my seat. It fascinated me to see the amount of farm land either side of the motorway. The old Burtonwood airfield came into view. No longer operated as an airbase by the Americans, the huge hangers were still used as storage bunkers. Renamed the Burtonwood Army Depot.

I spotted a car scrap merchant off to my left. A place I'd used before to replace the two front seats in my Mini. Leaving the motorway, Winwick Psychiatric Hospital off to my left I continued along the A49. A couple of miles further along the route I turned into the entrance. Houses either side. My research on the place suggested the sinking of the shafts had begun in the late fifties, a company from South Africa had been used. It had taken two years to complete. Both to a depth of eight hundred and fifty metres and twenty-four feet wide. No. 1 shaft, the downcast was used for winding men and materials. No 2 for winding coal using fifteen tonne skips. Coal production had commenced in 1964.

I slowed the car as I continued along the entrance; ahead a series of banners flapping in the wind. *Coal Not Dole* prominently displayed. Beyond which a cabin. I was half expecting pickets to appear. None did.

My attention now drawn to the scene ahead. Rising from the ground two huge white/grey concrete towers enclosing the headgear. Cold, box like, space age sprung to mind but in their own way iconic. I hadn't seen anything like it before. The only comparison that came to mind was the grain towers at Liverpool docks. The glass fronted buildings obscuring the base of the towers. These were the offices, baths, and canteen. What more would you want for a coal mine.

Originally four of us had accepted the offer to transfer to Parkside. The collieries Deputy Manager, Len Keech had explained to us on his visit to Cronton they were desperate for Deputies. Although I'd been acting as an Overman I'd transfer as a Deputy. My number one priority was to become an Overman at the first opportunity. Having sampled the role and the responsibility I wanted that to continue.

One of the four had backed out. Deciding to stay local. I and two others met in Don Gold's office. I wasn't sure how many of the NUM had transferred. By the time we'd completed the necessary paper work it was almost twelve o'clock. We headed towards the baths, carrying our pit gear.

At Cronton the officials and men changed and bathed in the same area. Not here. We had our very own separate baths. I was given a top locker, not really what I wanted. I noted my number, something I was unlikely to forget sixteen hundred. The main difference I noted here was the temperature of the baths. At Cronton it had always been red hot on the clean side. I recalled the first time I'd got changed there. I could feel my face was almost ready to burst.

Suitably suited and booted, we gathered outside. Here we were introduced to Harry Roach, our Union representative. Don introduced us as the Deputies from Cronton. I wanted to tell him I'd been an acting Overman. But thought better of it. Probably wasn't the time or place. He seemed a decent guy, clean shaven and wearing glasses. He'd show us his office later, he now wanted to give us a tour of the pit bottom area.

The route to the lamproom took us into a long rectangular hall. Harry explained this area was referred to as the crush hall. Fag stubs littered the floor, as way of an explanation for the smell of stale cigarette smoke. The last chance the lads would get to smoke before going down. The engineers offices were along here too. An array of drinking water taps along one side of the hall.

We arrived in the lamproom, everything we saw was on a larger scale to Cronton. The smells however were the same. The staleness of the hydrogen gas and the gentle hum of the batteries recharging. The ever-present smell of coal dust. The officials lamps were placed together. The yellow band surrounding each cap lamp easily discernible. I checked for number sixteen hundred. Twisting the cap lamp to release it I placed it around my neck. I next removed the battery from the rack and threaded my belt through the plastic sleeves. Placing the belt around my waist I temporarily secured it in position. The self-rescuers were on the opposite wall. Tightly packed together in their individual slots. I grabbed sixteen hundred. Once more threading it onto my belt which I now tightened and secured around my waist. Out of habit I checked the red wax seal on my cap lamp, then fastening to my helmet.

Harry was waiting for us outside the lamproom office. Four Eccles Protector Relighter oil lamps stood proudly waiting for their respective owner. The glow of the flame barely discernible against the glare of the polished metal surface of the lamp. I picked out sixteen hundred. The smell of colzalene emanating from the room behind.

"Lads like to keep im shiny." Harry was the first person to speak since we'd been in the baths. We each smiled. I'd never seen anything like it. Both the brass base and silver top competing for shininess top slot.

Following Harry around the corner we entered the Deployment Centre. I was half expecting to see Tommy Worthington, the Manager's Clerk. He'd often be stood in his suit and tie, passing out the respective brass and silver tallies to the Cronton officials as they passed through.

Harry continued to provide commentary on the underground layout. The mine was originally split into three sections, North, South and Mid Area. We'd be placed into one of the areas. Harry hadn't been told yet who was going where. Each of the areas under the control of an Undermanager. There were two Undermanager's, a third having recently retired.

I placed the brass tally onto the lamps handle. I kept hold of my silver tally. We continued forward along a covered passageway. A dirty white metal barrier running along the centre. Separating the route to and from the shaft top.

We stopped opposite an open door to our left. "Thay's control room. Not for much longer though. Havin newin built. State of art. All that Minos equipment bein installed." We entered. Again, the overpowering smell of cigarette smoke hung in the air.

"C15's maingate geet latch on." A young man sat opposite shouted into the microphone.

"Just checkin a stitchin Steve." Came the reply.

"Thanks, Keith." Having answered the voice on the tannoy Steve turned to face us.

"Owzthisel Arry."

"O- reet Mon."

"New recruits."

"I ex-Cronton lads come to join us." Steve lifted himself from his chair and walked across, shaking each of our hands in turn. He was dragging his left foot.

"Welcome lads. Welcome to the newest pit in Lancashire. Although we'll all be sat at home soon."

"Thanks Steve." We replied in unison. He looked towards me. I guessed what was coming next.

"Fuckin ell another Scouser." I laughed.

"Red or blue?"

"Only one colour for me." I replied.

"A red that's okay then."

"Oh, and by way." Harry interrupted. "There's barometer." He pointed to the rectangular box against the far wall. "Nice'n green as we like it.

Harry keen to keep moving continued. "Won't be long Steve just showing lads pit bottom circuit and if we get chance run along loco road. Want to be out before noon shift land."

"No problems alsithy. Oh, just beware Manager's on way out." No more was said we continued down the passage way. Once out of earshot Harry part turned to us.

"Good lad Steve. Was one of us. Bad accident on one of Florida faces. Lost part of his foot."

"Harry." I asked. "What did Steve mean we'll all be sat at home soon?"

"End of next month lad. Not been told big vote. Reckon we'll get the two thirds majority this time."

"Oh. Okay." I wasn't sure what else to say. I remember Norman giving me his view about the outcome too. *Something else to worry about!*

Exiting the passageway, we arrived at pit top. I shivered. The place was huge. Even for August it was cold. Possibly because it was the downcast shaft. But there was something else. I couldn't quite put my finger on it. Various rails underfoot made it difficult to decide where to place your feet. I wasn't sure what I was expecting, it wasn't this. The shaft was surrounded by various gates and fences. Signage littered the area. Against the shaft side a metal platform ran the full width. A set of metal steps either side. I wasn't sure what it was used for. My eyes distracted by the movement of the winding rope attached to the chains connected to the cage. It appeared so new. Not the battered two deck cage I'd been so used to. One, two, three, four decks. *For fucks sake!* I'd never seen anything like it. Now I understood the benefit of the platform.

"Koepe winder, cage and counterweight." Harry explained. "Platform allowing two decks to be loaded at once." The Banksman had his back to us. He lifted and secured the mesh gate. He turned. I recognised him immediately. One of the Cronton transferees.

"Alright Mick. How's it going la."

"Bloody ell, Colin, didn't realise you were here."

"Yeah, two weeks ago. Six of us. Mainly haulage lads." I raised my arms and received the regulatory pat down. I passed him my aluminium tally.

"See you around."

"I'm sure we will." I continued forward. Watching where I placed my feet. Pleased to see there was no gap between the shaft top and the cage floor. Inside the cage I grabbed the top rail. I was pleasantly surprised to see the floor and sides of the cage was solid. No obvious gaps exposing the drop below.

I turned to face my colleagues. Harry was explaining his role as NACODS North West Area President. I removed my tin of snuff and offered it to the group.

"Don't mind if I do cock." Harry offered. I took a pinch myself. Taking the brown powder up each nostril had now become a habit. Some might even say an addiction. Inhaling it smelt good. Replacing the surrounding aroma of oil and cold steel. I'd been a little too eager my eyes began to water. Without warning we dropped. I hadn't heard the shaft signals being exchanged. The cold air swirling about my body. We remained silent as we continued to descend. I'd counted two insets as we'd dropped. One unlit. As part of our secondary means of egress we'd be expected to travel them all. More than likely at a weekend. As the overtime ban was still in place men were still not accompanying officials on their regulatory underground inspections. It meant we doubled up at weekends.

Descending the shaft totally enclosed by the darkness, my hearing and sense of smell was accentuated. The cold intake air of the No 1 shaft devoid of the stale smells I'd been so used too. The sound of escaping compressed air too was missing. Within minutes we began to slow. I felt my ears pop. The shaft depth was twice that of Cronton although the time to descend seemed the same. I blinked as pit bottom came into view. The silence extinguished with the sound of voices and the slamming of vehicles being shunted.

We exited the cage passing a number of empties. An assortment of mine cars, full and half cuts, flats, and a couple of low loaders. Harry must have seen me looking.
"Like to clear empties first. Straight after dayshift have gone in. Then supplies in."
"I fuckin wish." A voice shouted. From behind a mine car a figure appeared.
"Ey up cocker." Harry responded.
"Can't get owt done with fuckin visitors up and down shaft."
"Owzthisel Durek."
"Not too bad owd lad and thee?"
"Can't complain." The guy talking, I assumed to be another official, short, and stout. He had an oil lamp hanging from the front of his belt. He was wearing a donkey jacket. A dark narrow moustache adorned his top lip. Tobacco stains emanating from either side of his mouth. He was smiling.
"Now lads let me introduce one of Parkside's many characters Mr Durek Moore." His fixed smile offered to us all as he nodded.
"What tha doin out ere?"
"Clearing shunts of empties. Been fall on face need timber and plenty of it."
"Reet then best get out of way. Let you get these up."
"No rush. Manager's on way out. Bin asked to hold cage for im."

The hooting of the loco just inbye caused a distraction.
"Speyk of the devil." We all turned to face inbye. The headlamps of the loco shining towards us. The loco itself seemed so quiet. That was because they were battery and not diesel.

We stood back as the Manager approached Harry. He was a big man. Wearing a dark blue boiler suit and holding a stick. His oil lamp barely visible under his white donkey jacket. He appeared old but not in years. A weary face etched with pain and suffering but there was something else. A hardness. He looked towards our group. I was certain he was looking at me. He stopped momentarily to chat with Harry. We couldn't hear the conversation. He was then on the move again. As he passed, he looked towards me again. I smiled. It wasn't returned.

"Patrick Creed. Best Manager I've worked for. Tells you as it is. Spent most of his time ere in every official position. No thidden agenda with that mon. Never cross him though. It'll be yer undoin. Been ere just three years now. Came from Golborne." Harry stopped talking he seemed reflective. "Bad doo that wah." I wasn't sure what he meant.
"What was Harry?"
"Explosion, 79." I was sorry I asked. We all remained silent for the next few seconds. "Well, we best be makin a move." We continued our pit bottom tour.

Two hours later we arrived back at pit top I shivered. Not the most exciting of days. We'd travelled the pit bottom circuit and walked the length of the locomotive tunnel. At least I now knew who the Manager was.
"Now lads I'm going to pass tha on to thi Undermanager. Don't forget if tha need owt tha know where office is. We followed Harry along a narrow corridor. I'd been allocated to the Northside.
"You're in there Mick." Harry pointed to a door, the plaque outside displaying the words **Undermanager**. "Mr Walters. Jack Walters. Men know him as JW. Tha be calling him mister." I nodded to my two colleagues and wished them luck. Leaving them I walked forward and knocked on the door.

"Yes man." I smiled. A Geordie. There were two gentlemen sat in their black. A set of Support Rules laid out in front of them. They both looked up. The Undermanager was the one wearing the white donkey jacket. His face expressionless. Eyes drooping not unlike a bloodhound. There was something else. I don't know what made me think it. Religious perhaps. Not one for getting flustered.
"Sorry to disturb you. I'm Mick Gibson ex-Cronton. Harry asked me to introduce myself. I removed my helmet.
"Oh right. Wasn't expecting you till end of week. What were you doin at Cronton?"
"Overman." I was pleased I'd got that in. Better start the way you mean to go on. The Undermanager turned to the guy sat next to him and smiled. It seemed to be his cue to respond.

"All full up in that department young man. You'll be starting as a Deputy until you've proved yourself. According to Don you're still at college, aren't you?"

"Don?"

"Don Gold, Personal Manager. You've met him already?"

"Oh yeah sorry. I've finished my degree. Hoping to start on my 1st Class ticket next month."

"A Scouser too I see."

"Yeah."

"Well, I'm Lenny Dunliffe. Mr Walter's Colliery Overman." JW was staring at me. I felt a little uncomfortable.

"Right lad if there's nowt else. Go get yourself a bath. You'll be with me tomorrow. I'll show tha round district." The silence that followed was my cue to leave.

"Oh, there is one other thing. My wife's about to have our second child. I need to book some rest days at short notice." Lenny looked up smiling.

"Bloody ell lad you've only been here two minutes and tha booking time off already."

"Sorry." I wasn't sure what else to say.

"Go on, go get thisen a bath." As I turned.

"W11's maingate." JW added.

"Oh right."

"You'll need dets." JW continued. *Fuckin dets. Shotfiring!* Talk about surprises. I wasn't just starting as a Deputy. I was being demoted to Shottie. I tried to maintain a look of neutrality. Although difficult. I suspected by the look on Lenny's face he'd detected my disappointment.

"Okay see you tomorrow."

☐

The next day I reported to the office for six. The place was heaving a mix of Overmen and Deputies. I received one or two smiles. Most of the lads had fags hanging from their mouth. None lit. I guessed JW was a non-smoker. I moved to the back of the office. Lenny was dishing out orders. He'd spotted me and winked.

"You one of the new starters?" One of the lads offered as he walked past.

"Yeah. Mick Gibson." We shook hands.

"I'm Gerry. Gerry Cook. I'll see tha round." He continued out soon followed by the rest of the officials. Lenny brought up the rear.

"Unfortunately, Mick something has come up. I must attend a meeting first thing. I'll arrange to take you around the district later in the week." I nodded. Not much else I could say. "Come on we'll head on to deployment." Lenny explained I'd oversee three contractors from the Associated Tunnelling Company or ATC as they were known. He'd arranged to meet the chargehand before going down. We were to construct a junction in an existing roadway, the

South Wigan Mines Access Intake. The junction would be the start of an intake road for the pits first heavy-duty face W11's in the Wigan Four Foot seam.

The chargehand Cornelius was a Lether. He was as thin as a whippet with a distinguished, grey pencil moustache. A kindly face but I sensed not someone you'd want to cross. His two mates Jimmy and Tommy were from Wigan. It was quite different hearing the various dialects from the men working at the pit. Working mainly with Scousers previously, anyone from outside the area was affectionately referred to as a Woolyback. I'd been told that many of the men were from St Helens, Wigan, and Leigh. Also from Widnes, Warrington, Coppull, Standish, Burtonwood, and several other towns. A sign of how many local collieries had closed.

On that first morning I travelled with my team on the loco manrider. I spotted Gerry in the back carriage. He was sat with a several other officials. He waved. I heard him tell his colleagues I was one of the new starters from Cronton. The conversation amongst the officials seemed to concern a meeting taking place with the Coal Board Chairman and our unions President and General Secretary. Something I wasn't aware of or the implications of such a meeting. I was sure I would find out at some point.

During the ride Cornelius explained their first job before starting on the junction was to build a working platform over one of the pits main coaling conveyors along the Wigan Mines Access Intake road. There were four conveyors positioned down the one in four brow. The first U conveyor which fed onto the No2 belt along No 3 horizon. U was followed by V then W and finally X belt. We'd be working opposite W belt. All the material required had been dropped off the previous day, including additional manriding platforms. That first day made me understand I was now an unknown to the Management team. As a shottie I was starting at the bottom. I was having to prove myself all over again. I'd have to produce a plan to get noticed. A plan I'd previously used at Cronton.

☐

I'd only been at Parkside for a week when Mrs Gibson gave birth to our second child, a little girl Lizzie. Work activities were put on hold as I took the next few days and following week off to look after our son Jamie. It was a time of change in the Gibson household. New job, new addition to the family and we were looking to move out from Liverpool and into Huyton. All this in addition to the miner's strike. The NCB and NUM were still meeting on a regular basis to resolve the dispute. After two days in hospital my wife returned home with our new addition, Lizzie.

Not being in work the following week either as I'd put in five rest days meant I was out of touch with what was going on in the dispute. So, on the Friday before returning the following week I made my excuses and popped back into work. I'd only be back in work for two days and then I was to attend Old Boston Training Centre for my Deputies refresher.

Initially I went to see Don Gold.

"Alreyt Mick. Thought tha was off this week lad?"

"I am Don just checking what shift I'm on Monday and Tuesday."

"Could av phoned in lad save the journey. Or is it tha's just too keen. Manager will like that." I smiled.

"Any idea where Harry Roach will be? Thought Friday was his day on the surface."

"Fuckin ell Mick you not heard?"

"Heard what?"

"NACODS called a special delegate conference Wednesday just gone. It wa unanimous. They've passed a motion calling for a national ballot. Week after next, Wednesday 26th September. Harry's got things to sort he has. If I wa betting man think tha might get the two thirds majority for strike action this time." *Like I needed to hear that.* "Government will be right fucked then."

☐

"How many dets did tha pickup Mick?"

"Twenty."

"Good lad. Shouldn't need them all. Best be on the safe side."

"Mornin tha two. Squeeze in here with me and Mick." Cornelius and I were sat in the front carriage. I moved across to allow Tommy to sit by me. Jack sat next to Cornelius. The ride into the top of the Access Road had now become somewhat routine. Most of the other officials sat together, Overmen and Deputies. Not knowing many of them by name I preferred to sit with my team.

"Fuckin ell Mick squeeze up." I duly obliged as Tommy placed the two pouches of powder by his feet. I was grateful for the additional passengers. The body heat generated more than making up for the cold downcast ventilation. It was different too, not inhaling the loco diesel fumes I was so used too. Fourteen tonne battery locos now the means of hauling the manriding carriages.

Over the previous week we'd completed the platform over W conveyor. Established a water and air supply. Horse heads and side ranters secured to the roof and sides. It was time to remove the first arch and begin setting the junction steel. It was a first for me. I'd been involved with building junctions before. Usually as the heading advanced or turning off for a face line. This was in an existing 16 x 17 arch roadway. The fact it was over one of the main coaling belts added additional responsibility.

Half of the junction steel had been dropped off by the haulage lads yesterday. Along with the corner brackets and bolts. We'd spent half of the shift rolling it under the conveyor. With very little room in which to work we made use of the space as best we could. There was also a dozen thirty mill heavy duty roof bolts. Half a dozen boxes of resin, four bundles of hessian bags and two packs of tin sheets.

"Have you got key?" Tommy asked. Cornelius patted the front of his overalls. I hadn't spotted it early. It explained the odd shape against his belly.

"Course I've got fuckin key." He responded smiling. Removing it he passed it towards me. "Seen one of these before Mick?"

"Certainly have. Mesh key."

"No flies on our Mick." I smiled. It brought memories back of Johnny Buckett and Tommy Oldcroft at Cronton. I'd completed part of my face training with the two on the Wint hole. I remember fondly Johnny filling hessian bags with the excavated coal from the small tunnel we were creating. The lad never stopped. A continuous stream of sweat falling from his face and chest. The smell of alcohol ever present for the first few hours of the shift. I could still smell the hessian bags.

We said little more as we jolted along the track. Ten minutes later the loco began to slow as we arrived at the top of the Access Road. We collectively fell forward as the loco came to a complete stop.

Discharging from the carriage's conversations continued as most of the men continued forward towards E3. Heading towards the next manrider, inbye to the Lower Florida faces. Tommy and Jack continued down the Access Road. Cornelius disappeared ahead; I waited by the locomotive. Within a few minutes he'd returned.

"Just sorting the next load of steel we'll be wanting."

"Oh right."

According to the Manager's Support Rules, we'd need the shorter roof beams first as we opened out the junction to its new width. The longest beams positioned perpendicular to the entrance of the maingate. Once we'd completed the junction and positioned the main stanchions, we could remove the legs. All straightforward until it came to firing to create room for the belt drive and Dosco Roadheader. I was trying to understand the best firing pattern to avoid damaging the main coaling conveyor. I had mentioned to Cornelius. He told me not to worry, "All in good time Mick." I'd only worked with the fella for two weeks, I'd taken to him immediately. His manner and speech was always reassuring.

As we approached the junction site, I could hear the bolt cropper. We'd previously experimented using oil on the arch plate bolts. Trying to release them with a ring spanner. To no avail. Cornelius, not wanting to delay the build managed to purloin the bolt cropper. As he continually reminded me, they were on bonus. Not that he would tell me the amount.

During that first week, the ATC Foreman Nick Arnold popped by to see Cornelius to check he had everything he needed. Hence the reason he was carrying the mesh key this morning. He'd also arranged a metal box to store the tools. Anything too big to go in the box we buried under the belt. There were too many folk passing by each shift to leave anything lying around.

Jimmy and Tommy had been busy. Four panels of weld mesh were visible on the platform. They'd completed cropping the bolts on the travelling side of the conveyor. Jimmy moved across to the tight side as Tommy dragged more slack bagging toward him. Within minutes the four bolts had been chopped through.

"Pass me thommer." Jimmy shouted. Tommy duly obliged. One hit with the seven-pound hammer sent the arch plates flying. One silently falling onto the black stuff below. I stepped forward placing my arm between the belt side iron and the greenline. Securing it from behind and placing it by my feet.

"Fucking ell Mick that were quick. Wouldn't worry too much. Magnet will sort at Pit Bottom."

"Never mind the magnet. Anything off this junction does not go out on the belt. Something gets caught in the chute and damages the belt. I'll be up for the high jump!"

Now with both legs detached from the crown. Tommy gave each a knock. Momentarily a cloud of dust engulfed the two lads. Followed by the clatter of mudstone hitting the platform floor. The crown settled nicely onto the horseheads.

"Pass me pick." Tommy began pickin above the displaced crown. "Don't look like we'll be needin any shots for this one Mick."

Once sufficient ground had been cleared for the roof beam, I gave the lads a lift to get it onto the horseheads. Followed by both legs. It was a struggle to get the tight side in position. Fortunately, the three ATC lads were all on the skinny side and managed. Jimmy had already broken the steel banding on the corrugated pack of steel sheets. He began to place them onto the platform. Watching the lads working they carried out each task without conversation each knowing exactly what was required. One of the many examples of teamwork I'd seen since becoming an official.

"Hold it." I shouted to Cornelius.

"What's fordo?"

"Aren't you forgetting something?"

"Oh them." He replied smiling. "Jimmy pass me drilling machine. Our Mick here doesn't miss a trick."

Once the roof bolts had been positioned, the corrugated sheets were slid over the roof beam. The hessian bags now filled with roof dirt. Packing complete we sat down on the platform, time for a pinch. These were certainly a good bunch of lads and knew their stuff. I wasn't sure how much I could trust them though. Particularly when it came to packing. Being on bonus certainly had its advantages, the downside however was taking short cuts. I certainly wasn't going to allow that to happen. Particularly as this was the entrance for the pits first heavy-duty face. I had no doubt visitors from far and wide would be coming down to see Lancashire's newest colliery's heavy-duty coal face. For the first time since being at my new pit I'd achieved something.

Later we sat down for snap. Although allowed twenty-five minutes we barely had half that. Most days I sat there and listened to the three lads exchange various tales. Cornelius as was his want always tried to include me in the conversation. Today's conversation about hare coursing. Although I suspect by the look, I got from one of the lads he was uncomfortable me listening.

"You got a dog Mick?"

"Yeah. Did have two. Had to have her put to sleep, quite old."

"What type?"

"Both mongrels. The one we've got now, Heidi, part Chow. Can tell as she has a black tongue."

"Do'y worm her."

"Yeah, every now and again. Missus deals with that sort of stuff."

"Suppose you buy those Bob Martin tablets. Fuckin expense." He paused as he extracted the chew he had recently placed in his mouth. "Me old fella used to work at Wood Pit. Loved his bacca. If he weren't chewing, he war smokin it. Never went to waste. Use it to for deworming our little Jack Russel."

"Fuck off. A dog chewing bacca?" I asked surprised.

"Nah ye daft cunt. After he'd finish with a chew, he'd shove it up the dog's arse hole. Dog wont appy. Certainly, got shut of them worms." We all erupted into laughter before Cornelius brought us back to the present.

"Cum on time we got back work."

The following day we continued where we'd left off. "Fuckin ell tha stupid cunt what think tha doin?" Cornelius suddenly shouted out. He was looking outbye along the belt line. I was alongside Tommy holding a hessian bag as he filled it

31

with the recently dropped mineral. A body lay sprawled on the conveyor. The lad had passed right under the platform. *Fuckin hell he was lucky there must only be eighteen inches of clearance.* I watched as he lifted his head. Turning he responded to Cornelius.

"Fuck off thee owd cunt!" Before he could respond another body suddenly passed beneath.

"Somebody's goin to get themselves killed Mick." I nodded in agreement. After all the trouble we'd gone to repositioning the platforms, men were still riding the belt.

"I'll pick up some extra signage when we get up."

"Fat lot of fuck that'll do. Someone will get injured before they take note." Jimmy added.

Arriving back on the surface and passing through the lamp room I headed straight to the Undermanager's office. The place was crowded. Most of the Overmen were gathered around JW's desk each vying for his attention with the end of shift report before disappearing off to the baths. I still found it fascinating how JW managed to take in all the information being verbally hurled at him without losing his temper.

"Alreyt Mick?" I hadn't spotted Lenny Dunliffe stood to one side. "Good shift lad?"

"Not bad Lenny. Completed the second got ground out for number three. That's on horseheads."

"What about the roof bolting?"

"Oh yeah. Two bolts drilled and positioned between one and two. Although I can't see what good there doing. Ground's solid."

"You know that, and I know that. But powers to be want them setting. Supposedly roof bolting will be playing a big part in our future. Or yours to be more precise."

I nodded. Lenny's comment was of no surprise. For the short time I'd been there several older officials were talking openly of taking the money now on offer and retiring. And that was me done shortest report to give. "Owt else?"

"Yeah, have you got any *no manriding* signs?"

"Lads riding under platform?"

"Fraid so."

"You'll never stop it. Best see Safety Officer. Met him yet?" I hesitated surprised by Kenny's comment.

"Yeah, I'll pop in on the way to the baths."

The next morning as the lads positioned one of the ten-foot legs on the tight side of the conveyor I took the signs I'd brought in with me to hang them on the getting off platform below. Satisfied I'd suspended them as low as possible without obstructing the stream of coal passing below, I wandered down to the next conveyor. The noise increasing as I approached the chute. I guessed the coal coming out was from L30's or L31's. Both faces in the Lower Florida seam. I still wasn't sure of the layout further inbye and which route coal from C15's travelled. What little dust produced exited the mouth of the enclosed chute. The lumps of coal falling directly on the middle of the forty-two-inch belt. The quality of which I'd never seen before. The banging and clattering of the coal louder now. The quarter inch hose suppling water to the enclosed spray neatly attached to the framework with plastic tie wraps.

Alongside the drive I could feel the heat generated by the single motor double drum drive. The smell of gear oil lingered in the air. I half expected to see evidence of leaking oil. There was none. Grease nipples amply supplied evidenced by the small blob of grease sitting on the outer edge of the tiny steel ball bearing. I stopped. There was something missing I retraced my steps to the gib end. It was there. A huge wiper blade. The length of orange neoprene reflecting the beam of light from my cap lamp.
I returned to the loop take up. Spying the carrying idler set feeding the belt back to the tension carriage. Removing my cap lamp, I knelt alongside. Shining my light to the tight side. It was spotless. *The fitters have obviously done a first-class job on this.* I stood back up. The sound of the Holman alerted me to my team outbye. Time to return to the job in hand. The problem was I was so fuckin bored. No disrespect to my team but I needed something more to do.

Before climbing onto the platform, I positioned my ear plugs. The single Holman on its shortened airleg was completing the second of two holes. A mist of oil and water spray hung in the air. I was horrified to see Jimmy who was holding the Holman not using any ear plugs. The noise was excruciating even with my ear plugs in place. I tapped Jimmy on the arm. As he faced me the machine came to a halt. A deafening silence followed. I was pointing to my ears His lips began to move. I couldn't hear him. I removed one of the plugs.
"What? What did you say?" Jimmy was asking.
"Why aren't you using yours?"
"What?" I waved the yellow sponge like material towards him.
"Your ear plugs."
"What?" He asked again. This time cupping one of his hands behind his ear. Obviously taking the piss. This was confirmed when I heard Cornelius snigger.

I hadn't spotted him and Tommy. They too were ear defenceless.
"Fuckin ell Mick bit late in the day for us old fuckers." Cornelius exclaimed.
"You'll pay the price later." I answered.
"If you're referring to tittinus, already got it." Jimmy added.

"Tittinus, your daft fucker." Cornelius interrupted. "You mean tinnitus."

"Yeah, that as well." The comment caused us all to laugh.

"Don't you be worried Mick we use these." Jimmy had extracted a ball of something black from his ear. "Cotton wool lad. Works a treat."

The dust generated hanging in the air caused me to cough. Cornelius tapped me on the arm. He'd cut me a piece of pigtail. His own concoction. Soaked overnight in Courvoisier as he'd previously explained. Jimmy replaced his cotton wool and continued drilling. I replaced my own ear protection. Didn't I just love these guys they didn't miss a trick.

Chewing on the bacca I was about to spit out. Suddenly distracted as I spotted a light disappear under the platform. I turned. "Not this time you fucker!" I shouted. Within two paces I'd reached the end of the platform. I jumped. Almost landing on the guy illegally manriding below. He turned towards me a look of shock and horror at the fuckin nutcase behind. Me.

"What the fuck do you think you're doin?" I shouted. No answer. "Hey." Louder this time. I spat the generated bacca juice onto the empty belt. Staring the guy out. I was angry, very angry. "We spend our time rearranging the platforms and you fuckers try and get yourselves fuckin killed doing that." I waited. We passed the repositioned getting on platform.

"What you doin out at this time anyway?"

"I've got an early note." He responded timidly. I didn't recognise him. For the first time I began to feel sorry for the lad. He was still in a state of shock.

We continued in silence. Five minutes later we stood up. The fluorescent count down markers suspended from the arches alerting us to the end of our ride. Maintaining our balance as we reached the getting off platform. For the first time I noticed he was carrying an empty powder tin. Obviously one of the heading lads from inbye. I reached down to touch my oil lamp. *Fuck I've left it hanging on the platform.*

"Right mister, name, and number?"

"Told yer I've got an early note." He passed me the paper. Three names and three numbers.

"Like I give a fuck." The sound of further bodies on the platform and the accompanying lights caused me to turn. His two mates, also carrying empty powder tins. I guessed they'd ridden under the platform too. By the size of one of them he'd have struggled to get under. I waited until they'd exited the ladder. I sensed the change in sound of the conveyor as the grey surface of the belt disappeared beneath the mound of black stuff.

"Ey up cock. What's up with tha?" The bigger of the two mouthed off first.

"I've just caught your mate here illegally manriding."

34

"And?"

"I'm about to fine him."

"And who are fuckin tha to fine anyone?" The big lad again. He walked towards me. Invading my space. He certainly was a big fucker. I touched the rim of my cap lamp.

"The Deputy for W11's maingate junction. Mick Gibson. The guy that doesn't want to ignore anyone illegally manriding."

"Fuck off." The big fella responded again. "Come on lads let's leave this wanker and fuck off. Rest of shift will be out soon enough." They began to walk off.

"You give me no choice. I'll let the Undermanager know…" I began to read their names and numbers off the note kindly provided by their colleague. "How about we start with a ten pound fine." All three stopped in their tracks.

"You can't do that." The smallest of the team who hadn't said anything up till that point answered.

"Watch me." I'd made my point but wanted to deliver a clear distinct message. "You heard about the two lads killed in Yorkshire last month?" I had their attention. "Illegally manriding through a set of airdoors mousetrap. The lad in front got stuck. His mate jammed behind him. Coal on the still moving conveyor buried them. Suffocating both in the process." I looked at each man in turn. They'd got the message. "I'll tell you what though. I'll give you a warning this time. No fine. But let everyone else know I will dish out fines if it happens again. That is until everyone gets the message."

"What say thi name is?"

"Mick Gibson."

"Well, I'll tell tha what Mick Gibson you can fetch fuckin pouches out thisen!" And with that all three men threw the pouches into the side of the road and walked off.

"Where the fuck av bin Mick?" Cornelius greeted me as I arrived back at the junction. "Bout ready to start charging yon oles. Want to get next beam up fore we leave."

"Come on then." I climbed back on to the platform. The lads had two sticks of P4/5 ready for me. Extracting two instantaneous dets I primed them both. Placing them individually into each hole followed by a second stick. Finishing off with the stemming. A little late getting out but roof beam five was now in position. We'd set the legs the following day.

The following days and weeks I became quite active. What with shotfiring and diving onto the belt to chastise illegal manriders. I handed out a series of fines to the more argumentative individuals. But by and large I just provided the majority with a good fuckin. The results became more and more obvious as the number of men walking passed the work area increased. I wasn't sure JW was particularly happy with the extra work I'd created for him.

☐

"Where've you bin Mick?"

"Just havin a look at the bottom junction. See how the lads are getting on replacing the junction roof beams." I sat down. Cornelius and his mates were having snap. A separate team of ATC men were working on the junction at the bottom of the Access. It must have been fifteen to twenty feet tall. Weight had come on and the beams were badly distorted.

"Must have taken some doin getting them roof beams into position. Don't you think Mick?" I knew what was coming next. Cornelius was always testing me. Trying to understand the depth of my knowledge and experience. Although I'd never told him, I was grateful. For the short time I'd been with him and his team I'd learnt so much. I suppose I should be grateful to JW too. Starting me off with these lads. It was all very well getting the next promotion and moving up the ladder. The stuff I was doing now I'd never learn in the classroom. It was also useful working with a team of contractors too. Something I'd never experienced before.

"I guess using steel roof bolts with an air hoist attached?"

"Fuckin ell Mick. Lifting them ten by eight RSJ's twenty foot in thir. I don't think so somehow."

"Go on then tell me how?"

"Straight forward really. Drive excavation in two lifts. Top half first. Meaning thi don't hav lift beams so high. Then take floor out and reset the longer legs."

"So how do you keep the beams in place when setting legs."

"That's clever bit see. You plate and bolt em first time round"

"Pity they hadn't bolted the surrounding roof. Would have stopped weight coming on."

"Nowt do with us Mick. Lazy fuckers who built it never packed above. Every time you walked through the place could hear stones falling on steel sheets. Deputy should have made em pack." Cornelius's comment causing his two mates to start laughing."

"Thanks for that."

"Any time Mick."

☐

Another area I found myself at a disadvantage was not knowing the personalities in the mechanical and electrical departments. At Cronton I'd gotten to know them all. From the top man down. Primarily on the back of projects or information I required for college. As I'd finished that was no longer the case. I had to find some other way. Now employed as a shotfirer that wasn't going to be easy. One opportunity arose when we had to find another manriding platform. Lenny Dunliffe had suggested we salvage one from an old Florida district. However, the bracketry required to attach it was a different size to the forty-two-inch structure.

"Leave it with me Cornelius, I'll sort it. You go get a bath."

"Tha sure Mick. It's no problem."

"No, I'll be fine." We'd just arrived on the surface. Walking along the overhead gantry towards the lamproom. We passed a number of men waiting to go down on noons.

"Tha'll need this mind." He passed me an oil spattered scrap of paper with sketch and measurements of the bracketry required.

"Thanks, see you tomorrow." We parted company in the lamproom. Removing my rescuer, I placed it in the rack. Turning I removed my lamp from the leather belt. Placing onto the empty shelf before placing the cap lamp onto the brass charging nodule. Turning onto the charging position.

From the lamproom I headed to the crush hall. The place wasn't too busy. We'd managed to get onto the first ride. The smell of cigarette smoke evident as the lads lit up.

The fitters office was alongside the electricians. I could tell which was which even if blindfolded. The fitter's had the regulation smell of oil and grease. There were a couple of lads standing around chatting as I walked in. The walls either side fitted with a wooden shelves littered with report books, bolts, and various sized tins. No one took any notice. There was an additional office further in.

"What can I do for tha?" A voice shouted from inside. I walked forward, dodging several pieces of sprocket and gear wheels. A red-haired lad was walking towards me.

"I'm looking for a shift engineer. Need something knocking up for a manriding platform."

"Pass ere lad let's a look." The guy was about my size. Fit looking. Probably another that played rugby. Which was no surprise. If it wasn't rugby, it was golf, or they sang in the choir. Others members of the first aid team. "Where's it for?"

"W11's maingate junction." He unfolded the scrap of paper.

"Who are you anyway?" I realised at that point not having my cap lamp or oil lamp he wouldn't know I was a Deputy.

"I'm the Deputy, Mick Gibson."

"How come I've not seen tha before?"

"Only started last month."

"From Cronton?"

"Yep, me and three others."

"Welcome to Parkside Mick. I'm Eric. Eric Greenland." We shook hands. "How's it going."

"Good thanks. Place seems quite busy. Can't imagine what's it like when everyone's working."

"Oh, it gets busier alreyt Mick. How soon do you want this for cock?" I smiled.

"Tomorrow?"

"Cheeky bastard. Are they all like you from Cronton?" Before I could answer. "Bloody ell Frankie whets think tha doin?" I turned to see who Eric was talking to. Initially I didn't see the guy stood behind me. He must have been about four foot tall. He had a fluid coupling sat on his shoulder. He was a fitter. The blackest fitter I'd ever seen. He lifted the coupling without too much trouble and placed it on the floor. "Fuseable plug entry damaged, needs fettling." He offered as a way of explanation. He looked up towards me. "You one of the new starters cock."

"You could say that." He raised his arm. I reached down and grabbed his hand.

"Mick this is Frankie Glow. Spends more time at pit than colliery cat."

"Good to meet you Mick."

"Likewise, Frankie." Once more we were interrupted as a guy in running gear walked in.

"Bloody ell Jeff you ran here?"

"Actually yes." He smiled. "Popped by to pass a rest day form in for next Wednesday didn't realise running club were away." Eric could see the guy he'd referred to as Jeff looking at me.

"Jeff this is Mick. Cronton lad just joined us. Mick this is Jeff Broughton Deputy Mechanical Engineer, marathon runner." I'd guessed as much. Wearing shorts, trainers, and a white vest. Across its middle in blue the name of the running club. *Leigh Harriers.* He offered me his hand.

"Bet you know my old mate, Frank B."

"Yeah. He's gone Sutton Manor."

"So, I heard. Right, can't stop. Good to meet you Mick. Catch you guys later."

"Anyway, cock what we owe the pleasure of you visiting our humble abode?" Frankie once more turning his attention to me.

"Mick's after some bracketry makin." Eric held up my piece of paper, which Frankie took. After a quick glance.

"When's wanting it?" I thought I'd take a chance.

"Tomorrow?"

"I'll leave it in hessian sack outside office." He offered.

38

"Thanks Frankie." I moved to one side as the noon shift began to enter. Each giving me a cursory glance. By my reckoning each wondering *who the fucks this?* Time, I moved on. "Thanks for your help lads."

"No problem, Mick. Enjoy." Eric offered. Frankie said nothing. He was now in conversation with one of the noon shift. Pleased with my first encounter with the fitting department I headed towards the officials baths.

☐

The following week I decided to try my luck with the electrical department. Now with the platform complete I wanted to establish a shotfiring station and make sure it looked the part. I'd have every Tom, Dick and Harry passing. That included HMI. I'd want to make a good impression.

Once up pit I headed to the shift engineers office. There was no one about in the outer office. Same design as the fitters, the shelves however were tidy. Report books neatly stacked. The smell of new cable. A combination of plastic and rubber.

"Who the hell are you? And what you doing here?" A voice from behind caused me to stop. I attempted to disguise my surprise. I turned slowly. The guy facing me looked quite important, the best dressed guy I'd seen to date. A dark blue suit, white shirt with plain blue tie. He was even wearing square gold-coloured cufflinks. His black moustache looked a little out of place.

"I, I, was after some insulated pigtails."

"Insulated pigtails. What do you think this is? Woolworths?" Listening to him mention the term insulated pigtails did sound rather strange. Perhaps it hadn't been such a good idea after all.

"Yeah, I…."

"Hiya Mick. What doin in here?" I hadn't heard a second person walk in the office. It was Glyn Amp, one of the assistants. I'd met him the previous week whilst we'd been setting up the junction. He was keen to understand when we'd need power establishing.

"Alright Glyn. You said pop in if I needed anything." The suited gentlemen looked a little put out he'd been excluded from the conversation.

"You too obviously know each other. Glyn I'm after Stan have you seen him."

"Yeah, he's over in the workshops." Without a further word the suited guy turned and walked out.

"Who the fuck's that?"

"Alan Fielding. The Electrical Engineer."

"Miserable cunt." Glyn began to laugh.

"Oh, he's alreyt really, can be a little touchy. What you after anyway?"

"Insulated pigtails."

"Yeah, think we've got some spare in the back office. What are they for?"

"Suspending the shotfiring cable."

"Fancy! Don't think I've seen them used for that before. Give us a mo."

Glyn continued into the back office. I waited. I had to give it to the electrical department nothing seemed out of place.

"There you go fella. Bout twenty there. If you need any more give us a shout." He passed me a hessian bag.

"Thanks Glyn, that's helpful. Just out of interest if Alan is the Engineer who's his Deputy?"

"Stan Boris. You'll like him. Not sure how long he'll be with us for. Talking about taking a job over in the Middle East."

"What mining sand?"

"Something like that." I left Glyn satisfied I'd gained a little more understanding. And I'd met the main man.

Out in the crush hall the place had begun to fill up. The air filled with the haze of cigarette smoke. I inhaled. The smell quite addictive. I'd never taken to smoking fags. Give me a cigar any day. As I turned, I thought I spotted someone I knew. Wearing a dirty white Donkey jacket. He looked smaller than when I'd last seen him. The giveaway was the unlit fag hanging from the corner of his mouth.

"Mr Keech!"

"Ay up Mick. How's it goin Marra." He remembered me, I liked that. He continued walking obviously no time for a chat. "Believe you're breakin in for W11's maingate?"

"Yeah, just setting up." He stopped to cadge a light from one of the lads passing.

"Ta Marra. I'll pop by and say hello next week sometime."

"Look forward to it." And then he was gone. I'd now seen the Manager in his black and Mr Keech. Come to think of it, I was yet to see any of the senior Engineers in their black. Must have lots of office work.

☐

The following day I waited, as was the norm to provide my shift report to JW. I'd tried already to pass it to Lenny. He advised I'd best wait. JW wanted a word.

"You got any empty powder tins in the district?" JW was talking to one of the Deputies covering W8's developments.

"Yeah, bout twenty. Lads won't carry'em out. Had'em loaded on the empties coming out."

"Why don't you get the lads to carry them out?" The Deputy, his name was Jack turned towards me and nodded. JW followed his gaze. He didn't look best pleased.

JW received the same comment from the lad out of V24's. Finally, there was just the Undermanager, Lenny, and me in the office.

"Mick you've only bin here man for two minutes. War tryin to get lads back to work not gan piss'em off."

"Mr Walters I can assure you I'm not trying to piss anyone off. The only lads I'm stopping time are those out too early."

"But they've bin given an early note by their own Deputy."

"Yeah, to ride the shaft fifteen minutes early not an hour!"

"They don't ride the shaft until fifteen minutes before. The Onsetter and Winder have all received clear instruction."

"They might not be riding the shaft but they're all in Pit Bottom. Imagine what time there setting off from inbye."

"But that isn't your problem."

"It is when I'm trying to fire a round of shots and I've got men passing through the junction." JW could see he wasn't going to win his argument. Shaking his head in frustration he turned towards Lenny.

"See you're confiscating the lads newspapers too."

"Yep, guilty as charged." Both JW and Lenny were distracted looking towards the office door. "The engine driver top of the Access haulage. Caught him the other day operating the thing whilst reading the paper. Dangerous if you ask me and a fire hazard." Both JW and Lenny seemed reluctant to answer they were still looking towards the door. I sensed whoever it was had walked in.

"And how do you suppose they'll wipe their arse, young man." I turned, startled by the loud authoritative voice. I didn't recognise him immediately. This time in his clean. The giveaway were his eyes. The hardness and determined look of a man in authority. Had to be the Manager. He returned my stare. Momentarily our eyes locked, only for a split second. I wasn't sure because of fear or respect. On my part.

"Jack, can you pop into my office when you've finished here."

"Will do, Mr Creed." And then he was gone. The three of us said nothing immediately. Lenny broke the silence.

"Go get bath Mick." He turned to JW. "Might be worth havin a word with Sid Large."

☐

3. NACODS Vote to Strike

"What time you in work today?" Annie asked me.

"One o'clock."

"You off Sunday?"

"Yep, all day."

"Good that'll make a change. Fancy goin Formby, let the kids see the red squirrels."

"You sure you'll be, okay?"

"I'll be fine, fresh air will do me good. Wouldn't mind poppin into the new Asda in Huyton village, this morning." I said nothing. "Good that's settled then."

An hour later. "Mick look over there." I turned towards where my wife was pointing. I knew exactly what she'd been looking at. "Aren't they some of the lads you used to work with from Cronton?" They were, I'd spotted them earlier. Three of them. Tony Ivor, Tommy Harris, and Pete Digby, smiling towards us. Standing at a stall collecting money for the striking miners. A huge yellow banner hanging above *Coal Not Dole.* There was even a flag providing a back drop to the stall. A red flag with hammer and sickle. Like the one in Johnny Helsby's office. It may have been the same one. "You got any spare cash on yer?"

"Come ed Mick. Show us yer cash." Tony shouted over. They knew the conversation me and the missus were having.

"I've only got a fiver."

"That'll do."

"But…. I."

"Yer tight sod. Give it here." Mrs Gibson held her hand out to me.

"Ta Mick. You're not the twat everyone thinks you are." Tommy now shouted. I smiled. What else could I do.

To avoid any further confrontation, I continued into Asda. Not that I expected any. They were three good lads, hardworking too. Always taking the piss. I'd done my heading training with them some years before. Jamie went with his Mum to see the striking miners. I questioned why I hadn't gone to see them. Maybe I was embarrassed I was still working. I'd justified previously in that I had a career ahead of me. Even though at Cronton we'd been given dispensation some of the lads decided to stay at home or assist elsewhere on picket duty. I had to admire them for their principles.

Annie was soon back with me. "Tony asked if you could get him a couple tins of beans. That's all they have now; beans on toast." I smiled. "Oh, and the other thing he mentioned. He said you'd all be out on strike soon. What did he mean?" *For fucks sake I was trying to keep that quiet.*

"He's referring to the union I'm in, NACODS. There's talk about another ballot of the members. I wouldn't worry, we only voted in April never got the two thirds majority."

□

"Mick someone to see you." Cornelius shouted up to me. At that moment I had my head above the last roof beams set. Checking for gas and the standard of packing. The regulation roof bolts already in position.

"Who?" I shouted as I jumped back onto the platform. I saw immediately who it was. "Mr Walters." Climbing down the metal ladder I shook his hand. It was the first time he'd come to see in person the work being carried out on W11's maingate junction.

"Morning Mick. How's it gan, man?"

"All good thanks Mr Walters." Cornelius and his two mates were keeping busy filling sand bags. I had no doubt they were listening intently as to why the Undermanager was paying us a visit this morning. "Reckon another week we should be something like and breaking into the gate itself." Jack Walters wasn't tall, softly spoken, hard to hear at times. Above anything he had such sad eyes. Even when he was laughing, he always seemed sad. He looked across to the belt. It was piled high with the blackstuff.

"Good. Expecting big things from this place. It'll be Parkside's first heavy duty face."

"Yeah, so I believe. Mr Keech mentioned it first time I met him."

"Right young man I shouldn't be keeping you." He turned to continue down the Access Road, suddenly stopping. "You might want to leave a little earlier today. Manager would like a word." *Fuck what have I done?* I didn't get chance to ask the question as JW continued inbye.

"Manager hey. What's tha been up to?" Cornelius asked as he lifted one of the filled bags onto the platform. His two mates were smiling.

"I suppose I'll find out soon enough."

As I was about to leave Nick Arnold appeared.

"Hiya Mick. How's it goin?"

"All good thanks. Sorry Nick can't hang about got an appointment with the Manager."

"What's tha been up to lad?"

"Exactly my question." Cornelius shouted down from the platform.

"Best take some of those report books with you lad."

"For what?"

"Down back of trousers." I smiled.

43

"See you lads tomorrow." I continued outbye.

The belts were running well today. Hadn't stopped at all. What was more pleasing I hadn't spotted anyone riding illegally. Climbing onto the manriding platform I looked inbye for a gap in the coal. I'd not seen so much coal on a belt ever. The satisfying rhythmic click with the accompanying smell of coal and belt. A satisfying experience for any pit mon. Still not sure of the main coaling routes and which coal face was delivering onto this belt. I had heard we had sufficient men working now with all four faces manned up. C15's, W6's, L30's and 31's. I had little choice but to jump on the existing stream of coal. Careful not to fall off in the process. Holding my oil lamp in one hand. I attempted to clear a space. The coal was damp but warm. I thought better than to lay flat. Lumps began to fall off the edges of the conveyor. I steadied myself in a seating position.

Within minutes I lifted myself. Balancing either side of the coal pile. Repositioning my oil lamp. Annoyed as small pieces of coal drop down the side of my boots. Arm outstretched as I reached the platform still moving at speed as I disembarked onto the getting off platform and making my way to V belt.

Ten minutes later I was at the top of the Wigan Mines Access. Stopping momentarily to empty my boots. It would be a walk out, too early for the loco. The cold intake air hit me as I entered the main loco tunnel. I shivered as the air hit my damp overalls. I picked up the pace creating additional body heat to offset the cold air. I was somewhat surprised to see several bodies ahead also walking towards the pit bottom. Within minutes I gained on them. Each moving sheepishly to one side as I passed. I didn't recognise any of them.

I spotted the pit bottom lights ahead. Partly obscured by more bodies. Standing further back from the shaft than normal. By the time I reached the group I could hear conversations taking place.

"It's that fucker Large."

"Cunt wish he'd fuck off." I continued through the throng of men. One or two objecting as I pushed my way to the front. Their objections soon stifled when they saw my oil lamp. Once I'd reached the front, I was even more surprised by what I saw. An official in dark blue overalls. He was about five three, Clean face, oil lamp hanging from his belt. He was holding a stick and smiling. I walked towards him.

"And where do you think you're going?"

"What's it look like. Up pit."

"What sort of example do you think you're setting?"

"Sorry?" I sensed the now silence from the men. Trying to listen to our conversation.

"An official riding the shaft early."

"Not through choice I might add. I'm off to see the Manager. JW's told me he wants to see me."

"Nobody's mentioned it to me."

"And who are you?"

"Sidney Large, Colliery Overman." I hadn't met all the officials yet. No surprise it was still early days. What I couldn't believe is how many Colliery Overmen the pit had. I was sure they outnumbered the Deputies. "And who would you be?"

"Mick Gibson recent transferee from Cronton."

"Oh, so you're Mick Gibson."

"Yep, the one and only."

"Go on then." As I continued forward, I heard movement behind. "Not you lot still early yet."

I hadn't given much thought as to why the Manager would want to see me. Although I had an idea. I'd made the decision already to stay in my black. It gave a better impression.

I had yet to go in the Manager's office. Although I knew where it was. During our first few days after arriving Harry Roach had showed us around the surface. He'd referred to the place as "Top Shunt." Which he'd followed up with. "Tha doesn't want to be goin in there too often." The thought of it now gave me butterflies.

"Excuse me. Where do you think you're going?"

My mind on other matters I hadn't spotted the blond-short haired lady sat in an office alongside the corridor. I turned towards her. Wearing a red chequered frock. She was in the middle of typing something. She looked quite stern as much as she could with a pretty face.

"Manager's asked to see me." I felt a little uncomfortable with the encounter.

"Have you an appointment?"

"I, I…" For some reason I couldn't get my words out.

"There's somebody already in there with him. Just wait there. I'll see if he's available. What's your name?" *Fuckin ell this is proving more difficult than I thought.*

"Mick, Mick Gibson." I watched as she picked up the phone.

"I'm sorry to bother you Mr Creed there's someone here to see you." She listened. "Yes, he's still in his black." Her expression hadn't changed. "Will do." Replacing the handset, she turned back towards me. "He'll see you now."

"Thanks." For the first time I'd noticed my mouth was dry. I'm not sure she heard me as she continued typing. The keys crashing down at speed. *Not one for chit chat then!* I continued forward running my tongue around my mouth trying to create some saliva. On reaching the office door I attempted to clear my throat. I knocked. Momentarily I felt as though I was back at school, outside the Headmaster's study.

"Come." The aroma of pipe tobacco was to greet me first. The smell reminding me of one of my uncles. To my right a desk, piled high with various report books. In the centre a plan of underground workings laid out various sized leather paperweights on each corner. Late summer rays of sunshine lighting up the room. The only sound, a large round clock ticking above the desk.

Most of the room was taken up by a large table. I recognised the Manager immediately. Another smaller guy was sat alongside. The Manager seemed taller than when I'd last seen him and younger. He was smiling. Wearing a tweed jacket, white shirt, and dark tie. He looked happy but still signs of an inner hardness. His receding hairline almost white. He had less hair than I had imagined.

"Take a seat lad." I hesitated, being in my black. "Don't worry about that sit. You two met?" He asked turning to the guy sat next to him. Neither of us answered immediately. The guy next to him looked younger. Grey curly hair and a colourful complexion. Suggesting he spent time in the fresh air. A kinder face too. He was wearing a denim jacket and opened necked striped T shirt.

"Mick this is Frank Prince, NUM Secretary at Parkside. Frank this is Mick Gibson a transferee from Cronton." Frank nodded towards me. I returned the acknowledgement. By the look on his face, I don't think he liked me. The conversation interrupted by the sound of men above us. The stamping of feet and conversation. The Manager pointed to the ceiling. "One of the benefits of my office Frank. Being beneath the lamp room I can hear the men when they come up pit." He looked towards his desk. On the wall behind it a large clock. It was one o'clock. "Particularly when they're early." His voice a little louder this time. Frank seemed to jump at his raised voice. He allowed his comment to hang in the air before continuing.

"Now lad, Frank tells me you've been upsetting his lads." It took me a moment to fully understand what he was referring to. And why he was referring to them as "his lads." Surely, we all worked for the Manager. It could only mean one thing.

.

46

"Illegal manriding?" My comment caused the Manager to raise his eyebrows and sit back in his seat. He turned to Frank. The man hadn't taken his eyes off me since I'd walked in.

"My lads tell me that ain't the case. First time it appened didn't even know the platform was there." I didn't answer. I wanted him to get his grievance out completely. Silence followed. Obviously waiting for me to answer. "The lads had been given an early note by their Deputy. They were carrying empty pouches out too." Again silence. "And you've been stopping the lads time." The Manager turned towards me. It was time for me to offer my explanation.

"Frank me and my team spent a week prepping the site. Repositioning the getting off platform with the relevant signage. Including I might add the countdown markers. We then salvaged an old getting on platform. Transported it to site along with the relevant signage. Not until that was complete did, we start on the junction. I'm pretty sure too, JW advised all his officials of this. Including the Mid-Area Undermanager, Howard Davies." I stopped momentarily to give Frank a chance to respond. Which he didn't. "The thing that annoys me the most is the trouble and time we went through to make sure everything was safe." I stopped to take a breath. "That being the case could only suggest one of two things. Either *your lads* are fuckin stupid or fuckin blind! I'm guessing they're neither." This time I waited for a response. Which again wasn't forthcoming.

"Until I'm instructed otherwise by Mr Creed I'll continue. Unless that is you want us to make an example of someone?"

My comment hadn't been well received. Franks face had reddened. He began gesticulating pointing towards me. He didn't seem the type of guy that got angry. "You can't just stop men's time. It's in our agreement they must be informed. At least three days advance notice."

"Not a problem. I'll get the Time Office to put a note up each week. Listing all those I've caught coming up early."

"For fucks sake Mr Creed. I thought Sidney Large was bad, but this fella takes the fuckin biscuit!"

After the meeting was over, Frank Prince left, the Manager asked me to hang back.

"How you settling in lad?"

"Okay thanks Mr Creed."

"Big difference to what you've been used to?"

"Do you mean the pit or what I'm doing?"

"Everything." With his last comment he sat back and reached for his pipe. Obviously ready to listen. The pack of Swan Vesta followed next. I waited until the puffs of smoke began to rise from his mouth. The fresh smell of St Bruno filled the room. His gaze now on me.

"Yeah, in some ways. I was hoping to get an Overmans role when I got here."

"All in good time lad. That reminds me that fella from Staff Training Malcolm Hughes, is planning on visiting. We need to interview you for the ET Scheme. You'll need to complete an internal application form." I'd heard of the scheme but thought it was only for student apprentices. To add further explanation, he added. "The shortened version. For you industrial students."

"When?"

"You're an impatient fucker, I'll give you that. As soon as I know, I'll let you know." He was staring at me now. I began to feel a little uncomfortable. This man certainly had presence. "Now listen lad and listen careful. I know you mean well. These lads are hurting. Forget the rights and wrongs of the strike. Some of these fellas have lost everything. They don't need their noses rubbing in. There's plenty at Area think we should teach'em a lesson. Afraid I don't go with that. It's going to take time to heal. We as management have an obligation to bring the strikers and non-strikers back together. There's no guarantee we'll do any of that. Between the Government, NCB, and NUM, they've made it right difficult, but we must try." The Manager's comments came as no surprise. I'd already spotted below that hard exterior was a man of passion and feeling. A moment of silence passed between the two of us.

"Yeah. I understand. I'm sorry."

"Fuckin sorry lad. I don't want you goin all soft on me." *Perhaps sorry hadn't been the best word to use.* For the first time since entering his office I began to feel at ease. That was soon to change as he picked up his fountain pen. "Time you fucked off I've got work to do."

Leaving his office, I headed towards the baths. The place was almost empty. Stripped I headed towards the showers.

"Heard the latest Mick?" It was Gerry Cook. His was in his clean inhaling on a fag. "Bout NACODS Special Delegate Conference."

"No."

"Motion been passed unanimously. Ballot set for 26th September."

"For what?"

"Strike lad. Coal Board being asked to withdrew the pit closure programme and them 15th August guidelines. Anyway, can't stop Harry's called meeting of executive."

Before I could ask any further questions, he was gone. *Fuck me! Strike. How will that work if I'm going on the ET Scheme?*

The following week I was at the pit for the first two days, then from Wednesday off to Old Boston for the Deputies five-day refresher course.

The refresher held every 3 years covered the duties of a Deputy. As well as lads from Parkside some of my old colleagues were there from Cronton including Shaun Galway. Conversation between us all concerned the ballot.

"What did I tell you Mick. Coal Board have fucked up big time."

"You think the ballot will be in favour of strike action?"

"There's nothing more certain."

Now back at the pit I'd travelled in that morning with several of the officials. Expectation was running high that the vote would be in favour of strike action. By the time I'd reached the junction the lads were already on site.

"For fucks sake Jack! Why has not oiled bolts. They're as dry as me Aunt Midge's cunt."

"Don't have a go at me. I thought Tommy were on it."

"Hey, don't be bringing me into it. Shouldn't be messin with thi auntie anyhow." Cornelius was standing on the platform, ring spanner in hand. His two mates just finishing a butty, having just arrived at the junction site.

"Where's the cropper?" I asked.

"Some cunt's nicked it. Jack never put it in box."

"Fuck me. It's have a go at Jack day, is it?"

"Should I try and arrange another?" I asked.

"Not to worry Mick. Nick's fetchin one in with him."

Hanging my oil lamp on the side of the road I clambered up towards Cornelius.

"If tha wants summat doin, do it theesen." He was now dabbing emulsifying oil on the arch bolts. "Fuckin cunts. Anyway, Mick how's coping with babbie scriking every neet?" I smiled.

"You'll be surprised to hear; we don't have that problem. Off to sleep at six. Wakes just before I set off. Missus gives her a feed. Different to lad. He was a pain in the arse. Never used to sleep."

"What's appening up there? Mothers meeting or what. Ere Mick grab this." I turned to see Nick part way up the ladder with the replacement cropper. The compressed air hissing from the connection. Tommy dragging slack and hanging it on the side rail of the platform. Passing the gun to Cornelius, I grabbed the ear plugs from my top pocket. Before I'd even placed them in position Cornelius had hit the trigger. Nick continued inbye. The *clunk, clunk, clunk*, of the machine's blade hitting the nut on the inch bolt, followed by *krr, krr, krr,* as it bit into the steel. Then *ping* as the nut flew through the air. The next three followed quickly in succession. I reached down as he moved to the opposite shoulder. I placed each of the split nuts into a hessian sack. Still warm to the touch.

As Cornelius started on the next four bolts, I looked inbye. The black stuff was now coming thick and fast. I wasn't sure from where. There was something special and satisfying seeing the belt full of coal. Still uncertain of the belt layout underground, although I was improving my knowledge during the weekend inspections. There were four faces producing. C15's, W6's L30's and L31's. A fifth currently being developed, L32's. I was suddenly brought back to the present as Cornelius connected the seven-pound hammer to the arch plates. The crown lurched forward. A pile of dirt dropping onto the wooden platform. The cloud of dust engulfed us both. Together we moved outbye. My mouth full of dust, I spat onto the belt below.

"Some weight on that one Mick. Doubt we'll be needing any dets." As the dust cleared, I peered to where the crown had been. There was now a two-foot cavity above. "Might want to be fillin some bags lads."

"Will do." Tommy responded.

By the time we'd got to the end of the shift, the fourth cross beam was in place, supported by legs either side. The corrugated steel sheets solid beneath the packing bags used to fill the cavity. I'd made sure of that. The number of men now walking passed the platform suggested it was time we were making a move too.

"Results just come in Mick." Gerry Cook shouted towards me as I reached the ground. "Eighty-two and half per cent in favour. That'll teach the bastards." It took me a moment to realise what Gerry was referring too. The NACODS vote had only taken place two days previously whilst I'd been at Old Boston.

"What? In favour of strike action."

"Yep. Harry's called meeting. Wants us in his office when we get up."

"That's our bonus in the cut!" Cornelius who'd been standing alongside me added. "Go on Mick. Get theesen gone. We'll put tools away." I didn't need any further encouragement. Positioning my oil lamp, I grabbed my Donkey jacket and followed Gerry to the manriding platform.

There was quite a gathering outside Harry Roache's office. Mainly the dayshift officials still in their black. I guessed the noonshift had already been briefed.

"She's fucked nah."

"I, following in Ted's footsteps."

"Is that it Harry?" Comments from the lads were flying thick and fast.

"Now hold up will tha. Let's be havin a bit of order." Harry shouted above the various conversations.

"When we striking Harry?"

"Lads will you hold on." I felt a little sorry for Harry he was struggling to make himself heard.

"What did I tell ye Mick." Billy Pete appeared alongside. I nodded.

"Nah listen lads will tha shut thi fuckin din and let Harry get a word in." The voice of Conna Michaels boomed out. He was a big fucker. The Deputy on E3 haulage. His intervention had the desired effect. Silence quickly followed.

"At last. Now first off there'll be no talk of striking." Harry continued. Conna had pushed his way through the throng and positioned himself alongside Harry. So had Gerry Cook. I think they both had something to do with the union too. "It's business as usual. Date for strike has been called for in another month. 25th October to be exact. There's plenty time for them discussions to continue."

Fuck and there's me thinking everything was getting back to normal. Six months into the strike, many pits working as normal. Although most of Yorkshire lads were still out. What would we do? Two kids and planning to move house next year. All that time spent at college and all for what? The situation for us all was a complete mess. What the fuck was I going to say to the missus?

"Right is there owt else from any of tha?"

"What bout poor George's Toyota Celica? He'll ave sell it now." I wasn't sure who they were referring to or the significance of the car.

"Nah, that's summat George'll ave deal with himself." Harry responded.

"Will we have our own picket line Harry?" Dan Jacks asked. I don't think he was serious. He was always taking the piss.

"I why not. I'll be with tha. Wouldn't want to miss you stopping Manager." Harry's final comment brought the meeting to an end.

Driving back along the M62 I contemplated not tellin the missus. She'd be worried sick. There again I had little choice it would be all over the news. Harry did say though negotiations were still taking place. There'd been ongoing discussion between NACODS General Secretary and the Chairman. What a complete and utter fuck up. After six months the Coal Board still hadn't managed to reach a settlement with the NUM. Whilst I'd been at Old Boston one of the officials from Bold Colliery had mentioned losing a coal face due to weight coming on. Another said they'd lost a face due to flooding. It was probably worse in other places that weren't having underground inspections. I reckoned the biggest problem both sides had was the Government. There was no two ways about it. The whole thing had become political. They were out to teach us a lesson. Regardless of the hardship faced by many still on strike and the poor bastards who were still trying to work. Each side believing, they were right. There had to be some means of compromise.

The management union BACM had three or four officials working at the pit. Senior management another ten to fifteen? Never enough to keep the place producing coal and certainly not enough to carry out the statutory inspections. I just hoped it didn't come to that.

My immediate problem was the missus and my ability to keep the money coming in. There was a possibility I could go working with my brothers. Two of them had their own landscaping company. Something I'd need to explore.

"You, okay?" Now that wasn't the response, I expected walking into the house. Annie was stood in the hallway. Cradling little Lizzie in a cream-coloured shawl. Something I hadn't seen before.

"Never mind me, how are you two? Where's Jamie?"

"We're both good. I'm going to have to wake her in a mo or she'll never sleep tonight." I walked across to give her a kiss on her forehead. "Jamie's in the garden. Playing with his war men. He's waiting for you to join him. Do you think you'll go on strike?" I suppose I had to be honest.

"Looks like it. Signs not good at the moment."

"How will we manage for money?"

"I was going to ask the lads."

"That's not going to cover the mortgage."

"I know but I've got the six-hundred-pound transfer money coming in next week. Plus, I'm in Sunday and…."

"Never mind for now best you go and see your son."

☐

I was back in work on Sunday. On a six twelve. The conversations amongst the officials were all about the result. I said very little. Listening to the various points of view. The majority were in favour and believed NACODS going out would bring the strike to an end. Particularly as several papers were reporting a split within Government on how the whole thing had been managed. Labour too were up in arms with what they now saw as the establishment of a national police force. One conversation from one of the older officials concerned picketing. He had a brother who worked in the Nottinghamshire coalfields. He'd been talking to him over the phone on how that would affect those pits that were still working. According to him he reckoned many of the officials would continue working. That's all we needed. I'd seen already the outcome of the split in the NUM. What would I do? I was due to go back to the Poly week after next, two day per week on a Tuesday and Wednesday to take my Manager's papers.

The following week I decided to have a chat with Harry Roach. I hadn't had much to do with him up to this point but from what I'd seen so far, he seemed level headed and more to the point said it as it is. After reporting to Lenny Dunliffe and before going for a bath I popped round to his office. Unfortunately, there were a number of officials already there. Gerry Cook too. He spotted me before I had chance to turn round.

"Nah Mick. Come to see Harry have you lad?"

"No, I'm fine. It's nothing." Gerry obviously knew I was talking shite.

"Go get a bath. We'll be out of here shortly. Make sure thi back here before three though. He's off to Wigan meeting with Executive Committee. National Secretary coming over to address the lads."

"Oh, right, thanks Gerry."

I was back outside his office within half an hour. The door was open slightly. I couldn't hear anything. Took a deep breath and knocked.

"Come in Mick." *How the fuck does he know it's me?* "Close door behind tha."

"Sorry to bother you, Harry."

"Thi's not bothering me lad. Only got ten minutes though. What's for do?" I wasn't sure how far I could go. Could I be open and honest with Harry? My initial hesitation caused Harry to add. "No beating round bush lad tell me what's on your mind."

"I'm not sure if you know but I'm due to start back at the Poly next week. Legislation for my Manager's papers."

"When's sittin examination?"

"Not till twenty first November."

"And tha's wonderin if thi'll still be able go college?"

"In a nutshell yeah."

"Still a way off yet though Mick. Negotiations still takin place with Coal Board. Might not come to a strike." Harry began to collect several papers off his desk.

"What do you think will happen."

"Nah lad I ain't got no crystal ball."

"Some of the lads mentioned another ballot taking place in the Nottinghamshire pits."

"I. Ave erd same."

"What if some of them decide to keep working?"

"Break strike lad?" Harry's voice now an octave higher. He pushed his glasses back along his nose. Staring at me intensely. "Be it on any man's conscience to do that lad. Need to be clear of consequences."

"Oh, sorry. I'm not suggesting I'd go through the picket line." I wondered if my questioning had gone too far.

"I'm not suggesting you would Mick being from Liverpool and all that." He paused for breath. "But you might be asked." His last comment hung in the air. I wasn't sure what or who he was referring too. "Right Mick if there's nowt else, I need to be makin move."

"Okay. Thanks for your time, Harry. Much appreciated."

"It's what am ere for lad. Me job."

Driving back home I wondered whether I was worrying needlessly. Harry was right still plenty of time for NACODS and the Coal Board to reach a deal. The size of the majority must have put us in a strong position. I mean surely the Government had no plans to destroy the industry. Although they'd given little thought to the problems they were creating for industrial relations. If a deal could be reached, it would obviously include the NUM. The problems facing the industry at this moment were on two fronts. The cheap price of oil and imports. That's what we needed to concentrate on.

There wasn't much I could do and worrying certainly wouldn't help. As my nan always used to say *worrying doesn't take away tomorrow's troubles. It takes away todays peace.*

Harry hadn't been wrong. The following week the Coal Board and NACODS reached an agreement on pay and the circular of the 15th of August was withdrawn. The strike hadn't been called off as discussion continued on the Colliery Review Procedure. Harry explained; NACODS were looking to have some form of independent arbitration in the review procedure if agreement couldn't be reached. The Advisory, Conciliation and Arbitration Service, ACAS, were now involved.

It was certainly obvious if agreement couldn't be reached and NACODS came out on strike the Government would be in deep trouble. There would have to be some movement on their part. There was unease in NACODS too. As in certain areas it was rumoured that if a strike was called some of the membership may continue working. It was the last thing our Union leaders wanted with what they saw happening in the NUM.

Days later agreement was reached when the Coal Board accepted the idea of an independent body. However, they still insisted on maintaining the right to make the final decision. Strike action was still a possibility. The final piece of the jigsaw would depend on the outcome of negotiations between Coal Board and the NUM.

I was working at least one weekend shift each week. I was getting to know the Deputies and Overman. All had their own views on what was happening in the industry. If a strike were called none of those, I spoke to would be crossing the picket line. One particular weekend the discussion on the situation became quite heated. Those I knew Gerry Cook, Dan Jacks, Bennie Lead were adamant if we didn't stand alongside the NUM there would be major consequences for the industry. Others including George Peters didn't believe the Government would betray the industry. It was the first time I'd spoken to George. This was the same guy that used a scrubbing brush in the showers, even on his face. Another guy I hardly knew was Jackie Flatt. Underground he was as bald as a coot. On the surface he had a mop of curly black hair. It was great for me to get a perspective on the current situation listening to these men.

☐

The following week I was back at the Poly. Only two days per week. Tuesdays and Wednesdays. Learning the ins and outs of the 1954 Act and the Regulations that came with it. Not dissimilar to what we learned when taking the Undermanager's papers. There was now however greater emphasis on learning the details from a Manager's perspective. The aim to be ready for sitting the exams for the 1st Class Papers in November.

It seemed a very short working week now. Before I knew it, Friday had arrived. Driving into work that morning news on the radio was continually providing updates on the bombing of the Grand Hotel in Brighton. Unconfirmed reports were suggesting up to thirty people had been injured and five killed. What had been confirmed was that the Prime Minister had survived.
In work it was the main topic of conversation. Several of the older men couldn't believe such a thing could happen in our country, others however, were not surprised. I was deployed that morning to the 320 brow. A first for me. Giving me the chance to meet several haulage lads.

That weekend I was working the Sunday, six till midnight. I travelled in with Derek Moore, Dan Jacks and Billy Pete. We stopped at the bottom of E3 for a chat before continuing inbye to conduct our inspections.
"She can't be well liked if they try and do something like that." Billy commented.
"Tha's not wrong there lad. Pinch Mick?"
"Thanks, Derek."
"Tha knows you can buy this in the canteen." Dan added.
"Mick doesn't know where canteen is. Probably best if he keeps out. Lads might lynch him." We all began to laugh.
"Listen I'll fuckin freeze if we stay here. Let's pop along to 19's return have a minute there."

Once we arrived, we positioned ourselves on several scrap wooden cable reels. It was certainly warmer I was eager to explore the lads thoughts on the strike. It was only just over a week before we went out. I turned towards Derek offering my opened tin of snuff. He seemed deep in thought chewing on his bacca, still with a grin on his face. Unlike his brother. Might have been the glasses he wore.

"For fucks sake Mick where d'you find that?" I ignored his comment and asked.

"What's the latest on our proposed strike action?"

"Chatting with Harry last week. Reckons President and General Secretary had a big fall out. Didn't help them both being off on holiday at the same time."

"Av herd some of the officials in Yorkshire are getting paid for staying at home."

"Am also told the odd shear of coal we're producing ain't being reported to Area."

"Mr Creed all over. Got get up early to catch that mon out. Stockpiling it'll be. Saving for a rainy day. Broke the mould after he made our Patrick that's for sure. Right Dan thinks it's time we made a move. Nearly half eight now. See you lads later."

After Derek and Dan had left Billy and I began to walk into the district.

"You get to many fancy dress parties?"

"Fuckin ell Mick every year lad. Love'em. Why tha askin?"

"Been invited to one New Year's Eve. Not sure what to go as."

"Only one outfit for me Mick. Straight out of my missus's wardrobe."

"What?"

"Yep. Dresses up as a women every time." I looked at Billy in disbelief.

"What with a wig, boobs and all that."

"You name it I wear it."

"What about your tash."

"Fuckin ell Mick that ain't comin off for no fucker." We both began to laugh as we continued inbye. The thought of the potential future strike on the back burner for now.

☐

Then totally unexpected the strike was called off. The agreed proposal between the NCB and NACODS removed the 15th of August circular and added an independent review body into the Colliery Review Procedure, CRP. Although the Coal Board were still insisting on having the final say. In addition, the pit closures at Polmaise, Cortonwood, Snowdon, Herrington and Bullcliffe Wood would be reviewed again under the revised CRP. Consideration too of the proposal to take out four million tonnes of capacity.

☐

I was surprised how quickly progress on the junction had been. I suppose being away at college two days per week caused me to miss some of this. I had given some thought on how we'd progress on the maingate but there was

56

something bothering me. I couldn't quite get my head around how we'd drill the tops. At Cronton it had always been straightforward but here. Everything was on a larger scale. It was the first time I realised why I'd been deployed to this role. My experience on these jobs was obviously lacking. This work was just what I needed. Only I hadn't seen that when I arrived. There was only so much bluff and bluster you could use to get through each shift. I'd been fortunate too. The ATC lads I'd been with had helped in that respect. I couldn't have asked for a better mentor.

"Morning Mick."
"Morning Cornelius." I'd just walked into the lamproom.
"How's college goin lad?"
"All good thanks."
"Learnt anything new?"
"Both days been covering the explosive regs." He began to laugh.
"I, learning how to do things by the book. Meaning we'd get fuck all done. That reminds me, you'll need dets. Twenty should do."
"I thought we'd be into a full face of coal after I'd left Monday."
"We are cock. Twenty is plenty. You won't need an exploder either. Soft lad forgeet to bring it out with him."

"You two coming or what?" Tommy shouted. The place was beginning to get busy with the bulk of the dayshift lads arriving. I was surprised how being away for two days each week allowed me to see things a little differently. There was no place like it. The lamproom and deployment centre. Men, all shapes, and sizes wandering in. Some wide-awake laughing and joking. Others still half asleep. Nursing headaches from the previous night. Jostling each other as the numbers built. The smell of stale sweat mixed in with alcohol and the obligatory smell of shit.
"Where's Jimmy?"
"Gone for powder. Told him we'd only need two cans. Four still in there." I shook my head. So much for me learning how things should be done correctly. Saying no more I headed towards the deployment centre to pick up my tallies.
"Morning Lenny, morning Billy."
"Mornin Mick, good to have you back."
"I mornin part timer." Little Billy responded with his usual joke. "I'll be fetchin yon sixteen be nineteens in later. Can you make sure your lads help to offload?"
"Yeah, will do. Can you ask them to offload at the entrance? The last lot they dropped off they left above the warwick."
"Fuckin ell Mick. Thy'll be askin em to set em next." Little Billy followed up still smiling.

Arriving at the junction I was a little dismayed to see the state of the place. Various lengths of steel lay outbye of the maingate entrance. Two shotfiring curtains, their yellow frame just visible beneath the main belt. The sight of which causing me to tap my left-hand side pocket. Checking I had the red sentry caps with me. Boxes of sand stemming lay scattered. One of the boxes partly open. A damaged plug laying in pieces alongside. I'd broke in to a sweat travelling down the brew but decided to keep my donkey jacket on for now. The cold intake air making its presence felt as soon as I'd stopped walking. The main belt was piled high with the blackstuff.

Most of the working platform was dismantled, haphazardly discarded under the belt. It was a little irritating trying to keep the place tidy when others didn't give two fucks. An additional Shelton arch had gone up from being there Monday. A pile of coal was still on the deck. Thin lengths of orange det cable lying in places. We were now using millisecs instead of instantaneous. There was the distinct smell of ammonia, they'd start clearing that first. How wrong was I. As soon as they arrived, Jimmy and Tommy grabbed a compressed air drilling machine a piece and began drilling. Cornelius spotted my surprise.

"Only way to reach tops Mick. Advance in two blows."

"Obviously." I blurted out. Proving my lack of understanding. Cornelius said nothing. He smiled which was response enough.

I reckoned it would be another hour before I'd need to fire. Wandering around the place I found the hundred shot exploder in the manhole outbye of the junction along with the four full pouches of P4/5. A brand-new coiled length of shotfiring cable lay beneath the pouches. The ramming rod and break detector were hanging from two cable hangers. Cornelius had mentioned on the way in some electrician guy had complained that the hangers were for cables only.

"Nah Mick almost ready." I'd used one of the empty pouches to collect the primed sticks of powder. "How many have you done?"

"Fifteen, as requested."

"Good lad." I wandered down. Tommy followed. He was carrying the other two canisters. Cornelius and Jimmy were busy coiling the compressed air bagging and placing the drilling machines away.

"Give us key Mick. I'll open these two." Tommy was kneeling. One of the canisters sat between his legs. I threw him my set of keys.

"How many sticks?"

"Two plus the primer." Tommy responded.

"Tha'll do no such fuckin thing. Don't want to be damaging main coaling belt. Getting our Mick ere in trouble." Cornelius added.

Extracting the first primed stick, I placed it into the drilled hole. Pushing it to the holes furthest point whilst holding the thin det wires in my left hand.

"Here Mick, we'll be here all day. Pass us some." Tommy was holding a spare ramming rod.

"My job thank you." I placed a second stick of powder in behind the primer.

"For fucks sake Mick. Yon mon lets us do it."

"Well, I'm not fuckin yon mon. I'll let you stem up if you're good."

"Our Mick likes to do things properly now he does." Cornelius added. He was standing behind me, placing a piece of bacca into his mouth. "Might let you try some of this later Mick. Soaked overneet in Courvoisier."

I wasn't trying to be awkward and had no doubt it would speed things up. The lads were more than capable. But what was the point of learning the legislation if I wasn't going to put it into practice. Plus, we were right on show to anyone passing. I remember arriving one morning with a break detector. Caused amusement amongst the three of them. I only used it once.

As I filled each shot hole, Tommy followed stemming up. Cornelius started connecting each in series. I was about to say something but let it go. Jimmy fetched me the shot firing cable. I coupled each of the two strands to the respective det wires. One final thing to do. Unclipping my methanometer I took a reading at the face of the heading. Carrying out the same procedure at roof level. Nothing.

"Right, who's being sentry?" I reached in my pockets for the red plastic cap. I knew it wouldn't be used as it should.

"I, give us ere Mick. Try this too." Cornelius offered me his tin of bacca. He'd already cut a short length.

"Thanks." I placed it in my mouth. The taste of brandy immediately hitting the taste buds. I didn't spit out immediately, wanting to savour the taste

"Good eigh?" He shouted after me as he proceeded inbye below the heading entrance.

Tommy and Jimmy followed me up brew. Connecting the cable to the exploder I lifted it out of the manhole. I looked down towards Cornelius. He acknowledged by waving his cap lamp. I repeated the same towards him. Looking outbye for the last time. I turned back, whilst at the same time winding the handle of the exploder. This was the part I loved best.

"Fire!" I shouted, a little too loud. No sooner had I pressed the button, lumps of coal flew out from the heading entrance followed by the dull thud of the blast. Smoke billowed outwards. Momentarily hanging in the air before being whisked away by the intake air. I was glad Cornelius had placed a few corrugated metal sheets to protect the belt structure.

"Fuckin ell Mick. Tha nearly burst my ear drums." He began to walk towards the heading.

"Let it clear first Tommy."

"It'll be gone by time I get there." I quickly uncoupled the cable and followed the lads down. Cornelius was already in position. The smell of ammonia lingered still. He'd positioned a short length of old conveyor belt at the heading entrance. Jimmy grabbed a shovel and knelt alongside the belt. Cornelius too was now kneeling as he began to shovel the loose coal towards his mate. Jimmy had taken the pick. Busily chopping away at the face dislodging any loose lumps.

Moving forward I visually checked the coal as it was being loaded. Misfires was always a concern. Particularly as we were loading onto the main coaling belts. Satisfied I moved back into the main intake. Leaning against the side of the belt I watched as the loose mineral was thrown onto the belt. I was taking no chances. Ten minutes later sufficient coal cleared I helped the lads lift the last of the Shelton crowns into position. Secured to the two-foot struts the lads returned to their original positions and resumed filling out. There wasn't much else I could do but keep myself busy tidying the place up. Within the hour they began to pull the drilling machines back into the heading.

"Mick just so you know. I'll be heading out a little early today need to check on mini panzer. Meeting Nick Arnold over on compound to arrange it loading up."

"You won't be needing it for a while though?"

"Ideally day after tomorrow. Tidy little thing she is. Makes life a lot easier than throwing it on belt. Could do with framework moving in this afternoon."

"Yeah. Saw that at pit bottom this morning. I'll speak with noonshift." I spat the last of the chewing bacca onto the belt. Once more piled to the gunnels with the black stuff.

"Fancy another Mick?" Cornelius had removed his bacca tin again."

"You trying to get me pissed?"

Once back on the surface. I left Cornelius to sort the mini panzer. I needed to arrange the journey in with the framework plus a bag of bolts!

The following day standing at the pit top I spotted Jimmy and Tommy. No sign of Cornelius though. According to the lads he'd gone across to the workshops to pick up the bracketry he'd had made for the mini panzer. I was surprised how many faces I didn't recognise. It was now nine months into the strike. The numbers returning to work was increasing by the day. I overheard JW telling one of the officials we were unlikely to reach three hundred thousand tonnes this year. One of the lowest annual tonnes since the pit had started production. I hadn't spotted any animosity between the men. The odd name calling and that was about it. I suspected there may have been other incidents. Working with the ATC lads I was somewhat isolated. I could only hope things got back to normal once the remainder of the lads returned. It was only a matter of time.

"For fucks sake!" Tommy shouted as we reached the junction. "Stupid bastards have only unloaded the steel inbye of where it's supposed to be. Been quicker fetchin it mesen." The haulage rope began to move.
"Don't worry. I'll get it loaded back up. Haulage lads are on their way out now."
"Stupid bastards."
"Fuckin ell Tom tha does go on a bit. Mick's just told tha he'd sort it." They both disappeared into the recess to have a butty before starting. In the distance I could see two cap lamps both stationary. They must have spotted me. Their lights began to frantically move about. At that moment, my attention was drawn to the belt. The click, click of the belting had been replaced by the duller sound as the coal heading outbye began to build. The lads on one of the coal faces were stopping over. The overtime ban was becoming a thing of the past.

I began to walk towards the journey, now just inbye of the steel. Raising my hand.
"Hold it lads." I recognised the two faces. Although I was unsure of their names. The smaller of the two reached across to the greenline suspended to the side of the road. Attached to the front bogie, two half cut mine cars and two flats.
"What's up nah?" He shouted as the journey came to a halt.
"Morning lads. Could do with that steel." I pointed to the stack under the belt. "loading back up and dropping at the junction."
"Not our job." The taller lad shouted.
"Little Billy wants empties out first thing. He won't be appy." Shorty added.

Shorty was now alongside me. Unkempt hair straggling beneath his helmet. A dried patch of bacca clung to the stubble beneath his chin. He must have only weighed three stone wet through. A good pan of Scouse wouldn't go amiss. He reached up to take the latch off. As he did so I grabbed the rolled-up newspaper protruding from the side pocket of his donkey jacket.
"Come on. I'll give you a lift." I offered.
"What's think doin? Not finished reading it yet."
"Let's say I consider giving it you back. Although we both know I'd be in my rights to confiscate it. Being a fire hazard and all that."
"Scouse cunt." The tall lad entered the discussion.

"Yeah, that would be me. Anyway listen. The longer we stand here arguing the longer it's going to take you to get out. Little Billy won't be happy."

"I and we'll blame you." I never responded the three of us stood there. Anybody watching, wouldn't have been mistaken if they thought they were watching us audition for a Mexican standoff.

"Come on. The sooner we get this done. The sooner we get going." The tall lad moved back inbye towards the empties.

Within twenty minutes we were done. The last of the steel offloaded. Plus, a bag of steel bolts. The empties began to move outbye.

"Thanks lads." I passed the rolled-up newspaper to Shorty. Surprisingly, I received no thanks. I moved away from the track and into the junction. Never comfortable standing below a journey on the incline.

The two ATC lads had been busy. Last leg set, they were now in the process of sheeting and packing behind.

"Morning all." I hadn't spotted Cornelius earlier. He dropped two hessian bags to the floor.

"Mornin."

"Right once tha two ave finished there let's get framework up."

☐

By the time I returned from college the following week two further sets of square work were in place. Plus, the partly built mini panzer. It looked quite impressive suspended over the main coaling belt. The white paintwork standing out against the dull brown surface of the steelwork. An additional steel framework over the conveyor supporting two lots of electric panels. Cables yet to be inserted. I guessed one of the panels was for the auxiliary fan. This I'd seen parked up on one of the shunts at pit bottom. Someone had chalked on the side of the flat *W11's m/g*. Cornelius and Nick Arnold had been in discussion the previous day. A second team of contractors would be here by the end of the week. They were to start on the return junction. I would be covering both teams. I was pleased about that. It would keep me busy without having to look for things to do.

College wasn't going too bad either. I was getting the hang of things. We'd spent some time studying past exam papers. Not that we could predict what we would be asked. I knew off by heart the various lengths of cable for the number of shots being fired. The lengths and distances of the various types of stonedust barriers. We spent a whole day the previous week crossing out sections of the Mines and Quarries Act 1954 that were no longer applicable. Adding what were termed *Statutory Instruments* to the various sections of the regulations. My original Part 2 book had now been replaced with sections A, B and C. Our lecturer kept repeating the term *reasonably practicable* meaning a legal requirement. It was the way he pronounced the word practicable I couldn't get it out my head.

It wasn't long before the mini panzer was up and running. Five metres in, the fan installation was next. I'd chalked on the arch legs where it was to be sited. Again, five metres on the outbye side of the heading. Whilst on stand siting the fan, we broke into the three-inch Victaulic water range and fitted the "T" piece we'd had made. It was our second attempt. I'd been given some duff information as to where the water range fed. First time we'd turned the stop valve off we received a barrage of abuse from a team of lads working inbye. They were in the process of re-ripping the junction at the bottom of the South Wigan Mine Access. To avoid creating the problem again, we fitted our own stop valve. Repeating the same for the six-inch compressed air range. Some of the equipment we used belonged to the ATC themselves. Including the mini Eimco bucket. I hadn't realised up until attending a talk at Leigh Miners that they had an office in Lowton. I'd driven passed it one day. For the first time it was beginning to look like a proper heading.

The second team of contractors arrived as planned. Spending my time with them setting up the platform over the belt, in preparation for the return junction. Pleased I'd stood my ground with the inbye officials continually complaining about the distance they were having to walk. Complaints increasing after we removed the getting off platform, repositioning below the return. I was still on the lookout for those illegally manriding, including some of the officials. I reckoned another ten yards and we'd be ready for the Dosco Roadheader in the intake, allowing the Eimco bucket to be used in the return.
A meeting station for both headings was now established at the maingate. Support rules, report books, firefighting equipment and first aid station established. The morphia safe I was having to salvage from W5's maingate, including tally boards restricting the number of men in the heading to nine. The exemption to increase to fifteen, I was told still with the inspector for approval. As yet we hadn't received a permanent fitter or electrician having to make do with the outbye lads.

As the workload increased my satisfaction level was to increase too. I got a real kick from seeing things happen. The shift passed a lot quicker. At the end of each shift before returning to the office I would wander over to the workshops to check on the progress on the items we'd requested. It was a good way of meeting new faces and understanding the parts they played at the pit. Providing my shift report didn't take long. Both JW and Lenny passed by the headings most days so knew exactly what was going on. There was one job however yet to be done. It was something I planned to do myself. It would give the finishing touches to the districts.

"Fuckin ell Mick. What's think doin?"

"Just grab it will yer." I passed two tins of paint to Cornelius as we waited for the cage.

"Oi." Cornelius shouted to Tommy as he tried to walk passed. "Take one of them off Mick."

"What we doin. Painting and decorating?"

"Pipe ranges lads. Tin of green and red for the water, blue for the compressed air."

"What's white for?"

"Manholes."

"What bout…." I patted the front of my overall.

"Brushes." Cornelius didn't look best pleased.

"Don't get fuckin paid for painting pipes Mick."

"Stop fuckin moaning. You don't need too. Just get me the tins to site. I'll sort."

Arriving at the heading I was pleased to see the afternoon haulage lads had unloaded a stack of stonedust. The lads had placed the tins of paint on top. I added my tin and the two paint brushes. I then wandered down to the return junction to watch the second team of ATC lads get started. The chargehand with this group was a guy called Donkey. I could only guess why.

"Nah Mick. Goin be needin some arches dropping off shortly."

"Yep. Leave it with me. You okay for everything else?"

"Fine lad. Think Nick Arnolds popping by later."

"Righto. You know where I'll be if you need me."

I headed back up to the maingate heading. For the first time I realised I was lathered. I hadn't stopped moving since I'd got to site. The cold intake air cut into my damp vest. I rebuttoned my overalls, increasing my pace. The noise of the fan grew louder as I approached. Clouds of dust began to flow towards me. *I'd fuckin told'em yesterday to use the wander hose when fillin out.* It was still early in the shift to be issuing a round of fucks but so be it! My anger rising as I approached the heading. The noise of the mini panzer and fan now combining. The click, click of the main coal conveyor to my right hardly discernible. I turned into the heading. As if by magic. Cornelius was standing on the pile of coal, wander hose in hand. Spraying the load already in the bucket and the surrounding area. Should I have expected anything less? He turned towards me smiling. "Cunt." I whispered under my breath.

It wasn't long before they'd started drilling again. I positioned my ear plugs and got on with the job of painting. As much as I tried, I still ended up with a smattering of green and red on my overalls. The smell overwhelming. Standing back to look at my handiwork I was distracted by a number of lights at the entrance. Placing the paint pot down I walked towards them. Instantly making out JW and Lenny. JW unusually had a look of concern. He seemed paler than usual. The third person I hadn't seen underground since I'd first arrived. Although I'd had the pleasure of being summoned to the Top Shunt some weeks previous. Standing there with his unmistakable blue boiler suit and white donkey jacket. He was pointing with his stick towards the roof above the mini panzer. His jacket moving to one side exposing the shiniest oil lamp I'd ever seen. *Fuck what's he spotted?* I continued walking towards the three of them. I was feeling a little uneasy. The smell of paint didn't help. The Manager's first visit that I was aware of to my district, and he'd found something amiss. My concern suddenly dissipating as he broke into a smile. His attention now drawn to me as I approached. JW too, now looked relaxed.

His deep penetrating eyes focused on me. The smile still evident but there was a hardness in his eyes. I'd spotted it the first time I'd seen him. A man you wouldn't want to cross.
"Morning gentlemen."
"Morning Mick." Lenny was the first to respond. I shook each hand in turn. "How's it going?"
"All good thanks. Reckon another couple of days we can start moving the Roadheader in and put the Eimco next door."
"Got another job lad?" The question from the Manager threw me somewhat. I didn't respond immediately. JW pointed to his own chest. Looking to the front of my overalls.
"Oh that." I smiled.
"Caught anyone else?" Without turning he pointed his thumb to W belt.
"No. Seems to have quietened down."
"And we're now getting all the empty tins out." JW added smiling.
"Good job, keep it up." And that was it. He turned and began moving inbye. The other two followed. I had expected him to come into the heading. Momentarily I remained fixed to the spot, savouring the moment. Had I heard right? Did he say *good job?* A compliment from the Manager. Fuck, I felt good.
"Aye Mick. What's for do?" Deep in thought I hadn't noticed the drilling had stopped. Cornelius had brought me back to the present.

~~~

4. End of the 1984/85 Strike

Before I knew it the New Year had arrived. I'd completed the 1st Class Certificate of Competency exam back in November. I think I'd done okay even though none of the old exam papers we'd been practicing with came up again. Christmas had come and gone. I'd worked four shifts over the holiday period including Christmas Day which hadn't gone down well with the missus. However, with the house move coming up at the end of the month that was soon forgotten.

I was still working in W11's. I rarely entered the canteen when arriving at work. Keen to get in and on with the job. Unless I needed a tin of snuff. I'd even stopped wandering into the Undermanager's office. He was rarely there at that time of the morning. Preferring to leave it to his Colliery Overman Len. I headed straight to the baths. Still a novelty that the officials had separate facilities to the men. The smell of the baths the same the world over. Stale sweat mixed with the ever-present odour of PHB soap. I undressed before climbing onto the aluminium bench to place my shoes and clothes into a top locker. It was a pain in the arse having a top locker but there was nothing much I could do about that. I was a newcomer to Parkside. I didn't want to start off as a moaning Minnie as soon as I arrived.

In one hand holding my soap tray and flannel, towel draped over my shoulder. In the other my bag of snapping. Something my wife prepared. I'd now settled on four rounds of bread usually containing cheese or tuna. Slipping into my plastic NCB flip flops I shuffled across to the dirty side. Very few of us hid our nudity. Something we all accepted. Bodies of various shapes and sizes, thin, fat, short, tall, whatever it didn't matter. The only part amusing was seeing the bald guys. In their clean many often supporting a toupee.

I sensed things were about to change. The Manager had sent for me during the second week back. It was only a short meeting. He advised me I'd need to apply for the Engineering Training Scheme, ETS, and get the application into Staff Department at Staffordshire House. To support my application, he had a meeting planned with Malcolm Hughes, from Staff Training. It was a strange meeting. Mr Creed seemed in a reflective mood. I hadn't said much, just listened. He made a point of telling me that a management role was a responsible position. It wasn't just about the men. It was also about something far more important. Family. As a Manager you were responsible for the men getting home in one piece.

On the social side me and the missus had attended several NACODS doo's whilst at Cronton. We now began to attend functions nearer to Parkside. The Manchester Geological and Mining Society holding a function in Standish at the Owls. We stayed overnight at the Beeches Hotel. One of the lads from Cronton, a university graduate Malcolm was there with his missus too.

By February, I was still covering both headings. The maingate now equipped with a Dosco Mk II Roadheader.
I hadn't noticed the first time I'd gone underground. Maybe because it had been August. How cold it was riding the downcast shaft. Grateful as the Banksman filled the cage. Cramming us against one another. Standing and drawing on the body heat from the guy in front and behind. Accepting the body odours of dried sweat and overall. The individual hygiene of the guy either side mattered little. No matter who you were or what position you held we were in this together. Dropping down into the bowels of the earth not knowing what the next few hours held for each one of us.

Although I'd never discussed this with any of my colleagues, Did any of us ever consider the dangers we faced each day? I don't think we did. It was a job, a way of life. Each one of us just got on and did what we had to do. Now though as the cage arrived at pit bottom, I shivered. At Cronton riding the shaft had taken place in the upcast shaft. Always warm with the variety of smells emanating from the inbye workings. Momentarily drifting, semi-conscious into the state between sleep and being fully awake. Here was different. The air was cold and fresh. From leaving the lamp room heading towards the pit top, the only respite nipping into the control room to check the barometer.

We moved as one as the cage entered the guide rails. Silence as conversations came to an end. Replaced by the mesh gate being lifted. The bottom two decks emptying first. Some men stamping their feet as they exited. Attempting to replace the cold that had seeped into their bones. We moved forward at pace, attempting to generate body heat. Blinking rapidly until our eyes became accustomed to the bright overhead lights and whitewash. The fog of condensation emitted by each of us dispersed as we moved forward. The crunching of the limestone ballast underfoot as we travelled either side of the twenty-eight-pound steel rails. The soft hum of the fourteen-tonne battery loco's in the distance. So different from the diesel equivalent.

Climbing into the manriding carriage. Happy to squeeze alongside those already in position. Conversations starting up once more. I watched as the guard in the back carriage waved his lamp to the loco driver. He confirmed we were ready for the off with two hoots on the horn.

☐

I'd been at Parkside for just on six months now. Much of my time on W11's junctions. For some reason that began to change. Arriving one morning I was deployed to W8's scour. Not wanting to show my ignorance, as I wasn't sure what a scour was, I went to look at the plans. It was a roadway driven through the waste of W5's. The same had been done for W6's, one of the current operating coal faces. Still as shotfirer, dets and powder the order of the day. The upside of this I was beginning to see more of the men. Getting to know who was who. Arriving back up the pit that day, there was a note on my lamp. Ron Gold had asked to see me before I went home. Surprised by the request and a little excited, I decided to call in before reporting to Lennie and JW.

I liked Ron. He was one of those guys you could take an instant liking too. You always knew when he was in the office. His voice booming down the corridor. "Nah young man, tha's a choice to make. Either tha gets back into work tomorrow…I'm not interested in your car. Get buzz. I that's right lad. Tha only lives at Platt Bridge. Tha's got choice. Outside King William or outside Legion. Thi choice laddie." He was still on the phone when I arrived at his ever-open door. He acknowledged me and beckoned me to enter. "Nah that's all I ave say about that. Or we can sort tha P45." He replaced the handset. "Tell tha what Mick. Wouldn't put up with it in my day. Nearly sixty lads a day no turning in. Sit thisen down lad."
"You asked to see me?"
"That I did lad. Where tha working this week?"
"W8's scour."
"Ah, that's good. Not too far from pit bottom. Need tha out handy tomorrow. Anderton House for quarter past two…"
"What for?"
"Bloody ell Mick. Give me chance finish will tha."
"Deputy Director, Evan Jacks want's see tha." That did get my attention. I straightened in my chair.
"What for?"
"I'm sure he'll tell tha when tha there. Think it's summat do with ET Scheme. Manager mentioned it tuther month." I sat there not wanting to move. Savouring the moment. "Summat else that'll help. Get thisen along to them mining talks at Leigh Miners."
"Right will do." I sat waiting for any other advice.

"That's it lad." I'd obviously overstayed my welcome. I stood.
"Thanks Don."
"Don't be late. Quarter past two sharp. I'd get out handy if I were tha."

☐

Travelling along Newton Road it was hard to believe just down the road was the North West's newest coal mine. I spotted the entrance to the ATC headquarters. I'd never been in but made myself a promise to do so one day.

It was only quarter to two. I was early. Turning into the entrance of Anderton House, small flakes of snow began to fall. The six-storey glass fronted building looked out of place. More suited to a Manchester or Liverpool office block. Its greatest feature was the sculpture outside the entrance. The head and shoulders of a miner, helmet, and cap lamp in place.

Mounted on a shearer disc; cutter picks included. Hands grasping a lump of coal. I wasn't into sculpture, but this feature was something special. I could never take my eyes off it. I was told it had been commissioned by Lord Robens in the sixties to mark the invention of the Anderton Shearer Loader. Named after the inventor James Anderton. Supposedly the father of the current Chief Constable of Manchester. First used at Ravenhead Colliery in 1952 and thereafter at Cronton. I'd first seen it when I attended my interview with Mike Penny to join the NCB.

Walking into the building that distinctive smell of office hit me. The smell of polished furniture. Glad to be in from the cold. I headed towards the reception desk. It was relatively quiet, save for the occasional sound of a telephone ringing

There were two receptionists both seemed reluctant to approach me. I wasn't surprised. Of all days I'd used the last of my Vaseline. Try as I might I could never remove the coal dust below my eyelids with just soap. Wearing a tie and jacket didn't seem to cut it either. The braver of the two suggested I take a seat. She'd call me when the Deputy Director was ready to see me.

I don't think I'd been in the building since attending Poly when I was taking my HNC. A gang of us used to meet up and catch the Coal Board bus for Staffordshire House. Stan the driver dropping us off outside the Poly on College Road. The place had hardly changed. I was sat facing the reception area, separated from the working area by a series of soundproof glass panels. I turned to see who was about. Not that I'd recognise anyone. There were a few. Still holding bits of paper. It was the only place outside the pit canteen I'd seen female staff employed by the Coal Board.

"The Deputy Director is ready to see you now Mr. Gibson." I checked my watch. Exactly two fifteen. She pointed to the glass double doors. "Top floor. You can take the lift or stairs." I heard the click as the door locking device was released.

"Thanks." She didn't respond she was glad she no longer had to look at the human panda.

Exiting the lift, I arrived on a circular balcony. At least half a dozen offices spaced around the perimeter. The Deputy Director's was adjacent to the Directors *I wouldn't have expected anything less.* Straightening my tie, I knocked to go in. Slightly nervous, although having done a shift underground tiredness made me less so.

"Come in." A female voice responded. To my surprise and before I could grab the handle, the door opened. The gentlemen stood in front of me was about five two in height, same as my wife. I recognised him immediately. He was smiling. One of those friendly easily replaceable smiles.

"Owsi gooin me ole shoe? Yo aurite?" two questions in quick succession. Before I could answer I was hit by a third. "Dyowannacupataye?"

"Hi, err yes please." I wasn't sure what I'd agreed to.

"Cum on in willyer."

I followed him in to an outer office. His secretary was sat at her desk fingers poised over a typewriter. She was smiling too.

"I'm on it Deputy Director."

We continued into his office. It was spacious rather big for one person. I suppose the further you moved up the ranks, the bigger the office. We sat opposite each other at a large table. It was used for meetings. There was an open file sat in front of him.

"Yoe a big chap Mick. What your mother feed yoe on? Raw meat." He laughed at his joke. "Bet no one fucks bout with yoe?" I smiled and nodded. *I bet no one fucks about with you either.* "Wheramya Mick since your move to Parkside?"

"Deputy, mainly shotfiring for the planned new heavy-duty face."

"Bloody ell lad. If wanting to get on yoe needs get into production. Should be an Overman by now." *Like I haven't been trying!*

"I have been an Overman, when I was at Cronton both on the coal face and covering afternoon shift."

"How old rayow?"

"Twenty-seven."

"Twenty bloody seven. I was Manager at twenty-seven. Coppice Colliery."

"Birch Coppice?"

"No, that's Derbyshire. Cannock Chase lad. Closed 1964. First Manager at Lea Hall tow. Are you in the rescue?"

"No."

"Bloody ell lad. Get theesen init. Pursue the experience." *Like I've got the fuckin time!*

"Tea gentlemen."

"Ta very much Gladys." His secretary placed two China cups and saucers onto the table. From being excited when I'd walked in, I was now feeling a little depressed. And there was me thinking I was doing okay.

"How yoe bin coping with strike?"

"Not too bad. Most of the lads have returned to work."

"Arr. It'll be over soon." Momentarily he stopped speaking, obviously reflecting on something. The silence causing me to feel a little uneasy.

"Only fighting for what they believe in. What about moving lad?" He asked changing the subject.

"House?"

"Pit! I and that will mean house."

"Yeah. Anywhere, I'm already applying for jobs." Once more he referred to the open file sat in front of him and began to rustle through some papers.

"Oh, right see what yoe means. Yoe have done some time in production at Cronton. In London Delph. Working under my old mucker Ron Groves. Good lad is he. Worked at West Cannock No 5. Cracking rugby union player, hooker he was at Mosely. Felt sorry for the lad when he had to choose sport or his career."

"Yeah." Something I was aware of.

"Not bin on ET Scheme I see."

"No."

"Need to get on a shortened version. No need bother with departments. Plenty of industrial experience I see." *Wow a compliment at last.* I now understood what he was looking at. I'd been asked by Malcolm Hughes to fill out a form, entitled *Review of Technical Assistants/ Industrial Officials.* There had been a section marked *Manager's Comments*, now filled in.

"I'm still waiting for the results of my 1st Class Certificate."

"Confident?"

"Yeah." What else could I say.

"See yoe got your 2nd Class. Bloody ell yoe had it five years."

"Yeah, took it after HNC."

"I like that." *Fuck me another compliment!* Closing the file, he looked towards me once more. "Any questions from yoe?" I was tempted to ask what the Manager had written but thought better of it.

"When will I start?"

"Yode go through selection process first." *Fuck I wish I hadn't asked.*

"You'll be fine. Right then Mick if that's it…oh and you'll be given a mentor not sure who'll that'll be just yet."

Within days of the meeting with Mr Jacks I began to be deployed to other districts W6's coalface and V24's face line drivage. V24's being the first face I was aware of in the Wigan 5'.

□

Although the miners' strike was still officially on, I watched as the numbers returning to work increased further. It was noticeable as we walked into the crush hall and then on to the lamp room many faces, I didn't recognise. Many returning to the jobs they'd previously had. Slotting into the daily routine without much effort. As officials we had been warned to look out for any intimidation between those returning and those choosing not to strike or returning early. I don't think it was as bad in the Lancashire coalfield as I suspected it was in South Wales and Yorkshire. I kept an eye on things nationally through the evening news. Appalled to see how some of the lads were treated by the Police. But also saddened to see how some of those who'd chosen to return to work or continue to work were treated by the strikers. It was a sorry state of affairs. Who was to blame the Government? NUM? Coal Board? How had it come to this? Had there been a way to avoid such a conflict?

One of the most important things I'd learnt since joining the ranks of junior management was to gain the trust of the men. They didn't have to like me. I had a job to do. Sometimes delivering the message no one wanted to hear. Not to be seen as a pushover but as the word implied manage. Towards the end of February, it was reported on the late news that over half of the NUM members were now back at work. It was only a matter of time before the strike was called off.

□

Returning to work on the Monday I was back in W11's. This time in the return and still on drill and fire. Today the place was buzzing. Walking into JW's office, Lennie had gathered us all together repeating the comment about intimidation. I wasn't sure if anyone would have the nerve to report such incidents. Who would? I guess the repercussions would soon follow.

Once underground I headed towards the manrider. I spotted Dan Jack's and Billy Pete in the distance. I followed them and squeezed in alongside. I was interested to hear what the older more experienced officials had to say about the end of the strike. As was his norm Billy was already in conversation with Dan when I climbed in.

"Problem for the working class now – defeating the miners won't just mean more pit closures. It'll be end of Unions power. Miners owt of way this lot will do what thy wants. Legislation changing too."

"Fuckin ell Billy that's a bold statement to make lad owd you work that out?"

"This lot av been planning this for years. Remember the 72 and 74 strikes ain't goin to appen again. You mark my words."

Billy looked towards me, recognising immediately my lack of understanding. "Nah Mick bit of a history lesson for you lad as you'd be still at school. Back in 60's miners hadn't been too badly paid. By the 70's that had all changed. They'd watched as the industry downsized both in number of pits and workforce. NUM called a strike after wage negotiations broke down with Coal Board. First time since 1926 an official miners' strike had occurred."

"First time them flying pickets were used." Dan added.

"Yeah, at some coke works in Birmingham. Government declared a state of emergency. Things were about to get worse. Some poor bastard got killed up in Donny whilst picketing. Strike lasted nearly seven weeks if I remember correctly."

"That be bout right. With a twenty-seven per cent pay increase."

"Then we had a repeat in 74. Three-day week and all that. Government made fateful mistake of going for election."

"Fuck, we're here already."

☐

By the middle of March, the return junction was complete. Ready to start driving the return gate Both headings now on two shifts. Nick Arnold had deployed Cornelius and his team into the return. It was getting towards the end of the shift. The lads had completed setting the first arch. I called them back to the junction, not happy with some missing roof bolts I'd got them to come back and complete. Solid coal, the Wigan Four Feet now facing us once more. I was checking steel availability for the following week. Noon shift were already on their way in.

I hadn't noticed a guy walk up behind me. He was just standing there waiting to get my attention. As I turned, he asked.

"Are you Mick Gibson?" The fella wasn't particularly tall but he more than made up with his width. He had a split lip, dried blood down the side of his chin. The area around his left eye was discoloured. Red, yellow, and blue. The black eye had yet to form. He looked one hard bastard.

"I certainly am." He smiled; just standing there staring at me. His gaze neither friendly nor threatening. I'd never set eyes on him before. I felt a little uneasy needing to break the silence. "Who do I have the pleasure…." Before I could complete the sentence, the guy had turned and continued his journey inbye.

How strange I thought. Turning towards the platform the drilling had stopped. All three of the ATC lads were looking towards me. Cornelius spoke first.
"You know who that is Mick?"
"No idea."
"Ged Shalla. Cock of St Helens."
"Don't want to be messin with im." Jimmy added.

☐

"Off on another jolly lad." I was standing in Don Gold's office. It was a Friday. He'd asked to see me. I'd spent all week in the Access Return. "Next week lad. Selection Board, Wolverhampton and tha gets an overnight stay." He passed me an A4 sheet of paper. "Joining instructions." My initial thoughts *three days before Easter* not ideal.
"I didn't know Coal Board owned property in Wolverhampton."
"Yeah. Fancy building at 46 Queen Street. Listed building too."
"Any idea what I'll be doin?"
"Usual stuff. Intelligence test, aptitude, written exercise, group discussion, individual problem solving, all followed by an interview." *For fucks sake!* "What's up lad tha looks a little perplexed I ave say."
"No, I'm fine." I wasn't really. It would involve an aptitude test. Not my strongest point.
"Must say though Mick. Might struggle with intelligence test." Don followed his comment up with a burst of laughter.
"Thanks." I responded laughing too.
"Tha still attending them papers like I told ye? Subsidence last month at Leigh Miners."
"Yep, I was there."
"Help tha get noticed them will Mick."

I hadn't done any prep for the Selection Board. The Manager had made it clear I'd need to get on it to progress. Arriving Tuesday morning, Don hadn't been wrong it was an impressive building. According to the plaque on the wall a Grade II listed building. Supposedly the first dispensary in Wolverhampton. I didn't know anyone attending which wasn't any surprise most were straight out of University. Little if any experience underground, in fact that wasn't quite fair. They'd all done their twenty days CPS, close personnel supervision. As I'd done ten years previously. Thereafter spending time at the pit with the various departments, surveyors, planner, ventilation, coal prep, engineering departments. I had enjoyed the group discussion. Each of us had a chance as being Chairman. I didn't rate one or two of them when we got into discussing the industrial relations problem. They'd have been better suited to the military. I tried pointing out the need to earn respect. They weren't having any of it.

That night we had a better chance of getting to know one another. Always helpful when the beer was flowing. I found it quite amusing to see one of the course co-ordinators entering conversation with each of us after are fourth pint. The conversation starting with something like. "Since you've been with the Coal Board what have you seen that you dislike?" For fucks sake it was like signing your death warrant. When I was asked, I was so tempted to tell the guy to fuck off. I didn't of course. Next day I didn't hang about. The interview seemed to go okay. I think the guy chairing the panel was old school. I got on with him.

☐

"Manager wants to see you like." I was facing JW; he was still in his black. Unusually his office was empty. Probably because I was late up the pit due to an electrical problem with the winder.
"Any idea why?"
"Didn't say man." I was still holding my report. "Best be gan." He put his hand out and took my report. He was still staring at me. His drooping eyes bloodshot.
"Right, I'll be off. See you tomorrow."
"Goodluck man." Fuck that sounded ominous. Still in my black I headed towards the top shunt. *I bet he's going to tell me I've not got on the ET Scheme. That means I'm in for a bollocking.*

The place was relatively quiet. Noonshift already underground. I'd said hello to Bennie Lead the afternoon Shift Overman. He'd been in the crush hall having a fag before going underground. I could feel the butterflies in my stomach as I approached. A shiver down my spine. *Why the fuck am I so nervous?* I spotted Don Gold outside the main entrance. He nodded.
"Go straight in Mick." I nearly shit myself. The Manager's secretary Susan Worth appeared from nowhere. She was smiling. I didn't know she knew my name. "They're waiting for you." *They're* someone else beside the Manager. I took a deep breath and grabbed the door handle. To be on the safe side I knocked anyway.

I was temporarily blinded as I walked in. The sun was shining brightly from the windows opposite. My eyes began to water. The combination of pipe and cigarette smoke obscuring the two figures sat at the table opposite. It took a few moments for my eyes to adjust. The Manager was smiling, he looked relaxed. He removed his pipe.

"Come in lad take a seat." I did as instructed. I could just make out the Deputy Manager sat alongside. "Think he's up for it Len?"

"Only time will tell Mr Creed." *What the fuck were they on about?* I wasn't sure I was allowed to ask. I waited, inhaling the intoxicating smell of St Bruno. I had visions of the beautiful young lady following the guy in the television advert. I wondered if Mr Creed had the same effect with his secretary.

"Looks as though you got through the Selection Board lad. You'll be receiving a letter to confirm." *Thank fuck for that.*

"Great." I finally plucked up the courage to respond.

"But your aptitude results were shite." He didn't look happy as he read from a sheet of paper. "A natural leader it says here. Natural chairman too. Get this Len says here he demonstrated a firm grasp of the industrial relations problem."

"Goin to need that Mr Creed." The Deputy Manager responded as he stubbed out what was left of his fag before replacing it with another. The ash tray opposite was full. They were both staring at me and smiling. "Mick it's time to prove yourself. Mr Creed has decided to promote you to a Face Overman."

They waited to see my reaction. I couldn't help but smile. Finally, I was moving up. I'd been at Parkside eight months. Not a bad move from Shottie to Overman, although technically I was a Deputy. I felt elated. Another step closer to my ultimate goal.

"Thank you, thank you. I won't let you down." I guessed I'd be on W6's. I'd already spent a couple of shifts on there.

"You'd best not lad." The Manager responded as he reached across for the box of Swan Vesta's. "Place needs shaking up. Only asking for two shears a shift. Men need sorting, need pulling together." From what I'd seen on W6's men seemed to be working together. "Mix of lads. Those working through strike and day oners." *What the fuck was a day oner?* I looked towards Mr Keech. He was on his third fag. He smiled and gave me a wink. "All good lads." The Manager continued. "Just need managing. Place only been running for a couple of weeks. Before you go best see Mr Davies. You'll be working for him now."

"Now?"

"From tomorrow. L32's."

"Good luck Mick." Mr Keech added.

The Manager said no more, striking his match. I watched mesmerised as the plumes of smoke began to rise. My nostrils eager to catch the smell once more. Mr Keech had disappeared from view again. Neither spoke. Just the sound of the Manager sucking on his pipe and the clock ticking above his desk. Think that was my cue to go.

Leaving the Manager's office, I was on a high. Face Overmen, I hadn't expected that. It was certainly something I'd been hoping for. Get this under my belt and then backshift Overman. Eight months it had taken me. Longer than I thought but wasn't surprised. The place had more Overmen than I could wave a stick at. Not forgetting I was starting the ET Scheme. Face Overman at twenty-six. I'd set myself a target of becoming an Undermanager whilst still in my twenties.

Before I knew it, I was stood outside the Undermanager's office, the door partly open. I could hear his voice, sounded like he was on the phone. I'd met Howard Davies previously. He often passed W11's as he made his way into his section. He often carried a pack of liquorice always happy to offer a piece, which I always accepted. He looked as though he was carrying the weight of the world on his shoulders. He seemed a gentle man. Too gentle to be an Undermanager, or so I thought.

"Will do Mr Creed." I listened as the handset was replaced. Knocking on the door I walked in.

"Hiya Mick, been expecting you." He was sat at his desk in his clean. The layout of the office little different from JW's.

"Hello Mr Davies."

"Call me Howard. Haven't got long, need to go, and pick my daughter up. Take a seat." I did as instructed. "See you're to become the Overman on L32's?"

"Yeah, only just been told."

"You must be excited?"

"Very much so. Meant to ask the Manager, what's happened to the previous guy?"

"There's no previous guy as you put it. George Thomas, District Deputy has been running the place." I recognised the name immediately but wasn't sure from where. "You'll have two other officials with you. Gate end Deputies, Freddy Clough, and Rob Flannagan." The names didn't ring any bells.

"How much has Mr Creed told you about the place?"

"Not meeting its target and men need sorting."

"That would be about the sum total of it. Ever managed a dispirit group of men?" I wasn't quite sure what he meant. My expression must have confirmed it.

"Strikers and non- strikers?"

"No, can't say I have."

"Can't believe he's thrown you in at the deep end. That's Mr Creed though. You'll either sink or swim." *Fuck that sounds ominous.* "Right any questions?"
"Not at the moment."
"If you report to Cayle Shelley first thing tomorrow. He's my Colliery Overman." He stood as he continued. "I'll see you when you get up tomorrow."
"Thanks Mr Davies."
"It's Howard." He leaned forward and we shook hands.

Driving home that afternoon I was so excited. My first coal face. The Manager had said how difficult it would be. At that moment, his comment meant little to me. Finally, after all this time my first Overman role.

"You're looking pleased with yourself."
"Never guess what?"
"You booked the holiday."
"No. I've told ye, I'll sort that out at the weekend."
"What then? Win on Spot the Ball."
"I've just been appointed Face Overman."
"More money?"

☐

5. Face Overman L32's

"See you're leaving us Mick?"
"Cornelius, I was hoping to catch you before you went down." I was stood in the deployment centre gazing at the list of men listed under L32's. "Only found out yesterday." I moved to one side as the dayshift began to make their way through.

Cornelius stopped talking. His attention drawn elsewhere. He looked concerned. I turned to see what had caused the distraction.
"Do you mind moving whilst I get my tallies cock." I recognised the guy instantly. I was good with faces not names. There was something different. His face absent of any bruising.
"Morning Ged." Cornelius provided the name. I stepped to one side to let him pass. I hadn't noticed the first time we'd met. His head seemed to rest on his shoulders, accentuating his width. His short stubby fingers grasping the tallies into his huge plate like hands. He moved on without uttering another word.

"Are you Mick Gibson?" A huge figure of a man appeared from behind. He was in his overalls without a helmet. Large head, longish hair. His distinguishing feature was his nose. Flattened to one side, coal dust scars across the bridge. *That must have been some accident.*

"Yeah. You must be Cayle?"

"No lad, Cayle's at dentist first thing. I'm Pete Mint."

"Rugby injury more like?" Lenny Dunliffe shouted across. "Time, he gave it up. Too old."

"Someone needs to tell him." Pete responded laughing.

"I'll see tha Mick." Cornelius patted my arm. "Good luck." He added with a smile.

"Right Mick." Before I could respond Pete was back. "Suggest you catch up with George Thomas, District Deputy. You been in there before?"

"No."

"E3 manrider. Head towards L19's. Next place along. As I say best get hold of George. You met him?"

"No." At that moment I felt useless answering every question negatively.

"Can't miss him. Permanent smile, biggest set of dentures at pit."

"And most expensive car." Lenny added.

George was waiting for me at the bottom of E3.

"Guess you're Mick Gibson?"

"You must be George." Pete Mint had been right. He was smiling, his teeth so white."

"Come on cock it's this way." We headed inbye off to our left, a few men ahead of us. The majority had continued down brew. George saw me looking. "L30's and 31's. Also 33's development." I nodded, now concentrating on the direction in which we were headed.

The place was very dark. A large stack of stonedust had been offloaded to our left, along with a dozen cans of Aquacent. The supplies covered in a layer of coal dust. "Derailment." George offered as way of an explanation. I ran my fingers over the top of the bags causing a furrow. The thirty-six-inch conveyor belt to our right had seen better days. It reminded me a little of Cronton.

I listened as George explained the set up and the team. Both gate end Deputies, Freddy Clough and Rob Flannagan had gone on ahead. I was trying to get a better understanding on the main personalities. Little if any conversation on the face not achieving its target. I'd deal with that later. I'd get George to walk me round the district. We hadn't travelled far. I was very warm. My donkey jacket wasn't helping. I could feel rivulets of sweat running down my back and chest. A cloud of dust hung in the air. Created from the men ahead, clogging up my nose and sticking to my face. The warm and stale smell of the pack was everywhere.

"Down there L19's." George pointed to a tunnel off to the right. "Longest face the pit ever had. Started producing in 1978 only stopping earlier this year, February. L30's started in same direction but had to turn it. Reduce strain on M6 motorway."

"Yeah. Been in there on a weekend shift with Billy Pete." I reached inside my jacket to pull my vest away from my chest. It was soaking. I wasn't sure whether it was just the temperature or my nervousness of not knowing what to expect. Ten minutes later I spotted the lit-up junction ahead. The gib of a conveyor and several pipes partly obscuring the lighting. Light particles of dust floating against the junction lights.

The meeting station was well laid out. A wooden bench, secured to the side of the junction, above which two six by two mesh panels with various support and transport rules attached. The top of the bench had an old piece of belting nailed to it. Alongside a fire hose container. Several spare hoses placed on the outside with a nozzle attached to the top hose. The stretcher container was on the opposite side. Suspended by pipe chain. There was something missing, or so I thought. The morphia safe, partly obscured by someone's jacket. Once again everything covered in a thin layer of coal dust. I'd need to understand the dust suppression arrangements. George wasn't the quickest of walkers. By the time we'd reached the maingate junction most of the men had already arrived.

Two groups gathered either side of the junction. The only other person I knew was Ged, he was stood in front of the larger group. Mostly young men. Some already stripped down to shorts and vests. The other group, older faces were sat behind a short guy. He was the image of Joe Gormley. Chewing bacca.

"Right lads. Let me introduce you to your Face Overman, Mick Gibson."

"How come you never got the job George?" Someone asked. He smiled at the comment.

"All in good time lad." I looked around to see what if any reaction would come from the others. To a man they were all staring at me. *Perhaps I should say something.* It was then I spotted one of the gate end Deputies. He was smiling. His helmet cocked to one side. A thick grey moustache above his top lip. Matching his exposed grey chest hairs. He was stood with the group headed by Ged. Whispering something to one of the lads stood alongside. "I'll be taking Mick round later. I'll do introductions then."

"Lads I'm lookin forward to workin with yer." I felt the need to say something.

"A fuckin Scouser." Someone shouted.

"Watch your snappin." Another commented.

"Hub caps their favourite." This brought the biggest laugh. All the comments from Ged's men. The gate end Deputy seemed to be enjoying it too. He had the biggest smile, something I'd need to sort later.

"What's want us do? Machines at number ten." The Joe Gormley lookalike shouted towards me.

"Cut coal, you daft twat." The biggest and ugliest of Ged's group responded. George leaned towards me and whispered.

"Big lad's Johnny Bastard ex Bold Colliery. He's on double ender. Tuther fella is Bobby Lunt. He's on single ender." *Fuck, I hadn't realised we had two machines on the face.*

"Hey, don't you daft twat me you cunt."

"Hold it lads. Let's have a bit of order. Think it's time we made our way in." I shouted as I walked forward. It seemed to have the desired effect. They began to move off. Some towards the return, the majority towards maingate. Ged walked towards me.

"Fuck me Scouse. Tha's only bin ere two minutes and nearly caused a riot." He walked off before I could give an answer.

"Where would you like to start Mick." George asked.

"You haven't answered me question." I hadn't noticed Bobby Lunt approach. There was another guy with him. I turned towards George.

"Take it in twice Bobby. Second time up to thirty chock and back in."

"Glad someone knows what for do." Bobby responded looking at me. Turning he and his mate continued along the maingate.

"Miserable sods them two. Be glad when they're gone."

"What do you mean?"

"Him and his mate Arthur Fanning. Looking to take redundo. Bout six of them. All worked through most of strike."

"Oh right. Out of interest I'm assuming a pre-shift inspection's been done?"

"Yeah, one of the regular nightshift Deputies. Jack. You'll get to meet him."

"Who's our return gate end Dep?"

"Rob Flannagan."

"What about the maingate fella?"

"Freddy Clough. He normally heads straight in with the rippers, Alf, and Jack."

"How long has the place been producing?"

"This'll be our third week. Officially we don't start up till May. Manager likes to keep some back for a rainy day. He's good at that gaffer is." Two lights approaching from outbye caused George to stop. "Noon shift here I, see?" He shouted towards them. The blue and red rims on their cap lamps was the giveaway.

"Alreyt George. See we've got a new starter." The smaller of the two responded. He was smiling. Dark intense eyes. His outstanding feature was his large flat nose. He had a good suntan.

"Mick, let me introduce Brain Token, our fitter and Dai Bando the electrician. Mick's the Face Overman."

"Morning lads."

"Morning Mick." Brian offered. "You've got a job on your hands. I'll see tha later. Need to head straight in. Got a bagging to change on the Hausherr." I received a muffled "morning" from the other lad.

"What's up with Mr Happy?" I asked as the two moved inbye.

"Missus fucked off with next door neighbour, only bin married six months."

"That's not good."

"Don't understand it. She was a minger, anyway, best get shut." George's comment caused him to chuckle.

"We heading in?"

"Yeah, in a mo, just need to make a phone call to Durek Moore. You met him yet?" He picked up the handset and began to dial.

"Think so on my first day. The guy with a permanent smile."

"I that's him. Always taking piss. Oh, hi Durek." Tom began to laugh. "Talking about tha not to tha. Listen pal, urgently need some cem and bent. Yeah, almost out. Thanks pal." He replaced the handset. "There's three of them you know. Brothers, David, and Norman. Durek your man if you need owt off main tunnel."

"You mentioned cem and bent. Where's the pumping station." George turned and pointed towards the return.

"Between the airdoors. Right cock tha ready for tour."

"Will be in a mo." I removed my donkey jacket. "This alright here?" I placed it alongside several other jackets.

"I, will be as long as lads don't know it's yours." Again, he began to chuckle.

He led the way, as the maingate belt kicked in. I wasn't particularly impressed by what I saw. The belt structure was all over the place. I stopped to make a note.

"Salvaged from 19's. Belt too." The distinctive *click, click, click*, as the stitches passed over the top rollers.

"Think we could do with Surveyors putting a line on for us. How come we never put any new rolls of belt in?" I asked as a damaged length of belt caught my eye.

"Mr Keech insisted we used the stuff from 19's." The sound from the belt changed. The black stuff began to appear. My first sighting of coal off L32's. I began to feel quite excited. *What a sad bastard am I?* "Chocks off there too."

"Mentioned earlier we had two shearers on face. Double ender and single. How come?"

"Need to keep maingate ahead of return due roof problems. Waste of time if you ask me. Better with just double ender."

"What about face length?"

"One hundred and eighty-five metres including gates. Seam just over six foot. Mudstone roof. Can get a bit friable need to leave tops, couple of inches. Below main band of coal tuther band of dirt, approximately eight inches then another eight inches of coal, then seat earth. Surveyors reckon on three twenty tonnes a shear. Mr Keech only asking for two shears a shift."

"I assume we're just taking the coal?"

"Nah. Tried that, base of chocks just sink into dirt. Spending too long digging them out."

I stopped abruptly. The sound of the conveyor had changed again. It was running empty. "I wonder what the fuck's up now?" Before George could make any comment, a voice shouted out on a tannoy.

"Breaking lump maingate end."

"That's Paul. Stageloader mon, good lad. It's another problem we have. Lumps."

"Tell you what, some stonedust wouldn't go amiss. What the fuck!" Looking inbye I could see part of a stonedust barrier. A number of shelves still stacked alongside the side of the road. "Please don't tell me that's the heavy barrier."

"That it is cock. Must remember to get some lads on to finish it."

"Fucking hell George, it should be in place now!"

"Only so much we can do cock." George seemed a little put out by my comment. "Couple lads finishing light barrier, then they'll be onto it."

"I don't fuckin believe it. Light barriers not even finished. Has the Undermanager been in yet?"

"No. No management have visited the place."

I decided to say no more. I didn't want to completely piss George off on my first day. I was going to need a couple of back up lads to sort this place out. Arriving at the partly built barrier I stopped to make some further notes. My mood lightened as the black stuff began to fill the belt once more.

"George, can we make sure we keep the entrance to the manholes clear too." I pointed to where some of the wooden shelves were piled up alongside a stack of stonedust.

"Will do cock."

We continued inbye just as the haulage rope began to move. I stepped to one side. "We got out own haulage team?"

"Nah. The supply team are the same lads supplying inbye. Use them as we need. Most of the stuff we send via the return. You'll see as we get further in, floor lift is a big problem."

"Fitter mentioned something about a bagging on the Hausherr earlier."

"Yeah. We've got one in either gate." We continued inbye.

"Mick, don't mind me askin, is this your first time as face Overman?"

"No. On occasion I filled in at Cronton." My answer wasn't a lie, but it wasn't the truth either. I'd probably only done the job for two weeks max. "Why do you ask?"

"Thought they'd have put someone in here with a bit more experience. Particularly with the team. Right bunch of characters we've got in here."

"Yeah. Mr Davies mentioned it yesterday. Strikers and non-strikers. He used the word dispirit."

"Howard Davies. Now there's not a nicer man have I met. Too nice to be an Undermanager. Can't see him lasting. You know we've got two chargehands?"

"Two? How come?"

"For the very reason you've mentioned. One of the reasons we can't get two shears a shift. Lads always falling out."

"Would they be Ged and the other fella?"

"Bobby Lunt. Yeah. Goin to have your work cut out there Mick. Need to watch your back. As I said earlier, think the lads at bottom end will finish at some point. Trying to get numbers down. Ged's the man you'll need to watch."

"I'm sure I can handle him."

"Just you be careful cock." I smiled. It was kind of George to offer me the warning. *Having worked with and managed Scousers for nine years I'm sure I'll manage a wooly back.*

We continued in silence. Passing the Hausherr, parked under the belt. An empty five-gallon drum of Aquacent lay alongside the track. I'd never seen a Hausherr in action. Only ever used an Eimco bucket. The machine looked so narrow. Ahead two lights appeared. George introduced the two lads as Bryn and Howard. They were completing the light stonedust barrier. Their usual place of work was on the dint. I made a further note. These would be the lads I'd use for slinging the belt.

Five minutes later George pointed out the face start line. The smell of packing material still lingered. Ahead the lights of the stage loader came into view just as the maingate belt began to slow.

"Outbye belts stopped." A voice shouted over the tannoy. I recognised the voice of a control room lad. I think his name was Steve. No sooner had the belt stopped the pre-alarm kicked in.

Brian the fitter and Dai Bando were sat in amongst the jumbo cables on the Pantech. They nodded as we passed. George introduced me to Paul Arnold our stageloader operator.

"Hiya Paul good to meet you." He nodded before turning to the tannoy and hitting the stop button on the stage loader.

"Outbye belts stopped." I turned to George.

"This a regular feature?"

"Who's got a latch on?" The control lad shouted.

"Just checkin a stitchin Steve." Another voice I didn't recognise responded.

I turned back to Paul. "How come there's no sprays on the stageloader?"

"Causes belt to slip." I wondered why the coal seemed dry. It also explained the amount of fine dust. Something I hadn't done was check the water sprays in the maingate chute.

"Belts can be a problem." George added. "But not the biggest problem. Mechanical and electrical give us most delays. Paul's reet bout sprays. Too much water and belt begins to slip. Turned over twice last week. Needs some new belt." *Fuck. No wonder we ain't getting two shears a shift.*

Without any warning the maingate belt kicked in. Paul immediately started the stageloader. The pre-alarm interrupting any further conversation.

"Right, think we need to keep moving. Good to meet you, Paul." I shouted. George continued to lead the way as we squeezed passed the belt and pantech. I began to perspire once more. The place was stifling. "What about gas?"

"Generally, point five at top end. We've got methane borers in as and when. Share them with L30's. Outbye generally about point two." I picked up the pace to get closer to George. I could hardly hear him. The continuous whining and *thump, thump, thump* of the hydraulic pumps just inbye, competing with our conversation. "Oops…. bloody ell." George shouted as he tried to maintain his balance. Grabbing hold of the stageloader spills he steadied himself.

"You, okay?" I could see the problem, the creamy white fluid running down the side of the hydraulic tank causing the floor to break up and creating a muddy slop.

"I, I'm good thanks cock. Brian's ordered a cut off valve. Need to chase up its whereabouts." I reached up to turn off the water feed. Looking inbye the leaking fluid had created a huge pool of grey mush.

The pump pack pipes to our left began to pulsate, causing the pipe chain suspending them to shake.

"That's good. Looks as though Durek got the mine car in. Mick just be aware, the two lads on maingate caunch, Alf and Jack Cherry are the biggest piss takers you could ever meet. Doesn't help they're twins. Never know who I'm talkin

85

with. But good workers." I looked towards the maingate platform perched over the AFC. There were three lights.

"Thanks for the heads up. Who's the third guy?"

"Gate end official. Freddy Clough." I looked again at the three of them. All sat down. The twins were each eating a butty. The guy with the oil lamp was scribbling something down on paper.

"Bit early for snap?"

"By looks of things from how we left it yesterday. Already set two legs." Impressive. I checked my watch. Just after nine.

"Early for a report, isn't it?"

"Tha'll get used. Freddy's our inhouse poet laureate." I wasn't sure I'd heard correctly but let it go.

As we continued inbye. The sound from the stageloader began to change. The dull *clunk, clunk, clunk* replace by scraping of flight bars on the pans. Looking towards the face line. The flow of coal from the AFC had stopped. A voice on the face DAC shouted "breaking a lump" immediately followed by the *krr, krr, krr* of a jigger.

"Alreyt Mick." One of the twins shouted towards me. "Place bit of a shithole doth think?"

"Which one's that?" I asked George.

"Alf. Always smiling. Jack has the serious face."

"I'm sure between the lot of us Alf we'll get it sorted." I shouted my response back.

"I'm Jack. Best get all clear from Ged first Mick."

"Don't need to Alf, I'm the boss." His response was drowned out by the AFC kicking in. The smile had gone though.

"Alreyt Mick." During the conversation with Alf, my gate end Deputy Freddy had climbed down from the platform. I turned to greet him. He was only small, wiry, light build. Long strands of hair hung below his helmet, the colour matching his unkempt pencil moustache. He reminded a little of the actor who played the part of General Custer in the film *They Died With Their Boots On.* Errol Flynn, it was. He had a fixed smile. He was chewing bacca. He seemed quite agitated, unable to keep still.

"Morning Freddy. Good to meet you. Any chance you could get the side ranters moved in?" He turned to look back at the caunch.

"Don't keep'em right up when firing." I used my cap lamp to identify each of the legs back from the face of the heading.

"Ten metres? I don't think so. And you'll be drilling next? Get'em moved in." The fixed smile remained. He was looking at me, I guess to understand if I was serious. He was still moving about. "Your lads work through snap?"

"Nah, Ged won't allow it."

"What they doin now?"

"Eating."

"That's my point. Get the side ranters moved in." I continued forward no longer waiting for a response. George followed.

I climbed up onto the face line. The smell of the newly formed pack filled the air. "Mick this is Les Peat and Colin Peach. On maingate pack this morning. Also, our back up shearer drivers." The two lads appeared from behind the newly filled pack.

"Morning lads."

"Morning Mick." They replied together. "You a red or a blue then Mick." The shortest of the two, Les asked.

"Only one colour for me."

"Must be a red then?"

"That I certainly am." A light just above began heading towards us. Les became a little agitated.

"Right need to get on. We've flushed the pipes out, need to extend now." And with that they were gone. The person approaching seemed to have put an end to our conversation. I soon understood why. The shear bulk of the guy was struggling to move forward between the chock legs. He was carrying a jigger pick.

"Nah Scouse. Talkin to my lads?" I smiled.

"Do I need your permission then?"

"No cock. Talk as much as tha wants but remember I give instructions. All come through me."

"I don't think so Ged. Seem to recall I'm the Overman." He was close enough to feel his breath against my face. He smelt of garlic. His light green eyes staring directly into mine. They never flinched. Eyes portraying no fear. I was beginning to feel a little uncomfortable with this direct confrontation. It seemed to last forever. He finally turned his attention away from me.

"We any mineral oil George?"

"Have word with Brian. Should have some near his box."

He gave me one last glance before brushing passed me and on towards the maingate.

"Tha wants to be careful there Mick. Don't want to be messin with Ged Shalla."

Continuing up the face, Tom introduced me to Arthur Fanning and Bobby Lunt on the single ender. We squeezed into the back of the chocks as they passed. I made comment regards the lack of working sprays on the drum. They said very little. Other than Bobby asking how much face experience I had. Out of earshot George explained laughing, how Ged referred to them as Cunt and Fanny.

Further up the face another guy was pushing over. I watched as he dropped the canopy of a powered support. Lowering his head and momentarily disappearing from view. Engulfed by the falling coal tops and dust. He advanced the chock towards the coal face. Scraping the dirt floor in the process. Stopping abruptly as it came to the end of the ram stroke. Gingerly he stepped out. Attempting to clear the top of the canopy roof of loose coal. *Good lad.* Then taking up his original position pulling on the control block causing the canopy to raise once more.

George provided a quick introduction. The lad, Cliff Johns had a kindly face and short black moustache, which you could hardly see. His face black as an ousel. The whiteness of his teeth accentuated against his blackened face. He didn't hang about, following the SERDs towards the maingate.

Stepping out from the chock line in the space provided, I walked across to the spills. The panzer was piled high with the black stuff, some of it fair sized lumps. Not enough however to cause stoppage at the maingate end.

"How come we keep stopping to break lumps?"

"Not this Mick. I should have pointed out when we came on. We got plenty of spalling at maingate end. Puts us in contravention of support rules."

"How do you mean."

"Prop free front distance."

"Oh right."

"Causing problem with roof too. Try to keep a few lads over put wooden dowels in." I nodded. Looking across to the coal seam the eight-inch dirt band Tom had described was barely visible. A combination of water and coal dust hiding it appearance. "Come on we best keep moving."

Continuing towards the return we passed two further men bringing chocks in. George pointed out these were part of Arthur Fannings team. They had little to say, so we didn't hang about. I was a little concerned to his comments being part of another team. Little wonder we weren't delivering the results. Although for the last ten minutes the black stuff hadn't stopped moving on the panzer. Lights ahead of us and the increase in noise as the double ender approached caused George to stop. I watched the haulage chain tension.

"Best hang fire here. Let the lads passed." He offered me an opened tin of Hedges.

"Thanks, don't mind if I do." I took a pinch, inhaling the brown powder up each nostril. Moving my oil lamp to the front of my belt I crouched down. George did likewise.

"Now cock just be aware of the big lad on the cutter. Mentioned him this morning. Miserable mean bastard. Never a nice word for anyone."

"Johnny Bastard?"

"That be im. Tuther lad David Butt. Really nice lad. Both ex Bold men."

"How does he get on with Ged?"

"Frightened death."

As George finished explaining, the cutter had almost reached us. The noise cutting out any further attempt at conversation. He moved forward to the next chock, easing himself into the back legs. I did likewise within the chock below. There was something exciting when in the presence of the shearer. The noise, obviously but also something else. The absolute power of the machine as it moved along the haulage chain. The *clunk, clunk, clunk* of both drums spinning, water sprays *pschitting* providing a fine mist of water against the drum. Droplets of water descending onto the front of the chock legs. Others landing on my face. The unique sound of the coal seam being ripped out from its carboniferous home. Having lain there for millions of years. Split by the carbide tipped picks doing their job. Crunching and grinding as the coal split, falling ahead of the disc. Gathered on the panzer below to start its journey to the surface.

A body appeared alongside. He was wearing a full-face mask, his face hardly visible through the dark wet smears of coal dust against the perspex. He couldn't have weighed more than three stone wet through. He looked like a character out of *Oliver*, a street urchin. He didn't smell much better. The odour of stale sweat swirled around my head. "Nah Mick." He offered raising his mask. "Never had such a good run. Must be you."

"Hi David." And that was the conversation over. He brushed passed, his orange overalls blackened and wet through. His attention drawn back to the front disc. Reaching forward to depress a brass button on the control block.

Ahead I watched as his team mate approached. No wonder the guy was such a miserable bastard as George had described. The lad was huge. Squeezing his body through the front and back legs as he travelled with the machine. I half expected the chocks to move as he passed through. Alongside me now, he was avoiding eye contact.

"Morning Johnny." I offered. He turned towards me; his face as black as the coal he was cutting. The sclera around round the iris as white as snow. He wasn't the best-looking lad I ever seen. Glaring at me he said nothing. Turning away he continued alongside the machine. Making a point of shoving me further into the chock legs. *Charming!*

For the first time I could feel a tight pain in the back of my thighs. My neck and back weren't doing much better. I readjusted my oil lamp before rubbing my right knee. It was taking a pounding from the base of the front legs and the narrowness of the walkway. I shouted after George to offer my snuff. He didn't hear me. Reluctantly I continued to follow. The dull thud of the fully loaded panzer now replaced by the clanking and scraping of the flight bars. Tugging at the front of my wet through overalls. I was soaked to the skin. I was a little envious of the lads we'd passed. Other than the shearer operators they were all in shorts and vest. My mouth too, coated in dust. I attempted to hawk up, unable to produce any saliva. *Must remember to pick up some bacca tomorrow.* There was no disguising it, I was completely fucked, and we hadn't reached the return end yet.

We hadn't travelled more than five chocks when the pans ahead began to snake across to the face.
"Mick, this is Phil. Phil Hale."
"Hiya Phil. Good to meet you." The smiling face that greeted me, appeared from in front of George. He only looked about twelve. Although his moustache made him look a little older. He offered me his hand.
"Hello Mick. You lose a bet?"
"How do you mean?"
"Ending up in here."
"Wouldn't miss it for the world."
"We'll soon sort that out." He smiled again and continued to follow the shearer.
Before I could say anything more, George offered.
"Really nice lad that. Most of them are. Come on let's keep moving. Time you met with Rob Flannagan. See what you make of him."

I was grateful to move back into the space between the front of the chocks and the spills. Ahead George had stopped again. One or two of the chocks ahead had already been advanced.
"Mick, this is Terry." I was surprised to see an older face. He looked out of place. And he wasn't sporting a moustache.
"Hiya Terry. Good to meet you."
"Likewise, Mick. If you don't mind need to catch up." I moved to one side to let him pass.
"Something I said?"
"Nah cock. Our man Terry is a man of few words." George offered me his open tin of snuff. "He was out for six months. Ged's never forgiven him. Terry's got personal problems." As George spoke, I began to rub the back of my

90

thighs. "Tight cock? Tha'll get used. Give it a week or two, we'll have you running up and down ere."

By the time we'd reached the return end I was desperate for a mouthful of water. I'd left my bottle in my donkey jacket now hanging at the Meeting Station. It was, however, some consolation to be finally stood upright again. It was quiet too. Just the background of muted conversation. The panzer on stand due to the outbye belts once more. I stretched; my back was in bulk.

The heading was about three yards ahead of the face. The three lads were in the process of pulling back the Holman drilling equipment. The tallest of the three approaching George and myself. I recognised him immediately. The recipient of a conversation with the other gate end Deputy.

"George, tha's got do something bout machine it's fuckin useless." I hadn't noticed it before. The machine he was referring to I'd never seen used, although I'd seen various models at Mining Exhibitions. A Webster cutter/loader it was referred to. This model seemed to be missing the drill rig. The detachable bucket was in place below the cutting head.

"Nah Graham, all in good time cock. Let me introduce you to Mick." I was beginning to take to George. Calm as a cucumber, with a permanent smile.

"Hiya Graham." I offered my hand. Which wasn't taken. He was a big lad, not as big as Johnny Bastard, but much better looking. He too had a moustache. "What's up with it?" Looking towards me he seemed unsure how to respond. Reluctant to speak to me even. "The machine, I mean."

"Nah come on Graham. Tha's not shy are thee. Mick won't bite." George added.

"Not frightened of no fucker me ain't." *Bet that doesn't include Ged?* We continued to stare at the lad. He was under instruction from Ged. Finally, he turned back to me.

"Cutting head. It's fucked. Can't get picks out. Bout as much use as tits on a bull."

Behind Graham I was alarmed to see his two workmates begin to prime the holes. "What the fuck are they doin?" I shouted

"Keep fuckin hat on Mick. Getting ready to fire." Ignoring Graham's comment, I walked forward. Laid on the floor three powder cans. Two with sticks of P4/5. The other with six primed sticks, ready for placing in the shotholes.

"Where the fucks the Deputy?" I shouted turning to George. For the first time that morning George's smile had evaporated.

"Out yonder." Looking outbye I could see a cap lamp moving about. Without asking anymore questions I paced towards the Deputy. He didn't see me approach, he had his back to me. He was singing to himself. I was angry, very angry.

"What the fuck do you think your doin?" My raised voice caused him to jump. Turning suddenly towards me. He looked completely surprised by my outburst. I recognised him immediately from this morning. He was about to answer. I hadn't finished yet. "You've got the men inserting the primed cartridges into the holes! That's your fuckin job." I hadn't noticed immediately. He was holding the exploder, one length of shotfiring cable already attached. "Are you completely fuckin stupid?" I paused for breath. Now composed he took the opportunity to respond.
"Saves time cock. Get job done quicker."
"Saves fuckin time?"
"Now hold on tha two." George appeared alongside. "Men listening. Not right falling out in front of them." George was right. I'd felt so incensed at what I'd seen and the potential consequences of Rob Flannagan's actions.

By the time I'd got back up the pit. I was fucked. No other way of putting it completely, one hundred per cent fucked. I was aching from every bone in my body. George had gone on ahead to the Undermanager's office with his statutory report. Before heading there, I spent a few moments gulping water down at the taps in the crush hall. The place was empty. Noon shift now underground. Lennie the afternoon shift Overman I'd passed in the deployment centre. The ice-cold water felt good. I swallowed allowing the excess to run freely from my mouth. Suitably replenished I continued to the Undermanager's office.

The place was almost empty. David was sat behind his desk, still in his black.
"How did it go then?" He asked smiling. I wasn't sure how to answer. Did he want the truth? In that the place was a complete shit hole. There was so much outstanding work to complete, I'd almost filled half my note book. Ideally the place should be put on hold till we'd completed all outstanding works. Like that was ever going to happen. The place was a tinder box of industrial unrest. The aggression amongst the men I'd never experienced before. I wasn't convinced the equipment we had in place was ideal, dependable even. "Grab a pew. Fancy a cuppa?" I grabbed one of the chairs against the far wall and sat.
"I'm good thanks David." I responded declining the offer. Before adding anything further the door to the office swung open.
"Bloody ell Mick. Three shears. Well done lad. Off to a winning start." Mr Keech offered before turning to David. "When you're changed, Manager wants a catch up on L30's top road."
"I was hoping to get away handy today."

92

"Sorry David. Gaffer's instruction. I'll see you shortly. Well done again Mick. We'll be expected that each shift now!" And with that he was gone.

David didn't look happy. He was staring at the phone. He suddenly looked back towards me. Smiling again.
"How did you get on with Ged?"

□

Later that week I received official confirmation from the Head of Staff Recruitment and Training Policy that my application for a place on the Board's Engineering Training Scheme had been successful.
Work continued pretty much the same, everyday a slog but this is what I signed up for. Taking the positives, I was learning a lot more about man management and travelling up and down the face I was getting fitter. The downside, however, by the time I got home I was fucked, always falling asleep.

□

I hadn't realised until Heidi our dog came back into the kitchen, I was late. Looking up at the clock it was already half five. I usually left at five. I grabbed the two rounds of toast I'd just buttered, not forgetting my Pink grapefruit *I'll eat these in the car on the way in.*
"Mick?" Annie shouted over the banister. I thought she'd gone back to sleep. I stepped into the hallway.
"What's up?"
"Can't you hear what's going on outside?"
"What?"
"Big domestic. Outside our house." I quickly made my way into the front room. We'd lived in the house for just on three months. We'd seen more dramas outside the house than we had in the six years we'd lived in Liverpool. The house a semi, located opposite the estate's shops. Still relatively private as there were two giant conifers in the front garden.

I expected to see a couple arguing. To my surprise there was a guy lying in the road opposite our gate. "Go on then run me over. See if I care." He shouted towards a green Ford Cortina. Partly obscured behind the conifers I could just make out a young girl sat holding the steering wheel. She had long brown permed hair. "I love you; I truly love you." He'd now raised his head. He looked distraught. I assumed she must have been his girlfriend. They didn't look married. The next thing I heard was the car starting up.
"She's going to run him over." Annie still providing the commentary from upstairs. I was sure she wouldn't, probably about to put the thing in reverse.

He'd then get up, fuck off and I could go to work. To my surprise she drove forward. The front of the car now over the top of his feet.

"Go on then do it. I can't live without you." He was now lying flat again.

"Mick you'd best get out there and sort it out. Before someone gets hurt."

I moved back into the hallway.

"Never mind that. I'm going to be late for work."

"Oh, my goodness she's driven forward again."

I opened the front door as quietly as I could, taking in the freshness of the early spring morning. The dawn chorus was still in progress regardless of the incident unfolding ahead of me. For the first time I could hear the girlfriend shout.

"Well, you shouldn't have been fuckin dancin with her."

"I know I didn't mean to."

"And fuckin snoggin her."

"She snogged me first."

"Like that makes a difference." I watched in horror as the car lurched forward once more. It looked as though I had little choice but to get involved.

I walked down the path to the front gate. Half the guys body was now under the Cortina. A tap, tap, tap on the window caused me to turn round. Annie was waving me forward. *What do you think I'm doin?*

"Excuse me." My intervention made no difference. They hadn't even noticed me. Insults still flying backwards and forwards.

"You're just a twat. Just like my dad. My mum warned me about fella's like you."

"I'm sorry. So, so sorry. How about we get engaged?" The guy still lying flat was looking up into the sky. An aircraft was flying overhead. "Let's go on holiday. Whit's just round the corner we could go to Benidorm."

"I'm goin nowhere with you Frankie you can fuck off back to dat tart you was dancin with." As much as I was enjoying the spectacle I had to get to work. There was coal to get.

"Excuse me." I shouted this time, finally getting Frankie's attention. He turned his head towards me.

"What the fuck do you want?" *Cheeky bastard!*

"If it's not too much trouble I'd like to get out of my drive. Some of us have a place of work to get to."

"Hey, don't you talk to my fella like dat."

"Dat's it girl you tell'm." To my complete astonishment the two of them had now turned on me. Frankie was still on his back.

"I'll tell you what then. Stay where you are, and I'll drive over your fuckin head."

"Hey you. Don't go threatening Frankie like dat. I'll call the Police." Frankie now having scrambled from under the car was standing facing me.

"Yeah you. That's threatening behaviour we'll get the busies on yer." Frankie added as he moved quickly to the passenger door. Climbing in he lowered the window. "Fuck off yer wanker." And with that they sped off.

Two weeks after receiving my confirmation letter for the ETS I was summoned to the Top Shunt. The Manager and Malcolm Hughes from Staff Training explained the detail of the scheme. It included attending two residential course at a place called Graham House in Newcastle-upon-Tyne. Dates had yet to be confirmed, although what was certain, it wouldn't be till next year. I decided not to mention it to the missus until nearer the time.

"Mick, tha knows we've got no steel."

"Mick, we'll need a fitter first thing. Hausherr's fucked."

"Mick, maingate pack will need pumping first thing if tha wants shearer to get in. Pump packing lads think Tekcem pipe blocked and they're nearly out of powder."

"Bloody ell Scouse what it must be like to be an Overman."

"Thanks Ged. I appreciate your concern." We'd just arrived at the meeting station. Questions from the lads were flying thick and fast. We hadn't got off to the best start. George was on a rest day, something to do with buying a new car. Leaving me, Rob Flannagan in the return and Freddy covering the maingate.

"Should you be underground with that." Ged raised his right hand. It was heavily bandaged.

"You're not suggesting I go on club?"

"No. What if you get it infected?"

"Just bruising. Cunt's ed was like fuckin granite. Need money. Not like tha cunts workin through. I'll be at panels if you need owt." I nodded as Ged moved off.

"Nah Mick. Am goin straight in with yon fitter. Try get Hausherr sorted. Soon as its moved I'll get lads relay track and take steel in." Freddy began. I nodded. Freddies appearance never ceased to amaze me. His long unkempt hair, goatee, and thin pencil moustache. He wouldn't look out of place on a college campus.

"Thanks Fred." I turned towards the crosscut. "Where's Rob?"

"Just left."

"Right, I'll catch you later. Rob!" I shouted as I headed towards the crosscut. I spotted him in the distance.

He was travelling inbye with the heading lads. As usual laughing and joking. Probably discussing last night's turn in the Labour Club. I never understood why he became an official. Always wanting to be one of the lads.

"Rob." I shouted louder this time. I knew he could hear me. He was just being his usual self. An awkward twat.

"What fuckin do now?" He responded. His team continued towards the airdoors.

"We'll see you in there Rob." One of the heading lads shouted.

He made no attempt to walk towards me. Just stood there with a face like a smacked arse.

"Listen fella, need you to do me a favour. Can you give the pump packing lads a hand and make sure they get the pipe unblocked? I'd do it but need to chase the haulage up, get another mine car of Tekcem and bent in."

"Can't."

"What do you mean can't"

"Lads want me fire caunch." I edged closer to Rob. Which was a mistake. As usual he stunk of alcohol. How the fuck he never got stopped by the Police driving to work.

"The lads have got to drill the place first. Anyway, I'm not askin, I'm fuckin tellin ye." He never responded. Standing there staring at me.

"You fuckin understand me."

"Fuckin ell Mick. No need to shout and you've spit on me." This fuckin man was the pain of my life.

"Thing is Rob. Every time I ask you to do summat we have to argue."

"Well, you should ask me a bit nicer."

"Fuckoff." He never responded immediately. Then out of nowhere we both began to laugh.

"That's better."

By the time I'd spoken to the haulage lads and returned to the meeting station I was lathered. I took a long swig from my water bottle. Letting it spill from my mouth and on to my chest. Leaning against the wooden bench I took another. The black stuff was now pouring out. The clatter and banging of the coal against the chute was a sound gratefully received. As was the sight of the inch and quarter pump packing pipes vibrating against the suspended pipe chain. The sight of water dripping caused me to walk across to the back of the jib. The neoprene wiper we'd fitted yesterday was doing its job. The formation of a stalagmite was testament to that. The blackened water falling freely as the neoprene did its job. I moved back towards the chute and poked my head tentatively alongside. Sure, enough the damaged water spray head was pissing out water. Tracing the half inch bagging back to the miniature brass valve I reduced the flow. I made a note to get it replaced. Before setting off inbye, I took a quick pinch of snuff, savouring the aroma as it filled my nasal passage.

I reckoned the machine wouldn't be far off the maingate end by now. We'd left it in cut the previous day. All things considered to how the day had started I was pleased. I began mentally to plan my day. *Travel the maingate first, check the loop for the next extension. Assuming they'd got the Hausherr working again leave sufficient time to park it under the belt. I'd need to use the men on the return dint tomorrow. Onto the coal face. Coal tops were beginning to thin from around number ten check. I'd need to check that out. Make my way to the return. Spying my chance to check the floor dirt.*

The loop looked as though we'd get away with it for another day or so. Looking beneath the bottom belt I'd need to arrange a clean-up. I continued inbye. The black stuff was still flowing freely. Occasionally a mound of white dirt appeared. I guessed the Hausherr was up and running. Cleaning out whatever was required to relay the haulage track. I wasn't wrong. By the time I'd reached the Bryn and Howard, the Hausherr was sat under the raised conveyor. The bogey and steel arches ready to go. Both men on their knees recoupling the rails and fish plates.
"Morning lads."
"Morning Mick."
"Well done. Steel next?"
"Certainly is."
"Catch you later."
"Aye."

Twenty minutes later, the lights of the stage loader came into view. I could see young Paul. His voice booming out from the tannoy I'd just passed.
"Hi Steve. Machine's at maingate end." Having removed the single ender the previous month, the double ender was proving its worth. Bobby Lunt and his lads had also taken early retirement.
"Thanks Paul. Is Mick with you?"
"Nah. He was outbye earlier arranging some supplies."
"Can you let him know, the cem and bent are now at the bottom of E3."
"Will do."
Another job sorted. The *click, click, click* of the conveyor grew louder as the pile of coal reduced to a trickle. I hadn't noticed him initially. There was a second person outbye of Paul. Sat on the jumbo cables. I recognised the shape but wasn't sure why he had his arm in the air.
"What's up Ged. Stretching exercises?"

"Fuckin ell Scouse tha's funny." Bringing his arm down he was examining his hand. The bandage now removed clearly showed how swollen it was. A mix of purple and blue, in places yellow had begun to emerge.

"Sure, you haven't broken your wrist?"

"No, I don't think so but it's fuckin sore."

"I'd call into the medical centre when you get up. Get Barry to have a look."

"Hello panels, hello Paul."

"Hi Alf."

"Is Mick with thi?"

"Yeah."

"Tell im machine's conked out. No power." *For fucks sake not a damaged cable.* "Tell him it's not cable. Think it's summat do with one of those micro progresses."

"Processors tha daft cunt." Someone added.

"I'll give tha daft cunt when I get hold of thi." Leaving Ged, I moved across to the DAC.

"Alf, Mick ere. Does…." I turned back towards Paul. "Who's electrician this morning?"

"Kenny."

"Does Kenny need anything?"

"Says he doesn't think so. Shouldn't be long."

"Mick, Les ere. Problem with twenty-two chock. Ram's fucked. Fitter's on it now. We'll chain it on but could do with one of spares running in from return if there's any left."

"Fuck is there anything else that can go wrong?" I said to no one in particular.

"All a ploy Scouse. Coal Board want close place." Ged was now alongside me, Having replaced his bandage. I ignored his comment.

"Paul do us a favour and give Rob Flannagan a shout. See if there's any spare rams lying about. Am sure I saw two the other day. By the way where's Freddy Clough?"

"Last I heard he war connecting up. Bout fire headin."

I said no more and headed towards the face. Almost falling as, I reached the hydraulic tank. The milky fluid as normal was falling freely towards the floor. The smell overpowering.

"Fuckin ell." I turned to turn off the water feed. Reaching the maingate end I could see Freddy perched on the platform. The smell of hydraulic fluid now replaced by the recently formed pack.

"Fred what the fuck are you doin." He returned my comment with his usual smile.

"Can't leave it Mick. All wired up, ast no choice. Waitin for yon machine fuck off." The man had an answer for everything. I had no doubt today's events would produce another poem. I continued onto the face. I was surprised to see Kenny heading towards me.

"Sorted fella?"

"Yeah. Thing is Mick I didn't do anything. Fettled itsen." Without warning the pre-start kicked in. The panzer chain drowning out any further conversation. The shearer was just ahead. Deciding to have a moment, I waited to let it pass. The *clank, clank, clank* and scraping of the panzer chain now dulled. The black stuff filling the panzer. A few lumps of coal spalling forward as the discs turned. I pushed myself further into the chock legs to avoid the water sprays, blasting out in various directions. Making a mental note to get the sprays cleaned out.

With Johnny off Cliff was assisting David on shearer duty. He appeared before me. His rag like figure moving between the chocks. Total concentration on the cutting horizon. The beam of his light picking out the narrow dirt band, six inches below the mudstone roof.

"Hiya David."

"Alreyt Mick." He shouted back.

"Just goin in the once?" I strained to hear his answer.

"Yeah. Give Freddy chance to drop the caunch. You know the tops are thinning again?"

"Yeah, I've heard. Probably run some split bars down end of shift. Could do with you cleanin out sprays next chance you get." He nodded. His eyes barely visible through the face visor. I patted David on the back as he passed. His dirty black overalls were soaked through. The noise of the discs reducing as it passed by. It was soon replaced by the return disc chomping out the six inches of remaining floor coal.

"Morning Cliff."

"Nay Mick. How's it goin?"

"All good thanks. I mentioned to David, not sure if he heard me. Next time you get chance check your sprays." Although looking at his disc they seemed in order. "Where's fitter?"

"With Les. Mick do us favour cock. Just check cable till we get into maingate." Reluctantly moving my arse out of the chock, I leaned forward to look along the spills. Bretby was doin its job. The double row of plastic nylon plates protecting the cable and water hose lying horizontal. Now uncoiling over that already lying in the spill trough. I moved forward. One of the U-shaped pins looked as though it was missing. I was mistaken. Everything in order I continued towards the return gate, easier now the pans had been pushed over.

It wasn't long before I spotted Les and the fitter coming towards me.

"Nah Mick. You goin into return?"

"Yeah, why?"

"Couldn't get hold of Rob. Pinch?" He passed me his open tin of Hedges. "Goin need two rams running down."

"Might be best if you get some more on order." Brian the fitter added.

"Thanks." I passed the tin of snuff back. "Fuckin ell Les how old is this stuff." I managed to say before overtaken by a bout of sneezes.

"I know. Left it in locker by mistake last week whilst off." Using the sleeve of my boiler suit to wipe the mucus now freely falling from my nostrils.

"How did you get on?" Les, Cliff, and David were into sea fishing. They'd hired a boat the previous week.

"More mackerel than you could wave a stick at. And a couple of tope."

"Whereabouts?"

"Rhyl."

"Fuckin Rhyl! Weren't they all dead?"

"Were they fuck. Loads of shark fishing goin on too."

"Get away with yer."

"I kid you not. Anyway, Mick as much as I enjoy talking shite, need to get those chocks in. See tha later."

I continued towards the return. My pace slowed now as I travelled along the chock line. My oil lamp alternatively hitting against the chock bases and my knee. I'd barely cooled down whilst talking to Les and Brian. The sweat began to pour forth once more. My chest was lathered. I could feel the perspiration now falling freely from my forehead. I stopped. This time for a proper pinch. The panzer began to slow.

"Breaking lump." A voice shouted out from the DAC. It sounded like Ged. I smiled. He wasn't going to let a broken wrist stop him working. Savouring the moment of my fresh tin of Hedges I gave some thought on my approach to Rob. We'd never really got on. I guess on his part I was the young up and comer. Never taking no for an answer and always pushing hard for a result. Rob anything for a quiet life. Wanting to be one of the lads. And that for me was his biggest problem.

Popping the tin back into my pocket I continued forward. Slower now. The panzer was still stationary. *Must be some lump.* I was tempted to shout something abusive towards Ged but refrained. I was nearing the top end. I couldn't hear any sound of the Webster or the lads drilling. Knowing Rob, he'd probably allowed them all to take an early snap. Something was bothering me though. I began to slow. It was too quiet. What the hell was it? I stopped. My ears now on hyper alert. *What the fuck was it?* I began to walk forward once again. I then stopped something wasn't right. *It couldn't be, could it? No fuckin chance.* I'd now reached the packhole chocks. I began to retrace my steps towards the maingate. Slowly at first. Moving backwards. Something was telling me to increase my pace. I turned and began moving at speed. Then. *Bang!*

The noise of the explosion washed over me. Unable to hear anything I watched in slow motion small pieces of stone fly passed me and onto the face. I was suddenly engulfed in dust. The concentration of which began to suffocate, coating the inside of my mouth. I contemplated throwing myself to the floor. There was no point. Instead, I sat on a spill plate where the chock had yet to be advanced. Removing my helmet, I began to rub either side of my head. Sound around me replaced by a continuous buzzing between my ears. A light appeared at the top end. Looking up, the air still laden with dust, the figure of a person was coming towards me. An oil lamp hanging from their side. It was Rob. The closer he got I could see his lips moving. He grabbed either shoulder. His face distorted with concern. Again, mouthing a sentence.
"Are you okay?" Behind more lights. He turned; I guessed giving instructions. I couldn't hear anything. The lights moved back off the face. Returning in seconds. The dust now cleared. It was one of the heading lads. This time carrying a water bottle. He passed it to Rob. Removing the top, he pressed it against my lips. I took a sip. Initially gargling before spitting out. I took another. The buzzing began to fade. Replaced by a ringing sound.

"Mick. Mick you okay." I looked up towards Rob. *What the fuck do you think? Stupid bastard.* The look on his face suggested he understood how I felt. He began to flap, which was no surprise. He turned away from me then back. Turning again he shouted to the lads. "Stretcher. Quick fetch a stretcher."
"I don't need a stretcher." I responded calmly.
"What?"
"I said, I don't need a stretcher." He'd finally stopped moving.
"I'm sorry."
"Fuckin sorry? Where was your sentry?" I remained sitting. A calmness had settled on me.
"I didn't think……"
"You didn't fuckin think." The calmness had only been temporary. "You didn't fuckin think. And Rob that's your biggest fuckin problem. You don't fuckin think." I could have continued but what was the point. He looked in a greater state of shock than I was. The pre-alarm kicking in stopped any further conversation. My head still felt numb. We both headed off the face and into the return. The heading lads gathered watching me as I walked further outbye.

Stopping as I reached the pile of chockwood. I sat down. One of them approaching me with his flask of coffee.

"Lucky there Mick."

"Tell me about it." He offered me a cup of black steaming sweet coffee. It tasted good. "Thanks."

Half an hour later and suitably refreshed I went to have a looksee for the rams. Having located them I gave instruction to have them moved nearer the face and to let the fitter know. Still undecided what to do with Rob. I was certain he hadn't intentionally tried to blow me up. I hoped that wasn't the case anyway. We did speak later on the way out. He seemed to accept he'd fucked up big time. The first thing he did when he got to the surface was head towards the Safety Office to pick up the red plastic safety caps. That was a first for Rob. I heard later the lads had given him a nick name, Bobby Bang, Bang!

"Bloody ell John! What you doin here?" The sight of John Meriden took me by complete surprise. John had been one of my Undermanager's at Cronton.

"Nah lad, how's it goin?"

"Good thanks John. I thought you'd gone Sutton Manor."

"I wa for a period. Been asked come ere. See you finally made it to Face Overman?"

"Yeah, just over a month now. L32's single shifting. All that mentoring you gave me finally paid off."

"Mustn't ave done too good a job. Manager tells me there's no consistency in production." I nodded at his comment. I liked John, he'd taught me loads. Never one for offering praise but I had to give it to him he was never back in coming forward.

"I'm working on it, you working with David?"

"Fuckin ell Mick, what's with all the questions."

"Where is he anyway?"

"Top Shunt." That sounded a little ominous. He'd been having a rough time of late. Particularly over L30's top road after the face had been turned. It didn't help with our performance on L32's either. "Where did the machine end up?"

"Top end. Bi-Di complete, ready to come down."

"Why weren't you coaling in overtime?"

"Couldn't get enough lads to stop over. Those that did used them on maingate end, roof bolting."

"David mentioned you were having some problems with the roof. Not learnt owt? Why don't you get them to leave coal tops?"

"Fuckin ell John. Think I'm fuckin stupid."

"Now lad do tha really want me to answer that?" Our conversation was interrupted as the door opened. It was David, he didn't look good. Thought it time I left.

"See you tomorrow." I didn't wait for an answer. Poor David.

⬚

"Ged could do with some wedges and half dozen lids."

"Am not tha gofer lad."

"Tha could be mine Ged."

"Nah Les, don't want to come down there and twat tha one?" I was stood with the two return end lads. All three of us lathered. We'd been running timber down to the fall area. Ged was sat in one of the packhole chocks, arms resting on the DAC.

"He could do with it Ged." One of the lads with me added laughing.

"Sorry Ged. Just joking." Les responded.

"Don't like them kinda jokes." With that Ged clambered to his feet. "Come on Scouse you're doing nothing."

"Cheeky cunt."

"Nah Scouse no need for that language. Where's bow saw?"

"On side there Ged by stack of chockwood." Graham shouted.

I followed Ged outbye, beyond the last lot of timber delivered. Split bars, wooden props, half dozen bundles of hessian sacks. The wooden wedges lay scattered alongside.

"I'll need to get this moved inbye." Ged never responded. The smell of wet timber more obvious now.

"Ever done this before Scouse?"

"I'm sure you're goin to show me." We both knelt opposite one another. Alongside a split bar resting and supported on chockwood. I grabbed the saw just above the pin. Ged was already holding the handle. Placing it six inches from the end he drew it back. I pulled on the return stroke, a little too hard causing his knuckles to smack into the timbers edge.

"Oops!"

"I'll give tha fuckin oops." I smiled. He smiled too. His small eyes glinting with a look of amusement. I hadn't thought of it before his eyes weren't dissimilar to those of a shark. Menacing even if I didn't know him better. I liked Ged he was a worker, straight and told you as it was. He never suffered fools; I think he liked me too a novelty in some ways. A young Scouser trying to make a name for himself as a junior manager. The men had respect for him too. He also frightened them because of his abrupt nature and his, at times, aggressive personality. Below the aggressive layer, I saw a kind and caring person. We had a mutual respect and understood the part we both played.

After sawing for twenty minutes, we were both sweating profusely. Perspiration dropping freely from our faces. Neither one of us ready to admit it was time for a minute. My shoulder was beginning to ache. My eyes stinging too.

"Snuff?"

"Knackered Scouse?"

"No. I was thinking more of you."

"Cheeky bastard. I, go on." He placed the saw to one side. I offered the tin. In the distance I heard the panzer pre-alarm kick in. I ran my arm across my forehead. "Water bottle's up there on side."

"Thanks, will in a mo. I'll tell you what you've certainly got them working as a team now."

"Yeah, they're not a bad bunch." I hadn't mentioned much about the strike. I wasn't sure if it was still a touchy subject.

"Were they all on the picket line with you?" He never responded immediately. Staring towards me. I wondered if I'd overstepped the mark.

"Yeah, all of'em. Accept Terry. Suppose you crossed?"

"No, actually. Cronton having already been closed before Corton Wood got dispensation to keep salvaging. By the time I moved here, pickets had given up."

"Had one of your lot join us on the picket line."

"Who would that be then?"

"Your poncy Leader of Liverpool Council. Used to turn up in his fancy crocodile skin shoes. Fancy gold watch and rings. Stunk of Brut." I laughed. His comment didn't come as a surprise.

"Heard you ended marching on Hobart House?"

"Yeah, pitched up for a week. Got put up in some couples fancy apartment."

"What? Southerners?"

"The hoity toity mixing with the hoi polloi. Got a kick out of mixing with the working class. Only stayed there two nights. She was always flashing me her tits. Wanted a threesome. Sure, her fella wanted me to shag him too. Fuckin southern nutters." I smiled. The thought of Ged in bed with another couple didn't quite add up.

"Do you think you achieved anything?"

"How do'y mean?"

"Pits are still being shut. Latest figures if you can believe'm. Lost another thirty-six and about twenty-five thousand men."

"Think it just goes to prove our point. She's doin what she always wanted to do. If you fuckers had joined us, we'd have won." I wasn't sure we'd agree on that point. Best I kept my gob shut. "I mean look at you. Going into management and all that. How long do you think you've got?"

"Come on Ged. They'll always need coal. Keeps the countries options open. Not wanting to rely on any one type of fuel."

"You watch. Talk now of privatising the CEGB. Anyway, it's fuck all to do with fuel. None of them are bright enough to look into the future. These fuckers are intent in bringing the Trades Unions to their knees. Don't want us lot causing 'em problems. Think they can do what they want now. During the strike kept talking bout miners being the enemy within. Using the courts, police, and media to portray us as revolutionaries. Load of bollocks. Vanguard of the working class we was. Do'y know there's still lads in prison trying to protect their jobs. Others with police records for the rest of their lives. Don't see any coppers being done for violent behaviour." He had a point. I recalled seeing the actions of the police at Orgreave.

"Hey you two. What doin? Havin a love in or what?" One of the return end lads shouted out towards us.

"Fuck off!" Ged responded.

"Think he's got a point though. Come on best get this to 'em." Ged never responded as we packed the wooden lids into the hessian bags. "Thanks for that. Gives another perspective on why things happened."

"Timing was wrong though. Union too divided. Ever seen them posters *Close a Pit, kill a community?* South Wales. Happening now, destroying villages. That daft cunt tellin people to get on their bike. Fuckin crazy. Could have been so different." And that was it end of conversation. We made our way back to the lads without another word being spoken on the subject.

□

The weeks began to fly by since John had arrived. He was becoming more involved with me and the operation of L32's. We'd agreed on a programme of performance improvement. Identifying the areas where changes could and should increase production. Removing the single ender had helped but we hadn't seen any consistency in production. Manpower wise, though, it had been a big help. This weekend we'd planned work on the Webster in the return.

"Nay Mickey, plenty goin on today lad?"

"Morning Cayle, yeah plenty happening." He had his usual big grin. Always smiling, well most of the time, unless Wigan had lost. Then he turned into Mr Grumpy, face like a smacked arse. I'd just walked into the Deployment Centre, cap lamp and self-rescuer in position. I was in the process of relighting my oil lamp.

"Don't forget lad, loco will be waiting, tha needs to get cutting head out as soon as possible. Workshops will be waitin." He passed me my tallies.

"Ta yeah got that covered. As soon as the haulage lads arrive at the bottom of E3 and shunt the first run, we'll have a flat ready."

"Ah morning George."

"Morning Cayle, morning Mick. See we've got no Ged this morning."

"No. Phoned in sick. Probably got the shit kicked out of him Saturday neet." I turned to Cayle smiling. *Like that was ever goin to happen!* "No worries though job in L31's has been cancelled. Teddy their face chargehand will replace Ged. Talking of which."

"Morning Cayle." Teddy nodded to me and George. I knew Teddy although he'd never worked for me. He reminded me of a panda. The layer of coal dust beneath his eyelids seemed to be a permanent feature. The thick black Mexican moustache added to his distinct features.

"Morning Teddy."

"Are you fuckers planning on going down today?" Derek Moore shouted. I hadn't noticed. Stood there talking had caused a hold up for the men passing through.

"Come on lads best we make a move."

"Righto Mick. I'll just go and pick up some dets."

"What for?" George seemed reluctant to answer at first. "Erm for the erm……"

"The maingate dint. I'll fetch a couple of pouches of powder." Teddy added.

"Okay see you at pit top." I continued forward in the throng of men. For a Sunday morning it seemed quite busy. I recognised several C15's lads too. As usual Keith Williams, Wilco, their face overman was with them. He waved to me. C15 the coal factory. What I'd give to be on there. The coal gave itself up. The face was the penultimate in the Crombouke seam. C16 planned for next year would be the last. They were fitting a crusher onto the maingate belts. Lumps being their main obstacle to increasing tonnage.

I had several jobs taking place that morning on L32's. In addition to the cutting head being repaired we had to remove a full pan at the maingate and replace with half a pan. I had two men on the Hauser Dinter in the maingate. The electricians were extending the armoured cable to create some slack on the jumbo cables plus a couple of lads moving the stone dust barriers inbye. If time permitted, I wanted to extend the loop. The two ex Hapton Valley lads manned the Hauser. They'd transferred with me from Cronton. You couldn't have wanted better workers. Problem however was understanding what they said.

Arriving at pit top the cage was in position. The two lower decks having been filled now suspended beneath the surface. The stair well to the top deck was already full. I continued forward the background noise filled with conversations of the men on the previous evening's antics. Gingerly stepping over the gap into the cage. Standing two by two in line we each faced forward. In position I grabbed the top rail. I said little. My thoughts on the jobs in hand. The removal of the pan my main priority. I didn't want the AFC getting fast on the ribside. I'd also ensure the following week we took additional shears off the maingate end to move the pans towards the return. The cutting head on the Webster should be relatively straight forward. Once removed Teddy was to take the haulage and get it back to the surface. Several picks had sheared off in the head affecting the cutting performance of the machine. The fitters had warned if we didn't get it sorted soon it would damage the gearing. Momentarily my thoughts distracted as the clatter of the mesh gate dropped.

Four decks now loaded. The Banksman made the necessary signals, and we were away. My overalls flapping as we dropped. Very few of us wore donkey jackets. The early morning being relatively warm for that time of the year. The conversations from earlier now subdued as we dropped into the bowels of the earth. For many of us it was a time of reflection as the air and anticipated smells whipped around us.

Without warning we began to decelerate. Finally stopping as the lads in the bottom deck discharged onto the landing. There was no Onsetter. I could hear Wilco barking instructions to his men. I detected the ever so light movement of the cage lifting upwards as the sixteen men discharged. Then the signalling to the winder. We began to move once more. I caught a glimpse of Wilco as we passed the inset, he was turning to follow his men inbye.

Exiting the cage at No. 3 pit bottom I moved forward at speed to join with George and Teddy. They were in deep conversation. Twenty minutes later, having travelled the Tunnel we reached the E3 manrider. No time wasted as the guard, using his stick hit the signalling cable above. We were away down the one in four brow.

It was another ten minutes after discharging from the manrider we passed L19's district before reaching L32's Meeting Station. Nobody hung about. Having been briefed earlier the lads made their way to the respective job locations.

"Mick I'll accompany Teddy and the fitter to the return. I've told haulage lads to have the flat in position."

"Thanks George. I'll base myself at the maingate. See you later." I began to walk off. "One other thing…." I turned back towards George. Too late he'd disappeared towards the cross cut. I could feel the change in air pressure as the airdoors opened. I'd wanted to ask about firing for the maingate dint. It was so unlike him. Usually hanging about at the Meeting Station with his flask of sweetened tea.

I gave it no more thought and headed inbye. The roadway was in good condition. The odd spot where the weight had come on causing the weld mesh to bulge out. I'd need to get bags of stone dust laid out. HMI had yet to visit. We could expect them at any time. I spotted two lights ahead, partly obscured by the swirling airborne stonedust. The two lads had made a start on dismantling the heavy barrier. Now standing on the conveyor structure removing the brackets.

"Now lads mind how you go. The dint will be starting up shortly." No sooner had I finished my comment the belt began to move.

"Fuckin ell Mick can thy see into future or what?"

"If only! I'd be doin the pools every week."

"Come on Mick. Who's tha kiddin. You wouldn't leave this job." His colleague added. We all began to laugh.

"If only I had the choice. Anyway, don't know if George mentioned there's two separate piles of dust stacked where the heavy and light barrier positions need to go."

"Yeah, he's already said."

"If there's time and you'll need to tie in with the Burnley lads there's a twenty-yard length of belt to go into the loop."

I continued passed the Hausherr. The Burnley lads nodded. Not ones for small talk. Five minutes later I'd reached the electricians they were sat on the jumbo cables eating a sandwich.

"Fuckin ell lads what we on. Breakfast overtime?"

"Nah Mick not expecting us to start work on an empty stomach are tha?"

"No just want to make sure we get the job done."

"Fuckin ell Mick, tha's always worryin. Take a chill pill you'll end up with an ulcer. Just like Manager."

The lads at the maingate had already removed one of the spill plates, now starting on the second. I was pleased to see they had plenty of room to work in with the chocks left back. Satisfied all the jobs in the maingate had either started or about to start. I decided to head up to the return. Having passed the shearer, I climbed back onto the pans and began walking up towards the return. Positioning my oil lamp against my right side I used my left hand against the spills to steady myself. Sweat was pumping out. I could feel it running down my chest. Keeping a careful eye on the coal face. Occasionally having to climb over the lumps of coal. I stopped momentarily to catch my breath. I was somewhat surprised to see a stationary light ahead. It was Brian.

"You got it off then?"

"Tha's fuckin jokin Mick it's as fast as my mates wallet on a Saturday neet. I'm acting as sentry. George's about to blow it off."

"What do'y mean. I thought you fetched a piece of kit to extract the head."

"Wouldn't budge it a gnat's cock." *No wonder George had brought dets. Nothin to do with the fuckin maingate dint.* I moved towards the nearest DAC.

"Hello……" The bang and thud of the firing caused me to stop mid-sentence. I looked towards the return gate. A small amount of dust appeared ahead. Then gone removed by the ventilation. I turned towards Brian. He'd opened a tin of snuff. "Don't mind if I do." I reached forward and took a small pinch.

"Yeah, help yourself Mick tha cheeky fucker." I ignored his comment taking an amount in each nostril. I began to move towards the return.

"I take it, it's just one bang?"

"I just the one."

By the time I'd exited the face the airborne dust had disappeared. All that remained was the lingering smell of ammonia. Teddy was stood looking at the face of the heading.

"Well would tha believe that mon?" I looked towards the spot his lamp was exposing. I didn't see it at first only the coal and the dirt band above. He raised both hands to grab whatever he was looking at. "Fast as fuck." It was the cutting head off the Webster.

"What the fuck have you done?"

"Aye Mick." George appeared from behind. "Said that was too much powder." His comment directed towards Teddy.

"I appens tha was reet George."

I wasn't sure who to direct my anger at. "For fucks sake you two. You've blown the thing to bits! What the hell are you playing at?"

"Fuckin ell Mick keep tha hair on cock." I turned towards Teddy. He was smiling. "We ain't blown owt up. At least it's off, just buried itself in coil. George pass me pick. I'll have it out in no time."

"Hello Mick. Hello Mick Gibson." My anger subsided temporarily as the outbye tannoy rang out. I shook my head as I passed George. He looked at me, his smile still in place.

"No other way to get it off Mick." I said nothing.

"Hi Control Mick, here."

"Mick, Cayle's been on. Workshops wanting to know how long you'll be with the cutting head." I turned towards the face of the heading. Teddy was swinging the pick into the coal surrounding the head. Even from that distance I could see his actions were making little difference.

"Shouldn't be long Steve. I'll give you a shout as soon as it's on the move."

"Thanks Mick. It's just the Blacksmith is on an early dart."

"What do you mean he's on an early dart?"

"Fuckin ell Mick. Joe's the pits star player. Got match on over at Golborne this afternoon." *Like I needed to hear that.*

"Hello Mick. It's me Billy at maingate end. Is yon fitter there. Lads off the Hauser has been on. Think he's saying one of the baggings has bosted. Needs replacing plus he's asking where's the nearest Aquacent." *Fuck so it begins. It never failed to surprise me when something went wrong everything fucked up.*

"Aye Mick, it's me Brian. If you've finished with me, I'll make my way. Any ideas where the oil is?" Once more I looked towards Teddy. He was still swinging the pick. He was now down to his vest. Discoloured as the sweat began to ooze out of his body. There wasn't much a fitter was going to do here.

"Thanks Brian. Yeah, we'll manage. Get one of the Burnley lads to fetch a couple of cans. There's a pile between the airdoors on the cross cut."

"Will do."

"Billy you still there?" I waited there was no immediate answer.

"Ey up Mick. What's up nah?"

"Just wondering how you were getting on with the pan."

"Fullen's out just movin the half back into position."

"You'll be done then by the end of the shift?"

"Not if I've got to keep answering the fuckin DAC." For the first time that morning I smiled. Bless him. Billy was never one to mince his words.

"Thanks Bill."

"It's fuckin Billy. Bill's me old fella."

"Thanks Billy." I had wanted to ask him how the electricians were getting on but thought better of it. I'd make my way round the district shortly. I'd need to check on the stonedust barrier lads too.

I walked back towards the others. Teddy had stopped swinging the pick. He was stood with a plastic bottle of water attached to his mouth. He looked as though he'd been stood under a dripper. George stepped forward.

"Don't think we've got much choice Mick." He offered nervously. "Goin to av blow the fucker out."

"Planning on putting a tracking device on it?"

"Sorry Mick what does mean?"

"Goin by your actions so far we don't know where it will fucking end up."

"Hello Mick. Hello Mick Gibson." Before George could answer I turned and headed back to the outbye tannoy.

"Hi Steve."

"Sorry to moider you again Mick. Manager's been on. Wants to know how you're getting on with the Webster." *Fuck I'd forgotten it was his weekend on.*

"All good Steve. We'll have it out shortly."

"Any estimate on completion." *For fucks sake Steve I'm not even sure if we'll need a new cutting head.*

"Yep, soon." Silence followed Steve knew I was talking through my arse.

The sound of the handheld compressed air drilling machine distracted me once more. I thought it best if I hung about until we'd got the thing moving outbye. I made my way back to Teddy, hanging my lamp on the side of the road I got behind him to help shove the machine forward. The tailings from the hole increased forming a pile on the floor.

"Steady Mick, don't want to be stalling machine." The drill rod began to slow. I moved back. The sweat was pouring from Teddy. A long-discoloured patch had formed on the back of his vest and he fuckin stunk. He must have guessed my thoughts.

"Curry Mick. Plenty garlic."

"You're not fuckin kiddin." I replied laughing.

"That should do it." He began to withdraw the drill rod. He returned it a couple of times to make sure the hole was cleaned out. "George?"

He was walking towards us, carrying a powder tin in each hand. The trailing strands of yellow wires suggested he'd already primed the sticks for the four holes.

I ran my tongue around the inside of my mouth and spat out. I could taste the coal dust.

"Chew Mick?" Teddy passed me a packet of pigtail. I bit a piece off the end. George had started charging the holes. "Think the one stick ill be enough." It never surprised me when the men offered their view on how much powder they used. They were the experts. We as the officials generally followed their instruction. Although I guess George wished he'd stuck to his guns earlier.

George moved back to retrieve the shot firing cable. Teddy completed stemming the holes as I connected the wires in series. We continued to work in silence. Without instruction Teddy headed across to the face line to act as sentry. Satisfied he was in position we moved outbye.

George had positioned the twelve-shot exploder behind a tall stack of chockwood. Connecting the cable, he shouted "Fire." Bang. We'd been closer than I thought. A few small pieces of coal shot passed where we crouched. We waited a few seconds before standing and walking into the cloud of dust. The smell of ammonia stung the back of my throat. The bitter taste absorbed in the bacca juice as I chewed. George positioned a dust mask before re-entering.

111

Teddy was already out. Walking towards us head leaning forward. He was carrying something.

"Thank fuck for that." I shouted laughing.

"I'll take it out then, shall I?"

"Yeah, I'll let haulage lads know." George responded. "You taking it all the way Teddy?"

"Yeah, might as well."

"Don't forget to come back." I shouted as I walked back to the tannoy. *Anything to get on land for a fag and cuppa.* "Hello Control. Hello Steve."

"Hi Mick."

"On its way. If you could let the manrider and loco lads know."

"Will do."

"Can you let the Manager know too."

"Why don't you give him a call thisel Mick."

"Nah, I'll leave that to you Steve thanks."

The rest of the shift went like clockwork. Couple of hours later we all headed out toward the manrider.

☐

6. The Misfire

By Wednesday of the following week things had gone well. Each day we'd managed to complete two and a half shears. I'd never class myself as being a negative type of person but when things were going well, I was always concerned at what may be just around the corner.

I stopped just beyond where the machine had cut into its bi-di. I felt fucked. But fucked in a good way. It didn't get much better than this. I sat myself down. Between the back legs of the chock. I hung my oil lamp between the front legs. The warm throbbing of the return hydraulic hose under my arse felt comforting. I was soaked through the thin cotton of my boiler suit sticking to my chest. I reached inside my pocket for my tin of hedges. Extracting a small amount, I inhaled up each nostril. Just the job, raw snuff. The menthol vapour clearing my head. Several of the lads had started adding Olbas oil. Not for me though. I was thirsty too, that would have to wait. My water bottle was at the panels. I became aware of my pink grapefruit tucked beneath my vest. I tapped it, although tempting I would savour that delight on the ride out. Instead, I replaced the snuff tin and exchanged it for the packet of tobacco. I bit a small amount and began to chew.

Give another ten minutes we'd be on our way down for the third. It never ceased to amaze me how the men's morale was heightened with the steady flow of coal. I know I felt better for it. Particularly now being able to take the piss out of the lads from L31's on the ride out. They'd encountered a series of geological problems of late.

"Hello Mick Gibson, hello Mick." Steve's voice rang out from the DAC I'd conveniently placed myself against. Leaning forward I spat out on the mound of coal heading towards the maingate.
"Hi Control, Mick here."
"Mick could you give Al a call at the maingate."
"Can't he talk to me on the DAC?"
"Just passing the message on Mick. You ready to start coming down?"
"Yeah, shouldn't be long now. I'll let you know."
"Right cock."

So much for havin a minute. I lifted myself, stretching in the process. Part standing, part crouching I headed back to the return. Al was the maingate Deputy. He'd been covering for Freddy, currently on the club. Recently passed out, he seemed a decent guy. He reminded me of the lead guitarist from ZZ Top. His long scraggy beard always exhibiting stains from the tobacco juice that fell freely from his mouth. Ahead I spotted the lights from the shearer lads heading towards me. This could be our best shift ever.
"Alright Johnny?"
"Fuck off." I wouldn't have expected anything less from the lad. There was an uneasy alliance between me and Johnny Bastard. He'd taken an instant dislike to me from day one. I could live with the obscenities. It was the threat of him removing my head that I kept my distance. Although I hadn't witnessed it; I guess Ged's threat of removing his head if anything happened to me had calmed the volatile relationship between the two of us.

I leaned back into the chock to let him pass. Crossing my arms across my chest ready to accept the elbow that was sure to come. How he ever managed to spend the whole shift travelling the chock line. The lad was huge. The gentle dig caused me to comment.
"Is that it?"
"Fuck off!" I smiled, leaning back as small pieces of the coal catapulted from the cutting disc. The water spray seemed subdued. I'd get them to clear the sprays when they got to the bottom. I stayed to let his mate pass.
"Bloody ell Phil where's Dave?"
"Top end with Bobby. Got some shit in his eye. Just getting it cleaned out."
"How have you got on this morning?"

"Set two. We're going to have to get the bucket sorted, attachment damaged."
"Yeah, I know. Plan to sort this weekend. Catch you later."

I continued up. Exiting the face line, I acknowledged Bobby. He suited his new name which he'd now accepted. He was standing over David with a bottle of saline eye wash. David, helmetless had his head back. He was sitting on a stack of chockwood.
"Fuckin ell Mick ast forgotten summut?"
"Phone, need to make a call."
"Up yonder. By the oil drums. Leckies moved it in this morning."
"Ta."

"Hi Paul, is Alan there?" I heard Paul shout Alan's name. I waited. "Why what's up? Something happened? Put him on. Hi, Al, what's up fella. A miss-fire! How long ago? For fucks sake! Stop the fuckin belts. Yes, fuckin now! I'm on my way." I replaced the receiver. Bobby had heard me shout.
"Owt up cock?" I ignored his comment and dialled the Control. A voice on the face DAC shouted.
"Stage loader locked out. Who's got the lock out on?"
"Steve, hi, yep, I know. We've got a fuckin problem, stop all the belts outbye. A miss-fire. Don't know yet on my way down now. I'll give you a shout when I've had a look."

I headed back towards the face. "Bobby any idea where George is?"
"With the supply lads on the cross cut."
"Do us a favour. Give him a shout. Ask him to meet me at the maingate end. We've got a miss-fire."
"Fuck, that's not good. Remember what happened last time." I never answered. I was fully aware of a previous incident. Police had got involved. Some poor old pensioner in Haydock havin lit the front room coal fire caused an explosion. Luckily, he was unharmed. Front room was a mess though. Police had found dets amongst the domestic product from Parkside. They'd threatened to prosecute the Manager. Fortunately, charges were dropped. I'm guessing we wouldn't be as lucky this time.

Within minutes I was half way down the face line. Passing the shearer. I received no comment from Johnny. He'd already positioned himself horizontal in the chock track. My oil lamp bashing against the spills as I travelled. Sweat once more oozing from every pore. I quickened my pace. The flashing red of the signal boxes providing further urgency to the situation.

"Hello Mick, hello Mick Gibson." I'd recognise those dulcet tones anywhere. I stopped opposite the next DAC. Reaching between the chock legs, I pressed the brass button.

"Hi Mr Keech. Mick here."

"Can you give us a ring Mick." *Does he fuckin think I carry a phone on my back?*

"As soon as I get to one Mr Keech."

"Steve's said you asked for the outbye belts to be stopped?"

"Yep, that's right." I just knew what was coming next.

"Stopping L30's, 31's, W6's and C15's."

"Yep, not ideal but until I get down there and see for myself…"

"But Mick…" Mr Keech stopped in mid-sentence. I could hear Steve in the background.

"Mr Keech, gaffer." Silence followed. I continued down. Mr Keech would have his own series of questions to answer now. The smell of the maingate pack confirmed my position. Within minutes I clambered down. I could see the twins Alf and Jack with shovels. Scratching about in the recently dropped pile of mineral.

"Geet another ere." Alf shouted. I looked across to where he was shining his lamp. Sure, enough a stick of P4/5 was poking out a drill hole.

"How many is that now?" I hadn't spotted Ged a little further outbye.

"Five." I moved up alongside Alf.

"Out of how many?"

"Twenty."

"Fuckin twenty. You normally only use half that."

"I thi reet Mick. Faulted ground above, thought we'd put in a few extra."

"How come no one checked before you started filling out?" I continued my pointless questions. Knowing full well I'd be asked the same.

"He did. Think he was a bit moidered. Belt lads found a bad stitching."

"How long were you loading out before you realised there was a problem?"

"Bout ten minutes."

"Half a dozen bucket loads?"

"I something like that Mick. Can't be one undred per cent certain."

"Someone's in for an arse reamering."

"Thanks Ged. That's helpful. Where's Al?"

"Up at panels havin a nervous breakdown. George is with em now."

"Can you get the lads off the maingate pack to check along…."

"Already sorted. Once they've checked maingate. I've told them to continue along cross cut to bottom of the E3."

"Thanks Ged, I'll catch you later."

I began to make my way to the panels. Mentally carrying out the arithmetic as to how far any unexploded shots could have travelled. So engrossed in doing the number I lost my footing. "For fucks sake!" I shouted as I slipped in the sludge beneath my feet. Just managing to grab the side rail.

"Mick." I looked towards Paul. "Phone." I guessed it would be Mr Keech. I used the side iron to avoid slipping again. Paul had covered the mouth piece. As I reached him, he mouthed the word. "Manager." *Fuck.* This wasn't going to be good.

"Mr Creed, Mick…" I moved the handset away from my head. I don't know how I looked but poor old Paul had gone white. The verbal onslaught continued. Who could blame him. "We've already…" He wasn't listening. He was on full transmit. I could hardly make out what he was saying. George appeared from outbye. He too looked in a state of shock. "Will do… Mr Creed, Mr Creed." He'd hung up. I turned to George. He raised his hand.

"And another." He was holding a primed stick of P4/5.

"That make's six. Where the fucks Alan?"

"Just outbye. Go easy on im Mick. Lads in a bad way."

"Fuckin bad way. I haven't fuckin started. Why the fuck didn't he stop the belts when he knew he had a miss-fire, can he at least answer me that?" George shrugged his shoulders and said nothing. He was right though. Me shouting like a mad man wasn't helping.

"The haulage lads are on the cross-cut belt. Pack lads on maingate belt."

"Right, I best have a look. By my estimate if the maingate and crosscut are clear, we can start the belts up again."

"Fraid not, got a bad stitching ain't goin last till end of shift."

"Fuck me. If it doesn't rain it pours. I'll check outbye. Once I'm satisfied, I'll let you know. We can run the belt clear. Get them two fuckers off the platform with the stitching machine ready."

"Alf and Jack." The look on George's face said it all.

"Use the tirfor if you have to. I want them both on the fuckin job." My comment caused George to smile.

"Mick you sure we shouldn't be checking up E3?"

"I'm as sure as I'm ever going to be. Might keep us all in a job too!"

I continued outbye. Al was sat towards the end of the pantech. He had George's flask in his hand. He looked up as I approached. His eyes blood shot. I wasn't sure how much tea he'd managed to drink. His hand offering involuntary movements. "Mick, I'm sorry, sooo sorry. I, I…"

"Al leave it fella. We'll get it sorted. You have a minute." George had been right. He was in a complete mess. "I've agreed with George we'll get the stitchin done. Make sure you get Alf and Jack on the job."

116

"What?"

"Yeah. Those fuckin two."

Twenty minutes late I'd reached the crosscut belt drive. The lads had found another three sticks. It felt strange with all the belts on stand. Just a haze of fine dust suspended around the junction lights.

"Hello Control. Hello Steve."

"Mick. How you fixed?"

"Good to go. Taking the latch off now."

"Thank fuck for that. Can you give the Undermanager a call. He's at 30's panels. Mr Keech too. He's at Strata Bunker."

"Will do. 32's won't be starting immediately. Bad stitch maingate belt."

"How long do'y reckon?" The silence suddenly broken as the belt pre-alarms kicked in.

"Say half an hour." No more was said. I had calls to make. And as I was later to find out, a visit to the Top Shunt too.

□

Like any holiday, it's over before you know it. I'd taken Whit week off. We hadn't planned to go anywhere, just days out, in preparation for our Lizzie's Christening on the Sunday. The biggest let down had been Wednesday evenings European Cup final in Brussels. Liverpool, already four times European Cup winners were this time up against the Italian champions Juventus. They'd lost one nil in controversial circumstances. However, the event had been overshadowed by the collapse of a retaining wall, killing thirty-nine fans. Why the hell the match was allowed to continue beggared belief.

The Christening had gone down a treat. After the church service we'd had a party back at our place. Must have been about thirty of us. Annie had done us proud with the spread she'd laid on. My only contribution supplying the booze. One memory I wouldn't forget was my nan sliding down the kids slide, pissed!

My mind wandered back to the days before I'd gone off. John Meriden had asked all his Face Overmen to hang back at the end of the shift. Still in his black, he'd been to see the Manager. I could tell by the look on his face he'd received a round of fucks. Another gentleman accompanied him. I recognised him. Something to do with the Coal Preparation Plant.

"Now lads this won't take long." He turned to the guy stood alongside. "This is Harry Smith, Coal Prep Manager." It was Harry's cue to address us.

"I've just come from a meeting with the Manager. We're having problems in the Coal Prep Plant. For some reason we're washing more dirt then normal!"

It wasn't till I'd arrived at work this morning that I'd found out L32's had been the reason. I'd been told the Manager wanted to see me. Waiting outside the Top Shunt I was about to knock on the door. It opened suddenly causing me to jump back. "You can come in now." I stood to one side to let the Manager's Secretary pass. The look on her face suggested the Manager wasn't in the best of moods. Taking a deep breath, I walked in. I tried to control my hands. The shakes had started already. My mouth suddenly dry.

The Manager was sat at his desk, reading a single sheet of paper. Unusually with no accompanying pipe. Mr Keech was sat at the far side of the large table. An unlit Players No 6 was moving about in the corner of his mouth.
"You've asked to see me Mr Creed?" He didn't look up immediately. The silence deafening. It seemed to last forever. Suddenly broken by the sound of a match being struck. He turned towards me. I could feel perspiration begin to run down my back. Grateful I was still in my black.
"Are you completely fuckin stupid?" I wasn't sure if it was a question, he wanted me to answer. I took a quick glance towards Mr Keech. Not that I could see him. A cloud of smoke blocking out his facial features. I could see his hand though as it reached across for his packet of fags.

"I'm sorry Mr Creed." Which meant I was stupid. "It won't happen again."
"Appen again?" He screamed at me. I heard Mr Keech's chair move. He must have jumped. "You don't think I'm goin to let you anywhere near that fuckin place again, do you?" Now I certainly wasn't expecting that. I'd only been face Overman for two months. "What do you think Mr Keech?"
"It's not as if it's the first time Mr Creed. We've got the ongoing arguments with the Face Chargehand." *Fuck me. That's a little harsh.* "He's managed to get the maingate end fast. More recently stopped production for the whole pit. And now this. How many chances does it take?" *Well, that certainly wasn't a ringing endorsement. If that's how he feels I'm well and truly fucked.* "And now he starts sending out more dirt than coal!"

I turned back towards the Manager. He was shaking his head. His angry glare still focused on me. "Ave never bin on face before lad? Ast done face training?" His comments cut deeper than anything he'd said to me before. Questioning my practical credibility. I returned his stare. My initial nervousness becoming less and less. The *red mist* had begun to descend. I could take a bollocking. Screaming and shouting but not my ability. I'd worked hard to get where I was.
He'd sensed he'd gone too far. I caught him wink towards Mr Keech.
"Go on. Fuck off out my office. That's your last fuckin chance."

☐

7. Her Majesty's Inspector

By the following week we were back into a full seam of coal. I was surprised to get an invite to the NEC in Birmingham after my bollocking. Mr Keech had organised a coach to take a number of us to the Mining 85 International Exhibition. Organised by the Association of British Mining Equipment Companies, ABMEC. I'd attended my first exhibition back in 1977, the first time it had been held at the NEC.

It probably wasn't the best day to be going. I had my first visit on L32's the next day from HMI. I'd spoken at length with George to make sure the place was suitably prepped. Fingers crossed he'd get it sorted.

The previous month's magazine, The Mining Engineer had certainly whetted my appetite. It wasn't just the foreword by the Chairman. It was the tone of the introductory message from the Energy Secretary. He stated the Government were fully "engaged in rebuilding the industry." Furthermore, he'd gone on to say, "I am confident that we can and should have a long-term competitive coal mining industry in this country." The 84/85 strike had caused huge suffering for those in the industry. Particularly for the NUM members from either side.

The forty-five-seater coach took us just under two hours to get there. The place was awash with stands. We were advised there were over three hundred exhibitors, many from overseas, including the USA and Canada. I was surprised to see equipment from the USSR and China too. Back in 1977 there had been a large number of Chinese delegates attend. This time there were even more. I guess selling equipment to China was helping their industry modernise.

On the Dosco stand there was a MK2B Roadheader. The first time I'd seen a Roadheader with star wheels for gathering the mineral. Another stand I saw something called a Metro-Bug. It was used for rectifying faults on loco tracks. The guy soon lost interest in our questions as there appeared several Chinese visitors all suitably suited and booted. Each sporting a badge indicating they were from the Coal Ministry of China.

Returning later that day the bus dropped us off at the pit. I popped in to the Undermanager's office to see if there was any further update on tomorrow's visit. Probably a bit late as no one was about.

☐

Deciding to go into work a little earlier this morning, I was on a high. It had been a good day yesterday. From what we'd seen and the conversations we'd had with reps on the various stands the future for the industry looked promising.

As I travelled along the M62 towards junction nine I glanced across to my right. The Ikea building was coming on a treat. It was surprising how quickly the building was going up. I had a similar thought as I passed the hangars off to my left. Wondering what plans the council had for the Burtonwood site.

Before I knew it, I'd exited the motorway. Ten minutes later I parked the car. Just after five, still relatively quiet. That would be short lived as the six o'clock shift arrived and the nightshift finished. Changed I headed to the lamp room looking to get an early ride in. I passed the control room hoping to go through without being spotted. No such luck.

"Fuckin ell Mick. Shit the bed." It was the nightshift, Overman, Bill. I smiled.

"Need to check a few things. Got the Inspector this morning."

"Tha's keen lad I'll give you that. Oh, and by the way George has been on. Won't be in today. Something wrong with his motor."

"You're kiddin. He's only just bought a fuckin brand fuckin new Toyota Celica."

"I knows don't shoot messenger Mick." I said no more. Not the start to the day I wanted. I just hope he'd prepped the district as I'd instructed Monday.

I was the only person getting into the cage after most of the nightshift had exited. No time to wait for a ride I continued along the main tunnel at pace. By the time I'd reached the top of E3 I was lathered. Stopping momentarily to take a pinch I carried on down. At the outbye end of L19's I stopped for a quick piss and mouthful of water. I was pleased to find a stack of stonedust and could see it had been laid out as per my instruction to George on Monday. Including several bags of calcium chloride. I'd get the haulage lads to spread them first thing.

Just outbye of the junction I walked across to the red semi-circular metal container. Above it a fire hydrant with a new replacement fluorescent sign attached to the arch leg. Inside the five fire hoses had been dusted down. A nozzle and branch pipe stacked alongside. I dropped the lid, instantly regretting it as I took a mouthful of dust.

Arriving at the Meeting Station I could see the place had been tidied up. The usual stack of newspapers had gone. The only items left on the wooden bench were the Deputy's report books. Even the copies of the Transport and Support Rules had been dusted off. "Good perhaps there was nothing to worry about." I said out loud.

Out of habit I removed my methanometer and took a reading in the GB. Nought point two just as we liked it. I began to relax. Looking across to the First Aid Station. Everything looked in order. I walked across to the morphine safe I reached down to my bundle of keys. One thing I'd found from experience the

Inspector always checked the safe. *Fuck I let George borrow my key on Monday.*

I started to head inbye along the maingate. The sound of the crosscut airdoors banging shut and the drop in pressure caused me to turn.

"Is that you Mick?"

"Morning Jack."

"Now lad who's with tha? Thought erd voices."

"No just me. You doin a pre-shift?"

"Yep. Tha may have to do some timbering first thing. There's a slip appeared round about." Jack stopped to extract his notebook. "Bout thirty chock. Couple of split bars should do the trick. Machine's just above."

"Okay, Jack thanks. If you don't mind, I need to keep moving."

"Tha carry on lad. Don't mind me. I've just got to do my report. Good luck with the visit. Just hope you don't get that old twat Mr Gray." His last comment caused me to stop. I'd heard tales about HMI Gray but thought he'd finished.

"He's retired." Jack seemed not to hear.

"Got many a tale bout that owd cunt. Used to ask some fuckin daft questions. Had him a few times myself. Nasty man caused many official to go on the sick. Thought it might be im when I heard George had phoned in…" Jack stopped talking as the phone began to ring.

"Hello. Yep, he's here." He raised the handset towards me. "Mick, Cayle."

"Morning Cayle. No dayshift not here yet. Who are you sending me as District Deputy? There's no one spare." *For fucks sake some choice, the poet, or Bobby fuckin Bang, Bang!* "Just a minute." I turned towards Jack. "You don't fancy stopping over?"

"Fuckin ell Mick. Am hoping to take early retirement. Don't want tax man after me."

"Hi Cayle. No, I'm talking to Jack. Anyway, thanks for the heads up. Do me a favour though. Give us a shout when my visitors get to the bottom of E3."

I left Jack and continued inbye. My spirits raised slightly seeing that some stone dust had been spread. Always watchful as to where the lads had put the empty bags. I checked each manhole as I moved inbye. Empty! That's a first. I was pleased to see George had continued putting the surveyors fluorescent tape on the belt slings. Pity they hadn't got some calcium chloride spread too. The dust lifting as I moved forward. I moved my lamp to my left catching the reflection of the manhole signs ahead.

The smell of the new hundred metres we'd changed the previous week caught my attention. The blueness of the outer skin reflected. Matching the blueness of the armoured cable on the blindside of the conveyor.

"For fucks sake." I shouted. I could now see where the lads had put the empty bags. Onto the belt. I looked back outbye. Sure, enough I could see another dozen or so bags. I retraced my steps and headed back out. Removing the bags, I placed them in a manhole. Noting the number. I'd get the haulage lads to empty it later. I continued inbye.

Ahead the heavy stonedust barrier came into view. I could see the stonedust on the shelves had been replenished. We'd checked the distance back from the face last week. So, there was no problems there. I lowered my head as I passed beneath. Checking there were no shelves missing. Probably need to get the Hausherr Dinter back out. The stonedust covered the rails beneath. My helmet accidently caught one of the shelves causing the dust to dislodge and drop down the back of my neck. "Fuck." I moved towards the belt to stand upright. Shaking my overalls. The dust was going nowhere. Sticking to the perspiration down the front and back of my body. I'd need to keep moving.

After another hundred yards I spotted the top of the Hausherr. It was sitting in a hole beyond where the rails had been disconnected. It's power cable suspended from plastic tie wraps and D links along the Tirfor's steel rope. A single electrical panel above the conveyor providing the power. There was a three-foot drop from where the lads had finished. We'd need to level it out before the inspector arrived. A little further on the belt was no longer on slings. Each of the belt stands now on wooden blocks. Intermittently I checked beneath the bottom rollers. It looked good. George had done well. The light stonedust barrier had been refreshed too.

The lights in the distance caught my attention. I was always surprised no matter which coal face I was on how eerily it seemed approaching the stage loader when it was stopped. The lack of the banging and scrapping of the chain was deafening. Perhaps it was our constant desire to see it running that caused this odd sensation. At the end of the water range, the damaged hydrant sign had been replaced. Beyond which hung three fire hoses. Each suspended separately from the pipe range. Looking towards the face it seemed further than seventy-five yards. I looked below the belt. Sure, enough two additional Victaulic pipes and collars lay on the floor.

There wasn't a great deal of room between the Pantechnicon and belt conveyor. Probably better if I'd gone the other side. I squeezed alongside the side iron. The electricians sandbags, usually piled in the loop of the jumbo cable had been removed. It was at this point the smell of the hydraulic oil hit me. The pumps were off, so unusual not to hear them running. We'd got into the habit of knocking them off at the end of each shift to avoid the leaks. I knocked the pumps on before getting down on all fours to check the belt tailend. It was clear. The melodic thump of the pump providing the reassuring background sound as I moved down towards the face. Beneath my feet a number of narrow trenches had been excavated. At least that would prevent the leaking Aquacent forming pools. I need to get the fitters to change the leaking bagging.

The maingate ripping platform looked tidy. *Shit, I hadn't checked the shotfiring cable.* I could see the end of it coiled and attached to the side rails of the platform. I just hoped Freddy had seen to that. There was a half-filled can of gear oil by the maingate drive. I'd need to get that shifted. The smell from the pack area caused me to reach across. The last bag was still warm. Condensations forming on the outer skin. I wiped my hand against my overall. I continued forward between the first couple of packhole chocks before climbing onto the panzer I looked back into the waste. The roof had collapsed. Fast up against the side of the pack and chock curtain. I stretched my leg over the spill tray. Steadying myself by holding onto the haulage chain I looked up along the face line. *Straight as a die.* Good. It had paid off getting the surveyors to draw me a face line each week.

I moved forward slowly at first. Picking up speed, confident the coal was standing firm. Occasionally checking the red numbers painted beneath the chock canopies. I slowed as I spotted the number twenty-eight. My attention now fixed on the roof between each canopy. Just as Jack had said. The roof texture changed at chock thirty. Small lumps of coal had fallen away from the slip area. A larger cavity was visible between chocks thirty-one and two. I followed the break back towards the face. The best remedy would be to keep it tight and keep moving the face forward. Not give it chance to settle. I'd learnt that much since being on L32's. Each face had its own characteristics. The secret was to recognise it and deal with it immediately. I sensed something ahead. Ever so slight. I was taking no chances. I quickly threw myself over the spills. I waited. Sure enough, a large slab of coal broke away on the face side. Spalling forward. Momentarily standing still before falling onto the panzer.

Now continuing through the chock line, I reached the shearer. I shivered slightly. The perspiration generated earlier had dried on me. I was tempted to take another pinch. Checking my watch however made my decision. The dayshift would now be at the bottom of E3. One last look at the shearer caused me to reflect on what I'd seen yesterday. A shearer on the Joy stand. It was the first time the thing had been on show the rep told us. The Joy 3LS longwall shearer. With its two, two hundred and fifty horse power cutting motors and chainless haulage I reckon it could do some damage on here.

Having passed the shearer, I climbed back onto the panzer. Again, watchful of any spalling as I moved at speed up towards the return end. I didn't stop again, the sweat once more pumping from every pore of my body. Finally, the top motor came into view. I climbed back into the chock line. This was a habit I'd gotten into never exiting the coal face directly off the AFC. I reached the top motor and extracted my methanometer. Reading point five, slightly higher than normal. Satisfied I returned the instrument to my pocket. Replacing it with my tin of snuff. The smell of which always felt better when I wasn't taking it continuously. Resting momentarily bringing my breathing under control. The silence was deafening, except for the gentle throb of the hydraulic pump. The smell of the return air so different than that of the intake. A mix of oil, pack, damp wood, combined with my own body odour.

I stood upright as I climbed off the coal face. The Webster bucket had been raised leaning against the face of the heading. There was a leg to set on the far side. The crown still resting on the horseheads. The side ranters were a little further back than I would have wanted. The trailing cable was suspended, again from a tirfor rope. I followed it back to the solitary electric panel. All seemed in order. I stopped momentarily. Unstrapping the water bottle from my belt. Taking a mouthful of the now warm water I let it run down onto my blackened chest. It felt good.

A mesh cage was in place behind the packhole supports. The suspended white plastic bag positioned ready for filling. I made a note for another pack of inch and a quarter pipes. Both the Tekcem and Tekbent pipes were further back than I would have liked.

The methane drainage drilling machine was dismantled ready for dragging forward. A length of pipe chain attached to the rear of the machine. Wrapped around the handle of the metal box in which the methane borers kept their tools, including drill bits. The lads had completed the last uphole the previous week and coupled it to the six-inch range. I'd need to get them back in. Currently we were sharing the drainage lads with L31's, far from ideal. The last of the standpipes lay scattered about the floor. There was an additional pack on the outbye shunt. The lads had mentioned fetching another role of densotape next time they were in.

On the opposite side neatly stacked chockwood, split bars and six by two mesh. Alongside the odd pack of wooden dowels and resin. Something else I'd need to order, just in case! A little further outbye I spotted the coil of shotfiring cable. Suspended from a cable hangar secured to the weld mesh. A twelve-shot exploder hanging below it. *Fuckin Bobby!*

124

By the time I'd reached the outbye end of the return the dayshift had arrived. Not that I could see them. It was Bobby Bang, Bang singing. Today's favourite *Blue Spanish Eyes.*

"Give it some Bobby lad." One of the rippers shouted. Lights appeared ahead.

"*Say you and your Spanish eyes will wait for me.*" Bobby continued.

"Morning lads."

"Morning Mick." A few of them responded.

"You doin the pre-shift." Bobby asked followed by his usual smile. He was sweating profusely. I immediately smelt alcohol. He'd obviously been performing at Lowton Social Club last night.

"You're so funny Rob. Who's signing today?"

"Freddy, he's your man. Said he'd see you at the Meeting Station."

"You know we've got the Inspector today?"

"Yep. Glad I'm not fuckin signing." *Not as glad as me.*

"Right, I'll catch you guys later." I began to move off, then stopped. "Rob, make sure you get the side ranters moved in. Keep a couple of the lads over to extend the pack pipes." I got no response. Not that I expected one.

Arriving at the cross-cut air doors. The outbye set were partly open. One of the doors had been damaged the week before. A pack of arches had caught it, damaging the hinges. I'd need to check where the replacement was. The joiners shop confirmed it had been made and loaded up. Standing on the outbye side I pulled it shut. Receiving a gob full of floor dust for my trouble.

The haulage lads were at the Meeting Station, as was Freddy still on the phone.

"Morning Mick."

"Morning lads. What's on the first run?"

"Steel and some chockwood." Arthur responded. Arthur was a big lad, ex Bold Colliery. Hoping to get on his face training shortly. Resolute too. He was certainly Deputy material.

"Any chance of pump pack pipes?"

"Yeah, next run down E3."

"Good stuff. You haven't seen a single air door on your travels?"

"Pit bottom back of shaft."

"I'll have a word with the Pit Bottom Deputy to get it moved in. See if you can get it to site on the crosscut. Let me know when it's there."

"Will do Mick." I was momentarily distracted as Freddy hung up the phone. He turned towards me.

There was something about him this morning that didn't look right. My suspicion confirmed when he extracted his tin of snuff. His hand was shaking. I stepped forward.

"Don't mind if I do." I took a pinch from the opened tin. Freddy never responded. He didn't look happy. "You, okay?"

"You know who the Inspector is today?"

"Not a clue."

"Fuckin HMI fuckin Gray." Freddy's response was so out of character. Since I'd known him. I could count on one hand the number of times he used profanities.

"And?"

"And! He's a fuckin cunt. A cunt with a capital C."

The phone began to ring. Freddy made no move to pick it up.

"Ello. Hi Cayle. Yeah, he's still with me. Yep, I'll tell him. Mr Meriden? I'll call him now. Oh, before I forget. Can we have the methane lads, holes a little behind. Excellent tomorrow will be fine. Don't worry bout me. Had plenty of visits from HMI. No never Mr Gray. Gray by name, Gray by nature. Thanks for the heads up. Are you coming in with them then? Well, no surprises there." I began laughing. "Catch you later."

I returned my attention to Freddy. He hadn't moved. "Cayle says lamp room have been on. The twelve shot battery needs returning." I watched as a bead of sweat appeared beneath his helmet, rolling down his forehead. "For fucks sake Freddy snap out of it. I'll be with you." Freddy finally began to move off. He looked at me and nodded. Beginning to make his way down the maingate. "Fred before you go. Just check the morphine safe. Make sure it's signed up to date."

I turned back to the phone to call the Undermanager. "Hi John, Mick here. You asked for a call. Right. Little unusual. Any idea why? Just wondered. I've had a look. Probably about ten minutes. Shouldn't be a problem. Yep, plenty of timber. Thanks, I'll see you later." *The Manager coming in with the Inspector and no Undermanager?* According to John it had been an instruction from the Manager. I suppose it's another test he's set for me. I turned to look for Freddy, but he'd gone in. I hadn't seen him check the morphine safe, I guessed he'd done whilst I was talking to John.

The call came through from Control the Manager and Inspector had descended the shaft. I'd spent the previous two hours on the face. Helping with the timbering and checking for any further deterioration in roof conditions after the machine had passed through. The split bars had done their job. The machine having passed through the area twice already was now heading towards the return. I made my way out along the intake towards the bottom of E3. The conveyor was piled with the black stuff.

I could see two lights in the distance. I could feel my stomach churn. Nerves! As they got closer, I could hear the clicking of their sticks against the rails. They seemed to be in no hurry. Just two of them. I recognised the shape of the Manager. The Inspector was quite short. They were both wearing white donkey jackets. I looked at my watch. *Where the fuck is Freddy?* I asked him to meet me at ten thirty. It was almost eleven o'clock.

"Morning Mr Gibson." The Manager greeted me.

"Good morning gentlemen." I had to look twice at the Inspector. He looked older than me grandad. Big bushy moustache. I raised my hand. "Good to meet you Mr Gray." His grip was so feeble. He smelt of moth balls.

"Do you ever worry about belt fires Mr Gibson?" His question took me by surprise.

"Yes, I…."

"Yes what? You have them inspected on a regular basis?" I wasn't going to get a word in edge ways. I looked towards the Manager. He returned my stare saying nothing. "Cat got your tongue?"

"No, I…"

"Well why have I counted six bottom rollers running in coal?"

"I'll get it sorted now."

"Not good enough young man." He continued forward to the meeting station. I followed. He began examining the Support Rules.

"What's happening on face lad?" The Manager asked in a lowered tone.

"Timber sorted, machines been through twice. Shouldn't be far off return now."

"Good that's what it wants. Movement lad don't give it chance to spall. Movement that's what it needs." The sound of the Inspector falling towards the wooden bench interrupted our conversation. He'd tripped over a bag of stone dust. He'd saved himself by throwing his arms forward. Unfortunately grabbing a copy of the Transport Rules suspended from the arches.

"Trip, stumbling and falling Mr Gibson, not good." *You're not kidding there.* Unexpectedly I caught the Manager shaking his head. He saw me look and in response rolled his eye balls. I knew exactly what he meant. *This guys a fuckin liability.*

He'd now moved across to the First Aid Station. "Now Mr Gibson. What would I expect to find in here?"

I left the Manager, who had now started to tap his stick against a metal sleeper. Moving across to where the Inspector was stood.

"Stretcher, blanket, and splints. Plus, a First Aid tin."

"Containing?"

"Bandages, padding, six large plain wound dressings, pressure bandage."

"Anything else?" I couldn't think of anything, thought I'd covered the lot.

"Erm…" I was distracted as the Manager cleared his throat. His stick now tapping against a packing bag.

"Sorry, thought you meant in the First Aid Tin. Two sand bags."

"For?"

"Head injuries." I was expecting at least to get a thank you. Although now, my bigger concern was where he was standing. Opposite the concrete morphine safe. He was tugging on the brass handle. *Where the fuck was Freddy?*

"Key?" I could have written the script.

"Unfortunately, Mr Gray, I've lent it to another official. As soon as my District Deputy, Freddy Clough, arrives…"

"Talking of which. Is he planning on joining us any time soon?"

"Yeah, should be on his way." I avoided looking towards the Manager. The Inspector now holding his Methanometer in the air.

"What would you normally expect to see?"

"Point two."

"I'm getting point three." *Well, aren't you the lucky one.* Replacing the instrument, we continued inbye along the intake. The Manager making a point of pointing to his watch. Like I needed to be reminded. He shewed me forward. At that point I was following the Inspector. He obviously wanting me to take control of the visit. The sound of the conveyor had changed too. The click, click, click of the stitching's passing over the top rollers had joined the tap, tap, of the walking sticks. I guessed the machine was at the tailend.

As I passed the Inspector, he was making a point of kicking the floor dust. Pointing to several unopened bags of calcium chloride. "Expecting them to spread themselves?" Before I could answer we'd reached the heavy stone dust barrier. I knew what was coming and was quite prepared. He stopped and turned to me. Using his stick, he gently tapped the first shelf.

"Heavy barrier, combination of lightly and heavily loaded shelves. Lightly loaded not to be closer than three feet and not greater than seven foot. Boards on each shelf not greater than fourteen inches. Heavily loaded shelf not less than fourteen inches and not greater than twenty." I paused for breath.

"All good stuff Mr Gibson. Why is there no dust on this shelf?"

"I'll get it sorted." I added both findings to my notebook. Fortunately, the remaining shelves looked okay. We continued inbye.

"Are we likely to see your District Deputy Mr Gibson?" The Manager shouted towards me. We'd reached the maingate dint. It was on stand. I didn't have the manpower today. The Hausherr was parked under the now stationary conveyor.

"I'm sure he'll be with us shortly Mr Creed."

"Who is it this morning? George?"

"No car trouble. Freddy Clough."

"Car trouble eh. Interesting."

The dint had been levelled out and the track reconnected. The Inspector was now poking around the Hauserr. He didn't seem concerned. We continued.

For the first time he was checking the manholes. I felt I had little to worry about on that matter. So, I was a little surprised when the Inspector stopped opposite one just outbye of the light barrier.

"Where's your nearest sanitary convenience Mr Gibson?" *Fuck it can't be!* I wasn't sure.

"Pit bottom." I answered with little conviction.

"Little wonder then." Looking to where his stick was pointing. The back pages of the Daily Mirror had partly covered a large fresh turd. The stench was overwhelming. *Who the fuck had done that?* I could hazard a guess but wasn't sure.

"I'll get it cleaned out." He never responded. I didn't dare look towards the Manager. We continued forward. Stopping once we'd reached the light barrier.

"Anything to say?" I looked up towards the first few shelves. They all seemed loaded with dust. I wasn't sure what he was after.

"Specification." The Manager offered.

"Oh, right yeah. Each barrier to contain not less than twenty-two pounds of stone dust per square foot of the average cross section of the length of the roadway. With this being the light barrier, it should be loaded with not more than twenty pound per foot length of each shelf. Each shelf board not to exceed fourteen inches." I paused. Taking a deep breath. I felt quite pleased with myself. Still able to quote from the Regulations after my recent legislation exam.

"How do you check?"

"Check?"

"The weight. I assume you know the roadways cross section?" I didn't. "Have you a set of scales?" The man had a point. I'd never actually seen anyone weigh the stuff. He never waited for an answer and continued inbye. I hadn't noticed earlier but my vest was soaked through, and we hadn't been travelling at speed.

A short while later the maingate conveyor kicked in. Soon followed by the sound of the conveyor hauling coal. At least seeing the black stuff piled high was something as was the lights of the stage loader ahead. I increased my speed needing a conversation with Paul ahead of the Manager and Inspector.

"Where the fuck is Freddy?"

"Gone out to meet tha."

"Well, I ain't seen him."

"Out via the return. Needed to drop some dets off with Bobby. Be honest with tha Mick, probably best tha keep im out of way. In a right mess he is." It couldn't get any worse. Freddy having a breakdown and Bobby borrowing dets. And fuckin George. I moved to one side as Paul reached across to hit the stageloader stop button.

"Who's got a latch on E3?" Steve in Control shouted. I looked outbye. The Manager and Inspector were having a conversation alongside the Pantech.

"Bet he's waiting for us now at the meeting station. Might be best if you give him a call."

"Hello panels."

"Hi Ged."

"Nah cock, is Mick with tha yet?" A latch suddenly appeared on the face console.

"Hi Ged, Mick ere."

"Bad news cock." I said nothing waiting for the next surprise. "That slip at seventy chock we thought wouldn't be a problem."

"Yeah."

"Just passed through it. Tops dropped out." That didn't sound too bad.

"Couple of split bars?"

"Fuckin ell Mick. I ain't finished tellin tha yet. Fell up. Reckon bout four, five-foot cock, over bout four chocks." I never answered immediately my head against the DAC. "You get that Mick?" With the stageloader on stop, the background noise was now replaced with the gentle buzz of the panels and throbbing of the hydraulics pumping. My head too was throbbing. I was having one of those moments when I wished I were somewhere else. On a beach even. Benidorm would be fine.

The maingate belt suddenly kicked in. Paul immediately started the stageloader.

"Yeah, got that. Take the latch off the face. Let's clear the coal off, ready for timber."

"Problems?" I hadn't noticed the Manager approach. My head still resting on the DAC.

"Yeah, bit of roof trouble at seventy chock. Just running the coal off and then run some timber down." The look I received said it all. I continued inbye towards the face. Closely followed by my two visitors.

"Just watch your footing. Bit slippy by the tank." I offered, the smell of Aquacent testament to that. Using their sticks in one hand and the other against the stageloader spills they navigated themselves through the grey sludge.

"Morning Mick." I looked up to see Alf and Jack smiling towards me. Before I could answer they turned away preparing to drill.

"Mr Gibson." I turned back towards the Inspector. He was pointing to the side ranter on the rib side. It was ten yards back from the face of the heading. Jack obviously heard the conversation as he climbed down to move it forward.

Climbing on to the face he asked me a question on the Prop Free Front distance which we'd obviously exceeded due spalling. At twenty and twenty-five chock, the double acting rams had been disconnected from the spills. One secured by a lifting chain the other using two load binders. At fifty-five chock there was gap between the canopy and roof. Which I reset, knowing full well, five minutes later it would drop again due to a faulty relief valve. By the time we reached the machine parked at sixty chock the lads had started running timber down. Stopping at the fall area, the Inspector took a sample of gas with his methanometer. Satisfied we moved on a little further. That was until he watched as Johnny Bastard was caught removing split bars off the panzer from the leading edge. Fortunately, the Manager missed the encounter. He'd hung back for a chat with Ged.

As we approached the return end, I was pleased to get a whiff of the completed pack. That however was the only pleasing thing we were to encounter. A methane reading over the top motor was almost one per cent. Bobby had already picked it up before we arrived. Seemingly the haulage lads had a derailment when passing through the airdoors. Unable to close them till the journey had been righted the gas had built up.

Bobby had developed a stutter from when I'd seen him this morning. Unable to answer any question posed by the Inspector coherently. It got worse when the Inspector discovered two joints in the shotfiring cable. The horseheads were over eleven yards back from the heading. It never helped when Graham said they never used them. His answer on the use of sentries when firing the rip and the use of the red plastic caps was pure text book. Although we both knew it was a complete fuckin lie. He asked about the number of safety lamps currently in the district. There were no concerns over stone dust. The place was whiter than white. The icing on the cake had to be when we reached the end of the visit. Just arriving at the meeting station Freddy finally caught us up. He was still shaking and looked as though he'd taken a shower. In response to the Inspector thanking him for finally joining us. Freddy was unable to respond, attempting to get his breath back. I wasn't sure what response to give. The visit had been a complete disaster. Probably the worse visit I'd ever had. In fact, there was no probable about it. It was the worse visit I'd ever had. It was the Manager who made the final comment.

"Come see me lad when you get up pit. Before going for a bath."

"Will do Mr Creed." With that they both walked off. I turned towards Freddy ready to give him a round of fucks. He looked pitiful, a complete fuckin mess.

"Sorry bout that Mick. Bit of a mix up. Owz, it go?"

By the time I'd reached the Manager's office it had gone three o'clock. Susan his secretary was in the process of leaving. By the look on her face, I guessed she'd been listening to the comments from the Manager and Inspector.

"Go straight in Mick. Good luck." *Fuck that sounds ominous.* I knocked, surprised how calm I felt. The fact I was both mentally and physically fucked must have been the reason. One of those occasions when you knew you were in for a good fucking. Parts of the brain seemed to close down waiting for the inevitable.

They were both sat on the opposite side of the table. I was momentarily distracted by the spread laid out on the table. It was a feast. Little had been touched. Four separate platters of sandwiches. A mix of ham, cheese, and tuna fillings. Two jugs of fresh orange, a large teapot, and a flask of coffee. Sugar bowls with white and brown sugar. Various plates of biscuits and a separate cake stand. Thick slices of Victoria sponge with a jam and cream filling. Madeira cake and my favourite caramel coated doughnuts. My taste buds had gone into overdrive. Saliva filling my mouth, I swallowed again as I sat down. Mr Gray was eyeing me suspiciously. I suspected the caramel doughnut was his favourite too.

"Mr Creed tells me you've been Face Overman for the last two months." I attempted to answer. "That is probably one of my worse visits to Parkside." This time he remained silent I wasn't sure I should answer with *mine too.* So, I just nodded. He then opened his notebook and began to list the things he'd found. I did likewise with my note book. Most of the points he raised, I'd already noted. The Manager remained silent other than the striking of a match, as he began sucking on his pipe. I felt a little dizzy as I inhaled the aroma. What I'd give for a cigar now. "Both heading neither had a lit safety lamp." I'd missed that. "And what of your two Deputies. Have they only recently passed out?"

"No, I …."

"It's just not acceptable young man." I nodded again. "I'll be back again in six weeks. I hope to see a marked improvement." And with that he turned to the Manager. "Thank you for your hospitality, Mr Creed. I'm afraid I need to be making a move now. Early start tomorrow. Off to Haig Colliery."

"Oh right. I'll see you out." He turned towards me. "You just sit there." His tone was not dissimilar to one that I use when talking to our dog. The Inspector never even said cheerio.

As soon as they left the room, I'd already planned my next move. Reaching across I grabbed the caramel doughnut and placed it whole into my mouth. As I was about to enjoy the delights of my favourite cake, the office door flew open.

"I have never bin so fuckin embarrassed in my life. What the fuck are you running down there? Hey. It's little wonder you don't produce any coal. You need to get to grip with the place lad. Pulling a stunt like that with a fuckin load binder." My taste buds were in overdrive again. Saliva was flowing down my throat. "Have you got nothing to say." He paused as he began to relight his pipe. I thought I was about to choke. "Well?" I shook my head what else could I do. By now the cake began to disintegrate, the icing melting. "Go on then fuck off out my sight." I didn't need any further encouragement. As fast as my little legs would carry me, I left.

The following day continued pretty much as it started. One delay after another. George had returned too. His smiley face had been the first to greet me in Deployment. The Toyota Celica was back in working order. Freddy and Bobby said little about yesterday's visit, both still recovering from the experience.

By snap time we'd lost almost two hours through lumps at the maingate end. Ged had positioned himself at number four chock with the jigger

"I'll tell tha what Mick." I was stooped alongside Ged in the chock line. For the first time I noticed the flaking white paint on a spill plate. Rubbing my thumb against it, exposing the rust. He shouted towards me. The sound of the panzer chain increasing as the last of the coal dropped onto the stageloader. The machine had landed at the return end. He'd just completed breaking another. The sweat was oozing from his face. His grey vest wet through. The smell of body odour and stale sweat mixed stronger than ever. The sweat on his face had caused some of the dirt to wash off, Exposing a large bruise above his cheek bone.

"Those lumps keep breaking off as they're doing, goin give us roof problems."

"How do you work that out?" I passed him my tin of snuff.

"Ta. Look at roof. See them hairline fractures." He directed my attention with his cap lamp. Leaning forward over the spills I looked up and could see exactly what he meant. "No coal to support roof. Chock canopies too far back to support."

"What do'y reckon?"

"Hello Mick. Hello Mick Gibson." The fitters voice shouted out from the DAC.

"Get some wooden dowels in. Try to keeping the coal from falling over."

"Yeah. Not a bad idea."

"Hello Mick, hello Mick."

I knelt to answer Brian. Spitting what was left of my chew onto the pans, leaving a bitter taste. I hadn't appreciated how much I'd been sweating since talking to Ged. It was a little concerning as I hadn't done anything physical. Could only mean one thing!

"Hi Brian. Mick here." I placed my ear against the white metal box. The sound of the empty panzer louder now.

"Just to let you know Mick problem with shearer. Maingate cowl won't turn problem with thidraulics." *Fuck that's all we need!*

"Thanks for letting me know Brian. Any ideas?"

"Checkin now cock."

"Brian…." I never got chance to finish my sentence I was suddenly engulfed in a cloud of fine dust. Followed by the dull thud of the roof opposite dropping onto the panzer. I swallowed a gob full. Attempting to hawk up. I spat out what remained. The dryness of the dust causing me to almost spew up.

"What did I tell tha." Ged shouted towards me. I couldn't see his face. Only the beam of his cap lamp penetrating the haze of fine floating particles.

Still kneeling alongside the tannoy the trickle of sweat down my chest alerted me once more to a previous concern. "Hello Paul. Hello stage loader."

"Aye Mick. Paul here."

"Do us a favour. Can you get hold of George and ask him to check the crosscut doors. Getting a little warm in here."

"Will do. Oh, just to let you know. Peter Mint's been on. He's on his way in. Where's best to meet you?" Pete was another of the many Colliery Overmen we had. I guess he'd been sent in by the Manager after yesterday's visit.

"Did he say which way his was comin in?"

"Nah." *Well, that's fuckin helpful.*

"Tell him I'll be at the return end."

"Hello Mick. Hello Mick Gibson."

"Hi Control. Hi Steve."

"You on the way down yet?"

"No problem with maingate cowl. Fitter's on it now."

"Any idea how long you'll be?" *Let me just check me fuckin crystal ball!*

"As soon as I know you'll be the first to hear."

"Just so you know 15's is on stand too. Damaged stitching on maingate belt." *Like I give a fuck.* I decided to ignore Steve's last comment.

"Fuckin ell Scouse popular today lad."

"Thanks Ged." I placed a latch on. "Paul I've put the lock out on." My head was throbbing like fuck. Ged and I moved forward to see how much ground had fallen up.

"Couple of split bars and chockwood should do the job." I suggested.

"Agree but if we don't stop the spalling, we'll av a bigger problem cock."

"Can you sort Ged?"

"Will do." I turned and began to make my way to the maingate.

"Thought tha was goin up to shearer?"

"I am. Just goin to get a mouthful of water."

"Do us a favour. Ask the twins to get off their arses and make their way to me."

"Will do."

As I stepped down from the faceline I looked up towards the ripping platform. Both Alf and Jack were sat eating a sarnie. "Lads hate to interrupt. Could you make your way onto the face? Need some timbering around five area."

"Fuck off Mick. We've just set one arch. Havin our jackbit."

"I'll let Ged know. It was him asking." I watched with amusement as they both immediately stood up. Discarding what remained of their sarnie.

I continued outbye. Careful where I placed my feet. A flow of white milky fluid was still covering the floor. The smell stronger now as I came alongside the hydraulic tank. Leaks every which way I turned. My water bottle was between the panels over the stageloader.

Coming towards me was Frankie Glow. "Bloody ell Frankie what you doing in here?"

"Aster not bin told. Mr Creed asked me to fettle tha lump problem."

"You got a magic wand or summut?"

"Wouldn't that be thy job. No av come to measure up. Put something similar in place we've got in C15's."

"What would that be?"

"Box bar with cutter picks welded on. Should do the trick." I wasn't sure how that was going to work but anything was worth a try.

"Hello Mick. Hello Mick Gibson." I could see Paul ahead shouting into the DAC.

"I'm here what's up?"

"Mr Keech has been on. Wants you to call him."

"Right Frankie, I'll catch you later. You know we've got a problem with the shearer."

"Aye. As soon as av done ere I'll make me way up."

Paul passed me the handset.

"Hello Mick. Hello Mick Gibson."

"For fucks sake Steve give us a minute." I said out loud shaking my head. "What the fuck now?" I passed the handset back to Paul. "Steve Mick ere."

"Sorry to moider you Mick but you've got one per cent methane outbye end of return." Before I answered Paul gave me a nudge.

"As tha said. Crosscut doors have been damaged. George is there now doing some repairs with the haulage lads." I nodded.

"Mr Keech, Mick ere. Yes, I know. On it now. How long? I'm guessing another hour." I held the phone away from my ear. "Pete no. Haven't seen him yet...."

"Hello Mick Gibson. Hello Mick." It was Pete Mint. Paul reached across to answer him.

"Peter, Mick's on phone. Shall I pass him a message?"

"Tell him, I'm at the outbye end of the return." I covered the mouth piece as the Deputy Manager continued to rant.

"I'll see him at the top end in about ten minutes."

"Mick says he'll see you at top end in ten."

"Not sure whether you heard that Mr Keech. Peter's in the return now. Yeah, I'll give you a shout as soon as we're done. No problem." I replaced the handset.

"Hello Mick. Hello Mick Gibson."

"Hi Brian." I reached between the panels opposite to where I was standing. Snatching my water bottle I took a quick swig. Swilling my mouth, I spat out. Listening to Brian as I took another gob full.

"Can't fettle cowl. Need parts. Lads doin a temporary fix." I guessed by that they would use chockwood to turn the thing over. "Is Frankie still with you?"

"He's doin some measuring up towards maingate end. Should I pass him a message?"

"I. Tell him not to bother coming to machine. I know what's needed. I'll come to him."

"Will do."

"Latch is off." Paul shouted as he started the stage loader. The pre alarm kicked in followed by the clanging and scraping of the flight bars. At least that was something. Coaling again.

"Paul, have you seen Freddy?"

"Outbye with George checkin doors." I left Paul and headed back to the face line.

Frankie was still alongside the tall spills. Tape measure in one hand, note book in the other. I relayed the message from Brian. Frankie nodded not making any comment. Fully engrossed with the job in hand. Continuing down towards the faceline I was pleased to hear the sound of coal falling from the AFC onto the stage loader. Two lights appeared coming off. It was Alf and Jack.

"Sorted lads?"

136

"What do tha think Mick." Neither one of them was smiling.

"You can go finish your snap now." Neither responded.

"Hello Mick." Paul shouted as I reached the first DAC.

"Paul?"

"George as bin on. Doors sorted."

"Thanks Paul. Can you ask him to check we've got plenty of resin and dowels in return."

"Will do."

"Ello Mick."

"Hello Bobby."

"Elec problems with Webster cock. Keeps cutting out."

"Where's leckie?"

"If tha gives me chance am on fuckin way up." Dai Bando interrupted.

"Thanks Dai."

Standing upright I turned to face the steady stream of the black stuff moving along the panzer. Completely covering the pans. A black river of coal. There was no better sight. I reached inside my pocket. I deserved a moment to myself whilst partaking. I took the opportunity to inspect the work the twins had done. Satisfied I continued towards the return. Passing the machine at one hundred chock. I acknowledged David and Johnny. Brian the fitter was alongside too.

"Frankie still there Mick?"

"He is but don't mither him. Measuring up." We both laughed. "Catch you later."

By the time I'd reached the top end, Pete Mint was already there. He looked as though he'd taken a shower.

"Hello Pete."

"Hi Mick." Without asking I offered my tin of snuff. "How the fuck do you put up with this?"

"With what?" He waved his arm in the air.

"And that cunt." I looked to where he indicated. A group of lads were stood around the Webster with the electrician. I knew he was referring to Ged. Like a lot of officials, they seemed to have a problem with Ged. I suspect because they didn't know him as well as me. Often seen as a bully.

"Oh, he's alright really. Just wants to be loved." I turned towards the panzer as it began to slow.

"Lock out on crosscut belt. Who's got a lockout on?" Steve in Control shouted on the tannoy. Soon followed by Paul on the DAC advising the face.

"Checkin a stitch." George provided the explanation.

Taking a pinch, myself I asked.

"What do I owe the honour then Peter?"

"Mr Keech asked me pop in. What with yesterday's visit and all that."

"No surprises there then."

"That fuckin man though. A complete fuckin wanker." I assumed he meant the Inspector and not Mr Keech. "The number of times he comes ere. We end up with half the officials goin on club."

"Ello Mick. Ello Mick Gibson." George's voice once more on the outbye tannoy. The sound of which meant only one thing.

"Give us a mo Pete." I climbed up and entered the return road just as the Webster kicked in. The heading lads and Ged gave a cheer. Slapping Dai Bando on his back.

"There you go cock. Knew tha sort." Bobby exclaimed.

"Hi George, Mick ere."

"Sorry cock, gonna ave to do this almost third of way through and coal coming back on bottom belt."

"Okay got that. I'll be with you shortly." I turned back towards Peter. "Sorry Peter I'll have to make my way out. You carrying on down face?"

"Well, I ain't goin back the way I came."

"Exercise 'ill do tha good. You lazy cunt." For a lad of Pete's size, I'd never seen someone move so quick. Ged never flinched. "If tha thinks thi man enough Pete. I'll let tha take the first swing."

"For fucks sake lads, leave it out." The two of them nose to nose. Well almost. Peter must have been two foot taller than Ged. The standoff immediately ceased when Pete smiled.

"Better things to do than waste my fuckin time on tha, cunt." He turned back towards me. "I'll see you at the meeting station." And with that he continued down the face line. I continued outbye, there was a stitching to do.

☐

8. The Oak Tree and the Willow

As was the norm, I walked into the Undermanager's office after most of the other officials had gone. John was sat there still in his black. The rim of either nostril coated in remnants of brown powder. A large open tin of Hedges sat next to his phone. John looked like shite. I'd watched the deterioration of the man's character over the last few months. And this was what I wanted to be? I must have been mad. I contemplated why I was still so infatuated by the job. I was beginning to think more and more it was a test for myself. I wanted to see if I could cope with the pressure and demands of the job. I wasn't helping either.

Struggling to produce two shears a day. Of late plagued by continuous mechanical breakdowns. The face fitter Brian Token had suggested the place was jinxed. John looked up towards me.

"Now lad what excuses have you got for me today?" Before I could answer his phone began to ring. He didn't pick it up immediately. He sat there staring. I think we both knew who it would be.

"Ello…" I watched as he lowered his head. Even with his face blackened by coal dust I could still see his complexion discolour beneath. "Will do…. Yeah, he's here with me now." He looked once more towards me. "Yes Mester." He replaced the handset. "Manager. Wants to see you." I never moved at first. Since I'd been Face Overman on L32's I'd spent more time with Mr Creed than my missus.

"Did he say why?" We both knew I was stalling.

"Does he need a reason?" John remained staring at me. "Might be best if you don't keep Gaffer waiting."

Reluctantly I left his office and headed towards the Top Shunt. I looked into his secretary's office. No sign so I continued. I hesitated before knocking. Something I could not get out of the habit of doing.

"You gonna go in or what?" I hadn't heard the person approach from behind. I recognised him but wasn't sure who he was. Other than being something to do with the mechanical department. He looked smart in his grey suit and tie. He had a kindly inquisitive face. I'm sure I detected a Staffordshire accent.

"Yeah, sorry." I responded somewhat embarrassed. I knocked.

"Come." I walked in. The guy behind me followed. The Manager was sat at the long meeting table. He was puffing on his pipe. "Take a seat lad." The Manager pointed to a line of chairs opposite. "Ah Mick thanks for coming." He offered to the fellow following. "You two met then?"

"Only just. Caught the young man loitering outside your office." The Manager smiled and looked towards me.

"Mick this is Mick Hobbit pits Mechanical Engineer." He continued to the other side of the table and sat next to the Manager. He smiled towards me.

"How do you do Mick. Gibson isn't it."

"Yes, it is."

"Suppose you wondered why I've asked to see you?" *I had assumed it was for another round of fucks.*

"Yes Mr Creed." Before he could answer there was another knock on the door. It was Mr Keech.

"Ah Len good of you to join us." The Deputy Manager still in his black entered the room. A lit fag hanging from the corner of his mouth. "How's it looking?"

"Good. Canna believe how low the place is. Lads doin a bostin job." As way of an explanation the Manager turned to Mick Hobbit.

"Lens been on V24's. Our first coal face in the Wigan Five Foot." For the moment I thought they'd forgotten I was there. "Another four shears today. Trepanners working a treat." I assumed the Manager's comment was for my benefit. "Nice top up until L33's kicks in."

Conversation over they all turned to me. Momentarily there was complete silence. Broken by the hum of men's conversation passing through the lamproom above. I wasn't sure if I was expected to say something.

"Mick we've decided to provide you with some additional support in L32's."

"On the back of the numerous mechanical breakdowns you're havin." Mr Keech added to the Manager's comments. I switched my gaze from the Manager. Mr Keech was holding the filter of his now exhausted fag in one hand. The other cupped and containing ash. The Manager reached across and slid a glass ashtray toward him. Nodding he placed the stub end and ash into it. Job done he reached into his top pocket and extracted his pack of Players No 6. Extracting one, he began patting his pockets down. Unable to find what he was looking for the Manager passed his lighter across. Mick Hobbit sat impassively staring towards me.

"Mick here, is goin to assign one of his Assistant Engineers to you. A young man by the name of Bob Black." I didn't recognise the name. The guys I was most familiar with were Brian Token, Frankie Glow and Eric Greenland.

"Good man he is Mick." The Mechanical Engineer added. "Been working on the design of W11's. Very knowledgeable lad." *He's going to have to be the shit I've been dealin with.* Again silence. I wasn't sure being knowledgeable was the only attribute he'd need.

"Cat got your tongue lad?"

"No Mr Creed, it has to be good news." The Manager picked up the lighter. Placing it over the chamber of his pipe. Sucking and drawing the air through the stem. The smell of the St Bruno and Players No 6 filled the room.

"So, I'm not expecting anymore fuckin excuses."

"No Mr Creed." Spell broken I shifted uncomfortably in my seat.

"Pop round to engineers office when you've had a bath. I'll introduce Bob to you."

"Will do Mick."

"Owt else lad?"

"No."

"Go get yoursen a bath then." I nodded. Mr Keech then turned to Mick Hobbit. "See the first load of sixteen-inch pipes have arrived.

"Bout fuckin time. I'm sure you can hear the noise from the compressed air range in No 2 shaft in canteen." My cue to leave.

☐

Three weeks later myself and Bob Black were asked to report to the Top Shunt. Since his assignment to 32's we'd continued to suffer with mechanical failures. It had been a baptism by fire. I don't think he was cut out for this type of work. Surprisingly, he'd never taken to Ged. His first week had started quite well and I was learning new things too. He'd set in motion a series of tests on the face equipment. Things I'd never considered before. The use of a chain tension transducer on the face chain. There was a correct level that fluid couplings needed filling to. All good stuff but thereafter!

I was still in my black when I arrived at the top shunt. Bob was already there in his clean. Stood outside the office door. Head bowed plucking up the courage to knock. I smiled. It was good to see I wasn't the only one.

"Hiya Bob. How are you fella?" He was as white as a sheet.

"Just a little concerned why the Manager wants to see me."

"Us Bob. He's sees us as a team now." The look on his face said it all. "This is a regular feature. High profile is L32's and not for the best results. Haven't brought any books along with you?"

"Sorry Mick, what do you mean?"

"You're in the trenches now fella. Books down back of kecks. Ready for the round of fucks we're about to receive. Amen."

"Whatever for?" Poor Bob he'd been working on projects since he'd arrived working closely with Geoff Smooth, the new Assistant Manager so I'd heard.

"You'll get used to it. One bit of advice though. Don't take any shit. If you think you're in the right. Tell him. He'll respect you for that." I didn't wait for an answer. Knocking on the door I walked in. Bob followed.

"You've asked to see us Mr Creed?" The Manager was sat directly opposite on the far side of the large table in the centre of his office. Mr Keech alongside. His face barely visible behind a cloud of smoke. He stubbed what little remained of his fag as we entered. Without being asked I walked forward and took a seat. Bob did likewise.

"Did I ask you to fuckin sit? What's think this is? A fuckin social visit." Bad move on my behalf. Looks as though he's in a right one today. Momentarily I reflected on the Manager's demeanour. It worked like this. He would take a hiding from the Area Director for any poor performance. He in turn passed that on to the Deputy Manager. Who in turn passed it on to the Undermanager. Mr Creed was somewhat different in this respect. He liked to dish out the fucks directly. Particularly as he'd completely destroyed my Undermanager, John

Meriden. My thoughts interrupted as Bob jumped up. In the process knocking his chair over.

"Who the fuck do you think you are? Coming in here and thrashing my office." The Manager screamed towards Bob. It was too much for Mr Keech. Both hands shaking he grabbed his box of Players No 6. Extracting one fag three others falling onto the table. He gave up trying to get them back into the box. Fag in mouth he used both hands to steady a Swan Vesta matchstick. The Manager ignored Mr Keech. He was enjoying the spectacle of Bob's performance. "Sit fuckin down!" He bellowed across the table once more. "And I suppose you think this is funny?" Fuck I was usually good with my facial expressions. My look of concern had been replaced by a smirk.
"Sorry Mr Creed. Got a bit of wind."
"Wind? I'll give you fuckin wind." His eyes gleaming with anger. And then he stopped. Like someone had clicked the angry switch off. He sat back in his chair. For a moment there followed a short silence. Nobody moved. Other than Bob's knees knocking together.

The Manager satisfied he'd set the scene. "Now you two. What have you got to say for yourselves?" I certainly had a few things to say. I wasn't sure now was the time or place. I'd shared my thoughts previously with Mr Keech. I looked towards him. His expression suggested the same. As did him lighting up another fag he'd retrieved from the table. "Well?" His voice a little louder this time. It was an ideal time for Bob to put his marker down. Or so I thought.
"I'm not quite sure what you mean Mr Creed." This certainly wasn't the answer the Manager was after from Bob. Confirmed as he slammed a clenched fist on the table. I watched as the two fags left on the table flew into the air. Before landing and rolling off onto the floor. My attention once more drawn to Mr Keech. He was having an internal debate as to whether he should retrieve them.

"I'll tell you what I mean!" His second clenched fist landed on the table. I doubted whether Mr Keech would attempt to retrieve them now. "Over the last two weeks we've had the face chain break twice. Clevis pins snapping on three chocks. We've had to replace the maingate gearbox, replace the tailend sprocket. The shearer keeps losing oil and the hydraulic power pack replaced. I've lost count on the number of double acting rams you've replaced. The grand finale last week the stageloader detaching itself from its base plate." Silence followed. Complete silence. As all the stoppages mentioned were mechanical, I was hoping Bob would answer. Without making it too obvious I tried to catch his attention. There was certainly movement from his mouth but no sound.

I watched as Mr Keech, stubbed out his fag. I counted three now in the ashtray.

"Well? Have you got nothing to say?" My attention was still on Mr Keech, he'd gone for a fourth.

"I think… I think… that's a little… un…. fair Mr Creed. The place is……"

"Un fuckin fair you say. Un fuckin fair." Louder this time. "I'll tell you what's un fuckin fair." Poor Bob he had tried. The Manager's response would put paid to any further comment from him. Perhaps I should add my two pence worth, ideally before the Manager said anymore.

"I think what Bob's trying to say Mr Creed." I don't think this was what he was trying to say. But guess it was worth a try. "You're talking to the wrong fellas. Perhaps you should be talking to the wankers that designed the place. The same wankers sat in an office somewhere suggesting the wrong specification for a seam of coal that requires something a little heavier duty." I realised then my comments were less than helpful. As Mr Keech's fag disappeared up to the filter. Replaced by a length of ash dropping onto the table.

"You cheeky Scouse bastard." Both fists once more landing on the table. "I signed off the design. Fuckin me. Colliery Manager. There's nowt wrong with kit. It's thi useless bastards that couldn't manager a piss up in a brewery. I'll not sit here and listen to this shite. If not, careful lad you'll be gone. Gone I say. Unless things start to improve." I sensed movement from Bob. I turned to see; he looked as though he was about to cry. "Come Mr Keech. Let's leave these two incompetent bastards. I've got better things to do with my time."

Without a further word spoke, the Manager left the room. Followed closely by Mr Keech. Bob now had his head in his hands. I said nothing for a moment. Reflecting on the comments that I'd made.

"Well, that went well. Wouldn't you say?"

□

"Tha seem nervous Scouse."

"Why would I be nervous." Ged and I were stood outside Mr Keech's office door. He'd asked to see us both. Production from the face was deteriorating by the day. As I went to knock Ged pushed passed me and walked straight in. Mr Keech was sat at his desk. The phone clutched in his right hand.

"Fine thanks. We can speak later." He replaced the handset. "It would be nice if you knocked first." Mr Keech was looking at me. Before I could answer.

"Nah Len what's bothering tha?"

"I'll tell you what's bothering me Ged fuckin coal or should I say the lack of it." Mr Keech's demeanour belied something else. He extracted a cigarette from the pack. Quickly lighting it he inhaled. I watched as the red tip moved along the paper towards the filter. The ash produced replacing the tightly packed tobacco. He saw me looking and flicked it into the already overflowing ash tray.

Mr Keech's office had an adjoining door to the Manager's office. I could only guess that the Manager was listening.

"Can't be blamed for the continuing geological problems at the main gate end Mr Keech."

"Mick I could run with that but there's more to it."
The adjoining door flew open without warning. Causing me to jump. I saw Mr Keech do the same. The only person not to move was Ged.

"Fuckin geological problems! I'll give you geological problems." The Manager stopped alongside the desk, his clenched fist landing with force. Both Mr Keech and I jumped again. Not Ged though.

"Nah Patrick, just you be careful you don't bust that duodenal ulcer." The Manager ignored Ged's comment as he continued.

"Who do we get rid of then? One of you will have to go!"

"Well as Scouse here is trying to make a career of it. I suggest it be me." For the first time since he'd walked in the Manager smiled. His change in demeanour also caused Mr Keech to visibly relax. He pulled up a chair and sat alongside.

"Go on Len tell them what geologist has had to say."

"Reckons the problems we continue to have at the maingate end is due to the pillar of a previous face above in the Ince seam. Suggests we get the intake end at an angle to cross it things should improve."

"Any questions?" The Manager asked.

"Is that it? After all this time." Ged was shaking his head. "Explains a lot. Now if you don't mind Pat, I've a buzz catch."

"Just make sure you keep that maingate in advance." Ged looked towards me.

"Think we can manage that." And with that he stood. I attempted to follow suit.

"Not you young man. I've another matter to discuss with you." Ged left the room. The Manager reached inside his jacket pocket and extracted a letter. He passed it to me. "Best have a read. It's self-explanatory."

It was one of those important letters, in a bulky light blue envelope. It was from Malcolm Hughes at Staff Training. I was to continue developing my supervisory and management skills as an Overman. Extend my knowledge of all aspects of colliery operations. Including the surface and especially financial and general management matters. Obtain an appreciation of the functions, organisation, and staff within Area. Also enclosed with the letter was an Area organisation chart, key contact numbers, and various colliery profiles. I would be expected to take the initiative to learn about functions from contacts with Area staff when they visit the colliery and ask him to arrange visits or short periods of secondment to the Area office you may require. I smiled as I read that part.

"Don't be planning any fuckin visits to Area lad. All experience tha wants is ere." The Manager was even a mind reader. I nodded. I'd need to attend the various local Institution of Mining Engineers meetings. *Missus going to love that.* Widen my general knowledge of the industry and management techniques, by regularly reading the Mining Engineer and articles and books on management. Confirmation of two residential courses, each of two weeks duration. At a place called Graham House in Newcastle-upon- Tyne. One classed as Technical, the other Senior. *Fuck that's going to go down well at home.* I'd need a plan of action to break that news to the missus. I was getting it in the neck on a regular basis on what was happening now. A short Area course on finance and a further two-week inter-area visit to a number of collieries in South Yorkshire.

It was a lot to take in, particularly with the Manager and his Deputy sat facing me. I finished reading and looked up.

"Nah Mick what does think then?" Mr Keech asked. I wasn't sure how many fags he'd smoked while I'd been reading. The haze of smoke obscuring his face suggested it would have been more than one. My initial reaction was I'd be ending up in the divorce courts trying to do all of that.
"Yeah, really good. Plenty to go at." I mustn't have sounded that convincing. The Manager once more hitting the nail on the head.
"Bet your missus will be pleased." They both began to laugh. "All in good time lad. Need to build on your face experience for now. Go on, fuck off and get a bath."

☐

We hadn't seen much of Howard Davies of late. Rumours abounded he was about to leave. John had been filling in for him quite a lot of late. From what I'd been told it wasn't permanent appointment. The job had to be advertised first and due process followed.
I liked John. Not one for sentiment but always good to chat things through. I'd learnt plenty from him at Cronton and very knowledgeable. I wasn't convinced however he'd get the role. Ron Groves had described him as a career Undermanager but that really depended on the Manager he worked for.
"Now lad how's it going." He seemed in a reflective mood.
"All good thanks John."
"Hear the Manager had words with you."

"Yeah. Not happy with what's goin on with L32's. Plus I've got a number of courses coming up. Didn't say when though."

"Graham House?"

"Yeah."

"Bit of advice lad on how you manage the men." He offered me his tin of Hedges. His large tin.

"Thanks." One of the many things I liked about John he always had fresh snuff

"I liken managing to being a tree." *A fuckin tree! Can't wait for this.* "The analogy I'll give you son is this. Some people think you should be all strong like an oak. Powerful, never giving an inch. But what happens when there's a storm?" Silence followed as I waited for the punch line. "Well?" I hadn't realized his last comment had been a question. Before I could answer. "It can snap. The branches break." I nodded. It was a fair comment. "But the Willow." I assumed this was a question. I'd seen many a willow tree when I was younger. Always near ponds where we used to fish as kids. I wasn't sure this was the answer he was looking for.

"Wat……"

"They bend lad." *Thank fuck he interrupted me.*

☐

"Remember lad. No fucks up. This could be the difference between having a career in management or ending up in safety." For fucks sake like I need to hear that. "Watch Tuffman. He'll try and catch you out, particularly as his boss, Deputy Director will be with him. Go on off you go I'll see you next Tuesday." The Manager picked up his pen and began signing off the statutory reports piled up in front of him. I left without uttering a word.

The news of the visit next week didn't give me much time to prepare. Fortunately, I was on overtime tomorrow dayshift in L32's. Changing the tailend sprocket. It'd give me chance to recce the place and Monday to sort any outstanding jobs. I wasn't too concerned. Ever since we'd started the monthly Face Management meetings any outstanding jobs we usually dealt with in a timely fashion. I was excited to meet the Deputy Director again. Particularly as I'd been accepted on to the ET Scheme. I headed straight to the Undermanager's office.

"No Mr Creed. Yes Mr Creed. Right Mr Creed." John was on the phone as I entered. He looked up towards me. His face said it all. Both of his nostrils were coated in Hedges. A large open tin of the very same lay alongside the phone. He moved the handset away from his ear. Even from where I was stood, I could hear the round of fucks he was receiving. I continued forward as he slid the tin towards me. I took a pinch then sat back onto one of the wooden chairs opposite his desk.

I continued watching John as he received the verbal battering from the Manager. He was still in his black minus his helmet. His tufts of long greying plastered to his forehead. The pit was now down to two Undermanager's. Howard Davies had left. Rumour had it he had family problems and no longer had the capacity to continue as an Undermanager. It hadn't surprised me when I was told he'd finished. John wasn't expected to fill the post. We were expecting a replacement from one of the local pits. Sat watching John I wondered how long he had left. *And I wanted to be an Undermanager!*

"Will do Mr Creed. He's with me now." He replaced the handset.

"See you've got Cannock mafia visiting next week?" His voice sounded deeper this time. Gruff even. I slid the tin of snuff back towards him.

"Mafia?" He laughed.

"Don't try to cross'em that's all. Thy'll end up with horses ed in thi bed." John seemed to find the whole thing amusing. The lack of my understanding caused him to change subject. "You ever met Tuffman before?"

"No."

"He's usually the person appointed as mentor to those just starting out on the ET Scheme. Looks as though you've drawn the short straw."

"How do you mean?"

"What I mean lad is he's a complete twat. I know of two lads already who packed the whole thing in. One's now in ventilation, the other safety."

"Thanks for sharing that." I reached across and took another pinch.

"Make sure you know your stuff. Particularly the equipment on the face. Loves to catch you new up and comers out." I liked John. Always ready to offer advice, although he'd become a lot more cynical these last few months. Probably the pressure he was under. "Right lad. Time you fucked off. Got a face installation meeting to attend to."

By the time Tuesday arrived we'd managed to put the finishing touches to the place and stone dusted. In the return there were several empties to get out including an old bucket off the Webster. Being on a single shift made life a little simpler. Knowing how we'd left the place the day previous and what we were coming onto. I'd spent most of Monday in conversation with the fitter and electrician. Attempting to improve my knowledge on equipment we were using, manufacturer, specification, and power requirements. I felt suitably prepared for the visit. However, from experience there was always something you'd get caught out on. The recent visit from HMI still upper most on my mind.

I waited at the Meeting Station. The Manager suggested they'd be underground around ten. My plan was to take them down the maingate first thing. We'd had a full turn out this morning. Even managing to man up the Hausherr dint. Although I'd suggested to George to get the lads slinging the conveyor first thing until we'd passed. Not wanting to choke my visitors with dust. We'd left the pantech further back than normal. Giving us a bit more room to pass the panels. The leak on the hydraulic tank had been repaired by Brian allowing the ground in that area to dry out.

The worse part of any visit was the wait. I'd spoken to Paul a few minutes ago. The machine was about to start cutting towards the return. Bi di complete. I was getting a little impatient still no sound of coal on the belt. I picked the handset up once more. Replacing it as soon as I heard the maingate belt begin to take the strain. Followed by the sound of coal hitting the chute and fall onto the crosscut conveyor. The water sprays kicking in as the additional weight of coal ran against the sensors. It was pleasing to hear but didn't remove the butterflies I could now feel in my gut. My mouth was dry too. Unfortunately, I'd left my water bottle at the panels. I'd refrained from placing a chew in. Not sure how this would be viewed by the others. For the first time I began to feel the cold intake air. I began pacing backwards and forwards. Stopping to take another pinch. I looked outbye again still no sign. Other than the black stuff piled high on the belt. Well at least that was something. Then in the distance, three cap lamps appeared. *Fuck here they are.* I could make out the Manager immediately. His height the giveaway. The other two gentlemen of smaller frame. All three carrying an oil lamp and stick. Each wearing dark blue overalls, and white donkey jackets. The tapping of the sticks becoming louder as they approached. The black stuff smashing against the side of the chute reassuring. Guaranteeing a good start to the visit. So, I hoped.

As they got closer, I could see the Deputy Director in deep conversation with the Manager. He was smiling. That must be a good sign. I coughed gently. Clearing my throat for the introduction. The other guy was looking towards me. He wasn't smiling. He reminded me of someone. I wasn't sure who. I stepped forward.
"Morning gentlemen. Welcome to L32's." I was about to add the words *the coal factory.* When the sound of coal dropping into the chute stopped. I watched with concern as the Manager's eyes darted across to the conveyor.
"Breaking a lump, maingate end." A voice shouted over the tannoy.
"Gentlemen, Mick Gibson. Mick this is the Deputy Director, whom you've met before." I raised my hand. The Deputy Director was still smiling.
"Owsi gooin me ole shoe? Yo aurite?"
"All good thanks Deputy Director."
"And the Area Production Manager. Mr Tuffman." This guy wasn't. He didn't look happy for some reason. Then it dawned on me. Who he looked like. He

was the spit of Frederick Forsyth, the author. I'd just finished his book *The Day of the Jackal.* I held my hand towards him. Which he didn't take.

"How come you ain't got a lump breaker?" He asked.

"We have, of sorts." I replied smiling. It probably wasn't the best answer to give.

"What's that supposed to mean either you have, or you haven't." I looked towards the Manager. He returned my stare. He wasn't giving anything away.

"We've had a box bar fitted with cutter picks attached."

"Ave not heard owt as daft." The sound of coal hitting the chute brought the conversation to an end.

"Where's machine Mick." The Manager added breaking the silence.

"On its way to the return for the second."

"Second?" Tuffman asked. "Time it is now should've been on number three, four even." *Fuckin ell this guy is a jobs worth. I'm in for some fun this morning.*

"Right then Mick. Cum on in willyer shall we have a looksee." The Deputy Director asked. He was still smiling. I nodded and began to walk down the maingate.

"I like travelling return first." I stopped in my tracks and turned towards the Production Manager. Neither the DD nor Manager made any comment.

"Return it is then." I began to retrace my steps. The situation was far from ideal. The Hausherr dint was on hold waiting for us to pass. Plus, I had a team of haulage lads with George heading out towards us. Mr Tuffman dropped in alongside me. The DD and Manager bringing up the rear.

"What quantity of air you got going round the district?"

"Four cubic metres. Hoping to increase it slightly with repair work on outbye doors."

"What you using?"

"To measure?"

"Anemometer."

"What type?"

"Just an anemometer."

"Thought you had your Ventilation Officers certificate?" This guy had obviously done his homework on me.

"I do."

"What about gas?"

"Generally nought point six at the outbye end. Top motor a steady point two."

"Methane drainage?"

"Yeah. Got a team in here every other day sharing with L31's. Unless there's a problem."

"Pattern?"

"As in up and down holes?" Before he responded the haulage rope began to move beneath our feet. "Watch the rope." I shouted. This was exactly what I didn't want. I was hoping the lads would be outbye by the time we travelled the return. To add to my concern the sound of the crosscut doors being bashed open. The inbye set first and then those nearest us. My heart sank as the front bogie appeared. I was tempted to grab the greenline off to my right. Two lights appeared either side of the track forcing each door open.

"Automatic doors I see." I chose to ignore Tuffman's comment. The haulage lads, Terry, Billy, and Punchy were good lads. Been with us from the start.
"Come on fellas what's your game?"
"Sorry Mick. Journey got away from us. Throwing some scrap steel on." Punchy answered. His face jet black as normal. Beads of perspiration running from his forehead. His flattened nose adding to his comical appearance.
"Bucket loaded Mick." Terry added. I guessed Billy was on the Pikrose engine. Punchy moved forward and pulled on the signalling cable. The journey coming to a complete halt.
"Likely fuckin story." Tuffman murmured. The sound of the middle doors being pulled to confirmed where George was.

He appeared along with his smile. "Morning Gentlemen."
"No wonder I keep receiving orders for new sets of doors George."
"Not from me tha won't Mr Creed. Make sure we protect that we do." George still smiling pointed to the length of old belting nailed to the inbye side of either door. I don't think it was the answer the Manager was looking for. I decided the best course of action was to keep moving.
"Right lads. Leave latch on till we pass."
"Will do Mick." I began walking inbye.
"If they get up to this when you're here, what are they doing when you ain't around?" Mr Tuffman was alongside me once more. "Transport Rules?"
"Four fullins or six empties." I counted the vehicles as I answered his question. Although technically these weren't empty. Particularly as we had the salvaged Webster bucket on the last vehicle.

"Well, well. Not have load binders here Mr Creed?" I'd spotted it too the bucket sat flat on the last vehicle was binderless.
"There's a pile just outbye of maingate." George shouted across.
"George come on. This is not how we operate. Get one of the lads to fetch a binder and secure the bucket before you go any further."
"I alreyt Mick." We couldn't have got off to a worse start and all because that cunt Tuffman wanted to travel the return first.

Once passed the last vehicle. I stopped to let my visitors get along side. The clash of intake and return air causing a cloud of dust to form.

"Right lads. All yours." I shouted. Punchy gave the greenline three sharp pulls. The journey began to move outbye.

"Good start Mick." The DD was still smiling as he said it. "A drag! Rare as rockinoss shit." He was pointing to the D link at the back of the last vehicle. I hadn't seen it before myself. And to be using it on the flat. As the last door closed the change in air temperature was evident. My body suddenly feeling the warmth of stale air. The smells too changed. A mix of packside, timber and that distinct smell of wood ash.

We'd almost reached the outbye end of the return. The place looked well. Even if I did think so myself. The colour coding of the pipes standing out. The green and red for the water range. Blue compressed air and yellow for the methane. Tuffman had obviously spotted them too.

"What purity you getting?" His lamp picking up the yellow band on the six-inch range.

"Fifty. Sometimes sixty per cent."

"That's good. Hence the reason you've got the deal with Crosfields?"

"Yeah, and the pipe range we paid for."

We turned into the return. Stopping twenty metres further inbye when I realised the Manager and DD had stopped.

"Probably discussing why Manager wants to pull out of the Lower Florida." Tuffman offered as a way of explanation. "You know after here and 31's have finished. L33's will be the last face."

"Yeah. Floor lift. You'll see when we get further inbye." I removed my tin of snuff. "Pinch?"

"Nah, never touch the stuff. Filthy habit. Suppose you chew as well?"

"Yeah."

"Proper pit mon heh. And from Liverpool. Think you've got it in you to become an Undermanager Mick?"

Blimey this guy didn't hold back. "I think so."

"You only think lad. You should know by now. Not going to be wasting the Coal Boards money if you only think. Do you know how much we spend on you lads to just get to Undermanager?" Actually, I didn't have a fuckin clue. "We did the sums the other day. Up to twenty grand there or there abouts. What with college, various course, field trips, ET Scheme, inter area visits etc. etc." The conversation coming to a halt as the Manager and DD reached us. I decided not to take a pinch. Replacing the tin in my pocket.

"All good yoe?" The DD asked.

"Yep." I replied.

"Just asked Mick if he's got it in him to become an Undermanager." Tuffman wasn't going to let this rest. I wish now I'd been a little more assertive in my answer.

"And what did yoe say Mick?" The two of them now. It was like a double act.

"Thinks he has." Tuffman again interrupting before I could answer. "Just explained how much it costs Coal Board to get'em there." Once more I looked towards the Manager for some reassurance. Nothing was forthcoming other than him raising his eyebrows again. Looks as though I'm on my own.

"What I meant…."

"I know exactly what you meant sonny. You said I think."

"Well, what I meant was…."

"I think." The man was now beginning to get on my tits.

"Perhaps we should just keep moving." The DD interrupted. I was sure I detected a smile from the Manager. We continued inbye in silence.

"This is where face started." The Manager placed his stick against the packside of the arches. We stopped. The DD walked across to examine the pack area a little closer.

"Any problems with spon com?"

"Nah. Not in the Lower Florida."

"All seams are liable but certain seams more liable than others. Mr Creed." Wow this was interesting. Tuffman was now disagreeing with the Manager. "Crombouke, Wigan Four and Five Feet, Trencherbone, Peacock, Plodder and Haigh Yard granted are the seams recognised in the Area."

"Well not in Lower Florida." Tuffman didn't respond he'd got the message.

We continued inbye once more saying very little.

"Hello Mick. Hello Mick Gibson." I spotted the tannoy just ahead of us. I increased my pace ahead of the others.

"Hi Steve. Mick ere."

"Just checking how you getting on. Lads on manrider asking what time your visitors want picking up. Paul tells me you've not reached panels yet." I checked my watch. Two hours had passed already, and we hadn't reached the face yet.

"Reckon another…" I turned towards where the other three were stood. They were in deep conversation. I was unlikely to get an answer from them. "Couple of hours Steve. I'll give you a shout once we're off the face."

"Got ye."

"Where's machine?"

"On way down for third. Ged's got the lads to work through snap." *Wow number three.*

"Thanks Steve."

I returned to the centre of the road hoping they'd heard that last comment. They were still in deep conversation. The Manager seemed quite animated. He was pointing towards Tuffman. I waited. Not wanting to interrupt. It was the DD that moved away first. He headed towards me.

"Right Mick. Shall we continue." The other two were yet to make a move. "Dayah worry bout them two. They'll catch us up." We continued to walk inbye. "Hear you're gonna Graham House start of next year. Technical Residential, isi?"

"Yeah. Mr Creed mentioned it last week."

"Just a heads up. Coal Boards Technical Director is giving a talk beginning of next month. At Leigh Miners. Thas worth gonna, good bloawke he is. My money's on him becomin next Chairman."

"Do you know the date?"

"I'll check when we get up. Subject's bout cost cutting."

"No surprises there then." Perhaps it wasn't the best comment to make. I didn't get a response.

"Best wait till the others catch up." The other two had started walking towards us.

"He's not such a baddin Mr Tuffman. He has your interest at heart. Seen too many lads fall by the wayside. Got be tough." I found it hard to believe how open and honest the DD was being with me. I took an instant liking to the man. Unlike the other fella. "Just saying to Mick here bout being tough as Undermanager." The other two had now caught up with us.

"Very true Deputy Director. Need to show the men who's boss." Tuffman responded. *Can't wait for you to meet Ged.* The Manager made no comment.

I began to move inbye once more. "What's happened here lad?" We'd only travelled a few yards when Tuffman began to point either side of the road.

"Where we started the floor dint. Save sending the dirt out and having to use empty mine cars. Plus, there no means of tipping it onto belt."

"What bout ventilation?"

"As long as we keep it up against the legs and no more than three feet high. No problem with gas so far. Air velocity up slight but no big deal."

"Something I insisted on." The Manager added. The comment put paid to any further discussion. We continued forward. Two hundred yards further in we passed the Hausherr Dinter.

"Where's panel for this thing?" I pointed ahead. It was sat on a pair of short RSJ's. The lads had accidently buried it once already. I'd got them to dig it out only last week.

"Who's return end Deputy Mick?"

"Bobby." *Oops!* "Rob Flannagan and Freddy Clough in maingate."

"Plus, the District Deputy we've already met. Little bit extravagant don't you think Mr Creed?" Once again, the Manager chose to ignore Tuffman's comment. I looked towards the DD. He winked.

We weren't far from the return end of the face now. The smell of the recently filled pack carried towards us. Intermittently mixed with damp timber. A pack of arches lay neatly stacked to one side. Along with struts and fishplates. I assumed the hessian bag on top contained the inch bolts. The sound of the Webster filling out onto the panzer and its tracking backwards and forwards. At least that meant everyone would be active and not sat down. I wasn't sure how that would go down with Tuffman. The lights ahead confirmed what I'd heard. Other than one. *For fucks sake! It can't be!*

Ged was sat on a stack of chockwood. He looked towards us as we approached. "Took your time Mick. Had me waiting at maingate for a time. Olden's couldn't keep up? Now Pat how you doin lad?" I needed this like a hole in the head. I wasn't sure how the Manager would react.

"All good thanks Ged."

"Bloody ell Ged. Not seen you for some time." The DD added.

"Evan you too. Afraid not been around much. What with strike and all that." The DD began laughing as did the Manager. I couldn't believe what I was witnessing. Ged knew the DD too and by all accounts they were on first name terms.

"Who the fucks he?" Tuffman whispered to me.

"Chargehand. Ged Shalla."

The Manager and DD sat down alongside Ged. Tuffman and I remained standing.

"Don't think you've met Derek Tuffman. Area Production Manager." Ged looked towards Tuffman without making any comment. Tuffman did likewise. The feeling towards one another must have been mutual. They'd obviously taken an instant dislike to one another. Tuffman moved off towards the Webster. I followed. The two of the return lads were walking towards us.

"Morning Mick."

"Morning lads. Where's Bobby?"

"Heard you were coming in. Fucked off towards maingate." One of them answered laughing. The Webster was still tracking backwards and forwards filling out.

"Who's that on the cable then?"

"Fitter. Brian. Had to change a damaged bagging. Can't hang about Mick bout to set legs." They continued outbye. I quickly moved forward to catch up with Tuffman.

154

"What's the machine your using?"

"Webster cutter loader."

"Model?" *How the fuck would I know that?*

"Hmm..."

"SL120." Brian responded. "Morning Mick."

"Morning Brian." Tuffman had made no attempt to converse with the lads. Obviously not comfortable with that side of things. Once more he moved forward. The look on Brian's face said it all. "I'll catch you later."

"One thing Mick. Can you check with George to get some more emulsifying oil. Almost out."

"Will do."

Tuffman was stood to one side as Graham continued loading out. I stood alongside. Tracking back in Graham spotted me. He stopped the machine.

"Alreyt Mick."

"Morning fella."

"See Ged's got his audience. Never known a guy talk so fuckin much."

"Bet you wouldn't say that to his face." Graham laughed nodding his head. He started tracking forward. I looked towards the roof. A crown was sat on the horseheads, struts already in place. Additional lights reflected off the airborne dust and on the face of the heading. I turned to see Graham's two mates returning. Each carrying a single leg a piece over their shoulder. The sound of the Webster increased as the panzer began to slow. I moved across to the face and nearest DAC.

"Hello stageloader. Hello Paul where we stopped." Before Paul answered Les shouted.

"Breaking a lump maingate end." I was so pleased that today of all days all the lads were communicating.

"You need a lump breaker." Tuffman had appeared alongside. I wasn't sure how to respond. We'd recently fitted one in C15's, by all accounts the crusher had certainly reduced delays. Which was ideal with the coal being sent onto to Fiddlers Ferry. Here, however, I was led to believe was increasing the domestic product. I guessed Tuffman would know this anyway. I decided to remain silent on the subject.

"You need to get tougher with this lot. Too easy from what I've seen so far. Remember who won the strike." The interruption on the DAC caused me to turn away.

"Mick, just to let you know. George's bin on. Couple of bad stitchers need doin on maingate belt." The message from Paul couldn't have been timelier.

155

Giving me chance to avoid answering Tuffman's comment. As I knew he wouldn't like the answer.

"Thanks Paul. I'll get him to arrange. Where's machine now?"

"Are you fuckin listening to me." I turned to face Tuffman. It wasn't the surprise from the anger of his comment. It was the shock at being dug in the side of the ribs.

"What?" I responded angrily.

"I said are you listening to me." This time he followed with a clenched fist wrapping my knuckles. The surprise at the physical abuse from this man was only matched by the dilemma I now faced. Should I respond by returning the compliment? I guessed that may result in something I didn't want to happen.

"Yeah, I'm listening and I'm trying to run a face. I won't get into detail about the strike cause in my opinion it was a complete fuck up in industrial relations. Showing who's got the biggest dick doesn't make it right. From what I've seen on here it's about working together. Not against one another. It's all very well being sat in a fuckin office in Anderton House or fuckin Staffordshire House with all your minions bowing and fuckin scraping to you. This is where it happens. This is where the action is. Not sat up there wondering what you're goin to have for fuckin lunch." I couldn't stop. This guy had so wound me up from the minute we'd met. And now the cheeky cunt was getting physical with me. Well, there's only so much I could take. The appearance of the Manager and DD caused me to stop.

"Warrayogooenonabou? Am ya okay?"

"Yeah fine. Mick's just explaining to me the merits of teamwork." There followed an uncomfortable silence. Broken by the DD.

"Well, are we moving or what?"

We continued down the face, no further discussion taking place between the two of us. Until about half way down I realised the Manager and DD were some way back.

"Right Mick tell me what you know regarding the product and market place." I was surprised at Tuffman's question, considering our little altercation earlier.

"I know the current demand exceeds our rate of supply. More than half the output is transported via the merry-go-round rail system to Fiddlers Ferry Power Station."

"Any idea its capacity?"

"Two thousand megawatt."

"How big are the hopper wagons?"

"Thirty tonne. Ability to load a thousand tonnes in less than half an hour."

"What about the rest?"

"High quality washed coal provided to our mix of industrial customers. Including Local Authorities, schools, hospitals, chemical works, textile firms and a number of other smaller companies that have converted from oil to coal. Local homes too. We supply thirty local merchants."

"You mentioned the deal with Crosfields earlier. Can you tell me anything else?"

"Crosfield and Sons at Bank Quay works six miles away. We're providing up to fifteen million therms per annum. In total Parkside provides seventy-five per cent of the firm's energy requirements."

"You have been doing your homework."

"You two not been falling out again?" The DD and Manager had caught back up with us.

The rest of the visit went without any further controversy. Even the introduction to Freddy. As ever however they missed meeting Bobby. The Manager seemed happy enough as did the DD. Which pleased me. I wasn't so sure about Tuffman, but would he ever be happy. His last comment to me when we were travelling the maingate.

"Face should be doing four, five shears a shift consistently." I didn't reply. The coal continued to come. The sound of the belt confirmed that. Occasionally I glanced across. The black stuff was piled high to the gunnels. I never wanted our journey outbye to stop.

When we reached the Meeting Station the DD turned to me and shouted.

"Thi coming out with us Mick."

"No need to get back." The noise from the chute was deafening. "Make sure that keeps coming." I raised my hand towards the chute.

"Good lad. I've enjoyed the visit. Just keep it up. We'll have you an Undermanager before you know it."

"Thanks. Like to think it's a team effort."

"May as well tell you before we leave. Mr Tuffman has been assigned your mentor. He'll be seeing you on a regular basis." *How fuckin lucky am I.* I nodded my head.

"Alsithy in bout months' time." Tuffman added.

"Do me a favour Mick. Just make sure riders ready for us."

"Will do Mr Creed." Final round of handshakes complete they continued outbye. I watched as they went, flexing the fingers on my right hand. Why the fuck Tuffman felt the need to crush my hand I could only guess. Turning, I headed back inbye as the maingate belt began to slow.

"Who's got the latch on?"

☐

9. The Accident

The previous week had been particularly tough. Not just with the big visit. Working over each shift and then back in Saturday morning on a six one. It was time I did something with the family. I'd checked the weather forecast for Sunday reckoned it was going to be another hotten.

"How bout we go for a picnic tomorrow." I mentioned to Annie that night after I'd put the kids to bed and read them a story. She'd come up later to wake me.

"Yeah. That sounds great. Aren't you tired though? You've been putting some hours in this week, and you worked today." I always appreciated when the missus made her positive comments. What she wasn't aware of things were about to change. I couldn't complain, we'd had six months on regular days. From next month the face would be going on two shifts. L31's had ceased production. We'd be joined by Colin Keys, the Face Overman and his Chargehand, Tommy Beddows, neither of whom I'd met before. There were changes afoot elsewhere too. W6's had finished, replaced by W8's. Plus the first face in the Wigan Five Foot V24's.

"No, I'll be fine."

"Where you thinkin?"

"Delamere Forest."

"Great stuff. The kids will be made up."

□

I was still on a high after the visit to Leigh Miners. The talk provided had given me renewed confidence in our future. It was obvious the industry would be on a smaller scale and there were tough times ahead, but at least there would be a secure and exciting future.

"How did it go last neet?" I was suddenly brought back to the present. George had climbed onto the open topped E3 manrider. "Cant move up Mick" He asked laughing.

"Sorry George." I responded sliding across the wooden slats against the metal arm rest. "Yeah, very good actually. The Coal Board's Technical Director is something else." Without warning the manrider began to move inbye. I grabbed the sides of my donkey jacket. Pulling it closer together, the change in temperature now apparent as Autumn moved closer to Winter. It didn't help the buttons to fasten my jacket were now missing.

"He's from round ere in he?"

"Yeah." I shouted in response, competing with the belt conveyor alongside. "Bold Colliery originally."

"Pinch cock?"

"Thanks." George held his tin of snuff towards me with one hand, the other shielding it from the swirling ventilation. We said little more travelling inbye. My thoughts still on last night's paper.

We began to slow as we approached the bottom of the one in four brow. I hadn't noticed the conveyor alongside had stopped too. "Ast spoke with Colin?" George asked.

"No. Problems?"

"Reckons we'll need some lads stop over. Get some dowels in bottom end. He's ere now. Let him tell tha." Colin was my opposite number now we were on two shifts. It was a different experience from single shifting. At least now it was a shared responsibility when we came to explain why were weren't achieving the desired production. I liked Colin and his chargehand Tommy. Two completely different characters. Colin must have only been in his thirties but looked a lot older. Such a serious demeanour compared to Tommy. He was always laughing, good natured. I could and was learning from them both.

"Planning on doin a full shift today, Mick?" He asked as I climbed out of the carriage. I smiled. Ahead I could see Tommy updating Ged.

"Think you've got plans for me doin an extended shift."

"Aye, ast George told tha. Maingate looking rough again. Anyway, init time George covered overtime for a change."

"Bloody ell Colin. Friday night's dance night. Him and his missus practicing foxtrot tonight. Big competition at the weekend."

"Seems to manage it when it's dayshift." I laughed. "Right. Machine's at thirty chock. Ready to come in for the first time. Tops getting thin. Spalling like fuck again. Hence the reason tops dropping out. Lads have put some dowels in but think it might be best if you get lads put some of them tandem dowels in. Pepper the place, Tryin fettle it"

It was a good call. Tony from Exchem had been to see us the previous week to explain how tandem dowels worked. One of the six-foot wooden dowels had a plastic sleeve stapled to one end. Drilling longer holes allowed you to insert two dowels. It reduced the downtime for dowelling. Simple idea but seemed effective.

"Okay, let's see how it goes."

"Alreyt Mick." Tommy Beddows was now alongside.

"Hiya Tommy."

"How'd tha put up with a cunt like im?" I laughed.

"Ged, he's an acquired taste." I looked inbye to where Ged was stood. He obviously understood what was being said.

"I'll give you acquired taste tha chaykee bastard."

"Come on lads, let's be making a move." The driver of the manrider shouted as he stood in the front carriage.

"Right Mick alsithy. You on at weekend?"

"Yeah. Sat twelve noon till six and Sunday early one. Six till one."

"Might see you at some point."

"I can't speyk, pair of greedy bastards. What you both saving for? Toyota Celica?" Tommy added as he climbed in alongside Colin."

"Alsithy."

The shift had started well. One shear complete, about to start on the second. I headed up towards the panels. Yet to break the news to my missus I'd be home late. I put a call through to control

"Steve do me a favour mate. Can you call my missus and ask her to get me a pack of Guinness when she's out today. Yeah, I know it's early in the shift, but I'm going to have to stop over. Want to get some roof bolting done at the maingate end. Yeah, I'm sorting that now. Machine? Should be at the return. Cheers fella. Speak later. Oh, don't forget, ask the nightshift to fetch me and the lads some snappin. Me plus four." I replaced the handset.

"Fuckin ell Mick thy missus must be very understanding."

"Yeah, used to it by now. Anyway, where's Ged?" I responded to Paul.

"Last time I heard he was at top end with fitter. Webster's acting up again."

"Hello Paul."

"Hi David."

"Machine's at top end. We're heading back down once lads have finished timbering." I leaned across to the DAC.

"David, Mick here. What about the bi-di?" As I finished the sentence Paul reached across and hit the stop button. The scraper chain began to slow. Followed by a calm silence. The sound of the hydraulic pump gently throbbing in the background. I leaned my head against the DAC. If we couldn't get into the return that would mean both ends falling behind again.

"Who's got the lock out on the x cut?" Steve shouted.

"Mick, Ged's told me. They've not moved up here. Still working on the Webster. Not moved all shift." *Webster cutter/loader fuckin complete waste of time. Spent more time on stop than operating.*

"Thanks David. Let Ged know I'm on my way up." As the maingate belt kicked in it was followed by the stage loader pre-start. I turned back towards Paul. "Do me a favour when George gets here. Ask him to arrange with the haulage lads a half cut with wooden dowels and resin to the return. Make sure it including those dowels with the yellow plastic sleeve."

160

"Just a heads-up Mick. Not sure you'll have any lads for overtime. Heard them talking on the way in."

"That's what they fuckin think."

I left Paul and headed towards the maingate end. Squeezing passed the Pantech I could feel the perspiration once more running down my chest. To steady myself I placed a hand on the inch and quarter rubber hose. Withdrawing my hand almost immediately due to the heat. Once passed the Pantech I slowed my pace. The floor a quagmire of dirt and leaking hydraulic fluid. In parts sliding I continued forward. Ahead the twins were lifting a crown onto the horseheads. They made no reply to my greeting as I passed beneath. In the pack area the lads had already hung the plastic bag. I could see lights further up the face as they helped with timbering the bad ground. Repositioning my oil lamp alongside my rescuer I climbed over the spills. The coal in places having already spalled. The very reason we had bad ground. The unsupported weak roof exposed once more. Keeping a careful eye on the face I moved forward quickly.

"Now lads. How's it goin?"

"Reckon another half hour or so Mick. We'll need some more chock wood and ideally another half dozen split bars."

"I'll sort once I get to the return. You okay to stop over tonight, Cliff?"

"Sorry canna do tonight Mick got practice. Big rugby match Saturday. Playing the Golborne lads. Beat them and we're in the semi's." It wasn't the answer I wanted. Cliff was one of my regulars for stopping over.

"What about you two?"

"Sorry Mick not tonight." Les answered. "Got summut on." His mate was shaking his head too.

"Snuff Mick?" Cliff offered. He could see I was disappointed by the response.

"I go on." Cliff held the already opened tin of hedges. I took a small amount between thumb and forefinger quickly inhaling up each nostril. Climbing onto the spills I lifted myself up between the chocks. The three chocks they'd been working on now tightly packed. Split bars running across the canopies above which a number of chockwood stacks filled the gap. I estimated about four foot in height. Further up the face another three to do.

I climbed back down. "Nice one. Can you make sure…."

"Fuckin ell Mick, not think we know. Machines set up ready." To confirm his comment Cliff shone his cap lamp onto the hydraulic drilling machine lying in the chock track. Baggings already attached.

"Nice one. I'll catch you guys later." I climbed back onto the pans. Grabbing the haulage chain, I continued up towards the return. I detected a slight tension in the chain. The sound of the pre-alarm kicked in. No sooner had it started it was silenced. I waited before jumping back into the chock line.

"David, Johnny where's my split bars and chockwood?"

"Fuck mop." I wouldn't have expected any other response from JB.

"On it now Cliff."

"Thanks David." The shearer operators response was enough to keep me moving along the pans. Stooped, I quickened my pace. Ever watchful on the face for any spalling but a little more relaxed as the middle of the face tended to remain intact.

There was one more job I needed to do before reaching the top end. I spotted the shovel standing upright on the back legs a little further ahead. Leaning between the chocks front legs I grabbed it. Moving back onto the pans I used it to scrap against the floor. Kneeling down to examine the exposed mineral. Satisfied I returned the shovel and continued my journey. The space available not allowing me to stand fully upright. My unnatural posture causing me to perspire more than usual. My neck began to ache. Twenty chocks further along I stopped for a minute. The sweat poured freely from my forehead. Ahead I could see the red flashing of the lock out box. I was near to the top end. I reached into my pocket for my tin of snuff. Extracting a small amount, I inhaled. Once more looking towards the return end. It was then I spotted one of the chocks sitting out of line. *Fuckin hundred and six chock. Should have been sorted on days!*

Replacing the tin of snuff, I moved forward once more. Leaning into the chock I could see the double acting ram, the clevis and ram still attached by a lifting chain to the spills. I removed my notebook. As I did so the pen fell onto the pans.

"Take your latch off Cliff. Timber's ready cock." I quickly grabbed the pen and jumped back in between the chocks. The pre-start kicked in. Quickly followed by the clanking of panzer chain against the empty pans.

"David do us a favour cock. Can you cut me a couple of lids." Cliff added.

I scribbled on the paper to get the ink flowing. Making a note to check where the replacement ram had got to. Popping it back into my top pocket I continued.

Having stretched the panzer, the lads were loading chockwood. Somewhat surprised to see movement from the figure ahead.

"Fuckin ell JB didn't know you had legs." The bulk of the man struggled to turn to face me. He was holding a piece of chockwood.

"Fuck off you cheeky Scouse twat." His black face contorted with anger. A piece of bacca fell onto his chin. "I'll shove this up your arse if you don't watch it." I took the opportunity to jump back onto the pans and move quickly passed

JB. He struggled to turn but still managed to hurl the piece of timber towards me.

"Better luck next time cunt."

"Fuck off!"

The shearer was a little further ahead. I climbed back into the chock line. David was throwing pieces of chockwood towards me. "Any idea where Ged is?"

"Sorry Mick didn't see you there. He's with the fitter. Webster's about ready to try."

That sounded like good news. "Sorry mate can I squeeze passed you." As he moved to one side I smiled. There was nothing of him. I'd suggested to him previously a good pan of stew wouldn't do him any harm. "You stopping over tonight?"

"Sorry Mick. Promised missus I'd be wom on time neet. Quiz neet at local."

"Fuckin ell Dave not you as well. What's up with you all. Thought you were saving for a B&B down South?"

"I am. Don't want to be doin it on my own. Spend any more time ere and missus will be gone." I laughed. He had a point stopping over till the early hours every time we were on noons was a lot to ask for. I certainly knew that from my own experience.

Finally, out into the return I was able to stretch I could see Ged ahead sat on the machine. The place was beginning to smell like a timber yard.

"Believe you've sorted it?"

"Yeah, me and my mate Brian."

"Could do with your help in persuading the lads to stop over."

"Why what's up?"

"They've all got summat on." Without another word being spoke he jumped off the machine. Crouching against the DAC.

"Les."

"Ged."

"You stopping over neet with Mick?"

"Sorry Ged, can't summat on."

"Les, you're stopping over." There followed a long silence. I did feel sorry for Les I could imagine what he was saying to the others. My priority however was the face. "Les?"

"Okay Ged. Will do." The response from the other two was the same. Other than David. He always put up some resistance but not for long. I was never sure whether it was to wind Ged up or genuine.

"Sorry Ged. It's like I told Mick. Quiz neet to neet." And to emphasise the point he added. "Grand finale."

163

"Grand fuckin final? David don't push me son. I'd be happy to come down there and throttle your scrawny little fuckin neck." Again, a long silence. Longer than normal. I watched as Ged scrambled to his feet. "I'll kill the little cunt." David must have been watching from below.

"Okay Ged, will do." I smiled. Ged on the other hand decided to go down the face anyway.

"Mick fuck off out way." Graham shouted towards me. He was driving the Webster towards the face of the heading. There wasn't a great deal of the shift left. I decided to continue outbye to make sure we had plenty of resin and wooden dowels.

One of the upsides of stopping over was the snappin the night shift brought in. Usually, meat and potato pies or my favourite small meat pies. Still warm and the grease seeping out. I remember when I was on back up at Cronton. On noons myself and Ernie would often stop over carrying the steel from where the haulage lads dropped it off. Taking it to the heading lads. When we got to the surface the snapping was waiting for us in the lamp room. A meat pie and pint of ice-cold milk.

I'd left the four lads stopping over at the maingate end. I went out to fetch the snapping from the bottom of E3. The manrider was already discharging the L31 face lads as I arrived.

"Alreyt Mick. One of tha lads must have an admirer. Canteen girls have sent tha two pies a piece and a sticky bun." He was holding a small cardboard box. One of those previously used for storing small cartons of milk. Each pair of pies were wrapped separate in white paper bags already stained form the leaking meat juice. The smell drifted across; I began to salivate. The buns collectively wrapped in a larger bag.

"Thanks, the lads will be pleased." I turned to head back towards L19's.

"Mick, how long reckon tha'll be?" The lad in charge of the manrider shouted across.

"Couple more hours."

"Alreyt. I've got a couple of runs of steel to fetch in. Say one o'clock?"

"Do for me. Thanks." I headed back. Once at the Meeting Station I had to stop. It was too much. I ate the first of my pies.

"Fuckin ell Mick hold off. They'll av it stalled." I was pushing against the back of Les. The fine black dust falling from the hole. The smell of burning now evident. I'd replaced Dave. He'd gone out to the stage loader for his sticky bun. He had a point. The drill rod had begun to struggle the return of tailings slowing too.

"Sorry fella. Want me to av a go?"

"If you think tha can manage it." Les responded laughing. I took the hand-held compressed air drilling machine, twisting it as he held the drill rod. Then replacing the three-foot rod with the longer six foot. I repositioned the drill machine and shoved it back into the hole. "Just a mo Mick." Les reached back into the chock line to retrieve his dirty plastic bottle of water. Gulping it down, oblivious to it spilling from the corner of his mouth. His lips returning to their natural colour against his blackened face. His eyes bloodshot. He held the bottle towards me.

"No, I'm good thanks." I wasn't really. My whole back was aching and my arms ready for dropping off. I couldn't imagine how Les and his mates felt. They were at it all the time.

"Snuff?" He took the tin from me. Inhaling through each nostril he passed it back. I shivered. For the short time I'd been stood there the sweat on me had begun to dry out. "Come on let's get goin. Another couple should do us."

I braced myself as Les put his weight against my back. The stench of sweat and body odours enveloped us both unable to discern our individual smells. I squeezed the trigger. Gently at first. Now rotating at full speed, I pushed it to the back of the hole. Les added his weight. Tailings began to follow the spiral of the rod. Falling to the floor creating a mound of fine dust. Within minutes the hole was complete. I began to move the rod backwards and forwards to clear the hole. Les removed the six-foot rod. Careful not to touch the Secopic drill bit he examined it closely.

"Mick we'll need to fetch some more bits."

"Yeah. There's a sand bag full of them by the panels we'll take em out with us. I'll drop em in the workshops get the lads to sharpen them." We placed half a dozen tubes of resin into the hole. Using a single dowel, I pushed the resin in as far as I could. Les held another wooden dowel, the plastic sleeve already in place. I positioned the second into the sleeve. Matching up the two chamfered ends we pushed the lengthened dowel into the hole. The tubes of resin continued to the back of the hole. A final shove ruptured one of the tubes. Placing the adaptor into the machine we placed it onto the protruding dowel. I squeezed the trigger. Slowly at first. The dowel moved forward. Squeezing the trigger further the dowel span faster, resin began to fall freely from the hole. The intoxicating, smell of the epoxy resin increasing as Les exerted additional pressure on my back.

"That should do. Come on let's clear up and fuck off."

□

The following week as we arrived at the bottom of the E3 manrider Colin pulled me to one side.

"Mick, can I ask tha something in confidence." I knew what was coming.

"Fire away fella." He looked around before continuing.

"When tha phone yon mon when tha gets back up pit. Canst make sense of what lads saying."

"Pissed you mean?"

"Sounds like it to me."

"You get used. The best of it is, whatever you tell him he never remembers. Shame really, he's a good man. Working with him for a few years now. Reckon he's under a lot of pressure from the Manager."

"Not likely to get the permanent position then?" I had given this some thought. Particularly as the job for Howard Davies position had been advertised recently. I'd even applied for it. Not that I would get it, but I wanted to show willing."

"I thought at one time he would. Not so sure now."

Arriving back on the surface and having showered I popped into the canteen for a new tin of snuff. Steve from the control room was just ahead of me. The smell of bacon and the sound of eggs being fried filled the room.

"Alright Steve"

"Hi Mick. Don't often see you in your clean." I laughed. He had a point. "Mick if you don't mind me saying. Don't ask me to phone your missus again. Got a right gob full I did."

"When you on about?"

"Last week, phoning up to get you that pack of Guinness. Give me a right gob full she did. Said you needed to be home on time and help with the kids." I was surprised by Steve's comment. So unlike Annie.

"Sorry about that mate. She must have been in one."

"Sounded like it. If you don't mind me askin, is she a lot older than you?"

"Only a couple of years. Why do you ask?"

"Oh, nothing really."

"Mick, what can I do for you?" One of the canteen ladies interrupting our conversation.

"Large tin of Hedges please Mary."

"I'll see tha Mick."

"All out of Hedges, I'm afraid."

"I, see you, Steve."

"Got M^C Chrystals but only the small tins."

"That'll do."

Forty minutes later I arrived home. Annie was in the kitchen making tea.

"Hiya. Dad's home." I shouted.

"Hiya love. Tea won't be long."

"Okay. Where's the troublesome twosome?" I asked as I headed towards the living room. They were both glued to the telly, watching Rainbow. It looked as though Bungle was throwing a wobbler. "Hello you two." Neither turned, although I did receive a short comment from Jamie.

"Hi Dad." We'd recently invested in a VHS video player. It had the ability to record programmes. Rainbow being the kids favourite.

I headed back towards the kitchen.

"How's your day been?"

"Kids mostly. Been in all day with the weather being so rubbish."

"Tell you what. Why don't we go Chester Zoo at the weekend, haven't been there for ages."

"Yeah, think the kids would like that."

"Remember last Friday when I asked you to get me some Guinness."

"Yeah."

"Were you annoyed with me?"

"No why would I be?"

"Just wondered."

"Oops. I know what you're on about. Mum was here when the pit called. I couldn't get to the phone quick enough. She was giving some guy a mouthful on the other end." I began laughing, knowing the mother-in-law as I did. Someone you don't want to be getting in an argument with.

"Has it caused a problem?"

"No not really." I was sure Steve would get over it.

☐

Climbing into my car, I couldn't remember the last time I'd left the pit so early. From starting work at six, I was away by ten thirty. Leaving George in charge, we'd already completed one shear. I was off to Anderton House again, this time to meet my Supervising Officer, Derek Tuffman. After my last visit to Anderton House with the DDM, things had changed big time, finally getting a permanent Overmen's position. What surprises would be in store for me this time?

The Manager had asked to see me the week before to advise me of the meeting. Mr Creed was now aware of my application for the vacant Undermanager's position, advising me I wouldn't be getting an interview. It had already been decided who would be replacing Howard Davies. I guessed that wouldn't be John Meriden but thought better than to ask.

Turning into the entrance, the place seemed busier than last time. Probably because it was a Monday. It was a dark miserable day, as the six-storey glass fronted building suddenly appeared from behind the line of trees. Instantly I could feel my gut began to move. *For fucks sake man get a grip.* It settled a little as my favourite sculpture came into view. It conveyed all that needed to be

167

expressed. The grit, determination, and fortitude of a miner. It was and always would be special to me. I struggled to find a parking spec, having to walk a little further this time to the entrance. Time to straighten my tie. The sculpture, however keeping me company as I walked forward.

Inside the place was heaving. The smell of polished furniture competing with the various aromas of aftershave. Conversations filled the air, the constant ringing of telephones in the background. I spotted a tall gentleman in a long black trench coat move away from the reception desk. I recognised his face but wasn't sure from where. I took the opportunity to move into the vacated space.

"Good morning. Mick Gibson to see Mr Tuffman." The young lady smiled, a kindly smile, exposing her white teeth accentuated by the ruby red lipstick. She checked some papers lying on the desk.

"He's expecting you. Go straight through. Second floor." That was my first surprise of the morning. "Have you been before?"

"Yes, thank you." I turned towards the glass double doors. I was met by a number of envious stares from those waiting. I guessed most of them were reps attempting to persuade the powers to be to buy from them. The young receptionist had timed it to perfection. The doors locking device clicking as I reached the handle.

Walking into the lift I hit the relevant button. *Second floor heh!* Black trench coat man joined me.

"Morning." I offered. He never responded, not even to look at me. My black eyes never helped. I left him at the second floor. He remained. *Gosh he must be important.*

I was surprised to see the Area Production Manager waiting for me outside his office. Smiling. Surprise number two.

"Good morning, Mick. How are you young man?"

"Good thank you, Mr Tuffman." He was shorter than I remembered. I felt a little uncomfortable as he was still smiling. He looked even more like Freddy Forsythe. Blue blazer, regulation brass buttons and plain beige slacks. Light blue shirt with matching tie. A blue chequered kerchief protruding from his top pocket. His brown brogue shoes were the finishing touch. I had to give it to the guy, he was certainly a smart dresser.

"Come on in." He turned towards his office. "Drink?"

"Coffee. Black no sugar."

"Just the way I like it. This is Penelope my secretary."

Penelope was sat at a desk as we entered. The layout identical to the DDM's office. A large typewriter the only item on the desk.

"Two black coffee's Penelope."

"Yes certainly, Mr Tuffman." She stood. Blimey she was gorgeous. Long black hair with matching long mascaraed eyelashes. She was wearing a black frock, clinging tightly to the curves of her body. *I guess Mr Tuffman spent plenty of time in the office.*

The inner office was off to the right. "Come in grab a pew." It was quite sparse, containing a desk, a large round meeting room table with chairs either side. An opened pack of King-Sized Marlboro Red cigarettes lay open against a glass ash tray. It contained a single stub. *Obviously not under the same pressure as Mr Keech.* Before sitting he took a Manila envelope from his desk. From it he extracted a copy of the National Coal Board Internal Application Form. It was the one I'd recently completed for the ET Scheme.

"Started with the NCB as a Student Apprentice. How come you ended up on Mining Craft?"

"Failed my first year OND. Transferred to Technicians Final."

"Hence the reason you took HNC and gained your Undermanager's papers."

"Yeah. Then Degree to take my Manager's papers."

"Says here you're still waiting for the results from the exam held in November last year."

"That was correct at the time. I applied to the ETS, January this year."

"For the length of time you spent at college, you could have become a doctor." I wasn't sure how to answer the question. He had a point though. "Do you mind?" He'd removed a Marlboro from the pack.

"No not at all." He removed a small gold coloured petrol lighter from his trouser pocket. Flicking the lid back, a bright yellow flame appeared. The tip of the cigarette glowing brighter as he inhaled. Releasing the vapour from his nose and mouth. The smell richer and sweeter than the usual fags the lads smoked. A series of smoke circles appeared. Not dissimilar to those produced by the mother-in-law from her Woodbines.

"Coffee gentlemen." It was now a tossup from watching the circles of smoke or Penelope.

"Thank you." I said. By the time I turned she was already leaving the room.

"See you've been applying for Undermanager's jobs in Nottinghamshire and Yorkshire?"

"Yeah."

"Not happy with Lancashire then?"

"No not at all. It's just I've been told if I want to progress in the industry I should be prepared to move." He nodded his approval.

"What about your missus? Would she be happy leaving family and friends behind?" I'd never ever had the discussion with Annie.

169

"Oh, yeah. One hundred per cent behind me." His smile suggested I was talking bollocks. His questioning seemed to go on forever.

"What's this about a visit to the Ruhr Coalfield? Learn much?"

"Yeah. Gang of us went over. See how they operated. Biggest surprise was the numbers of men manning the coalface."

"Unlike here you mean?"

"I'd like to think we'd be classed as more efficient." He reached forward to stub out what little remained of his Marlboro.

"Don't have strikes." I was beginning to feel hot. The room now a little stuffy. I wasn't sure how to answer that. The knock on the door coming to my rescue.

"Your eleven thirty is here Mr Tuffman."

"Thanks Penelope. Won't be long." He stood and walked across to open the window slightly. "I think Mick for the time being you continue as Face Overman and keep applying for shift Undermanager's jobs. Get some interviews under your belt." I was feeling quite relieved. The meeting hadn't been too bad.

"Yeah, will do."

"There's one thing however I'd like you to do for me." He was now staring straight at me. "When you're back in work tomorrow. Pick out the biggest hairy arsed ripper and give him a good kicking. Create a walk out. Show'em who's boss." I remained silent, not sure I'd heard correctly.

"Did you…?"

"Yes, I did."

☐

I was off the next day. Me and the missus were off to Whiston Hospital. We had an appointment with a doctor whom I'd been referred to for my vesectomy. The instruction from Mr Tuffman still playing on my mind. Surely, I'd misunderstood him. Why the hell would anyone want to piss the men off again. It was only seven months ago since the strike ended. I decided to leave taking any action for the time being.

It would be another two weeks before I was reminded by the Manager of the action I needed to take. Having done so we got the desired result. I hadn't kicked any of the rippers. My preferred target, Johnny off the shearer was the man.

"Well Mick, that proved popular."

"I know George. I just hope the noon shift don't follow suit." We'd just arrived at the Undermanager's office.

"Now lad. Manager wants to see us both." John stood as we entered. Unusually John was in his clean. I wasn't sure if he were aware of the instruction I'd been given. I certainly hadn't shared it with George or the other two officials.

"See you tomorrow, George."

"Aye that tha will."

I followed John out of the office towards the Top Shunt.

"Don't mind me asking, where you off to?"

"Anderton House." No further information was forthcoming. Obviously, something he didn't want to discuss.

"Go straight through. He's expecting you." Susan offered as we passed her office.

The Manager was sat at his desk. "Take a seat gentlemen." He waited whilst we removed two chairs from beneath the meeting room table. Placing them opposite his desk. "Right lad tell me exactly what happened." I did as requested. Leaving out the bit when I'd kicked Johnny and his attempt to knock shit out of me. "Did they leave the place safe?"

"Yeah. Once Ged had told them it was a walk out, he told both rips to set any outstanding steel. Packs were complete anyway." I glanced across to John. He was staring down at the desk. He looked like shite. "Panzer and stage loader were already clear of coal."

"What about electrician and fitter?"

"No, they didn't go." The Manager nodded, reaching for his already prepared pipe. He struck a match and began to draw on the stem of the mouth piece. Strands of smoke drifting from the corner of his mouth. I was anticipating the smell of St Bruno. He returned my glare.

"Go on then. Fuck off, get a bath. Let's see what tomorrow brings." I climbed out of the chair, half expecting John to follow me. He was now looking towards the Manager.

"What time you seeing him?"

"Two o'clock Mr Creed." I'd lingered a little too long. The Manager glanced back towards me. I quickly left without hearing another word spoken. *Who the hell was John meeting?*

The next few weeks as we approached Christmas passed without incident. Little more said of the walkout. It was as if nothing had happened. John too, seemed more relaxed. Whatever had taken place at Anderton House seemed to have lifted a weight from his shoulders. There was talk of us replacing the panzer chain over Christmas. It was badly worn; the fitters were struggling to keep it tensioned. For whatever reason, the job was cancelled so I decided to take the whole of Christmas off, except for an overtime shift on my birthday.

Time spent with the wife and kids would gain me some brownie points. I was yet to tell the missus about the two residentials in Newcastle-Upon-Tyne.

~~~

1986

Start of the New Year saw a second team come across from L31's. Headed by the Overman Tommy Aldridge and his Chargehand Tommy Millet. Cayle had already given me the heads up that Tommy Millet and Ged had history. Something to do with the strike. It wasn't long before I saw the animosity first hand. We were on noons. As the manrider reached the bottom of E3 many of the dayshift were already there. Mainly because of an electrical fault on the No 3 Pikrose.

Tommy my oppo was at the front. Black as an ousel. His grey tash too. He was smiling, chewing bacca, the juices running down the side of his chin.

"Alreyt Mick?"

"All good thanks Tommy. How have we ended up?" I wasn't actually *alreyt*. Before leaving I'd made Annie a cuppa and gave her the news of my residentials. The first coming up at the end of the month."

"Left half dozen lads stopping over. Completing bi-di at maingate."

"What's that then? Two and a half."

"I lad. Had three if we hadn't had the electrical fault on signal box. One of baggings on thirty-nine chock bin dripping on box. Not sure for how long…" A commotion across from where were stood caused Tommy to cut short our conversation.

"You fuckin cunt."

"Least I don't look like a cunt, you fuckin Pikey." Ged and Tommy Millet were squaring up against one another. Tommy and I stood watching. Although Tommy was bigger than Ged, I didn't rate his chances. Millet resembled a pirate. He could have doubled for Blackbeard.

"Alreyt you two. Let's av some order." Connor Michaels shouted as he walked towards them. He'd been acting as guard. "Come on Ged get thisen and men moving." I decided to walk over. I'd seen enough of Ged over the last eight months to know when the red mist had descended.

"Ged. Come on fella let's be making a move." He looked across to me, his eyes unblinking. He reminded me of a shark I'd seen on television, in one of those Jacques Cousteau episodes. I wouldn't rate a shark's chance the mood he was in. His right fist was clenched shut. It seemed like forever but finally. I watched in relief as he unclenched his fist and smiled towards me. He turned and began making his way inbye.

"Yeah, go on fuck off." Millet's comment caused Ged to stop.

"Hey. Get on the fucking manrider before I put tha on stretcher." Connor had grabbed Millet's arm and shoved him forward to the nearest carriage. And that was it spat over.

"For fucks sake John how, we supposed to manage that?" I'd just walked into the Undermanager's office. I was up early for a First Aid refresher. Colin my counterpart off noons didn't look happy. John Meriden was facing him. Still in his black, both nostrils coated with snuff. Some had dropped onto the front of his boiler suit.

"Sorry lad. Manager's given a clear instruction to cut weekend overtime. You'll have to replace it between shifts. I've got Teddy to load the first lot of thirty metre lengths."

"It's goin to take us over two weeks. The things breakin every other shift." Colin spotted me enter the office. He was shaking his head. "You heard Mick?"

"No. What's up?"

"Our plan to change the full panzer chain this weekend has been cancelled. No overtime. We're expected to change thirty metre lengths between shifts on afters!" That certainly wasn't good news. Not with the trouble we were having of late. I turned towards John.

"Out of my hands." And with that Colin turned and walked out, I followed.

"It'll cost us you know."

"Yeah. It'll take us longer. Not takin into account the delays." Colin seemed not to listen.

"By the way Mick, that slip at return end has spread up the face. Don't look good. If that drops out, you'll know bout it."

I'd never seen Colin like this before. I could well understand him though. I went for a bath. George was just leaving.

"You heard?"

"I Teddy mentioned it to me."

"Tomorrow when you come in hang back at pit bottom. Get as many of those half cuts with the panzer chain towards E3. I'll have a word with Connor Michaels. We'll get as many moved in as we can.

"I, will do cock."

The next day when I arrived in the lamproom I was surprised to see Tommy Aldridge.

"Alreyt Mick."

"Morning Tommy. What you doin up so early?"

"Workshops cock. Still haven't had the tensioning device back for coupling panzer chain."

"Colin tellin me avin use chockwood to tension chain. Slipped last neet nearly took Tommy Beddows ed off."

"Fuck me, That's not good. How did he get on yesterday."

"Did okay. Two shears and a thirty-metre length of chain. Reckons he could have done two lengths if he'd had more chain."

"Yeah. Got George on that this morning."

"Ast Colin mentioned slip to tha at top end."

"Mentioned it yesterday. I was going to have a look at it this morning."

"Hardly moved. Big fucker it is. Just make sure lads know bout it."

I decided to head onto the face via the return. On the rider I'd mentioned the same to Ged. He accompanied me in.

"Nah Scouse what's this bout you goin off on jolly, again."

"I can assure you it's no jolly."

"Fuck off Mick. You can't kid a kidder." He responded laughing. "What's missus had to say bout it?"

"She's over the moon. Second residential within a matter of weeks." We said little more as we continued inbye. I was in some way going to have to make it up with Annie.

As we arrived at the top end. Graham shouted towards us. "Ged ast seen slip on face?"

"Just comin to av a look now cock." I was ahead of Ged and climbed straight onto the panzer.

"Mick. I'd get thisel back in chock line. It's a big fucker tha knows." That was me told.

"Thanks Graham. Will do."

The slip was running at something like sixty degrees to the coal face. Some seven foot in length. I could only guess how far it went up. For some reason, this thing wasn't moving.

"You be careful now." Ged had leaned forward over the spills. Running his hand along the fault line.

"It's like glass. How's the face line lookin?"

"Last drawing, I got off the surveyors, maingate was leading. Just over five metres."

"Might be worthwhile doin a couple of long bi-di's see if we can get through it."

And that's what we did. Not that it made any difference.

The following morning there seemed less cars in the car park than usual. A thin layer of ice sat on each one. For some reason Colin's car was still in its usual place. I guessed Tommy hadn't made it in and he was covering. I began to walk across to the main entrance. It was absolutely freezing. A trail of vapour following me as I moved forward. The place seemed eerily silent. Mr Keech's car was parked up outside his office too. I would normally head straight to the baths. Activity outside John Meriden's office caused a change of plan.

"Fuck me Harry what you doin in at this time?" The NACODS union rep had just left John's office. He didn't look happy.

"Ast not heard lad?"

"No, I've only just come in."

"Colin's in tensive care. Lad's fetched him out last neet." Harry needn't have said anymore. I could imagine what had happened. "Can't hang about lad. Got go see family." With that Harry went. I continued into John's office. He was in his black.

"You heard then?"

"Yeah. Just bumped into Harry."

"Inspector's here this morning. First thing. Best make sure everything's in order."

"What about night shift?"

"Sent home."

"Any idea what happened?"

"They'd finished coaling. Replaced one length of chain, tried for another. Thing got fast. Colin was at top end, saw the problem. Climbed onto the panzer to sort. According to one of his team, time was pressing." I wasn't surprised by John's comment. Colin leading from the front as usual. "And then this solid lump of dirt dropped. Mick it was huge. Must av weighed half a tonne." John had obviously been in to see for himself. "Couldn't shift the thing. Took them two hours to get it off the lad. Had to use pull lifts and lifting chains. Then another two and a half to get him out." John said no more. He seemed wrapped up in his own thoughts.

"Right, I'll get on. Make sure we're ready for Mr Gray."

"Won't be him. Retired. It's a new lad, Van Gogh."

Little wonder the face team were subdued. Word had got out. I sat with Ged on the manrider.

"Surprised the poor bastard's still alive." He offered as I passed him my tin of snuff,

"I wonder if we could have done anymore?"

"Like what? Dowel it? No chance. Something like that, you move forward or wait for it to drop. I wouldn't question yoursen."

We said little else and headed straight to the return. The lump of dirt had been pulled off the face. I guess using the Webster. John hadn't been wrong it was huge. Not so much the length of it but its depth. My stomach turned at the thought of it. It didn't help to see blood splattered on the underside.

"For fucks sake." Was Ged's first comment. "Never had a chance." As we stood there, the return end men began to pass. No one said anything other than taking a cursory glance at the lump of dirt. I never pushed to get coaling. I wanted it to be when they were ready.

The Inspector arrived in the district at ten. Accompanied by the Manager. The place required little prep work. Just stonedusting. The Inspector seemed very sympathetic to what had happened. The only thing he pointed out was a side ranter, some ten yards back. I had it moved forward whilst he was still there. Taking a look at the lump of dirt he shook his head. The Manager said little. From what I'd heard he rated Colin very highly. After they'd been to look at the resultant cavity, they never bothered going through the face they left the same way they'd come in.

I waited at the meeting station to see Tommy Beddows and his team. They'd all turned in for work.

"Alreyt Mick."

"Yeah. Do you need me to stop on?" I asked the District Deputy, Jack.

"No, we'll be fine."

I watched as the team entered the district. Total silence as they passed. I couldn't imagine how they felt. The look of pain and hurt etched on each face. Tommy was near to the back. I never recognised him initially, the first and only time I'd never seen him smiling. He looked up as he passed and nodded. I so wanted to talk to the man but held back. He'd speak when he was ready.

I was about to walk off. A cap lamp in the maingate caught my attention. It was Tommy walking back towards me. He sat, not looking directly at me.

"He just wanted to get the job done. You know what he was like. Saw thopportunity to get a second length in. I was a little further down face. Knew something was wrong when we asked why latch was still on. Didn't get an answer. I made my way to the top end. The lump was the first thing I saw. Mick it wa huge. Then fuck me, I saw his legs. I began shouting his name. One of the lads further down the face must av heard me. Told him we had a buried mon and to get all the team to top end." I said nothing. He turned towards me I wasn't sure if he was waiting for a response. Tears welled up in both eyes. He was reliving the whole ghastly incident all over again. I wanted to stop him. Turning away once more he continued.

"I couldn't get passed the thing on the panzer. Had to climb back into the chock line. I was still shouting his name. I immediately saw movement. His right hand was trying to grasp summut. I gave him my hand. He opened his eyes. And do know what he said Mick? Do know what he fuckin said? *"Tommy I'm done for."* For what seemed an eternity I waited for him to continue.

"By now lads had reached me, plus the Deputies. Jackie checked the cavity. Said there was nothing else likely to fall. Six of us got round the thing and tried to lift. No fuckin chance. Thought bout using chocks. Gave that up as a bad idea. We'd need pullifts but where do you get a set of pullifts when you fuckin need im? Took us forty-five minutes to find a set plus lifting chains. Jackie went out for morphine. Av bin on some situations Mick but this was the scariest, lifting that lump of fuckin dirt without making his condition worse." Tommy stopped again. The memory of the event still raw.

"Listen Tom, think it best if you leave it there."
"No Mick I'm good." He cleared his throat. "Lads began havin a debate if we should wait till Jackie got back. Told'em to get it lifted, quicker we got lad on the surface the better. As it started movin he began to groan, relief like it was finally being moved. Then the fuckin chain slipped. The poor bastard began to scream like you've never heard. The sound will stay with me till the end of my days. Finally fuckin Jackie arrived, flappin like mother fuckin hen. Decided to put morphine in his free arm. Daft cunt lost half of it, shaking like a leaf but finally got it in. Started lifting again. Poor bastard must have bin unconscious. Never moved. Thank fuck Connor Michaels arrived. Brought haulage lads in with stretcher." He stopped again deep in thought. The outbye belts kicked in. The sound of the remaining coal on the belt hitting the chute. The generated cloud of dust raising slowly before being picked up by the main ventilation and taken back into the intake. I passed him my tin of snuff.

"Ta cock. The minute it was off his body, me and Connor reached beneath, part lifting, part dragging the lad. Colin never looked as though he weighed much he certainly didn't now. His body was broken. His left arm looked shattered. Hangin in opposite direction it should av bin. Got im into return gate. Kept checkin his pulse, he felt so cold. Connor strapped his arm against his body. Started scriking again he did. Connor had fetched in with him another ampoule of morphine. Jackie said he shouldn't av any more. Steve from control let us know ambulance had arrived and a doctor was on his way in with Night Shift Overman. Second injection given we loaded him on stretcher and off we went. Rode him out on belts till we got to bottom of E3." He returned my snuff tin "He'll never work underground again."

☐

10. *Pipes Down Shaft*

The following week, Colin's team, and Tommy Alridges were moved onto the start-up of L33's. Another week would have seen Colin out of L32's. We were back to single shifting. It was also the twelve-month anniversary since the end of the strike. The event was mentioned in most of the newspapers. Over the previous twelve months we'd lost another twenty-three pits and over twenty thousand of the workforce. Not good news, however the industry had produced an additional fifteen million tonnes on the year before. Had the NUM been right? The numbers were down but at least the annual tonnage was back where it needed to be.

One issue that had bothered me from the day I'd started as Face Overman was the relationship between those men who had worked through the strike and those that had stayed out for the full duration. As junior management we had been instructed to watch out for intimidation and the use of the word scab. On L32's I'd been lucky in some ways. The groups of men had been separated. Primarily because the face had operated as two teams. It wasn't ideal, however, it kept conflict to a minimum. It certainly hadn't contributed to an efficient production unit. Over time however the offer of voluntary redundancy had caused a number of the older members to take early retirement. This and the removal of the SERDS had solved the problem. So now we were working as an effective team except for one older fella, Terry.

Ostracised by his so-called team mates because he hadn't stayed out for the full twelve months. At snap time, if we weren't coaling, he would sit alone on the face and eat in isolation. I'd found it convenient to put him on pushing over to avoid working with the others. Not ideal but it suited both parties. I'd approached Ged on several occasions about the matter. During our private conversation, the term scab was used. I'd used the argument that the strike was now something in the past. He would have none of it. "Once a scab, always a scab" was his stock answer.

I'd often given thought to this on-going conflict. Twelve months later I suppose to the outside world, the healing process would have sorted it by now.

But it wasn't the case. That was the sad part of it. Who was to blame? British Coal were under pressure to reduce cost. Competition from cheap North Sea oil, natural gas, and nuclear. The Government had got their way. Destroying the power of the NUM allowed them to now dictate industrial relations policy with little objection from the TUC. All good stuff but what of the men who'd given their all to keep the pit's open?

"Morning Terry. How are things with you?"
"All good thanks Mick." Terry was sat in the chock line just above half way. A blocked chute on the Access Road had brought all the outbye belts to a stop. I was travelling up from the maingate.
"You wouldn't tell me if things were bad anyway. Pinch?" I sat down alongside. Resting my arse on the looped bagging between the chocks.
"No thanks."
"What? No thanks you don't want a pinch, or you wouldn't tell me if anything was wrong?" He laughed.
"No. I might be havin a bite to eat if we don't start up shortly." He hadn't quite answered the question and I had no intention of pursuing it. I replaced the tin and reached across to the DAC.
"Hello Control. Hello Sid. Any idea how long we'll be?"
"Beltmen are on their way Mick. Shouldn't be long now."
"Sid, might be worth tellin L33's to break their lumps before sending them out."
"Now mister Gibson. Don't be casting aspersions."
"Like kettle calling pot black." An anonymous person shouted. Followed by.
"Tuther way round you daft cunt."
"Isn't that telly programme?" A third person shouted.
"Bloody ell Mick you've caused something there." Terry added laughing. "May as well have me snap now."
"Not a bad idea." I leaned back towards the DAC. "Ged...."
"Nah lads. Might as well get a bite to eat." Ged interrupted. I smiled. He'd given the instruction himself.

"You two seem to be getting on well together."
"Yeah, a lot better Terry. Better than when I'd first started on here. We still have our moments though."
"I think we spent more time walking off then coaling in the early days."
"Don't remind me. I'm still not happy how you're being treated though."
"Don't worry about me. I'll manage." I wasn't sure if I could push it but thought it worth a try.
"Do you regret breaking the strike, Terry." Silence followed I wasn't sure he would answer.

"Not one bit. It wa necessary. Needed the cash. I do regret losing friends on the back of it." I remained silent. There was more to follow. "My circumstances are a lot different to most of these lads. Don't know if you know? My missus has a heart condition and just before strike daughter come to live with us. Husband fucked off. They have a disabled child. My little granddaughter. A real beauty she is. We love her to bits. Daughter couldn't afford the rent on her own. Just me and the missus big house plenty of room. Seemed the obvious solution. Most of lads on ere got a second job. Had summut fall back on. Like Alf and Jack at bottom end. Not me though. Had three mouths to feed." I waited nothing followed.

"I don't blame yer."
"Hey, now Mick, don't be feeling sorry for me. Don't forget those poor bastards in the pit villages. Likes of South Wales, Yorkshire, and Nottinghamshire. Imagine being a scab in them places. Must be awful. Round ere folk come from all over. Local, Wigan, St Helens, Liverpool even." He smiled towards me after his last comment. He had point, something I'd never thought about. "Bet British Coal never considered that. All very well asking you lot to keep an eye on lads being intimidated. What about when they've returned home? Who keeps an eye on them there? I'll tell tha, no fucker. Left to fend for themselves. Me I live in Culcheth. Posh there you know Mick. No mining folk. Although we had an Area Director living there once."

"Outbye belts have kicked in. Take the lockout off." Paul on the panels shouted.
"Fuck off havin me snap."
"No tha fuckin not your cutting coal lad."
"Okay Ged."
"Got to give it to Ged. Certainly, knows how to motivate his staff. Not even Jonny Bastard would argue." Terry shouted towards me as the panzer pre-alarm kicked in.
"Certainly, got a way with words."
"Hello Mick. Hello Mick Gibson."
"I'll see tha later Mick."
"You certainly will. And thanks for the chat, Terry. Given me something to think about." He never responded as he moved away. He looked sad. I wondered how long he'd continue. He must have been one of the oldest lads still working.

"Hello Mick Gibson. Hello Mick." Some things never altered though. I reached down to the DAC directly opposite.
"Hi Sid. Mick ere."

"Mick, can you give us a call when you're by a phone. Nothing urgent."

"Will do." *Nothing urgent?* If it weren't urgent, he'd have told me over the phone. It usually meant the Deputy Manager or Manager!

Changed and now back in my clean I headed towards the Top Shunt. I'd made the call to Sid when I reached the return. Mr Keech had been after me and wanted a call. He'd told me when I got up the pit. Manager wanted to see me. I asked why. Which either he didn't know or more likely didn't want to tell me. The usual butterflies had entered my stomach. The intensity increasing when I reached his office door. I raised my hand to knock and then hesitated. I attempted to clear my throat.

"He won't bite you know." Somewhat embarrassed I turned to see Susan Herrington. Alongside her Sister Kish. They were both smiling. "He's expecting you. Just go in." I nodded and turned quickly I could feel my face begin to flush. Knocking once I never waited for a reply. I walked in.

The Manager was sat at his desk. It was one of those rare moments when he didn't have a pen in his hand. Replaced with his pipe. I loved the smell of St Bruno. Sat at the meeting table was Mr Keech. Both smiled towards me. Unusual to say the least but not as unusual as Mr Keech without a fag in his gob.

"Now lad. Come in, take a seat." The scene played out in front of me shouldn't have been a surprise. Over the last week an atmosphere of pleasantness had broken out. The atmosphere at work was evident to us all. The pit was on target to hit over seven hundred thousand tonnes for the year better than we'd done the previous two years. L33's had started on time. Operating with four faces. What more could any of us want. But these two smiling. It was a little unnerving.

"How many today lad?"

"Three, Mr Creed."

"Started to get a bit of consistency." Mr Keech added.

"Not before fuckin time Len." And there's me thinking how well this was going. I shifted uncomfortably in my chair. "Suppose you're wondering why I've asked to see you?" I remained silent. I had asked myself the very same question more than once or twice. I was sure the answer would come shortly. "When you get back from your residential."

"Another two weeks away Mr Creed?" I smiled. The very same question had been asked by my missus. It hadn't gone down well.

"That's right Len. The lad here's off on his senior residential next week."

"If he comes back."

"Oh, I'm sure he'll be back. Got big things planned for the lad. We just wanted to let you know few more weeks we're promoting you to District Overman."

The look on my face must have conveyed my thoughts. *Fuckin District fuckin Overman!* "Don't forget lad you've still to complete the Scheme. Haven't you got an inter-area visit coming up too?"

"Yeah, middle of April for two weeks." Another piece of news I was yet to tell the missus. I hadn't decided the best time yet.

"Well, we'll see how things pan out when you get back."

They both sat there waiting for a response. I wasn't sure what they wanted to hear. The silence had made Mr Keech a little uneasy. He reached into his jacket for his pack of Players. Mr Creed took the opportunity to strike up and relight his pipe. I took the opportunity to inhale the smell of pipe tobacco.

"You on this weekend Mick?" Mr Keech asked as he took the first drag on his fag.

"Yeah, Saturday and Sunday." I wasn't sure whether I should tell them about the rest day I had booked.

"What about the Bank Holiday, Easter Monday."

"No, I'm off plus a rest day on the Tuesday."

"Bloody ell lad. You'll only have been back two minutes and you're taking rest days. Payin him too much Len."

"I'm in hospital Tuesday. Vasectomy." My revelation caused them both to sit back and contemplate my statement.

"And you've only booked a day?"

"I've heard it can be quite painful. Not the operation, the after effects." The fact I only had one rest day left wasn't something they'd be interested in.

"Come on Len I've better things to be doin other than talkin bollocks." The Manager's comment caused us all to laugh. Time, I left.

☐

The following Tuesday, the day for my vasectomy had arrived. It was also April Fool's Day, not ideal.

"Are you sure just taking a day off will be enough?"

"Little choice love. That's all my days used up."

"Good luck. Make sure they don't cut it all off."

"Thanks for that."

"I'm only kiddin."

"I know you are. See you shortly."

Forty-five minutes later Annie arrived at the ward to take me home. Operation complete, my bollocks now supported in a jock strap. They felt a little tender but not too much pain.

The following day I woke at five and felt like a pee. I jumped out of bed. Something I wish I hadn't done. I was in agony. The slightest movement and that included walking sent a searing pian through my testicles.

"What are you going to do? You'll have to throw a sickie." Annie suggested.

"I've never been on the sick in my life."

"Well, there's always a first time."

"I'm not even sure what you do."

"All you need to do is phone in. Think you get three days. Just fill a form in when you start back."

"I can't take three days off. What will everyone think?"

"Well, if you've got a better suggestion, I can't wait to hear it."

Later that day, after my phone call, I received a call from Don Gold. He suggested it might be in my best interest to turn up for work the next day and stop on the surface. He'd find me something to do, for the next two days. I was grateful as it would give me the weekend too, to fully recover.

"Well how is the gelded Scouser. I did tell you it would be painful." The Manager commented as he entered the Personnel Manager's office.

"Yes, you did Mr Creed." I answered struggling to get to my feet.

"Now lad don't get up on account of me. You get yourself right. Don't want to be getting any dirt into them wounds. May have to have the lot taken off."

"I that's right Mr Creed. Tell the lad." Don responded chuckling as only he knew how. "You haven't seen him walk yet Mr Creed. Looks like he's in one of those so-called Westerns about to draw his Colt 45. Go on Mick show Mr Creed." I thought Don was joking. Obviously not, they were both looking at me expectantly. *For fucks sake!* I took two steps forward. The pain was excruciating.

"Now lad av seen enough. Sit thisel down." The Manager offered. "If tha thinks tha's got problems wait till tha pubics start sprouting." He turned towards Don. "Av tha told im bout next week?"

"Just getting round to it boss. Goin to get Mick ere to make out the notes and put on lamps."

"Why what's happening?"

"Update on industry lad. Gentlemen from Area Industrial Relations Department will be presenting at Old Boston. Calling it a Team Briefing. Monday, Tuesday next week."

"Will that be our very own designer of parachutes?" Don asked.

"I mister. Our very own Tom Brian. Lad's destined for big things."

"Certainly not running a cattery." The Manager's comment caused Don to erupt into uncontrolled laughter. I never had a clue what the fuck they were talking about.

After the Manager left, I got down to writing the notes for the visit to Old Boston. Not all the officials would be going but a fair selection, including me. Don got Eric, the Manager's clerk to hang on the lamps. There was little else required during the afternoon.

"Figures just through Mick for last year. Pit produced just short of seven hundred and fifty-five thousand tonne, with an OMS of two point three tonnes. Men on books now at one thousand six hundred and thirty-one. Not bad goin given circumstances."

"How do you mean circumstances?"

"Bloody lads on club." I had previously heard the absentee rate was on the increase. "I'll av get letter sent out. Ast heard bout Haig Colliery?"

"Yeah, one of the lads mentioned it." Don seemed not to have heard my comment, he was still on transmit.

"Closed end of last month. Last deep mine in Cumbria it wa. Mark my words Mick lad big mistake. There's millions of tonnes of good quality coking coal under the Irish Sea. They'll be back for it one day. So called replacing it with Nuclear – I don't think so. Too dangerous for my liking already had one fuck up in '57. Think by changing its name us ordinary folk will forget. Well, I'll tell tha what lad. Call it what you want Calder Hall, Windscale, or Sellafield all fuckin same to me. It won't replace coil!"

☐

What I found remarkable about Old Boston Training Centre whenever I visited were the memories that came flooding back. The first time, over ten years ago. Transport then was a red bus, the 320, I'd pick up at the bottom of Bluebell Lane, in Page Moss, Huyton.

I could still see Val, as he liked to be called, spitting blood onto the ground. Advising me and a group of other sixteen-year-olds that this was the result of pneumoconiosis. Something none of us had heard of before. Then there was Frank the Training Centre Manager. He walked with a limp due to a false leg. We were told he'd lost it in an accident underground. There was a younger guy too, Keith. Always busying himself with one thing or another. He seemed an ambitious character.

I slowed as I reached the entrance road. Leading to the arch railway bridge beyond which was the old pit.

There were plenty of cars parked up. I checked my watch. I was a little early. I headed over to one of the large classrooms off to my left. Someone had pinned to the door a label *Team Briefing*. Inside I recognised several faces. An assortment of Deputies and Overmen. Some colleagues from Cronton too. Along the back wall a couple of long trestle tables covered in a thick white table cloth. Two huge metal teapots alongside the unmistakable white porcelain canteen mugs. There had been four large round plates of biscuits. Two now empty, the others heading that way. I needed to get in there and quick.

At the far end of the room was a desk. Sat in front of a large blackboard. Written on the board were a few titles, alongside chalked in red several figures. Bang on nine the door to the classroom opened. In walked two guys. Both suited and booted. There appearances couldn't have been more different. The taller of the two was as bald as a coot. The shorter guy a mullet of jet-black hair with a matching thick Mexican moustache. What would the taller fella have given for some of that hair. I reckoned he'd have been happy with the tash alone.

Their entrance caused us to move to the seating area facing the blackboard. Once we were all sat, the short guy coughed slightly. The way you do to get everyone's attention. At the same time the bald fella lifted two folded sheets of card. He stood them upright facing us, each containing a name and their job title. The bald guy was Graham Vann, Head of Manpower. And the Mexican Tom Brian, Head of Industrial Relations.

"Morning Gentlemen." Tom had a thick Wigan accent. "Glad tha could join us today. We've got plenty to get through over the next couple of days. It's important you take note as the very future of the coal mining industry relies on each one of you playing your part. *Bloody 'ell – heavy stuff!*

Over the next two days we learnt about our competitors. Oil, natural gas, nuclear and something I hadn't heard of before, seaborne coal. The 1974 Plan for Coal had heralded a whole new future for the industry, however it had been a little too ambitious. Back in 73 the oil price had gone through the roof, but things had now changed. The price had reduced, the UK now had their own supply from the North Sea. Including natural gas. The rising oil prices had made the exploitation economically feasible. Nuclear still in its infancy was proving a reliable source of electricity supply. Seaborne coal, however, was different. The likes of the US, South Africa, and Australia had invested heavily in their own industry. The additional quantities of coal no longer required. The point was hammered home that we don't sell coal we sell energy.

Once again, the term Gigajoule was mentioned. The unit of energy. Used to measure our efficiency against the competition. Another acronym I'd not seen used before was mtce – million tonnes of coal equivalent. Again, it helped to better understand where the industry stood against the competing fuels. I wasn't surprised to see that the likes of the US, South Africa, and Australia could produce coal at £1.00/GJ. Landing it at our ports pushed the cost up to £1.50/GJ. Most of the pits in the Western Area were producing at one pound fifty. This was increased by a further fifty pence to transport to the CEGB's power stations. Seaborne coal was attracting the attention of the UK's coastal power stations. Fiddlers Ferry being such a power station! We'd need to cut cost to remain competitive.

It had been a good two days. Meeting up with former colleagues and now a better understanding of what was required. We all readily agreed it was something we could achieve.

Later that month the news headlines concerned a major nuclear disaster in Ukraine at the Chernobyl Nuclear Power Plant. One of the reactors had blown up causing large amounts of radioactive material to disperse into the atmosphere. The results of which effected large areas of Europe. The radioactive cloud spread as far as Scandinavia. Initially up to a hundred deaths had been reported, although that number was expected to increase. Once more it put a major question mark against the safe use of nuclear in providing power. It could only add to the benefits of using coal particularly as the UK had an abundance of it. The future looked promising, and I was getting impatient for my first senior role.

Then totally out of the blue at the beginning of May, the Manager sent for me. He suggested there was an opportunity for me to become an Assistant Undermanager on noons. I was excited at the prospect although a little surprised. The Colliery Overman on noons Bennie Lead seemed to have that shift firmly under his control. I was still hoping for my own shift to manage. I began to suspect the Manager may have been trying to manage my expectations. I'd lost count of the number of positions I'd applied for up and down the country.

At home, now I was back on regular days, had allowed us to get into a routine which pleased the missus. However, my sleeping pattern was all over the place. I suspected it was due to the amount of time I was spending on the coal face chasing coal. I had thought of asking my colleagues but felt too embarrassed to do so. I wasn't just on L32's during my working shift. I was now spending time there whilst a sleep. One particular night…

"For fucks sake!" I lay there momentarily, eyes closed. Hoping I hadn't woken any of the family. The dig I received in my ribs suggested I hadn't been so lucky.

"Mick what the hell do you think you're doing? It's half four in the morning."

"I'm sorry love, bit of a nightmare."

"You've been tossing and turning all night. At one point you started slamming your fist on the duvet. Then you started laughing. Are you okay? Is there something worrying you?" If only she knew.

"Again, I'm sorry. I'm fine. I'll get up now anyway. Fancy a cuppa?"

"You know I'll never say no to a cuppa."
"Be back with you shortly."

I headed downstairs to the kitchen, letting the dog out first for a wee. Switching the kettle on I stood there revisiting my recent dream. I'd been on the face. It had been a good dream. For the first time we'd had four shears. When I'd woken, I felt in such a good mood. Until I realised it had been a dream. I couldn't tell the missus. She'd think I was nuts. Although I had my suspicions, she already did.

□

"Hello Mick, hello Mick Gibson." "What the fuck's up now? Give us a mo Brian I'll be back with shortly." I wasn't in the best of moods. Having already worked the Sunday morning on the face. I'd been called in on nights to cover Brian the fitter and two men. The job on the face changing the cutter disc had run over. They couldn't get anyone to cover the night shift, so they called me. Being the face overman on L32's I hadn't had much choice. Not that Mrs Gibson saw it that way.
"Hi Steve, Mick here." I never received an immediate response. "Steve, Mick here."
"Sorry Mick, all over the place at the mo. Can you give me a call?"
"What's up?"
"Just give us a call." That certainly didn't sound like Steve. Not one for abrupt answers. By the sound of things, there were other people in the control room. I climbed back on to the panzer and headed back up to the shearer.

The shearer was positioned two cuts back from the face. A number of Dowty props in position supporting half a dozen; three by three's. After coaling on the Friday, the lads had peppered the face side with wooden dowels. Brian and two of the facemen were in the final phases of torquing the bolts up. The old disc was sat in the return, waiting to be loaded up.
"Problem Mick?"
"Don't know yet. I'll be back with you shortly." I climbed back into the chock line.

"Steve, Mick." As I waited for a response, I could hear a number of voices. I was sure I could hear the Deputy Manager.
"Just a minute Mr Keech would like a word."
"Mick. We've got an emergency."
"Practice?" I interrupted.
"No Mick, no fuckin practice just listen will you." I waited. "There's been an incident in No 1 shaft. A pipe's dropped into Pit Bottom. Shaft is out of action."

187

As Mr Keech relayed the message, I'd recalled seeing the three shaftsmen, harnessed up waiting to go in as we were about to go down. I was aware they'd been hanging a new sixteen-inch compressed air range. "We're clearing the pit as we speak. Get your lads out to No 2 shaft immediately.

"Will do." I then heard the Manager's voice.

"Just a minute Mick." They were obviously having a discussion. "Manager's asked if you'll do us a recce at No 1 Pit Bottom. Need to understand how bad the damage is. Oh, and be careful. We haven't had any contact with the shaftsmen yet." *For fucks sake!*

Fifteen minutes later the four of us were at the bottom of the E3. There were several men already sat on the manrider.

"That everyone from your place Mick?" Billy Pete shouted over to me.

"Yeah, that's it from my side." I watched as one of the nightshift manrider lads used his signalling rod to hit the two parallel signalling wires above his head. The carriages dropped back before moving forward. We were off. I sat deep in thought. I pulled my donkey jacket tight around my chest. The ventilation whipping passed my head as we sped outbye up the one in four brow at speed. The air around us clear from the haze of small dust particles that usually hung in the air. Several conversations taking place around me. *What sort of state would the shaftsmen be in?* I recalled an incident some years before. A young lad had committed suicide throwing himself down the shaft. It had taken a few days to collect his body parts. The Police had been involved too. Some poor constable having to ride the shaft with the shaftsmen. Even then he was still missing his right arm. That was found some weeks later in one of the insets. I shivered at the thought of it.

Fifteen minutes later we'd disembarked the manrider. Then travelled the short cross cut to the loco road. I joined a number of my colleagues in the back carriage.

"What fucks happened Mick?" Billy asked.

"Believe Manager wants tha go see damage?" Gerry added.

"A pipe's dropped down shaft. Wants me go and check out the damage." I wasn't sure how much I was to supposed to say to anyone if anything at all.

"A fuckin pipe Mick! That's not what I've heard." Gerry responded. "From what Onsetter's told me, it's the whole fuckin lot."

"When did you speak with im?"

"Bout an hour ago. He'd ran full length of tunnel. Shit his pants. Said it sounded like an explosion." The sound of the loco signalling was soon followed by us all moving forward as it pulled away.

"Fuckin knew summut would go wrong."

"What's meaning Billy?"

"I was talkin to Randy one of shaftsmen last weekend. Tells me they weren't happy with the way things were progressing."

Billy went on to explain how the work was done. A total of seven pipes were coupled together at pit top. Attached to a winch and then lowered down shaft. The shaftsmen riding along the descending pipes on top of the cage. Building the range from pit bottom up. Each pipe fifteen foot long and sixteen inches diameter weighed nearly three quarters of a tonne. Once the seven pipes were alongside, they'd signal pit top and manoeuvre them into position.

"Tell tha what. Them lads must have nerves of steel. Must av!"

"What securing them with? Must be summut stronger than pipe chain."

"Fuck off tha daft cunt. Fuckin pipe chain. Lads were using proper designed brackets."

"How the fuck did they secure bracket like. I'm told the shaft walls on both shafts are twelve-inch solid concrete."

"Holman, then resin and bolts. Shaftsmen reckon in place some of the concrete was rotten. Keep finding chunks of it in sump."

"Fuckin Holman. How supposed to use Holman in shaft? Unless they've got them extra-long legs." We all began to laugh. I hadn't said anything up to this point, just listened. I was still contemplating what I'd find at pit bottom in the way of body parts.

"They used bracket as template. Marking the shaft wall."

"Bet they weighed summut." Billy ignored the comment and continued.

"Randy say that war worse part of job like. Once Holman was set up on top cage. As they started drilling and pressure applied with leg, cage would start to move across shaft. Nearly lost one of his mates one night right off top of cage. Changing bits every half hour. Concrete was that hard."

The change in the loco speed indicated the end of our journey along the tunnel. The view outside of the manriding carriage was obscured by a cloud of dust. Not moving. It didn't taste good either, each of us covering our mouth. The smell was different too. The cold air laced with the smell of steel, oil, and ochre. There was something else different too. Complete darkness. We lurched forward as the loco came to a complete halt. Momentarily no one said a word. Sat there just listening to what sounded like freely flowing water. There was something else too. A hissing sound.

"Does want me to come with tha lad?" Gerry broke the silence. "Let Billy take lads through loco tunnel to No 2."

"Yeah, if you don't mind." I wasn't quite ready for what I might find alone.

"You okay with that Billy?"

"Yeah, all good. Come on then best be making a move."

Gerry and I stood back as Billy led the way around the back of No 1 shaft. The lads followed him. Each looking towards the unlit pit bottom. Gerry and I began to walk forward. It was becoming clearer now. The dust beginning to settle. It was so unusual seeing pit bottom in complete darkness. We'd travelled no more than a few yards when a number of pipes came into view. Some still coupled. Along the level I counted at least twenty. A further six were bent double. One single pipe lying on top of a now flattened mine car. The intensity of the ochre smell greater now. Brown water flowing freely from what I guessed was the six-inch pump range.

"Fuckin ell Mick, tha'd av to see it to believe it cock." Gerry was holding his cap lamp, directing it to a thick length of steel rope sat up in the air. "Guide rope"

"Guide rope? How the fuck do you work that out?" I was somewhat surprised by the certainty of Gerry's comment.

"Lay of rope Mick. Bin on many a job with shaftsmen when they've been changing em."

The closer we got to the pit bottom the greater the destruction. Loops of blue and yellow armoured cable lying across the floor. Lengths of six- and three-inch pipe lying alongside. I swung my cap lamp left and right. Looking for what? And then my worst nightmare. "Gerry." I held my lamp stationary.

"What's for do Mick?" He followed the beam of my light.

"Fuckin ell Mick you had me going for a minute. It's a fuckin helmet. What's expecting to find in it? A fuckin ed!"

I felt somewhat embarrassed. I'd been so concerned about the shaftsmen.

"It's probably the onsetters after he made a run for it." I began to laugh. More from relief than anything else. "Do you ere that Mick?" Gerry was shining his lamp towards the shaft. Above the sound of the leaking water there was a tap, tap coming from somewhere in the shaft. We both scrambled forward climbing over the mangled mesh shaft gates. Split and flattened five-gallon drums laying everywhere. The smell of various oils filling the air. Not quite reaching the opening as the number of damaged sixteen-inch pipes increased. It was now obvious that most off the pipes had landed in the sump. Various lengths sitting above the inset. At least half a dozen lying across the shaft.

"Must be shaftsmen."

"Thank fuck. Still alive." We got as close as we could. "How they goin to get them out?"

"Mergency winder lad." We started moving away.

"No doubt bout it Mick. Ave to use cutting gear."

"What?"

"Yep, ave to get exemption. No way of pulling them free. Looks as though shaft wall damaged too." I turned towards Gerry. He was kicking a lump of thick grey concrete. Several more pieces lay scattered amongst the pipes.

The arch roadway looked little different than normal. Other than a couple of missing or smashed whitewashed lagging boards caught by the falling pipes. Three adjacent panels had been upended. The attached armoured cables still in place. I doubted whether they'd still be flameproof. Various lengths of chain hanging down. A length of loco track no longer straight. The steel sleepers sitting perpendicular to the floor. There was also a taste that I'd never experienced before. I could only describe as metal and whitewash. I hawked up a few times as we continued our examination. The smell too was of cold metal. The sound of the leaking pump range began to reduce, replaced by the hissing and fine spray of the high-pressure firefighting range.

"Hello Mick. Hello Mick Gibson." We both turned. The sound of Steve's voice surprising us both. I headed to the side of the road. Once more encountering a number of obstacles. I had to stretch my arm through two damaged pipes to reach the tannoy.
"Steve, Mick ere."
"How we lookin?"
"Can't see us manriding this shift." I caught Gerry shaking his head. It probably hadn't been the best thing to say considering who'd be in the control room. I attempted to correct my fuck up. "A mess Steve. One big fuckin mess. Pipes, steelwork, cables you name it. Oh, and not forgetting what looks like a severed guide rope."
"It is a guide rope." Gerry added.
"There's also something else Steve. We've heard a tapping sound in the shaft."
"Yeah, we know. Manager and Mr Keech are over there now. Made contact with the shaftsmen. Not sure what state they're in yet. Sent for the emergency winder. How long do you reckon?"
"I assume you mean before we sort the pit bottom out?"
"Exactly that." I personally didn't have a clue. I looked towards Gerry.
"What do you think couple months?"
"Nah with the right lads should have it sorted in say a month I reckon."
"Bout a month Steve. Might be worthwhile getting someone to turn off the water feed. They're going to have to drain the system to carry our repairs."
"Yep, thanks Mick got that."
"Well, if there's nothing else, we'll make our way out." There was no response. I completed some notes on what we'd seen. "Come on think we're done here. Let's be making a move."

"I lad, nowt else we can do ere. Tell tha what though. Imagine if men had been travelled shaft when pipes dropped." I shuddered at the thought of it.

Back on the surface we headed to the lamproom. I was surprised to see JW there. Still in his clean. Not often I saw him about at weekend. His was with one of the Colliery Overman. "Try Teddy Costa again. We'll need a fork lift operator asap. Manager's gone fuckin ape." I moved a little closer to them both. Another first. I don't think I'd heard JW swear before.
"Anything I can do to help Mr Walters?"
"Not unless you're able to operate the large forks, man." I never responded as we both knew the answer. I watched as he walked off. I wasn't sure what the forks would be required for but decided to take a look. There seemed more men had arrived. The canteen staff had obviously been alerted as the lights were on. Four o'clock on a Monday morning ordinarily the place would be empty.

I headed outside. I'd never seen the emergency winder before. I'd overheard one of the lads mention it was travelling down the M1 motorway from Mansfield. From what I remember from college an annual visit of the winder was supposed to take place each year. Looking towards the outside of the No 1 Tower there seemed to be quite a lot of activity. I now understood JW's comments. The concrete plinth the winder was to be positioned had disappeared from view, beneath various clumps of overgrown vegetation and two small shipping containers. That explained the forks. I didn't recognise any of the men hacking away. I decided to head back to the shaft top.

As I approached, I could clearly hear the Manager's voice on a loud hailer. "Now lads emergency winders on way. We'll have you out in no time. Just lowering down a little sustenance. Try and get flask to Randy too." In the distance I could see the Manager leaning over the shaft side. He obviously had no problem with heights. Alongside him Mr Keech. He was holding a coil of shotfiring cable lowering something down towards the men. There was at least a dozen other men standing watching.
"Flask of coffee Mick with a good dose of whiskey." I hadn't seen Stevie the Banksman approach me. I turned to acknowledge his comment. "Hadn't even started work. Three of em on top of cage I'd just lowered them down. Doin a quick recce before starting. Fuckin ell Mick. Noise you should of erd it. Screaming too. Good job they all had harnesses on. Poor old Randy fell off. Still hanging now. Other two lads tried pullin im up. Can't manage weight."
"You've got to be fuckin kiddin."
"I kid you not. Thought we'd lost him."

Our conversation ended at this point. A series of blue flashing lights adjacent to the Tower. "Winder's here Mr Creed." One of the lads shouted.

"Is Teddy Costa here yet?"

"On his way boss." The Manager turned to Mr Keech.

"Len, can you sort. Tell Teddy if the winder's not in position within half an hour, I'll be suspending him over the fuckin shaft myself!" Poor Teddy. He was in for a round of fucks. It was always a relief when somebody else was getting it up the arse.

I wasn't sure what else I could do so I thought it best to follow Mr Keech. In case he needed any additional info on what I'd seen at Pit Bottom. I still couldn't get out of my head that Randy was still suspended in the shaft. Stevie had said when the pipes dropped the cage was just above the first inset. By my reckoning Randy had a drop of nearly a quarter of a mile beneath him. I shivered at the thought. What must be going through his mind? Heights was not my strong point. I struggled at the best of times just getting into the cage. To be left dangling in total darkness. From what I remember of the lad he wasn't the lightest. How long would the harness hold him for? I had to stop myself thinking about it anymore. It was making me feel sick.

"Mr Keech. Here's my notes on what we've seen."

"Thanks, marra."

"Anything else I can do?"

"Nah, don't think so Mick. What shift you on tomorrow?"

"Days."

"I'd get yoursen gone lad. Not sure yet what we'll be doin over next few weeks. Let's see what the Inspector says. Priority is to get those lads out."

"Aye up Len." We both turned as Mick Hobbit appeared. "We've cleared the site just securing the winder now." *Looks as though Teddy will be safe now.* By the look on Mick's face, I don't think he felt the same way.

Up till that point I hadn't noticed the number of men in clean boiler suits and NCB donkey jackets. Mr Keech saw me looking.

"Area staff Mick. Descended on us like flies. Not sure what fuckin use thy are. Had to get canteen Manageress call her girls in."

"Right then. I'll see you tomorrow."

"Len!" The Manager shouted across.

"Ta Mick." Leaving me he headed back towards the Manager.

Walking back to the main building I came across a group of men I didn't recognise until one turned his back towards me. All wearing dirty white jackets. The guy had a label pinned to the back advising he was part of the area shaft team. They seemed to be having an argument amongst themselves.

"Well, some fucker's goin ave do it."

"Am tellin ye. I ain't."

"Me fuckin neither."

"Nor me."

"What bout you Baz?"

"Yeah?"

"Well done Baz Cutlass. You are the man."

"What? What ona bout?"

"You've just volunteered to go down in kibble."

"Am I fuck."

"Ain't that right lads."

"We all erd it. Right, we did." The lad they were referring to as Baz Cutlass did not look happy.

"But…."

"No buts Baz. It'll be good experience for tha."

Driving back home that morning I tried to recall what the 1972 Act restricted the number of men working underground with only one shaft. In a heading it was usually nine and with exemption up to fifteen. But a shaft. It was either twenty or thirty. What about those poor bastards still in the shaft? I tried to think what it must be like, hanging by a single chain in total darkness beneath. He'd know exactly how far it would be to the bottom of the shaft. And what of the comment Pete had made. What if the pipes had dropped whilst manriding? It didn't bear thinking about.

Arriving at work the next morning it was somewhat of a surprise to be told by John Meriden to return home. Talking to a number of lads they reckoned it had taken over eight hours to get the shaftsmen safely back to the surface. The Area shaft team had been increased to help get the shaft back in working order. I spied my chance to see what was happening around the Top Shunt. Surprisingly for that time of the morning the place was heaving. By the look of the number of fancy cars outside guessed they'd be Area staff.

The following day John directed a few of us to report to the Surface Foreman, Teddy Costa. I'd never met Teddy in person. Only spoken to him over the phone. Usually, to give him a round of fucks if I hadn't received the supplies we'd ordered.

I headed across to the compound. It was a glorious early spring morning. The sun hadn't fully risen but had exposed enough of its brightness to suggest it would be another scorcher. The heat on my back felt good. The air filled with birdsong. Mainly skylarks. I stopped to watch a number of them rise high into the air before dropping out of sight. I breathed in the intoxicating smells of the surrounding countryside. How lucky were we? To experience the simple pleasures in life when usually we'd be a couple of miles underground.

From the pleasant distraction my mind returned to the here and now. The place was heaving. I spotted several of my lads off L32's. They were loaded three-inch pipes onto a flat. Sat watching them was Ged. He saw me and waved. I began to walk towards him. I hadn't spotted a small guy in blue overalls right alongside me. He looked mithered.

"Excuse me mate. Could you tell me where I'd find Teddy the Surface Foreman?"

"That would be me." The guy had a kindly face but looked worried. I suppose he wasn't used to having all these pitmen in his compound.

"And who do I have the pleasure of speaking to?"

"Mick Gibson, L32's Face Overman."

"Oh finally." He smiled. "I get to meet Mr Angry." His comment took me by surprise. I wasn't initially aware of what Teddy was referring too. And then I remember the previous month me shouting the odds to get some materials underground. I felt a little embarrassed.

"Oops yeah. I remember. Fall on the face needed the timber." I held out my hand which he took. Good to see he didn't hold a grudge.

"Well, I can certainly make use of you. Every time I turn my back the lads stop work."

"Who could blame them. On a day like this." I don't think Teddy took kindly to my comment. He was obviously under pressure to get material underground to assist with the pit bottom repairs. "What are they asking you to get down?"

"Pipes, rails, armoured cable you name it. Just had a call to get some electrical panels loaded. Only arrived this morning from Area workshops. Priority to get power back on to pit bottom."

"Everything going down No 2?"

"Some of it. I'm told we'll be using No 1 shortly. Completed replacing guide rope yesterday. Still some repairs to do in shaft. Couple of cables to replace and damaged pipes."

"Right then. I'm yours to do as you wish." By the look on Teddy's face, he wasn't sure if I was taking the piss. I waited.

"Well, if you wouldn't mind getting some of those lads over yonder." He pointed towards where Ged's men were working. "Could do with the bank of panels loaded. Fork truck driver's over there now. Electrical compound."

"Yep, I'll sort that. I'll get Ged to organise. What else?" The worried look had inexplicably returned to Teddy's face.

"Yon mon sat down. That's Ged Shalla?"

"The one and only."

"Oh right." I remained silent wondering why the interest in Ged. Didn't seem I was going to get an answer.

"I'll make a move then. Oh, one other question. I was told Cayle Shelley was here?"

"Yeah, sat in Portacabin supping coffee hasn't moved since first thing."

"Morning Ged. See you're busy?"

"Nah Scouse chaykee bastard. Not often we see sun at this time of day. Believe you've seen damage?"

"Yeah, not good. Right fuckin mess. Undermanager reckons we'll be back on the face next week with a skeleton team. Try and get some coal off."

"Thought we'd be restricted with number of men underground?"

"We will. Must have got an exemption from the Inspector. So don't get too used to being sat there in the sun."

"Fuck off!" He replied laughing. "Coffee over there wants some panels loaded I hear?"

"Who the fuck's coffee?"

"Teddy Costa."

"Why you calling him coffee."

"Fuckin ell Mick. Thy needs to get out more. Had the finest coffee when we were on a rally in London last year. Place called Costa; some Italian guys just opened the place. Cappuccino. Vauxhall road." The look on my face must have said it all. "Ever bin London Mick?"

"No can't say I have."

"Anyway, can't sit here chatting all day. Might make me Colliery Overman. Let's get some panels loaded."

Once I'd had a wander around the Compound, I got a better appreciation of the layout. There's was obviously a logic to where each set of materials were stored. Of the items observed I was surprised by the amount of electrical tackle lying about. Of greater interest were a set of new face supports. They were huge. I'd never seen anything like it.

"W11's." Teddy had reappeared. "Pans over yonder." He pointed to a corner of the compound I was yet to see. "They're big too, heavy duty."

"When are they going down?"

"JW was hoping to have them moving this week. Obviously shaft incident has put paid to that."

"Never appreciated how vast an area the compound was Teddy. And it looks so orderly."

"You just remember that next time you're screaming and shouting at me down the phone."

"Yeah, I will." I responded a little embarrassed. "Out of interest what stops you getting the stuff underground?"

"Load binders. Never get them back." My mind wandered to the bottom of the E3 there was a pile of them stacked in a manhole. Extracting my notebook, I made a note.

"I'll see what I can do to help the cause."

"That would be much appreciated. Why don't you go and get a drink? See your mate, Cayle."

"That fucker still in portacabin?"

"Never moved."

"Right then, I'll go join him." I began to walk away from Teddy until I remembered something else that had been niggling me. "Sorry Teddy something else I don't understand. The last pit I worked at Cronton, the surface was plagued with cats. I've not seen a one since I've been on the surface." My question brought a smile to Teddy's face.

"Not surprising really. Couple of years ago now. One of the surface electricians and his mates decided to try out a parachute he'd made from top of No 1 Tower. Couldn't get any volunteers so decided to use one of our many cats."

"For fucks sake was it killed."

"No but the experience didn't go down well. Never saw it again. Must have told his mates. They went with him."

"Who the fuck would do such a thing?"

"Did him no harm. Went into personnel at Area. Head of Industrial Relations now."

"Tom fuckin Brian?"

"The very same."

"I've met him."

By Wednesday we were allowed to go down and onto the face and take a shear. From what I was told the coal produced was not being reported to Area. Think while we were stopped Manager was trying to build a small stockpile. The Thursday and Friday I was back in the surface compound. I had always assumed that the skips in No 2 shaft were purely for coal winding. It was a shock to find that above each skip there was also a cage for manriding. Not a four deck just double. Then beyond all expectation the following Wednesday we were all back underground.

11. The Manager Visits L32's

Over the coming weeks things got back to normal and we started riding the No 1 shaft once more. The refurbished pit bottom looked little different to that before the pipe incident. Other than some additional whitewashing you'd never have known the difference. I'd inquired as to the fate of the shaftsmen. I was told they'd finished. In fact, during one of my regular visits to the Top Shunt I'd bumped into the head shaftsman, Randy. I didn't really know the man, other than to say hello. He was waiting to see the Manager as I came out. He didn't look well, white as a sheet. I don't think he recognised me. Poor bastard. I wonder how anyone would feel left for five hours dangling in the shaft.

The other change that took place was the appearance of a new Mechanical Engineer, Bill Maskill. No announcement he just appeared. Rumour had it Mick Hobbit was now at Area. Heading up the Maintenance and Reliability department.

Although L32's face performance had improved it hadn't taken long for things to get back to normal. Breakdown after breakdown and the return of the bad ground at the maingate end. The pressure on John Meriden continued unabated. He looked completely and utterly fucked. On dayshift he was there before I arrived and still there after I left. On many an occasion when the phone rang, we watched as John hesitated before answering. The shouting from the other end caused him to sink further and further into the chair. We wondered how much more he could take. Howard Davies's replacement was still to be announced. One thing was certain it wouldn't be John.

The whole episode had got a lot of potential Undermanager's questioning whether this was the career they wanted. Joe Kitchen, a colleague I knew from college had decided enough was enough. He was now happy to remain as an official. There was no way he was allowing work to take over his life. But what of me? Had my view changed? If anything, it had increased my desire to attain that position. A challenge to myself. I believed I could take it. It wasn't going to happen to me. I guessed John would be next. Once a Manager found a chink in your personal armour he'd keep hammering until it had been breached. That's when you were fucked!

Then without warning it happened. Arriving at work one morning, a new Undermanager had been appointed. Geoff Hoffman he was sat in John Meriden's office. But what of John? Had he been side-lined too? It wasn't till I came up the pit later that I saw him. Sat alongside the new guy Geoff.

It seemed no matter how much pressure was placed on John he had no intention of resigning. He was a fighter. In fact, it was an apt description. Each morning he looked punch drunk. Even the humiliation of now working for Geoff. I tried to have a private conversation with John. He was having none of it. All he would say is the Manager had asked him to take the role of Undermanager "Special Duties." In my eyes a nonjob particularly as the first project he'd been given was to restart the installation of pipes in No 1 shaft.

One particular shift I'd unusually come up pit on time. Having promised to take the missus, her mum, and our kids to the Albert Dock in Liverpool. The Tall Ships were in town. It had been some time since I'd passed the noon shift heading in. Having deposited my lamps and rescuer I went straight to the Undermanager's office. Walking along the corridor I could hear Billy Britain's voice. Which wasn't unusual. I reckon he talked in his sleep. Billy another good Deputy, always with a funny tale to tell. Today was no exception as I heard him laugh at his own comment. The cloud of smoke drifting from the Undermanager's open office door suggested there was more than one in the audience.

"I'll tell tha. No fucker would answer it." More laughter. "In end ad to pick it up mesen." He was stood in the office with three other officials, including Gerry Cook. Gerry acknowledging me as I entered. All three smoking fags.

"Alreyt Mick."

"Hi Gerry." I looked towards the two empty chairs behind the desk. "Where's Geoff?"

"Billy's just bin tellin us. He's in No 1 sump wit John."

"Manager sent them in with a couple of lads." Billy added. "Cheese weights fast. Spillage from skips had caused a build-up. Had to stop winding till we fettled it. As I was on pit bottom went with'em. Little mini panzer in there, crackin piece of kit. Only problem yon mon keeps ringing 'em. Asking for update like."

"By yon mon, you mean Manager?"

"Mick, I kid you not. He was givin them a right thommerin. It got to point were neither would answer phone. Just grabbed a shovel and ran off." Billy's guffaws were intoxicating we couldn't help but join in. "At one point, Geoff started humming some fuckin sea shanty pretending he couldn't hear me. Thought Gaffer was goin to av an epileptic fit or summut. No wonder he's got fuckin ulcers." We all began laughing again.

"Always good to see a happy workforce." To our surprise the Manager had appeared at the door. I wasn't sure how much he'd heard. "Where's Mr Hoffman?"

"Not rightly sure Mr Creed. Billy ere was last to see 'em." Gerry answered on our behalf. We all turned to Billy. Billy seemed frozen, unable to speak. His mouth still open from his last comment. "Billy, Manager's askin tha question."

"I, I …."

"Come on lad spit it out." The Manager offering further encouragement.

"Left em in sump. Still shovelling reckon another half hour or so will have cheese weights clear."

"When they come up, tell'm I wish to see them in my office and not to bother getting changed."

"I will do Mr Creed." The Manager turned and began to walk off before suddenly stopping and turning back to our group.

"Good to see you showing concern over my medical condition Billy." Poor Billy he began to shake. His mouth opening and closing without any sound We waited until the Manager was out of earshot before uncontrolled laughter took over once more.

I didn't see much of John after that. I had my own problems, back to twelve-hour shifts and the continued onslaught of fuckings from the Manager. Then one day he'd gone. I wasn't sure where to. It was quite sad really. I'd learnt quite a bit from John. Some of his own observations and comments may have helped him if taken on board. I didn't dwell on it too long. Priority was to ensure my next promotion.

"Mick phone."

"Who?"

"Mr Keech." I took the phone from Paul. I was lathered. Sweat pouring from every pore in my body.

"Mr Keech. Yeah, new one's there now. How long? Reckon another thirty, forty minutes. Yeah, will do." I replaced the handset. "What does he think I've got a fuckin wand." I began to kick the belt stand beneath the panels.

"Fuckin ell Mick. Steady on lad you'll have a coronary cock." Paul was right. Pointless getting worked up because of a damaged shearer cable. New one was on site now. Hopefully, we'd beat the time I'd given Mr Keech. I'd arrange to get the old one run out in overtime. I made a mental note. There was a second damaged cable. Under the belt opposite Meeting Station. I'd lost count the number of times I'd asked George to get it loaded. It was so fuckin annoying though. We'd got off to such as good start. Not even snap time and we were half way down on our second. I took the opportunity for a quick pinch. Passing the tin to Paul. The place was deadly silent, save for the hydraulic pumps.

I grabbed my bottle of water. Swilling out my mouth. Then hawking up what bacca remained in my mouth.

I was continually reminding the lads to keep the spill trough clear. The build-up had caused the Bretby to climb up before falling to the floor. Then it got snagged on a chock ram after they'd pushed over. Fortunately, we'd had a spare cable in the return. Only fifty metres back from the face. I'd got the haulage lads in overtime to move all supplies forward last week. Then we had a fuckin big argument how we'd get the spare to the shearer. The lads had wanted to run it down on the panzer. I was taking no chances. Risk damaging the spare. No fuckin way. I'd personally carried the brass pummel end to prove the point. My wet overalls were testament to that. I'd left Ged to organise the swap over whilst I let the powers to be know what had happened. The call from Mr Keech was expected.

"Hello Paul. Hello panels." The DAC burst into life.
"Hi Ged."
"Is Scouse still with tha?"
"Certainly is. I'll put him on." I looked towards Paul shaking my head. He'd got the message.
"Go on Ged pass your message. He can hear tha."
"He's not goin to like it."
"Fuckin ell Ged just fuckin say what the problem is." I shouted out in exasperation.
"Go on. He's listening."
"Cable's too short. Bin labelled up wrong."
"Too fuckin short!" I shouted causing Paul to move away from the DAC. Jumping up I could feel the anger inside of me rising. "What do you mean too fuckin short?" I screamed into the DAC.
"No other way of putting it. Too short cock." Ged responded calmly.

The noise of jangling keys knocking against a First Aid tin and oil lamp caused me to look outbye. My cap lamp caught the gleaming smile and white of George's dentures.
"Alreyt cock." He asked Paul as he approached.
"Just found out spare cable's too short. Ged's bin on."
"Good job I've just fetched a sparein in." I wasn't sure I'd heard right.
"A spare shearer cable George?" I asked.
"Yep. Bloody yon mon, Teddy had loaded two. One for us and one for L33's put'm in same mine car. Usual excuse. Short of empties. Got the lads to offload and put it in a half mine car with some chockwood. Lads hauling it into return as we speyk." At that very moment I could have grabbed George and given him the biggest hug of his life. I didn't though.

"You little darlin." My response caused him to chuckle. I turned back to the DAC. "Ged. Get the short cable into the chockline. We'll run it out later with the damaged one. Get the lads into the return. Spare one on its way."

"Fuckin ell Mick. That were quick cock. Sure, it's a longan?" Good question I hadn't thought to ask. I looked again to George.

"I longan alreyt. Took us forever to shift."

"Ged good to go!"

"One other thing." Ged responded.

"What fuckin now?"

"He's worse than my missus for talkin." The comment from an anonymous voice caught me by surprise.

"Oi Cliff I'll fuckin av tha makin comments like that."

"For fucks sake Ged it weren't me honest."

"Les then, you little cunt."

"Not me Ged." Les responded a little too quick.

"Ged. Me again. What other thing?"

"You comin up ere to carry pummel end?" His comment caused me to stretch my back it was still aching. I checked my watch. We'd lost half an hour already.

"I'll leave it to you. You're the experts."

"Ere get this down tha cock." George passed me a cup of his steaming hot sweetened tea.

"Don't mind if I do. Thanks George." Twenty minutes later.

"Hello Mick. Hello Mick Gibson."

"Hi Control. Mick ere."

"Mr Keech bin on. What's latest?"

"Nearly there Steve. Just goin back on to check."

"Right. I'll let him know." I turned back to Paul.

"Best get the outbye belts started."

"They haven't changed cable yet."

"You know that, and I know that. Let's not let the fuckers on top know, heh. Just get the fucker going." I liked Paul. He was a good lad but sometimes he felt the need to question my decisions. I continued down towards the maingate. Alf and Jack were in their normal position. Again, eating snap.

"You two got fuck all to do?" Not often I got the first word in.

"Now our kid. How's yer sen?"

"Good thanks Alf. Where's Freddy?"

"Gone up return. Bobby short of dets again. Needed borrow some." I shook my head. "Have seen his latest poem Mick?"

"The Arrogant Overman?"

"I. He's done another."

"Not as good as first." Jack added.

"I'm sure I'll get to see it. Right if you don't mind, I haven't got all day to chat with you two."

"Mick, just before you go. Jack ere reckons thy could ave put tuther cable on. They do have some stretch in them." They both began to laugh.

"Fuck off Alf."

"Hello Scouse." Ged's voice rang out from the face DAC.

"Best get move on Mick. Don't want to keep your mate waiting." Ignoring Alf's comment, I climbed onto the face.

"Ged?"

"Best get theesen up ere."

"Why? What's up?" I got no response, which suggested he didn't want Control to hear. This wasn't good. I adjusted my oil lamp to the side of my belt and climbed onto the face panzer. Not forgetting to check the faceside I began to move up the face at pace. Twenty chocks further I needed to navigate a large slab of coal sitting over the pans. Another five minutes lights ahead alerted me to the proximity of the shearer. I could see Ged standing just below it. He was holding something in his hand. As I got closer, my cap lamp reflecting off the brass exterior.

"What the fuck?"

"My thoughts exactly." It was the pummel end, minus the cable. "Almost reached us. Coming down nice as pie. Before we knew it. Stopped. Panzer still running, flight bar ripped it right off. Nowt we could do."

"I don't fuckin believe it." A number of lights above the machine directed towards me. No one said a word.

"Me neither cock."

"Hello Mick. Hello Mick Gibson." Steve's voice filled the silence.

"That's all I fuckin well need."

"Hello Mick Gibson. Hello Mick." I stood not moving to answer. My head was throbbing, sweat once more tricking down my chest. What should I do? I'd need a minute to think. Get this wrong and I was in for a right old fucking. Time to pass this shit on to someone else.

"Who was on the other end?"

"That's the best part. Fuckin Bobby Bang, Bang, and the Poet."

"No fuckin surprises there then." Lifting my helmet, I wiped my forehead attempting to stop the sweat dripping into my eyes.

"Hello Mick. Hello Mick Gibson."

"Do you want me to get that?"

"No, I'll sort it." I climbed back into the chockline. "Steve, Mick here."

"Any update? Manager's been on." *Time to pass the buck.*

"Fuckin update. Fuckin update. I'll give you a fuckin update and you can pass it on to the Manager. That fuckin man that calls himself the Surface fuckin Superintendent has only sent us a short cable. We only find out once it's been fitted and start attaching the Bretby."

"Fuckin ell Mick take a breath." Ged's comment caused me to do just that.

"It's a complete and utter fuck up. That's what it is. A fuck up. No other way to describe it." I screamed into the DAC.

"Think he got message cock!" There was no immediate reply from Steve.

Then finally.

"Have you got another?"

"On it now. Hello panels. Hello Paul."

"Hi Mick."

"Is George still with yer."

"Yeah."

"Can you put him on."

"George ere Mick."

"That other cable you mentioned earlier. Can you get lads to move it to the return? Now!"

"But Mick as I said before it'd labelled for…."

"Fuckin now George. Fuckin now!"

Two hours later we finally got going again. I stopped over with half of the lads to keep coaling. We ran out the three cables. The two damaged and the shorten. I made sure we loaded all three plus the one from under the belt. The pummel too, I'd have to explain that at some point but not today. The noonshift haulage lads were told cables out was a priority. Whilst loading the cables I caught both Freddy and Bobby trying to sneak passed the Meeting Station. I had a quiet word with both. I think they both understood how I felt.

By the time I'd got up the pit most of the dayshift had gone. There was only Chris in the control room. I guessed Bennie had gone to get changed. I headed towards the lamproom. I was completely fucked. Aching from every bone in my body. The tops of my thighs from running up and down the face. My arms and back from dragging and loading cable.

The lamproom too was empty. I placed my oil lamp on the table outside the office. Having removed my lamp and rescuer I continued into the crush hall. The mid-afternoon sun was streaming through the top windows of the crush hall. Another late summer scorcher. Momentarily blinding me. I spotted the water taps. My mouth was dry. Removing my helmet I placed my head below the spout, allowing the clean, fresh, cold water to fill my mouth. The pressure of it blasting between my teeth. Gargling for a few seconds I spat out bits of bacca.

Then head back down for another refill. This time swallowing. It felt good, really good. I replaced my helmet. My chest now soaked through, I headed towards the Undermanager's office.

Geoff was sat suppin tea from a large white porcelain mug. He smiled when he saw me enter. "Good ere init."

"Why would you have it any other way." I responded.

"Go and get a bath. There's nowt else tell me is there?" Before I could answer I sensed someone walk in behind me. Geoff's eyes confirmed another visitor. I turned. The guy standing there looked familiar. Jet black hair, his sideburns had flecks of grey. Dark blue patterned suit with a lighter blue shirt and matching tie. The most striking feature were the large golden cuff links prominently exposed on the cuffs of the shirt.

"Hello Geoff, I'm not interrupting you, am I?" He looked towards me, it was more of a sneer. I recognised him. Then I realised who he reminded me of. The guy off Tiswas with Spit the Dog, Bob something or other. I returned his stare.

"No Alan, what can I do for you sir?"

"Seems we've had another damaged cable on L32's." Geoff afforded me a quick glance. I don't think Alan spotted it. "Making a habit of it. Thing is the damaged ones are not being returned to the surface. Mr Creed has deemed fit to reduce my budget on consumables. I can't keep buying new. Can you get your people to get the damaged ones out?" Geoff once more looked towards me. This time maintaining eye contact.

"Yep, already loaded. Priority this afternoon." I responded. Not that this guy paid me any attention.

"Straight from the horse's mouth." Geoff replied. Not that I'd ever been called a horse before.

"Might be worthwhile explaining to the Neanderthal's to be a little more careful." *Cheeky bastard.* Before I could say anything, he'd turned and walked off. Geoff had just taken another mouthful of his tea. Almost choking as he began to laugh.

"Who the fuck was that?"

"Alan, Alan Fielding, Electrical Engineer."

"I thought the other fella. What's his name. Stan Boris, thought he was the Engineer?"

"Stan thinks he is. No, it's Alan. Certainly, has a way with words. Might want to mention to Ged bout being a Neanderthal."

"I think we should let that one go. Right. I'm fucking off for a bath."

"See you tomorrow."

"I that tha will lad."

The baths were empty. I removed my boots. It felt good, the smell however wasn't. Climbing up to my top locker I extracted my towel and soap tray. Completely stripping off, I threw everything into the locker. I'd suddenly remembered I was taking the kids to Pex Hill, an old sandstone quarry on the way to the Hillside in Widnes. I'd promised the missus. I was late already.

Standing below the torrent of hot steaming water blasting against my exposed skin. I stood motionless. Eyes closed. I threw my shoulders back. The aches from earlier seemingly gone. Reaching behind me I increased the flow of hot water. Opening my eyes momentarily to watch the dirty black residue running over my feet onto the concrete floor. Back into the white tiled channels.

My mind wandered back to the comment from the Electrical Engineer. I wonder how often he got underground. If at all. These fuckers were a law unto themselves. The guy at Cronton, Lenny, hadn't been the same. In fact, I thought he was one of the face electricians he spent that long underground. Calling us Neanderthals *cheeky bastard.*

"Tough shift lad? Turn tha round. I'll do thee back." It was Bennie. "Owt else they needs taking in?" I placed both hands against the tiled wall.
"Just make sure you get the damaged cables out."
"I, Geoff mentioned same. There you go. Clean as a whistle." I turned back around.
"Thanks Bennie."
"Best you get moving lad. You're spending more time ere than Frankie Glow."
"I think I'm some way from that yet. I'll see ye." I continued to stand there after Bennie had gone. The hot pounding spray of the water on my back massaging the aches and pains away. I began to reflect on Bennie's comment. There was no doubt I was spending a lot of time at the pit. More time on L32's during the week than I was spending at home. Being so excited at being appointed as the Face Overman. The responsibility and exhilaration when achieving. Whatever the task. Having the authority to make decisions that were mine alone.

I arrived home an hour later.
"You're late. Thought you'd promised to take the kids out?"
"That I did and that's what we'll do. Where are they?"
"In the back playing. Thanks Mick I know you must be tired, the kids were so looking forward to it." Unexpectedly Annie walked across and gave me a peck on the cheek. "Kids, Dad's home. Time to get ready."
"Daddy."

"Hiya you two. I hope you've been good for Mum." I responded to Jamie and Lizzie as I lifted them up together.

☐

"Hello Mick Gibson. Hello Mick."

"Fuckin ell Paul ask him what he wants." I shouted above the noise of the stageloader and coal dropping onto the maingate belt. I was sat opposite the panels.

"Hi Chris, Mick can hear tha."

"Could he give me a call. Tell'em it's important."

"For fucks sake!" I responded again. Having only just sat down with a cup of hot coffee with sugar. Kindly provided by Brian the fitter. I was not best pleased at being disturbed.

"Chris, Mick here. What? When? Okay." I replaced the handset.

"Problem?" Paul asked.

"Not yet. Any idea where George is?"

"Outbye somewhere checking supplies."

"Right do me a favour. Give George, Freddy, and Bobby a shout. Ask'm give you a call. Tell'm Manager's on his way in and I've gone out to meet him."

"Where is he?"

"Bottom of E3."

"Fuckin ell Mick that's not much warning."

"Chris reckons he'd originally planned to go to V24's. Must have changed his mind." I took the last gulp of coffee. "Can you also give this back to Brian." I passed Paul the empty plastic cup. The noise from the stageloader began to increase. The dull thud of a fully loaded pan now replaced by the rackety, rack of flight bar on the steel pans. It then began to slow. Paul reacted in an instant.

"Who's geet stageloader locked out?" There was no immediate answer. Just the noise in the distance krrrr, krrrr, krrrr, of the jigger pick.

"Breaking lump maingate end." I recognised Ged's dulcet tones immediately.

"Ged Mick ere could you pop up to the stageloader."

"Why don't tha fuckin pop ere."

"Can't mate. On my way out to meet someone special." He'd got the message by the silence that followed. "Right Paul let the guys know and for fucks sake try and keep the coal coming."

"Will do."

I began to head outbye at speed. The last time the Manager had been on 32's was late summer last year. He'd accompanied the Deputy Director and Production Manager. It hadn't been a particularly good visit. *I wonder why today?* I was a regular visitor to the Top Shunt he hadn't given any indication the last time I was in.

I was a little concerned I hadn't been round and done a full recce of the district. Normally leaving that until later in the shift. From what I'd seen yesterday the place hadn't looked too bad. Probably could have done with more stonedust spreading around the junction opposite the Meeting Station. I wasn't about to kid myself though. There was always something to line you up for a round of fucks

By the time I'd reached the Hausherr dint I was lathered. I felt for the pink grapefruit down the front of my overalls but thought better of it. I was out of bacca, forgetting to call in to the canteen first thing. I quickly extracted my tin of snuff. Looking about the place the lads had left it in a reasonable state. The dint wasn't manned this morning. I'd used the lads on pump packing. I'd agreed with George to leave the belt suspended in the air. Parking the Hausherr beneath, enabling the haulage to pass. It looked okay and certainly took away the problem of having to clean the bottom rollers. The change in sound coming from the belt suggested they'd sorted the lump and we were coaling again. The click, click, click of belt stitching over each top roller, replaced by the silent passage of fully loaded belt.

I shivered. The fresh intake air had replaced the excess body heat I'd generated. The dampness of my vest beginning to feel uncomfortable for the first time. Time to keep moving.

Both sets of stonedust barriers had been moved in the previous week. Something we were doing on a regular basis now face production had increased. The arched roadway looked a little patchy from the stonedust spread. I made a mental note to get it done again. It wasn't the most efficient way to spread the stuff by hand. Manholes were all clear. It had taken sometime but finally we'd got the lads to take the empty stonedust bags out on the haulage. Always preferable to hiding in the manhole or sending them out on the belt. Walking again at pace alongside the belt the structure now at waist height. The black stuff piled high. I reached across to the mix of large lumps and smaller mineral. Quickly extracting a handful. It was damp. A consequence of us cleaning out the sprays on the shearer on a regular basis. And as important replacing when required.

I wasn't far now from the Meeting Station. The lights of the junction I could see clearly. Then into view came two further lights. I'd only been expecting one. They were looking towards me. I soon made out the bodily shapes ahead. One was carrying a stick and wearing a white Donkey jacket and blue overalls. It was the Manager and George. His ever-present smile with his whiter than white dentures. I'd put the smile down to one of two things. When he picked up his weekly pay chit or climbing into a brand-new Toyota Celica. It must be catching; the Manager was smiling too. Not a regular occurrence from my experience.

"Good to see you, George. Perhaps we'll see you later."

"Aye that thy will Mr Creed." The Manager had given George his prompt to fuck off. "Alreyt Mick?"

"All good George." I looked for any expression of concern. There was none. Just his permanent smile from his clean face. He headed out towards the return. Which suggested the Manager would be visiting the face via the intake.

"Morning Mr Creed."

"Morning lad. How's it going this morning?" The Manager's question was unusually softly spoken. His face black. It made him look old and tired. Weary even. I couldn't for one minute imagine what pressure he was under. Certainly not after the incident with the pipes. I'd gotten to know the man for the short space of time I'd been employed at the mine. Not surprising the amount of time, I spent in his office. He was as hard as nails, scary even. He didn't suffer fools. From experience if you put the effort in, even if sometimes you failed, he'd support you. I had huge respect for the man.

"All good thanks Mr Creed. Shearer on its way down for the second."

"Come on then take me round your district."

"Might be best if you leave your jacket here."

"Good point lad." We began to move inbye.

The sound of the black stuff hitting the chute was always a comfort. Moreso with the main man alongside. "Oh, just one thing." He'd stopped pointing back to the junction. I thought we'd got off to too good a start. "Good move that." He was pointing to a stock pile of stonedust. "Saves the panic when you've got a visit."

"Thanks." I took the compliment. However, the reason we'd done it was due to a derailment. It had been heading towards the return we just hadn't got round to reloading it.

"How's Frankie's chute?"

"Doing a great job." I wasn't likely to say anything else. I'd gathered Frankie was held in high regard by the Manager. A relationship I guessed went back many years. To be fair, however, since it had been fitted, we'd had very little trouble with chute blockages. He turned back towards me.

"That and others making a real difference to our larger coal product. Local companies can't get enough of the stuff. You aware of the gas we sell to Crosfield and Sons lad?"

"Yeah." I loved the way he kept referring to me as lad. It was like being with my dad.

"Three million we spent laying a six-mile pipeline."

He began to tap his stick against the rails. A signal to get moving. We continued inbye. The sound of his stick hitting the rails accompanied the conveyor.

I stopped after a few yards. The Manager a little further back. He was walking slower than normal. I waited till he'd caught up.

"You okay Mr Creed?"

"Yeah, why shouldn't I be?" He was giving nothing away as usual. We continued in silence until we'd reached the heavy barrier. "Might be a thing of the past soon. Got some of those new water barriers for W11's. Going to give them a try."

"So, I've heard. Frank's mentioned it." I smiled at the thought of seeing Frank Newton, the Safety Engineer. I often saw him in the clean canteen. When I'd first arrived at the pit, I thought he was the Manager.

On reaching the Hausherr dint. It was my turn to stop. Wanting to explain, before I was asked, why it hadn't been manned up.

"Short of lads for pump packing."

"One of the many reasons we're pulling out of the Lower Florida." He seemingly ignored my explanation. "Floor lift. L33's will be the last after this place. As will C16's in the Crombouke. Future will be in the Wigan Four Feet and Ince Six Feet. Just the two areas going forward, Mid and South." He looked towards me. The blackness of his face accentuated the whiteness of his eyes. They were bloodshot. He looked old, a lot older than he was, maybe late forties approaching fifty. I could only guess. It wasn't a question I was likely to ask. The silence that followed suggested it was time to continue inbye.

"How you and Ged getting on?"

"Okay, I guess. Give him a good slapping now and again. Keep him in place." The Manager began to laugh. I waited for any further comment. There was none. I'd long suspected that being made up to Face Overman on L32's had been a test. A test to see whether I was up to the job. Not just managing the face but also managing the men. It was all very well shouting and using your position to get things done. It was also a matter of gaining their trust and respect. Showing them, we were all in this together. It didn't work with them all. There was always the odd twat to deal with. Mine happened to be the ex-Bold lad Johnny Bastard.

Twenty minutes later, I could see the stageloader lights. The conveyor was still piled high with the black stuff. I couldn't believe my luck. The coal hadn't stopped coming since I'd been with the Manager. It was like being in a dream. It wasn't often you got moments like this. The gentle hum of a fully loaded belt in the background providing reassurance.

There were two individuals standing opposite the panels. Paul for one and I guessed with certainty who the other would be. His cat like smile greeted us as we approached.

"Nah Pat what do we owe the honour?"

"Come to see where all this coal is coming from Ged." I continued passed Ged ignoring the gentle dig of his elbow in my ribs. It was a tight squeeze getting passed him the control console and bank of panels. Thought it best if I left the two of them in private for a catch up.

"Hi Paul. How far down are we now?"

"Bout thirty chock. Problem though Mick, goin to have to stop shortly pack hasn't gone off."

"Why the fuck......" The clanking from the stageloader chain began to increase as the weight of coal reduced.

"Reckon them daft fuckers have put too much Tekbent in." I looked outbye toward the Manager and Ged. They'd taken little notice still deep in conversation.

"Well why don't they add more fuckin cement?" I wasn't sure why I was telling Paul this. "I'll go and have a look."

Fuckin knew this was too good to be true! I almost slipped as I travelled at speed towards maingate end. The hydraulic tank as per norm was overflowing. The white creamy fluid running down the side of the tank. Turning grey as it mixed with the coal dust. I stopped momentarily to switch off the flow of water. The floor beneath my feet now a mud pile. Brian the fitter was soon alongside.

"Alreyt Mick."

"Am I fuck!"

"Relief valve cock. Bin in touch with Bob. Sending one down with noon shift. Soon av it fettled." One of Brian's many qualities he never got flustered unlike some.

I continued down to the maingate pack. Alongside the lump breaker Frankie had fitted, I stopped to make a note. All the cutter picks were missing. Just the box bar left. I'd begun to perspire once more. The smell of my body odour worse than normal. I could taste too the salty perspiration above my top lip.

I couldn't see the packers Cliff and Les. However, Alf and Jack were sat on the maingate platform. Having set the first arch of the shift they'd decided to have their snap.

"Alright cocka?" Alf shouted down towards me. The two of them looked like a pair of gargoyles. I could never understand how the two of them always looked fresh. Ged had mentioned they ran a paper round before coming to work.

"How's yer sen Mick?" Jack added.

"Not fuckin good!"

"Dost tha want summat eat?" I ignored any further comments. They just loved to take the piss.

Climbing up onto the face I was hit by the smell of the plastic packing bag. Mixed with the unmistakable aroma of the Tekpak. The red flashing light of the DAC directly opposite. I was a little concerned as I still hadn't seen any sign of the packers. Somewhat relieved I spotted two cap lamps behind the chock.

"For fuck's sake lads. What the fuck is goin on?"

"Fuckin ell Mick. Nowt do with us." Les appeared he had his worried look on. "It'll be them two fuckin wankers on machine."

"I and who put 'em on?" His mate added.

"Thanks Cliff, that's helpful." I moved passed where the lads were standing and prodded the bag. Two thirds of it had begun to solidify. The top was still liquid. "You know I've got Manager with me?" I didn't receive a reply. "Why don't you just add cement?"

"Fuckin ell Mick. Dost think we're thick. The fuckers av gone and blocked cement pipe."

"Fuck, shit, wank!" I wasn't sure what else to say.

"Nah Mick. Don't be gettin theesen all worked up." Cliff responded. "Knob eds have found blocked pipe. On with changing it now."

"How long?"

"Should only be another five."

"What you goin to do? Just add cement?"

"Nah, don't work like that Mick." I watched with concern as Les extracted a Stanley knife. Before I could say anything else he sliced just above where the pack had begun to harden. The white Tekbent gushed out causing us all to step back.

"For fuck's sake Les what yer doin?" He never answered immediately. He and Cliff began to unclip the top of the bag from the mesh. Allowing the top third of the bag to now sit on the stuff that had gone off.

"Watch and learn Mick and whilst thay's at it pass me the half bag yer standing on." I hadn't spotted it earlier. I was standing on what Les had described as the half bag.

"Pump pack station lads av been on Les. Pipe sorted. Ready when you are." Paul shouted over the face DAC.

The lads took the bag from me and began to hang it. "Mick, tell'm we'll be ready in two." I relayed the message from Les. My attention now drawn to a light advancing from up the face. The scrawny figure could only be Dave off the shearer. He saw me looking.

"Good ere init." He said smiling before turning to his colleagues. "How long's reckon?"

"Fuckin ell Dave not you as well. Got enough on ere with fuckin Mick mitherin." We all began to laugh. "Mick tell'm start pumping."

"Paul let'm know to start pumping. Are the other two still talking?"

"Will do and yeah." At least the Manager hadn't had to see the fuck up.

"Best get back and wake that lazy cunt." Dave's comment interrupted by the splash of the Tekpack pouring into the newly hung bag. I had a vision of Johnny lying on his back. Helmet covering his face.

"Dare you tell'm to his face." Les responded laughing.

"Might just do that. Take lock out when you're ready for us." Dave shouted before disappearing back up the face.

"Snuff anyone?" I offered as we watched the bag fill. The distinct sound of the splashing liquid hitting the base of the newly hung bag. Reducing as the area filled. The smell I'd picked up earlier back again now but fresher.

"I go then Mick."

"Chew as well Mick?" Les offered.

"We'll make a proper pit mon of Mick yet Les."

"I, bout time he started buying some himself." I smiled and nodded in agreement. I'd gotten to know these lads quite well. Don't think I could have asked for a better group. I'd been lucky. The team a mix of completely different personalities worked well together. We'd miss Dave since he'd announced he was leaving to start a B&B in Devon.

"Right Mick, take lock out off." The pre alarm kicked in.

"I'll see you two in a mo. Better go and see where Manager is."

Climbing down back into the maingate I shivered. The cold intake air apparent once more.

"Alreyt our kid." Alf shouted from the platform. They were setting up the hand-held hydraulic drilling machine. I ignored his comment as the coal began to drop once more off the panzer on to the stage loader. The black stuff was alongside me as I reached Frankie's pickless lump breaker. A large lump held stationary as the flight bars beneath ripped into its lower half. The coal began to build. Now reaching the top of the side plates. Each time a flight bar hit the lump the bar moved ever so slightly. The high tensile bots holding it firm. I looked around for the jigger and then. The sound of coal being smashed, splinters began to shoot off in all directions, followed by clouds of dust. The flow of coal behind began to force the obstructed lump forward. Its resistance finally thwarted as the box bar removed the top half. Causing it finally to pass under.

There was still no sign of the Manager. Brian had disappeared too along with the leaks from the hydraulic tank. He'd obviously done a temporary repair. I continued forward. Paul was sat between the panels having his snap. Further outbye the other two were still in deep conversation. Although I doubted whether the Manager had, had chance to say anything. It looked as though Ged was still on transmit.

The Manager looked towards me as I approached. "Hey Ged, any chance you could give your gob a rest. I'm sure Mr Creed would appreciate it."

"Fuck off Scouse." Our comments caused the Manager to smile, which was always a result. So too was him standing.

"Right Ged, thanks for the catch up. Looks as though Mick wants me to keep moving." No more said we continued inbye. As we reached Paul the Manager stopped.

"Now lad, how's your old man?" Paul somewhat surprised to be spoken to, hesitated before answering.

"Okay, thank you Mr Creed."

"Pass him my regards." *Well, I never!* The Manager knew, Nick Arnold, the ATC Foreman was Paul's old fella.

"I will Mr Creed." I winked at Paul as I passed. The poor lad was in a state of shock. With a workforce of over a thousand men, he'd know that. I was suitably impressed.

The black stuff was still coming thick and fast. So was the leak from the hydraulic tank. So much for the temporary repair. The unmistakable smell of the Aquacent. Before he could make comment. I reached up and turned off the water.

"Relief valve. Got a replacement coming down with the noonshift." Using his stick to help him pass over the mud pile that had once more established itself beneath. The last thing I needed was the Manager slipping over.

By the time we'd reached Frankie's lump breaker I was alongside the Manager. Once more perspiration was oozing from every pore of my body. We stopped.

"One of Frankie's?"

"Yeah…."

"Isn't it missing something?"

"Yeah. I've got a replacement on order." Which wasn't a lie. I'd just need to follow up to where it was. Workshops were currently inundated with work due to the imminent start-up of C16's and W11's. The Manager hadn't mentioned to me W11's for some time. He had suggested some time ago I would take charge of the place. I hoped my performance on 32'S gave him the confidence I was ready for bigger things now.

"What was the problem with the pack?" *For fuck's sake did this guy never miss anything?*

"Blockage, sorted now." That was all the detail I was willing to give. I never liked giving too much away when we'd had a fuck up. Surprisingly, there was no follow up question. We continued forward.

Ahead Alf and Jack were busy drilling once more. No sarcastic comments offered this time. It was an affect the Manager had on certain individuals, finding it hard to converse with the boss man. Ged being an exception.

An array of lights emanating from the faceline and the noise of the shearer picks ripping coal suggested the machine was about to enter the maingate. Alf and Jack ceased drilling and moved back. Huge slabs of the black stuff surrendering ahead of the maingate disc. Falling onto the panzer, some lumps spilling into the maingate. This was one of the moments I loved best. The huge double ender hauling itself into the roadway. The noise deafening. The absolute power of the machine for all to see. The fine spray of water shooting in all directions as the maingate disc began to raise itself to its highest point and cut out much of the roadway's profile. We stood and watched the spectacle ahead in silence. I bet we all felt the same. Dave, the cutter man, face black as an ouzel, safety goggles smattered with coal dust and spray busily prodding the control block with his improvised handle. A short length of wooden dowel. I caught sight of JB skulking on the faceline, glancing occasionally to where we stood. The slabs of coal had now entered the stageloader. I just hoped and prayed the pickless box bar did its job. The grinding and crushing sound gave me my answer. I gave it a cursory glance. What was left of the slab passed beneath. *Thank fuck!*

The disc began to drop towards the ribside. Profile complete, I watched Dave prod another brass button causing the cowl to raise itself. Passing through ninety degrees it fell to the floor as the machine began to haul itself in the opposite direction. I took the opportunity to glance sideways at the Manager. The whites of his eyes accentuated by the blackness of his face. His expression had changed. Replaced by that of excitement, contentment even. We must all have felt the same. A sense of achievement. After all this was why we were all here. To "win" coal. He must have sensed my look. I turned away, hoping he hadn't seen me staring. The noise now reducing as the machine moved out of sight. It was a signal to keep moving before the machine entered for a second time to complete the bi-di.

Climbing onto the face I took a quick glance towards the pack. Satisfied at what I'd seen. The smell too was different, the heat too evident as it solidified. No sign of Lcs or Cliff. They'd moved further up to assist in advancing the chocks. The Manager was leaning over the spills, lamp shing towards the roof. Satisfied he turned back towards me. He followed as I led the way. This time in front of the chocks yet to be pulled in. The AFC now fast up against the coal face.

"How's the floor dirt?" The comment caused me to stop. *Oops.* I turned. The Manager was smiling I don't think he expected an answer.

"All good Mr Creed. I check it regularly."

A little further along we moved into the chock line. Two of the face men appeared. Advancing the supports working their way towards the maingate.

"Morning Mick, Morning Mr Creed."

"Morning lads." The noise from the shearer hauling itself back towards the maingate prevented any further conversation. I settled back into the next chock to let the shearer operators pass. I watched as the Manager did the same. Extracting my tin of snuff, I stretched across to offer it to the Manager. We were then engulfed in the noise and spray from the maingate disc. Dave appeared, eyes barely visible in his protective goggles. Looking up towards the roof profile. From previous conversations he'd explained to me how he used a small band of dirt, hardly discernible to the naked eye as his guide to where he placed the disc. He smiled and was then gone. Shards of the black stuff flying in all directions. The carbide picks chomping and releasing the mineral. I moved my head to one side to avoid the flying debris. The experience as always was exhilarating. Huge slabs surrendering before the disc, sliding forward towards the pans. Some falling forward joining that already cut heading towards the maingate. Others waiting to be smashed before continuing outbye. The long flat surface of the cutter was now facing me. I was pleased to see the lads had cleared most of its surface, now replaced by the newly extracted mineral. Using both arms I covered the front of my body as Johnny appeared. I needn't have bothered. He paid me no attention. His eyes clearly fixed on the return disc. I guessed the presence of the Manager had dissuaded him from any physical attack on the Face Overman. It wasn't too good an opportunity to miss. Clenching my fist, I gave him a light kidney punch. Perhaps not hard enough as there was no response.

Pulling myself up I continued forward. Ahead, Terry was pushing the pans over.

"Alreyt Mick?"

"Yeah, all good thanks."

"Bloody ell. See you've brought Gaffer in with tha." I watched as he offered his hand to the Manager. Which he took. I was suddenly distracted spotting the Bretby moving along the floor. I quickly moved forward to lift it back into the spills. Large lumps of coal lying in the bottom of the trough. I'd need to get the thing cleaned out. Last thing I needed was another damaged shearer cable. I was now out of earshot from the other two. I guess they'd known each other for some time. It wasn't a surprise I recalled a conversation with someone when I'd first arrived at Parkside. He reckoned the Manager held a unique record in the Lancashire coalfield. According to him Mr Creed had held every official mining position at the same pit. From Shotfirer to General Manager. Wow that must be some record.

I waited as they continued their conversation not wanting to interrupt something I guess the Manager very rarely got time to do. Whilst waiting I contemplated my position. I'd been Face Overman nigh on fifteen months. I was now ready for something bigger. Was this an appropriate time to pop the question? I wasn't sure. Mr Keech had suggested there may be a possibility of managing a shift. Wouldn't be the nightshift. Tony Ramsbottom already filled that position. Noons was probably the only option. Currently covered by Bennie Lead. Lights appeared ahead, I put my thoughts to one side. I watched as chocks began to drop, then advance forwards. It was Les and Cliff. Ordinarily I'd have assisted. I didn't know the Manager well enough to understand how he would have viewed that.

"Alreyt Mick. Taking your time today?"

"Yeah, just waiting on Terry. Plus, I had Ged earlier telling the Manager his life story. Tell you what. He can fuckin talk your Chargehand." Les smiled. It was a game I loved to play with the lads. Continually having a dig at Ged. Trying to get his men to agree but I could never get any of them to say anything derogatory. Loyal to a man or maybe it was pure and simple fear of what he would do, if he caught them talking out of turn. Whatever the reason, I just loved to play the game.

"Looks as though you're on the way." I turned to see the Manager finally approaching.

"Quick question Les. When Dave gets his B&B you planning on taking shearer duties?"

"No fuckin chance. Work with that fuckin nutter. Nah, I'll leave that with Colin Peach."

"Okay, just wondered. Catch you two later." I continued towards the return, still within earshot of the two of them.

"Morning Mr Creed."

"Morning lads."

I took my time travelling between the chocks. The continual bashing of my oil lamp against my knee I was finding quite annoying. Ordinarily I'd be travelling towards the return on the pans. Spying my chance when the panzer stopped. Not today, however, we were having the best run for some time.

The sweat was now pumping out of me from all over. I decided to stop and let the Manager catch up.

"You must be pleased?" He asked as he reached me. I wasn't sure what he meant.

"With the face?"

"No with everything." I felt a little uncomfortable. It wasn't something I found easy to discuss. Compliments from Mr Creed.

"Yes and no. Always room for improvement."

We continued outbye with little more being said. Not until we got to the outbye end of the crosscut.

"Well Mick, you coming out with me?"

"If you don't mind. I'd need to go back in. Couple of things I need to sort."

"Understand and well done." Again, it wasn't something I was used to. Not sure if I preferred the arseholing and abuse I usually got. This was a little unnerving.

"Thanks Mr Creed." Once more I was tempted to ask the question of my next move.

"Not sure if Geoff has mentioned to you about the consultants?"

"Consultants? What do you mean?"

"Seems we're moving into the modern world. Hobart House has decreed that each of the Area's need to better understand the workforce. After the strike top brass want to better understand the general feeling of the workforce Director has been instructed to carry out what they're calling a staff survey." *What the fucks one of them?* I thought better than to ask. He began to laugh.

"Don Gold becomes an Assistant Manager."

"What?"

"Assistant Manager Personnel."

"That should please him."

"I'm sure it will. Catch you later."

☐

"Morning Mick."

"Morning George."

"Managed to sort anything?"

"Yeah. Cayle's sending us Vinny. Just gone back for dets. Picked up ten misen just in case."

"What was up with Bobby then?"

"Threw up in baths. Dicky tummy." I shook my head. A likely story. Probably still pissed from last night. The jerk and clashing of the manrider carriages interrupted our conversation. The locomotive began to haul us inbye. I pulled my Donkey jacket tightly in against my body. Unable to fasten as I'd lost all the buttons. The cold intake air from the downcast shaft swirled in amongst the carriages. The carriage was full. Bodies packed in tightly against one another at least provided some heat. Even though it was summer, standing around at Pit Bottom caused the cold to get into my bones. I was fuckin freezing.

"You heard about Vinny, Mick?" Freddy Clough asked as he offered me his tin of Hedges. "Need to go easy on im Mick. Not in the best frame of mind."

"Fuckin ell Freddy. You'd think I was a complete twat with you lot." The silence that followed may have given me the answer.

We'd started having problems with the maingate again. I'd arranged with Ged to get the shearer already in the tailend to go in again before heading back down. Give us a bit more time. George would chase the haulage lads to get another run of timber in. I passed the tin back to Freddy. Inhaling through my nostrils cleared my head immediately. The aroma pleasant enough. I planned to head straight into the maingate with Freddy. There were legs to set and pack to pump on. I'd concentrate on the timber and if needed get some wooden dowels in.

An hour later, timber complete, the shearer headed down towards the maingate. I was still on the face watching as the black stuff continued to flow. Sat between the chocks, I took another pinch. My body sweat had almost tried time to get moving again. I could smell it too. Lifting my arse off the warm comforting loop of inch and quarter bagging I began towards the tailend. The slowing of the panzer caused me to reach towards the DAC. I needn't have bothered.

"Breaking a lump." Les shouted from the maingate. It was pleasing to see how quickly the lads reacted to any stoppage.

"Come on Les. Be doin lad. On for big bonus this week." Ged shouted.

"Yeah, get a fuckin move on you little shit." Another voice added.

"Hey Graham. Don't be talkin to our little Les like that."

"Sorry Ged." The command this fella had over these lads never ceased to amaze me. I'd previously asked him why he hadn't gone on a Deps course. His answer had been terse and straight to the point. "And leave the NUM? Don't fuckin think so Scouse. You may have betrayed your working-class roots but not me lad." I never brought the subject up again.

"Come on Les. Get a move on lad."

"Fuckin ell Ged. Tryin our best."

"Can't be doin much, time spent on DAC." The pre alarm covered any further conversation. I continued towards the return.

"Now Ged. How's it lookin?"

"All good Scouse. I'm heading down to maingate for me jackbit." The expression on my face caused him to add. "Stop fuckin worryin. Lads are working through plus they'll stop over if required."

"Nice one."

"Tell you what though Mick. Bobby's replacement Vinny don't look in best of shape."

"What do'y mean?"

"With im earlier. Wanted to slit me wrists. The fuckin lad's in a bad way. Thought he were goin to start scriking." I recalled Freddy's comment from earlier.

"I'll have a word."

"I best do that. Graham says keep catchin him staring into waste. I'll see tha later."

Climbing off the face into the return, the lads were busy setting steel. The clanking of the empty panzer chain being thrown over the return sprocket louder now. An empty pump packing bag hung ready for filling off to my left. No sign of Vinny. Ged's comment causing me to peer into the waste.

I shone my lamp outbye. I didn't see anything at first. Then I noticed a lamp to the side of the road. Someone sat down. I continued outbye. It was Vinny. I didn't know the lad that well. Other than to say hello when we passed in the baths.

Hi Vinny. How's it goin?" He had his head turned away from me.

"Shit Mick, if you want to know." He turned to face me. His eyes reddened. The dampness of tears still apparent.

"Fuckin ell fella what's up?"

"Me and missus split up."

"Oh, I'm sorry to hear that. What happened?" Not that it was any of my business. I didn't know what else to say.

"Ever bin Graham House Mick?" *Oops* Did he need to say anymore.

"Twice actually. When I was on the ET Scheme."

"Heard of the Tuxedo Princess?" *Heard of it? Me and my mate Jimmy were nick named the Captain and his mate.* "It's a night club."

I slowly lowered myself to the floor. Sitting on a wooden prop. I extracted my tin of snuff. This I had to hear. "Pinch Vinny?"

"Ta Mick." I waited. Think I could guess what was coming. "Sandra was her name met her first time we went aboard. Had a few drinks, started kissin. One thing led to another. Went there every neet. Said she loved me. Said I was the man of her dreams." I wanted to ask if he was paying for the drinks. "Spent a fortune on Champagne. Said she loved it." *Bet she did.* "Even told me where she lived. With her mother she said. Split up with her husband. He was a ripper at Westoe Colliery. Marrying him had been a mistake." Vinny placed his head in his hands. He began to gently sob.

"Listen mate. You don't have to tell me anymore." I did feel a bit of a shit prying but was enjoying the story so far.

"We've got no kids Mick. Missus can't av im. No big deal I suppose. We've always got on together. She's got her interests, I've got mine." I interrupted.

"Chew?"

"No thanks Mick." Vinny still looked upset, although the tears had stopped. I bit a piece off the end of the pigtail. I readjusted my arse on the prop as he continued his story. He obviously needed to talk with someone.

"You might find this hard to believe. We never actually did anything. She'd only let me kiss her. Said if I were serious things could go further. Said she was no slut."

"Hello Mick. Hello Mick Gibson." The tannoy to the side of the road blasted.

"Just a minute fella. Let's see what's up." Reluctantly I climbed to my feet. We were obviously getting to the interesting part. "Hi Steve. Mick ere."

"Durek's bin on. There's only one mine car of chockwood in the shunt."

"Ask im fetch that in. Will have to do. Do me a favour Steve. Get hold of Teddy. Ask him to load another two for noonshift to get in. Plus, a couple bundles of hessian bags."

"Will do. Where's shearer?" I looked towards the tailend. The three lads were sat down. They'd set the steel and were havin their snap. I could hear the panzer.

"Should be on a bi-di. I'm in the return."

"No worries, Mick. I'll give panels a shout."

"Sorry bout that. Go on you were saying she was no slut." I sat back down spitting the mouthful of bacca juice I'd produced onto an arch leg. My aim was improving.

"Bloody ell Mick tha must av more to do than listen to me." *I have Vinny,* however.

"No mate you carry on. Better out than in as they say."

"I used to get butterflies in my belly. Finishing at the end of the day. We'd all go up and get changed ready for tea. Then queuing up for the phone." *I remember it well.* "Few minutes talking to the missus. Before you knew it, taxis had arrived. Tuxedo Princess here we come. They call it the Boat up there."

"Oh, do they?" I feigned surprise.

She was always there before me. With her mates. Soon as she saw me, she'd come running over, hugging me then snogging. We were like a couple of teenagers. Mick I was in love!" I couldn't help but feel sorry for the lad. His face beaming at the memory now sat in his head. "We were there for two weeks. When I got back, I couldn't get her out of my mind. That weekend I was

on a Sunday late. Twelve till seven. I had lieu days in for Monday and Tuesday.
Me and the missus had planned to spend a couple of days together. What with
me having been away for two weeks. Fortunately, she couldn't get time off. She
works at Winwick down road. Know where I mean?"

"Yeah. Mental hospital just as you get off the motorway."

"I just thought fuck it. I'm off. Packed me bags. Left her a note. I had her
address. Semi. A placed called Whitley Bay."

"Yeah. I've heard of it."

"Got there. Took me about four hours. Found her place quite easily. Right on
coast." He stopped obviously building up for the finale. In the silence that
followed I realised the panzer had stopped. *For fucks sake!*

"Sorry Vinny. Just a mo." Standing back up I shouted to the heading lads.
They were now back on their feet. "Hey lads where we stopped?"

"Ged's bin on. Wants some timber sending down."

"Right, I'll be with you in a mo." *Fuckin roof in again. That's all we fuckin
need.* I turned towards Vinny. "Listen fella, sorry I'm going to have to go." As
much as it pained me. He was sobbing again.

"She was still fuckin married. Five kids. Told me if I didn't fuck off, she'd call
the police. Best of it is. Her husband was asleep upstairs. He was on night shift!
Bitch, fuckin bitch!" And there was me worrying about a bit of timbering.

"Fuckin ell Vin. Don't know what to say. You back with your missus then?" I
regretted making the comment as soon as the words left my mouth. The upside
from my perspective I'd got him to talk about it. And now he was angry which
was no bad thing.

"No. Staying at me mam's. Missus not sure she wants me back." *No fuckin
surprises there then.*

"Sorry Vin. I'm going to have to go. You have a minute here. For what it's
worth get her some flowers."

"Tried that. Threw'em back at me."

"What about Champagne?"

"Fuckin ell Mick. Never thought of that. Now that's an idea." I left Vinny and
continued towards the face line. If I couldn't make the grade of Undermanager,
I could always become a counsellor.

□

12. *Bennies Apprentice*

Having picked up my lamp and rescuer I headed towards the Deployment
Centre. It was a week since Mr Creeds visit. As I entered, it was unusual to see
only Derek and Stuart. "Morning gents."

"Morning Mick." Derek replied. There was no response from Stuart. Nothing unusual there he was such an ignorant bastard.

"Where's Cayle?"

"With Geoff." Derek's answer was somewhat of a surprise Geoff like JW never arrived until after the six o'clock shift had gone down.

"Big day Mick?" Stuart added.

"Think you best pop down to see Geoff, wants a word."

"Problems?"

"Don't know. Just asked that you see him before you go down."

"Might be in for another fucking Mick!" Stuart added laughing. Ignoring him I turned to retrace my steps.

"Morning Mick. Goin wom already?"

"Morning George. No Geoff wants to see me. Shouldn't be long. Save me a seat on rider."

"Will do cock."

Arriving outside Geoff's office I could hear Cayle's raised voice. The door was partly open. He didn't sound happy.

"And what the fuck am I supposed do Geoff?"

"Orders from Gaffer." I hesitated, hoping to hear more.

"How long for?"

"Cayle, I don't know. Only found out misen last neet. Called me at home."

"Well, I'll go see him." I heard Cayle move towards the door. I wasn't quick enough. "He's ere now, listening at door." I attempted to respond. I'd not seen him like this before. I moved to one side as he pushed passed me. I thought it best not to reply and continued forward.

"Morning Geoff. You asked to see me."

"Morning lad. Grab a pew. Drink?"

"No, I'm okay thanks. What's up with him?"

"I'm pulling you off L32's. Not sure how long for yet." I guessed what was coming. Little wonder Cayle had been upset. "I'm making you Senior Overman in Mid Area." The Manager had sort of intimated this was coming. The surprise was how quick it had happened. I wasn't sure if Geoff was happy about the new arrangements.

"Wow, okay, yeah." Not the best fuckin answer I wasn't sure what else to say.

"If you go see Derek, he'll show you the ropes."

"What about Cayle?" I was a little concerned how this was going to work with him in his present state of mind.

"If he'd waited and let me explain. C16's installation. Need a bit of a push on that. Got to be ready to go beginning of September. He'll be working with Keith." Therein lay another problem. I wasn't sure Keith liked working with anyone. "Sure, I can't get you a drink?"

223

"No, I'm fine. Best get back up and let George know."

"Should keep him happy another quarter shift each day." I watched with surprise as Geoff removed his false teeth, top and bottom. Something I'd always guessed was the case. "Fuckin bacca." He reached into the desk drawer to extract a small pen knife. There was no embarrassment as he began picking bits of bacca from between the teeth and flicking on the floor.

"Right then Geoff. I'll see you later."

"I that tha will lad." His face seemed smaller with the dentures removed. "If tha see yon daft cunt. Tell him get his arse back in ere."

By the time I'd got back to the Deployment Centre the men and officials had gone. Derek and Stuart were already on the phone to the respective districts. Both with mugs of tea in their hands.

"Want a drink Mick?" I turned to see the Lampman. This must have been part of their morning ritual.

"I, go on that would be nice thanks. Black coffee, no sugar." I walked up and stood alongside Derek. He was standing opposite L32's board. I watched as he removed the names of the Hausherr Dinter men and placed them under the tab marked cross cut haulage. He relayed the message into the phone.

"Well, I'm sorry George it's tough tits and Mick ain't there." He turned towards me and winked. His face as always full of mischief. "If tha be wanting any timber that's best, I can do."

"There you go Mick."

"Oh right, thanks" The Lampman passed me a mug. At some point in the past, it had been white. I took a sip. It tasted fine. I wasn't sure what I'd catch though. The Lampman was still watching me. "That's good." Satisfied he turned and walked off.

"Chance to prove yourself George. Might make it permanent." He turned again towards me smiling. "Right. Now fuck off I've got things for do." He replaced the handset. Stuart was still deep in conversation.

"Listen yon mon. You'd think there were plenty goin on." Derek nodded towards Stuart. "He's only got W8's and that poxy installation. How's our Cayle? Bet he's not a happy bunny. Last time yon mon was on face was when he took that news reader round L19's. What's her face? Anna Ford." Before I responded he began to walk off. Come on let's see them other cunts." I assumed by "poxy installation" he meant W11'S and "them other cunts," the shift engineers. I followed Derek out towards the crush hall. "Careful with what Lamp mon gives tha. Dirty cunt never washes his hands after he's been for shit." I emptied my mug as we passed the cold-water drinking taps. Leaving the mug there too.

"Morning you two." We'd entered the shift electricians office first. Both Glyn Amp and Alan Volt were sat at the desk. From what I could see it was a plan of C16's electrical installation. "Do you know these two Mick?" I nodded.

"Certainly do." Glyn looked up.

"Morning Durek. Could do with those armoured cables moving in. Morning Mick." Alan never acknowledged either one of us. I had history with Alan recognising him for what he was. A lazy cunt. Glyn on the other hand seemed a good lad. He got things done.

"Best av a word with our Mick ere."

"Why what's for do?"

"Mick ere, is the new Senior Overman for the Mid Area." For the first time Alan raised his head. He eyed me suspiciously. I smiled. It wasn't returned.

"Congratulation Mick. Yeah, the three, three still at pit bottom. We'll need em for weekend."

"Thanks Glyn and yeah I'll sort."

"Feel sorry for poor old Al though." Poor old Al ignored Glyn's comment.

"Right owt else?" Derek was eager to keep moving. He was still holding his notebook with pen poised.

"Overtime list. Make sure I've got a couple of men Sat and Sun. Want to get the panel build up complete." Derek noted down Glyn's comment.

"Right best be doing. Don't want to keep Geoff waiting."

I followed Derek into the fitter's office. Eric Greenland was sat at the desk writing.

"Nah Billy no mates. Where's everyone?"

"Morning Durek. Bill's called a meeting first thing. Behind schedule with the sixteen-inch compressed air installation."

"I don't be wanting anymore fuck ups there lad."

"Tha's not kiddin there Durek. Nah Mick what's tha doin ere cock?" Before I could respond.

"I'll see tha later Eric." Derek and I both turned to see Frankie Glow. He was carrying a sprocket, balanced on his right shoulder. I don't think I'd ever seen Frankie empty handed.

"Fuckin ell Frankie. Where's tha goin with that?"

"W8's maingate."

"They were still shearing last time I inquired." Derek continued.

"Not now tha daft cunt. Between shifts. Right, I best be doin." Standing there I felt quite uncomfortable. Now part of a world I hadn't experienced before. So used to being in the think of it. Barking orders. Now stood like a spare prick.

"Mick ere's the newly appointed Senior Overman for the Mid Area."

"Bloody ell lad tha's only been ere two minutes." I smiled.

"It's only temporary."

"Tha wants to make sure its permanent. On a fuckin good screw yon men."

"Fuck off tha chaykee cunt. Come on Mick time we fucked off. Nothing else from you Eric?"

"Nowt ta."

No more was said as we headed back down to the Undermanager's office. Geoff was sat at his desk, having changed into his underground gear. He was puffing on a cigarette. Both feet on the desk alongside a pack of Park Drive. I watched how his eyes closed each time he inhaled. Obviously enjoying the moment.

"Owt, you want getting in Geoff?"

"I Durek steel desperate both headings L33's and that new muff coupling at pit bottom for Mick's old place. That reminds Mick. Can you pop in to see Mr Keech. Wants to see you before tha go down."

"What now?" I asked.

"No idea lad."

As I turned to leave the office Cayle walked in. If I thought, he looked bad before he looked even worse now. I tried to gain eye contact. Unsuccessful I continued out. This was certainly one relationship I didn't want to lose. I got on well with Cayle, enjoying the banter we had. Only yesterday he'd offered to let me have a set of Dinky cars and race track his lad had finished with. It was going to be a surprise for our Jamie. I planned to go round and pick it up on Friday. That freebie seemed unlikely now.

I found it a little unsettling heading towards Mr Keech's office with it being alongside Top Shunt. Deadly quiet at that time of the morning. The smell of freshly polished furniture more obvious. It always reminded me of the area outside the Headmasters office at my first school. I was conscious of the time too. Normally the Manager appeared this time of the morning. I'd bumped into him previously. Not looking in the best of moods. I'd offered him a good morning but got no response. The experience was one I'd like to avoid.

I knocked on Mr Keech's door.

"Come." An opened pack of Players No 6 lay on his desk, alongside a box of Swan matches. I counted three stubs in the tin ashtray. There was a fag hanging from the corner of his mouth. He face partly obscured by the exhaled smoke. He was on the phone. "He's here now. Yeah, saw him mesen. Face like a smacked arse he'll get over it," the Manager was already here. Cayle had obviously been to see him. "Right Gaffer see you shortly." He replaced the handset.

"Nah Mick. How are you lad?"

"All good thanks Mr Keech."

"I know it's probably a little sudden pulling you off 32's but we thought it time you got a feel for the other aspects of management. It's only temporary. Manager's got other plans for thi. Try not to wind any fucker up. Get to understand what goes on. It'll seem strange at first." He wasn't wrong there. "Tha'll get used. Position's neither one thing nor tuther. Anything you want to ask?" There was one thing. The day rate for Face Overman and Senior Overman wasn't vastly different. However, I'd got so used to the extra quarter a shift each day I wondered if I was still able to book the same.

"No, I'm good."

"Good lad. Try not to cause any walkouts." He was smiling as he stubbed out the cigarette. He reached across to the open packet. "That's all. See thee later."

As I left the office I was tempted to go and see the Manager and thank him. I thought better of it. Best if I just go with the flow for now.

"Nah Mick, congratulations seem to be in order." I hadn't spotted Sidney Large walk through the main entrance. He was smiling. The same smile he used if he was greeting someone or docking time. I hadn't seen Sid for some time, now he was working in the control room. According to Gerry Cook it was for his own safety.

"Morning Sid. How nice to see you and thanks."

"Bet Cayle's taking it well?" He was still smiling. "Watch he don't knife tha in back."

"Thanks for that Sid."

By the time I got to Geoff's office the place was empty. I headed back to the Crush Hall. I was in two minds as to whether I should leave my water bottle attached to my belt. Thought it best I keep it with me. Checking the time, it was almost eight o'clock. They'd all be at the shaft side. I hurriedly made my way, passing the old control room. I was looking forward to seeing Bennie later to give him the news. I slowed as I reached the gantry leading to the shaft. I'd just made it in time. The cage had landed. Geoff was stood with Cayle and Derek. JW too with Stuart. I entered the cage last. Nobody spoke other than the Banksman shouting towards us as he dropped the gate.

"Have a good day gentlemen." As we dropped at speed, I was deep in thought. Yesterday I'd come up the pit as a Face Overman. Today I was going down as Senior Overman. Not a massive change and still only temporary but the main thing. Things had started to move. I satisfied myself with that.

The days following my appointment went quicker than expected. The hardest part was hanging about first thing. It took me time to realise that it was now about listening. Picking up pieces of information that would help my thinking when underground. I hadn't appreciated the men employed at Parkside had come from several pits now closed. Some I hadn't even heard of. The likes of

Robin Hill and Chisnall Hall. I began to pick up the various dialects too. I was soon able to differentiate between Wiganers, St Helens, and Leythers.

Visits from the Manager to C16's maingate and face installation and Deputy Manager to L32's I was expected to accompany them. It soon became apparent this was a very different way of managing. For the first time I wasn't directly in charge of anyone. The other Overmen and Deputies were employed to do that. Some better than others. This was more about communication and the smooth operation of the shift. Some days due to staff shortage I reverted to the Face Overman role.

This, however, no longer held the excitement I had once felt. Having tasted the role of Senior Overman, I wanted it more. I was being exposed to the various areas of the mine that I'd never encountered before. Places and situations different to what I'd been used to. The acceptance of others of me in this new role wasn't a given. More than ever, I had to earn it. Screaming and shouting to get things done wouldn't work. Although I still had my moments, particularly with the engineers.

Working with Ged and the lads on L32's had helped me better understand and more importantly how to manage. I continued to apply for jobs up and down the country. I wanted those at Area to know I was prepared to travel anywhere to further my career. Something I knew would help me progress to my goal of becoming an Undermanager. I still remembered clearly that day eleven years previously at Bold Colliery where my epiphany had happened.

Something else I experienced for the first time. When directly in charge you can see the results of the decisions you take. Good or bad. This role there was never any direct feedback if the face had completed three shears. Or we'd wound a thousand tonne in the shift. This was about the smooth running of things. The time you could be effective was when things went wrong. Times when you were called upon to use experience to solve a problem. I recognised that I didn't know it all. Or would I ever? There were guys down here who'd spent many more years mining coal who was I to compete. This was about using their experience and knowledge to solve a problem. What I craved for more than ever was my own shift. Which I recognised was the next move.

In August, a new Chairman was appointed. It bode well for the future notwithstanding the fact he was also a Mining Engineer, having studied the subject at Birmingham University. Under the last year of the previous Chairman, we'd lost another twenty-seven collieries with nearly thirty-six thousand individuals choosing to take voluntary redundancy.

The new mantra for the coal industry was "customers buy energy not coal." A term I'd heard back in April at Old Boston Training Centre. It was now the case that imported coal from Australia, South Africa, Poland, and the USA, was consistently cheaper than oil.

Power stations were now reverting to burning coal rather than oil. Primary energy consumption in the UK during 1985/86 was at its highest since 1979/80. Coal was once more the single most important source of fuel. Accounting for thirty-six per cent of total energy consumption. Of that the CEGB took over eighty million tonnes. The chemical industry was the second biggest user of British Coal. The Board's main objective was to breakeven during 1987/88 and by 1990 reduce the heavy burden of interest rates and become self-financing.

The Coal Industry was still in direct competition with gas, oil, nuclear and imported coal. Due to the world energy requirements reducing large quantities of seaborne coal became available at prices of twenty-two to twenty-six pounds a tonne. This was of particular relevance to our coastal power stations. Fiddlers Ferry included. The size of our future industry would depend on our quality and price.

☐

Towards the end of the year the Manager sent for me. He said there was a possibility within the next three weeks I would be appointed Assistant Undermanager on nightshift. Tony Ramsbottom had become Undermanager at Florence Colliery. It wasn't guaranteed as yet but he was hopeful to get it signed off at Area. And was I up for it. Did he really need to ask?
The news was most welcome something I'd been aiming for ever since I'd arrived. The only major issue as I saw it was telling the missus I was going on regular nights.
Then days later I was let down big time. The appointment wasn't going to happen. To say I was pissed off would be an understatement. It was the second time since I'd been there had caused me to fall out with the Manager. Not the ideal approach to take but I had been so looking forward to it.
Then without warning, things changed again. Mr Keech sent for me. I was to join Bennie Lead on regular afternoons. It wasn't ideal but at least it was something. I liked Bennie too, which helped.

The start of each shift with Bennie commenced with a visit to the pit bottom cabin. The place smelt damp; the smell of whitewash and disinfectant ever present. Here the young Onsetter Karl would share his huge flask of strong tea with Bennie and the pit bottom lads. The lad must have added a two-pound bag of sugar each time he filled the flask. Little wonder Karl's teeth looked black. Bennie's opening comment was always.

"Now Karl does not think could do with more sugar?" Instantly those around him began to laugh. It was the same each shift. I began to join in too. I found the spectacle comical. Initial conversations centred around who Bennie was shagging. It then moved on to sport and not always about rugby league. All the pit bottom lads seemed to enjoy American football. The Super Bowl final was due in four months, all had a view who'd be participating in the final. After my first week the routine of sitting in the Pit Bottom cabin became frustrating. I needed to be doing something.

"Hello Bennie. Hello Bennie Lead." The tannoy positioned on the far wall blasted out.

"Fuckin ell Steve does not know this is Bennie's prep time?" His comment caused the lads to laugh in unison.

"Do us favour Karl see what Steve wants." Both Bennie and I were sat behind a large table in pit bottom cabin. The rest of the team sat opposite.

"He can ere tha." Karl responded.

"Bennie, L32's is on stand. Gassed out in the return. Haven't started up yet. Might want to send your apprentice." Bennie turned towards me smiling.

"Tell him okay."

"Oh, and Mr Creed has asked you give him a call. Might be best if you do that in person. Let your secretary get on with his own job." All the lads began laughing once more.

"Fuck off." Bennie shouted to no one particular

After the call to the Manager, "Nah mucker time we were making a move. Manager wants me in W11's. You okay sorting 32's?"

"Yep, suits me fine."

I'd only been gone from L32's just over a month. They hadn't replaced me. George had taken on the role of Face Overman with Freddy Clough still covering the maingate and Rob Flannagan in the return. The face had another month to run. Still plagued by geological problems and now gas. It was still single shifting. Ged's team would transfer to L33's. There were no plans to salvage the chocks.

Leaving Bennie at the top of the Wigan Mines Access, I continued inbye. Before long I'd reached the maingate of L19's. I did miss my role as Face Overman. I liked being in charge. The biggest kick I got however was having to make a decision. Sometimes I got it right other times not. It was all part of expanding my experience. I wasn't sure the role as Bennie's apprentice was as rewarding. Now removed from the action and little control over decision making. The role was about monitoring, overseeing the shift activities.

Documenting the results and reporting to senior management. If things went wrong, you were sometimes called upon to make decisions. Then again most of the officials in charge had the confidence to make their own. They didn't need some new up and coming youngster telling them what to do.

Still deep in thought I'd arrived at the meeting station. Memories flooding back of my first day as L32's Face Overman. I smiled. I hadn't a clue what lay in store for me.

The place looked so dark. The wooden bench on the junction corner was strewn with discarded newspapers. Something I'd tried to discourage. Old M&Q booklets containing copies of reports. The cleaner beige coloured booklet was currently in use. Confirmed by the blue carbon paper protruding from the middle pages. The extended gib from the maingate conveyor looked abandoned. Stringers from the belt hung loosely, in places encrusted with dried dirt. Even the junction looked smaller.

"Alreyt Mick." It was George. His ever-present smile still evident. I hadn't seen him approach from the crosscut.

"Hello George. How's it goin?"

"Should be startin up again shortly. Barometer's helping. Crosscut doors were damaged. Got the return lads doing some hardstopping. Bobby Bang, Bang was with them. He's gone back inbye to check the readings." He passed me his tin of snuff.

"What were you getting?"

"Two and a half per cent over the top motor, three per cent at the outbye end. Got Bobby to run some brattice along the back of the return chocks. Had little effect. Call came through from the haulage lads, they were transporting the old bucket off the Webster along the crosscut. Hadn't checked the height of the thing before passing through the doors."

"Hello Mick, hello Mick Gibson." The tannoy interrupting George's explanation.

"What you reckon then?"

"Bout another twenty minutes." I moved across to the tannoy.

"Hi Steve, Mick here.

"What's latest?"

"Another forty minutes should see us going again."

"Oh right, thanks. Can you give Mr Keech a ring too, in his office."

"Will do." As I moved across to the phone George continued his explanation.

"Don't think it helps being on one shift. Got my suspicions Ventilation department have reduced our air pushing more towards L33's." I wasn't sure that was true.

"Hello George. Rob here. Down to point eight, heading inbye to check over top motor."

"Thanks Rob, I'll get belts running and tell the lads we're almost ready." George replied.

"Hi George, we're back at point five over top motor." It was Freddy Clough. "Latches off lads. Let's get coaling."

"Got that." Steve shouted from the control room. "Tell Mick that was the quickest forty minutes I've ever known."

Ignoring Steve's comment, I put the call through to the Deputy Manager.

"Hello Mr Keech, Mick here. Yeah, got that. Yeah, I'll make sure they stop over." I looked across to George. He was smiling, nodding in agreement. I wasn't surprised. I'd noticed last week a brand-new red coloured Toyota Celica in the car park. "Yeah, I plan to." I could hear a voice in the background. No mistaking who it was. I pictured Mr Keech with his Players No 6. My thoughts interrupted as the pre-alarm of the main gate belt kicked in. I replaced the handset.

Immediately coal began falling from the thirty-six-inch belt. The sound of the coal hitting the chute sounded muffled. Small lumps of coal missing the belt completely. Falling between the side iron and belt. I walked across to take a closer look. Coal dust swirled in all directions, momentarily hanging in the air.

"Yeah, I'll get one of the lads out to clear the spillage." George offered as he followed me.

"For fucks sake, one of the side plates is missing." It had been replaced by a length of belting. Each lump of coal hitting the belt caused it to move to one side.

"Damaged, replacement bottom of E3. I'll send one of the lads out to pick it up." I shook my head. From the amount of coal lying there it was obvious the plate had been missing for some time. I moved back following the line of the quarter inch bagging. Reaching up I turned the brass on/off valve. I watched in dismay as the fine sprays of water shot in all directions. None of which landed on the coal.

"Careful Mick. Belt ill start slipping."

"George, I have to say. It's a fuckin disgrace."

"Nah hold on Mick. We've only a month to run then were out of here. Seems pointless spending money on replacing everything."

"George, it's about safety and standards. The Deputy Manager is hoping the place is going to cover off the shortfall from L33's. That'll never happen if you let the place go to rat shit."

A light ahead caused me to stop. No more was said until the person was up on us. I didn't recognise him.

"Hi." I offered.

"Alreyt Mick. Come to clean up."

"Mick, this is Randy Shakespeare, one of the trainee Deps. He'd doing his shotfiring training with Freddy ex Bold Colliery."

"Good to meet you, Randy." I wondered if Freddy was showing him how to write poetry too. "How long you got left to do?"

"End of the week. Then I'm across to S31's developments." Our conversation was interrupted as the sound from the conveyor changed. The continuous hum of the conveyor laden with the black stuff was replaced by the clink, clink of the belt stitching passing over the top rollers. George moved across to the tannoy.

"Hello Paul, stageloader, Are we stopped?"

"Just breaking a lump at maingate end. Ged's asked me to mention we need some more mineral oil. Jigger's puffin and pantin like me Aunt Midge."

"Will do." I smiled. This should be interesting I hadn't spoken to Ged for some time.

"Right Randy good to meet you and good luck." I began to move into the maingate. George followed. "You still got the lump breaker over the stage loader?" He began to laugh.

"Nah that went ages ago. Picks kept breaking. Just left the box bar. Creating more problems than it was worth. Chucked it."

We continued inbye. The roadway had taken a hit. Both with floor lift and weight coming onto the arches. Weld mesh in numerous places bulging forth. Walking forward I was surprised how easily the floor dust lifted. Coating the inside of my mouth and nostrils. Like everywhere I'd seen since coming into the district the place was black.

"Stonedust?"

"Struggle to get haulage down ere. Anything for the maingate we send via the return." He had a point the thirty-five-pound rails were all over the place. "Even tried reversing the belt. Turned over." I lowered my head as we passed under the heavy barrier. What dust was still on covered in a fine layer of coal dust. I steadied myself holding on to the belt side iron. It seemed pointless asking if it was in distance, I stopped. Sweat was oozing from every pore on my chest causing the airborne dust to stick.

"Pinch?"

"I go on." Passing him, the tin of Hedges I noticed both the water and compressed air pipes hanging oddly. Guessed they were robbing lengths of pipe chain to hang inbye. In contrast to the armoured cable. "Coaling again." George added as he passed me the snuff. The sound of the conveyor changing once more.

"What if you get an Inspector?"

"Unlikely. More interested in seeing W11's. Getting some visitor's in there I believe."

"I that's true. What about you, any plans for the future?"

"Funnily enough I was discussing with me missus the other day. Can't see me goin on much longer. There's just the two of us, house paid for. Thinking of getting one of those motor homes do a bit of travelling. Never really holidayed in this country. Normally do Benidorm twice a year. It's becoming a young man's game. Pressure to take cost out. Not sure where it will end." George had a point. I'd watched with interest the number of older men take the money. L33's was the last face in the Lower Florida. C16's would be the last in the Crombouke and then it was down to the Wigan Four Feet and Ince Six Feet.

"Right think we best keep moving. Need to arrange overtime."

Fifteen minutes later I could see the panels ahead. I recognised immediately the lad standing there.

"Nah Scouse how's it going?"

"All good Ged. You?" He seemed in a reflective mood.

"Thinkin of finishing."

"You're fuckin kiddin me?"

"You know where this is goin Mick?"

"Go on tell me."

"Privatisation cock. Not sure I want to be part of that. Brother-in-law works at Pilks reckon he could get me in there. The offer of redundancy is on the table." I was disappointed to hear Ged's comments. So, unlike him. In my eyes he'd always been a fighter. Ever since the end of the strike many of the older lads were taking the redundancy. We'd lost over three hundred men since the end of the strike with another three hundred planned to go.

I spotted Freddy Clough in the distance. Deep in thought sat on top of the jumbo cable doodling pen poised. Either that or he was writing another poem. I'd heard there was one entitled the Arrogant Overmen 2. I was yet to see that.

"Hello Mick. Hello Mick Gibson."

"Hi Steve."

"Mick, Bennie's bin on. W belt's turned over asked if you could make your way there."

"Where's Bennie?"

"No 2 Pit Bottom. One of the skips stuck in shaft."

"On my way." I turned to Ged. "Sorry wish I had more time to chat."

"No worries, Mick. Catch you later."

⊔

"Dad it's been snowing. Can we go out." I was in bed; in that place you get to from being fully asleep and half awake. It was my son I heard first.

"Dad we can play Star Wars." Followed by his sister. For a change I'd been having a good sleep. Opening my eyes, I checked the bedside clock it was only six thirty. I turned towards the kids who were now on the bed still in their pyjamas.

"Can we Dad please?" Mrs Gibson was alongside me. She hadn't moved. She was either still asleep or kiddin me not wanting to get up. I sat up lifting the pillow as I did so and shoving it behind my back. I grabbed the two of them and pulled them in towards me.

"Come on give your old Dad a cuddle." They both giggled as I gave them a hug. Lizzie struggled free. Looking towards me with her big brown eyes. She'd only started talking for the last month. I was still waiting for her to call me daddy.

"Mummy let us stay up late last night to watch a video."

"What was that darlin?"

"Never Ending Story daddy." Her brother added.

"Wow, I know the one you mean. Where they both get chance to ride that big dog."

"It's not a dog."

"Oh, that's right, it's a Luck Dragon, it's called Mallor."

"No Daddy, I've told you before. It's Falkor." Jamie hadn't been happy with my answer.

"Oh sorry, I stand corrected."

"You're not standing you're lying-in bed. We want you to get up." Lizzie added. There was still no movement from Mrs Gibson. The next thing I heard the heavy breathing from Heidi as she walked into the room.

"Looks as though Heidi needs a wee. Come on let's get some breckie."

Jumping out of bed I grabbed my dressing gown; we headed downstairs our Heidi leading the way.

"Right let's put the telly on while I sort the breakfast. The Rainbow video was still in the recorder. I pressed play. Bungle, Zippy and George appeared. They were discussing what the word *independence* meant. Kids settled I headed to the back kitchen, letting the dog out for a wee. It was bloody freezing; snowflakes began to fall. Time for the heating. I'd light the coal fire later.

I left the kids eating breakfast in front of the telly I returned upstairs with a cuppa and piece of jam toast for the wife.

She hadn't moved. "Mornin darlin cuppa? Annie?"

"Oh." She let out a loud yawn. "Never heard you get up." I sat on the edge of the bed still holding the tea and toast. "Give it here. What time did you get in last night?"

"Must have been just before midnight. Bit of a problem with one of the main coaling belts."

"Does that place always have problems?"

"No not all the time. Goin through a bad spell at the moment." There then followed a short silence. I guessed what was coming next.

"Mick I'm sick of this. It's like being a one parent family." It was pointless responding. I sat and listened. "You're never here. I must do everything on my own. I miss you. The kids miss you. Can't you get a proper job. Before you know it, the kids will be grown." The silence that followed I was expected to fill with an answer.

"It won't be forever."

"That's what you always say. When you started at Parkside you said things would be different. Better. Spending more time together. I'm only young I need a life. All you seem to do is work, work, work. Is the pit more important to you than me? Even, when you're here your half asleep if not sleeping. We don't have any social life." I felt like shit, she looked so unhappy. I hadn't told her yet. In a couple of weeks there was a Leigh and District Mining Society Dinner Dance. She seemed to like the pit doos.

"But it's the way things are love."

"No, it's not. My mates from Plesseys have husbands that start work at a reasonable time and get home on time. Not you there's always something and that something is pit."

The sound of the kids bounding up the stairs put paid to any further discussion. Before leaving for work later that morning I made an effort to play with the kids. Sword fencing with yellow plastic tubes. The pretend light savers in the garden. I played the part of Darth Vader which I had no doubt the missus would approve. As usual I let Luke and Princess Leila defeat me. Annie watching from the back-room window. Her demeanour hadn't changed. When I suggested she pop round to her mum and dads. It hadn't been the best of suggestions as she'd been there yesterday and the day before. Something which she had already told me, but I'd forgotten.

"Right, you two. Time Dad was off to work. I'll see you tomorrow."

"But Dad it's only early we haven't finished playing."

"I know but Daddy has to earn some pennies."

"I hope you're not suggesting I don't do anything. Just because I don't earn any money." I realised too late it hadn't been the best thing to say in earshot of the missus.

"No, I didn't mean it like that dear."

"You and mummy havin an argument dad?" Jamie added.

"No son. Sometimes grown-ups have little disagreements."

"Tell you what. Why don't you pop round to my parents. I'm sure dad was off today."

"Your parents are a complete waste of time. Always finding an excuse for not havin the kids. I didn't tell you that your mother last week made a detour of our house just to avoid us. The kids saw her and banged on the window. She just ignored them. She has no interest in her grandkids." *I think it's time I fucked off!*

"Right, I'll be off then. See you tonight." I never waited for a reply. Grabbed my jacket and headed out.

"Mick?" I turned. Just in time to catch the plastic bag with my snappin flying towards me.

"Thanks, darlin." I followed up with an imaginary kiss. It wasn't returned.

☐

W11's coal face had been operating for two weeks, I had yet to see it. Bennie spent most shifts there. It was something to do with proximity to pit bottom. I was usually in C16's or L33's, sometimes S31's developments. It was Parkside's first heavy duty face an investment of five million pounds. With a planned daily output two thousand two hundred tonnes.

"Any chance we can have a wander into W11's."

"Hope you're not planning to piss on my patch." Bennie responded laughing. I was stood alongside him as the cage began to slow.

"Would I dare?"

"Fuckin hope not."

"Afternoon gents." The onsetter shouted as we came to a stop. I reached forward to raise the mesh gate.

"Hey what for doin? That's my job."

"Oops sorry."

"Our Mick's in a bit of a rush today." As we stepped out the cage Bennie passed the onsetter a brown paper bag. He was stopping over. Bennie had brought him a couple of meat and potato pies.

"Thanks, Mucka."

"No problems fella. Just make sure we get all the empties up before we start bringing anything down."

"Will do Bennie."

We continued forwards towards the pit bottom cabin.

"If you don't mind, I'm heading straight in."

"Fuckin ell cock tha's in a rush alreyt." The fact was I hated wasting time sat in the cabin suppin the most awful sweet tea. I never had the heart to tell Bennie the truth.

"Give me chance to pop into the headings later."

"Bloody ell Mick tha'll not make old bones cock. Don't forget you're doin call neet. Good experience talking to Manager." *Fuck!* I had forgotten.

"Lookin forward to it." *Like fuck was I but I suppose it had to happen at some point.* "See you later."

I continued inbye walking the main tunnel. Before I knew it, I'd reached the South Wigan Mines Access Intake. The sound of coal hitting the chute greeted me as I reached U belt. I'd built up a little sweat during my journey, this now increased as I passed the conveyor drive. Heading down the brow I looked across to the forty-two-inch conveyor. The black stuff was piled high. I guessed all three faces were in full cut. I travelled on the opposite side to the belt. There were still large lumps of coal lying on the floor. The remainder of what had been cleared after the belt had broken the previous month. I'd been away on holiday with the family. From what some of the guys had said when I got back, we'd been lucky. Two men that had been manriding that afternoon had managed to jump to safety. The other fella hadn't been so lucky. They found him wrapped up in the belt, a broken fibula and fractured radius the result. Manager had instructed all the stitching's on the Wigan Mines Access belts to be vulcanised. An outside company were due in this weekend to complete the final two joints on X belt.

I spotted two lights ahead of me as the haulage rope began to move. There were several empties to clear out of 11's return before the lads began to bring supplies in. JW had asked we get a spare shearer cable into the return plus a pack of steel before we started on the maingate. Moving into the manhole above the maingate warwick I waited.

"Ey up Mick. Do us favour cock. Can tha lift warwick."

"Will do." I moved across to the concrete filled metal bucket. Pulling down hard on the wire rope until I was able to place a foot on it. The white painted RSJ lifted with ease. "Fuck!" I looked at my middle finger. A loose strand of wire had broken the skin. *Need to remember gloves tomorrow.* Turning back to the warwick, the fluorescent red stripes reflecting in the beam of my light. Behind the front bogie six empties. I was pleased to see the flats had been loaded with several old arch legs. The two-half cut mine cars with empty five-gallon oil drums.

With W11's starting up the big push was to break the pits face output record. And with assistance from L33's and C16's the weekly output record which would inevitably lead to an improved OMS. The targets set had created huge excitement with the men. That was more to do with the bonus generated. Something that had become consistent since the end of the strike. The two young haulage lads were bringing up the rear.

"Owzthisel Mick?"

"All good thanks Ronnie. I'd be a lot better if the two of you were outbye of the journey."

"Fuckin ell Mick. We've only just seen tha and your dishing out fucks." Ronnie laughed at his reply.

"Only thinkin of your safety."

"Pinch Mick?" His mate Reggie asked as he came alongside.

"Don't mind if I do." I responded releasing the weight gently to the floor. Ronnie reached across to the greenline. The journey came to an immediate halt.

"For fucks sake Ron I can't speyk. What's done that for? Tha's put lock out on now."

"Shut tha fuckin moaning. Wants to see if our Mick ere wants a brand-new set of hub caps." Ronnie and Reggie weren't their actual names. They could get hold of any item for at least half the cost you'd pay in the shops. In fact, I didn't know their real names. They seemed happy with the label *the Krays*.

"No, I'm fine. Thanks for the offer though. For fucks sake." I'd just inhaled the snuff offered. "Fuckin olbas oil!"

"Can get you some of that too."

"No thanks."

"There's no pleasing some folk. Any way can't stand round ere all day Mick got job to do. Oh, by the way, where's our Bennie? Asked if I could get im a set of Ray-bans for when he's off Benidorm with his mate. Tenner that's all it'll cost im."

"Was at pit bottom. He'll be down here shortly. You'll probably catch im at the top."

"Latch is off." Ronnie shouted down towards us.

"Alsithy Mick."

"Make sure you keep top side of the journey."

And with that the lads continued outbye. I stayed alongside the manhole a little longer. I was never keen travelling below a journey even with a warwick in between.

As I approached the maingate junction my mind wandered back to when I'd first started at Parkside. Just over two years now and this had been my first job. Working with the ATC lads, Cornelius and his two mates. I wasn't sure what he was up to now. A few of them had transferred across to Bold Colliery. How time flies it only seemed like yesterday. I'd been their shotfirer working on both junctions. And this now was the result the pits first heavy-duty face. From conversations with the Manager at that time I always believed I'd be one of the Face Overmen in here. Not to be. Having completed that role on L32's. That would have meant not having the privilege of working with Ged and his men. Something I wouldn't have missed for anything.

"Hello Control. Hello Steve. My men are timbering before the shearer complete its bi di." The unmistakable tones of Charles Henry. I'd been so wrapped up in my own thoughts I hadn't realised the coal had stopped. My ears now receiving the unmistakable click, click, click of the empty belt.

"Thanks Charles. Any idea how long you'll be?"

"Hopefully not too long old boy."

"Just an idea would be good Charles. Deputy Manager will want to know."

"Oh, tell him. I don't know. Say an hour?"

"A fuckin hour! I thought you said you wouldn't be long?"

"Oh, go on then. You've twisted my arm. Say half an hour max."

Bless didn't we just love Charles. I walked across towards the tannoy. There were two at the Meeting Station. One for outbye along the Access Road. The other for W11's gate roads. "Hello Norman. Hello Norman Moore." Norman was the District Deputy, younger brother of Derek. I usually informed the Deputy when I was about to enter the district. It was a lesson I'd learnt when accompanying the Fire Officer at Cronton. We'd entered a district without informing the Deputy Joe Moss. He wasn't too pleased. In the ensuing argument we were barred entry.

Whilst I waited for a response, I took a moment to look around the Meeting Station. The place was immaculate. Not surprising. The Manager had impressed upon everyone the place would be high profile in the Western Area. Rumour had it we were about to get new Board Chairman. Parkside had been pencilled in as one of his first visits.

"Hello Mick. What's for do?"

"Norman okay to come in via the maingate."

"What's askin me for Mick. Tha's fuckin boss. Just fetch theesen in." I just loved the Moore brothers. Three of them in total, always ready for a laugh.

"Thanks Norman. Will you let Charles know?"

"I will do. He's on face timbering." No surprises there. Charles was always in the thick of it.

As I began walking inbye the sound of the conveyor changed. A sure sign they were coaling again. The drive's two 400 hp motors pumping out the heat as I passed. The air filled with the smell of new electric cables. *Some half hour that turned out to be.* The roadway was in excellent condition. The arches standing perfect. A thick layer of freshly applied stonedust sitting in the web of the crowns. The road was perfectly straight. I'd heard it was the first place the linesman went each morning. Even the track lay in a perfect line. JW had used the same guy brought in to relay the main loco track. Ex British Rail. I'd met him once on nightshift. No sign of floor lift. It was still early days, but the Wigan Four Foot seam was not expected to give any problems in that area.

The belt now began to drop down from the back of the loop. All slung at waist height. The black stuff piled high once more on the move. I stopped momentarily to pick up a handful of coal from the conveyor. Still warm but now damp. It was so different to what we'd mined in L32's.

The steel corrugated sheets surrounding the arches now gave way to mesh panels. Still in the same condition as the day they'd been crimped to the crown and legs. Nothing had been left to chance. Ahead the getting off platform for manriding already in place. It made sense. The men and officials wouldn't be walking out. Why not make it a manrider from day one. Removing my cap lamp, I shone it along either side of the road. The blue armoured cable carrying the 3.3 KVA supply strung perfect. Connected to the transformers situated in the Access sub-station which had been extended to accommodate the additional new transformers.

The three-inch-high pressure Victaulic water range coloured coded with the red and green bands. Suspended by matching lengths of pipe chain. Coupled together, not with the usual split link, but with short quarter inch bolts. The blue banded six-inch compressed air range no different. On the opposite side the perfectly formed manholes. Each with the green, fluorescent numbered indicator. Above which the brand new Tekcem and Tekbent pipes. Vibrating backwards and forwards as the respective fluids passed through the line. I hadn't noticed the water barriers above my head. It was the smell of the plastic containers alerting me to their presence. I turned back towards the conveyor. The black stuff still piled high. The words of the Manager ringing in my ears when I'd first arrived. "this would be our big hitter." From what I'd seen so far left me in no doubt.

Ahead the lights surrounding the stage loader. It looked huge. To my right supported by a steel platform over the belt, two separate banks of panels. Everything about the place was big. I recalled seeing some of the chocks loaded at pit bottom ready for the journey inbye. The canopies loaded separate because of their size. The bases had what was described as lemniscate linkages at the rear of the base.

JW must have been so proud to have this in his section. Any Undermanager I guess would feel the same. Such Potential. I was now level with the face start line. The plastic pump packing bags protruding between the mesh panels. The smell of the Tekpak lingered. I ducked beneath the return wheel of the rope haulage. Secured to the side of the road with an inch and quarter rebar. I was now at the outbye end of the Pantechnicon. The longest I'd ever seen. A coiled loop of jumbo cable sat on the first flat. Secured either side with purpose-built horns. I smiled. On L32's we'd used tie bars bolted to the flat. The reflection of the lights caused me to blink. The place was so white. Everything so new.

"Alreyt Mick."

"Norman, how good to see you again." He offered me his already opened tin of snuff. "Thanks."

"Listen cock tha's no need to ask permission to come into my district. It's not like I'm going to say no."

"Yeah, I know. It's just habit."

"Where's your side kick Bennie. Still sat on his fanny at pit bottom?"

"No, he'll be on his way by now. Where's machine anyway?"

"On its way back in. Charles old boy had taken it on a long bi-di. Tryin to get ahead of the bad ground. I say bad ground. More to do with tops breaking…"
The maingate conveyor began to slow.

"Who's got latch on No 2 belt?" Steve's voiced rang out on the outbye tannoy. Immediately answered.

"Beltman's checking a stitch." It was Bennie. "I'm with im now."

"Nice if you could tell us beforehand."

"Fuck off Steve. Think I'm a clairvoyant." Bennie responded.

"What's best bet for the two o'clock at Haydock, Satday?" Somebody else shouted.

"How would Bennie know. He'll be shaggin." The banter continued as I travelled towards the coal face.

I waited as the shearer entered the maingate for the second time. The machine was huge. It oozed power, the noise so loud. From what I'd been told it had cost nearly a million quid. The all electric two thirty Kilowatt BJD. Huge lumps of coal spalling onto the panzer as the disc approached. Roof coal began to drop. I was mesmerised as the coal gave itself up. The coal tops dropping out I likened to L32's. I was leaning against the spill plates. I hadn't noticed Bennie approach.

"Alreyt mucker."

"Hiya Bennie. Just thinking, might be worthwhile getting the lads to put some roof bolts in before machine comes in again."

"No lad. What tha's wanting is some advance. The place just needs moving forward. Not spent millions of pounds to hang bout putting wooden dowels in."
I wasn't sure about Bennies thoughts. Bolting in my mind wouldn't go amiss.

We continued watching. Completely enclosed by steel. The lemniscate linkage shield powered supports had cost nearly four million pounds. These provided structural stability by removing all horizontal forces from the hydraulic legs. There was no way of seeing the waste with the full rear shielding and side flaps. The theory was heavy duty faces were producing thirty per cent more coal than the conventional faces.

The visit to W11's had been everything I'd expected and then some. Little wonder the Coal Board was investing in this new equipment. It had been a real eye opener and satisfying to see it in action at the pit I worked at.

As I was to call the Manager, we left a little earlier. I'd have stayed longer but wasn't sure if that would have been for the right reasons. We said little as we travelled outbye via the return. Bennie had arranged the manrider to meet us at the top of the Access Road. The black stuff was pouring out. Each belt we rode, it was a struggle to find somewhere to sit. It wasn't until we'd climbed off U belt the coal began to ease.

"Fuckin ell Mick, call to Manager should be a gooden neet. All three faces haven't stopped. Steve reckons we'll clear two hundred skips too."

"Yeah, can't wait."

"For fucks sake what's up with tha. Uncle Bennie's shown you the way. Don't forget, his bark is worse than his bite." He began to laugh. I smiled, already my mouth was beginning to feel dry. *Must remember to have a drink with me before I start.*

Back on the surface we headed straight for the baths. Still a little nervous I consoled myself with the fact, any information I needed to pass on to the Manager would be written down on Bennie's pro forma. By the time I was changed I headed back towards the control room. Bennie was already there, having a chat with Steve. He was half way through a meat and potato pie.

"Yours is there mucker." He pointed to a white paper bag alongside a white mug of tea.

"Cheers mate." There was nothing nicer than a warm meat and potato. Not too hot just warm, the way I liked it.

"Big neet toneet Mick." Steve offered.

"For fucks sake Steve leave the lad be. It's only the Manager." Bennie's comment created laughter between the two of them. I joined in, not because I thought it was funny. Just trying to hide my nervousness.

The last of the noonshift officials had just arrived on the surface. Most of them already sporting an unlit fag.

"Has got leet Bennie." Bennie threw him his plastic lighter.

"After tha Danny." Norman shouted over.

"Bout fuckin time got tha own." Both Deputies ignored Bennie's comment.

"Big neet I hear toneet Mick?" *For fucks sake! Did everyone know?*

After weeks of listening to Bennie making the call to the Manager, the bravado and confidence I'd been building up for this very day, disappeared as soon as Steve passed me the phone. My hand suddenly started to shake. Why I don't know. Attempting to hide it, I used both hands until I had the ear piece firmly in place. The sound of the Manager's phone ringing seemed exaggerated. I was unaware of his domestic arrangements, wife, or kids. I wondered if they hid specifically at that time of night. He may have a sound proof room they kept well away from. Bennie's pro forma was on the desk in front of me. I avoided picking it up. My left hand had now taken over the shakes. The unanswered ring tones continued. I looked towards Bennie. *Perhaps he was out?* My mouth was now dry. Swapping hands, I picked up my mug of tea just as the ringing stopped. I quickly swapped hands again, accidently spilling tea onto Bennies pro form.
"Hello." Silence "Hello." I attempted to soak up the tea with another report. "Hello Mr Creed?" I watched in horror as the ink denoting number three against the column marked W11's shears spread creating the number eight.

Finally, I received a response. He was asking for the report. Taking a deep breath, I began. I sensed both Bennie and Steve were now watching. I was talking too quickly. The Manager stopped me mid-sentence when explaining the number of arches, we'd set in S31's intake. The tea had obscured the number two, it looked like a four. I sensed Bennie move across. He too had picked up the wrong figures being given.
"Evening." The silence in the control room broken by the sound of Bill, the nightshift Overman entering. He was answered by a *shush* from Bennie. Bill nodded apologetically as he realised who I was talking to.
"Sorry Mr Creed, two not four. Skips?" The figure was completely illegible. I recalled Bennie mentioning two hundred but that was earlier in the shift. I turned back towards Bennie. He had his back to me now whispering something to Bill. "Erm… that would be…" Looking towards Steve I mouthed the word *skips.* He held up a piece of paper. "Three hundred." The line went dead.
"Fuck, Steve can you phone him back. Been cut off." Bennie turned towards me.
"Nah lad. He'd finished with tha."
"Was that it then?"
"What you expecting, an applause or summut?" I replaced the handset. *Thank fuck that's over!*

By November things were buzzing at the pit. W11's had started to do what had always been planned. It culminated in breaking the pits individual face output, achieving thirteen thousand six hundred and twenty-three tonnes. Which in turn broke the record for the weekly saleable output, twenty-seven thousand six hundred and twenty-seven tonnes, lifting the overall output per man to nearly five tonnes. Bonus at the pit was at an all-time high. We all readily agreed the place was well on its way to becoming another million-tonne pit.

For my part regardless of the assurances provided by the Manager, I was still looking for my first Undermanager role. My completed supply of Internal Application Forms were filled out and ready to go. Although I had changed tact. I'd now begun applying for the Assistant Undermanager roles.

≈≈≈

13. Night Shift

The start of the year continued pretty much as we'd left 1986. The first week we'd had a damaged cable on W11's and then a few days later a broken face chain on C16's. I'd been together with Bennie for almost four months now. I wasn't sure what else I could learn. Desperate as always for my own shift. I continued applying for jobs up and down the country, the latest for an Assistant Undermanager's position in Nottinghamshire. The Manager's recent conversation with me to take over on nightshift had yet to be realised. The big national announcement on the industry was the establishment of the British Coal Corporation to replace the National Coal Board. Since arriving at Parkside two and a half years ago the number of pits had dropped from one hundred and seventy to ninety-four. Deep mined output reducing from one hundred and two million tonnes to eighty-six million tonnes. The biggest surprise was employment down from one hundred and forty-eight thousand to seventy-five thousand, an unbelievable fifty per cent reduction.

The upside of regular noons meant most of my weekends were free. Except for Saturday when I was exhausted, getting over the previous week. Last weekend had been an exception. We'd spent it with my brother-in-law and his family decorating Annie's parents' house. Then on the Monday I'd stayed late to cover off changing a spill plate on W11's maingate end. Bennie had given me the option. Stay and cover off the work with Charles or come up usual time and give the noonshift report to the Manager. Guessing the news of the damaged spill on 11's would be a surprise to the Manager I stayed underground.

This weekend we had nothing planned or so I thought. After our sleep in me and the kids went downstairs to get breakfast ready. My first job was to get the coal fire going. The kids loved watching. Old sheets of newspaper scrunched up, placed between the kindling on top of which the large lumps of coal. I struck a match. The kids were mesmerised as the flame took hold. All three of us watched as it quickly spread to the bits of wood. Whispers of smoke began to appear from the coal. The smell began to increase as a backdraft caused some of the smoke to enter the room. I quickly grabbed a sheet of paper. Holding it across the fireplace entrance. It had the desired effect.

Satisfied I positioned the fireguard. "Remember you two. Don't go near the fire." Neither responded. They were in the trance like state watching as the coal began to glow. I knew what they were waiting for. I'd done it myself as a kid. The blues and yellows appeared, as the gas from the lumps of coal were released.

"Dad?" I turned. Jamie had followed me into the kitchen.

"Yes son."

"We still goin Sormby tomorrow?" James was still unable to pronounce the letter f. I smiled he sounded so cute.

"What?"

"Mum said we were going tomorrow." *Fuck!* I'd forgotten that. Formby was about forty-five minutes away heading north and on the coast. We'd often go for the day out in the summer, but this was February and very cold.

"I think it's a bit cold. What about Speke Hall?"

"Dad, you promised. I want to go Sormby. I want to see the red squirrels."

"Little chance of that son. They'll all be hibernating."

"But I want to."

"Tell you what. Go inside with your sister. I'll bring your rice crispies in. We can watch Rainbow while we have breakfast." No more was said as Jamie disappeared out of the kitchen.

Ten minutes later I headed into the living room carrying a tray with the two bowls of cereal. The heat from the fire filled the room.

"There you go Lizzie breakie."

"Do fink Heidi looks like Bungle?" Lizzie was having the same problem pronouncing her th's. She was sat in front of the telly with her arm around Heidi.

"Yeah, she used to. Not so much now she's had all her fur cut off." I still couldn't get my head round the fact the missus had chosen to have the dog's coat cut. I'd argued against it and lost. "Come on, sit up at the table. Time for breakfast. Where's your brother? Jamie?" I shouted into the hall.

"I'm here Dad." He answered as he clambered down the stairs. "Mum said we are going."

"Going where?"

"Formby. Like we promised the kids." Mrs Gibson added as she followed Jamie down the stairs. That was me told then.

We arrived later that morning. There was hardly any traffic on the road. The car park opposite the sand dunes was empty. No surprises there. Ahead swirls of fine sand whipped into the air. A strong wind was blowing in off the Irish sea. The swaying clumps of marram grass were testimony to that. It felt good to be in the car. I'd had the heater blasting out during the journey.

"Can we have an ice cream mummy?"

"I don't think we'll see any ice cream vans here today son. Too cold."

"Can we take our picnic with us?"

"I think it best we leave it in the car. Bit too windy out there darling." *Windy?* I reckoned with the cold temperature and wind chill; it must have been minus twenty. Arctic sprung to mind. I restarted the engine. The cold had already begun to seep into the car.

"We're not going already, are we?"

"No son. Daddy's just keeping us warm." I looked into the rear-view mirror. The kids were both peering out the windows. Their breath creating condensation on the glass. Heidi was looking towards me over the back seat. She was already beginning to shake. The dirty blue grey sky hung low, the dense thick clouds adding to the winter darkness.

"Well, are we getting out or what?" Annie asked. I for one didn't really want to. I was quite comfortable where I was. The dog felt the same way.

"Yes, mummy let's go and see the waves." Jamie shouted excitedly. Lizzie hadn't said anything up to this point. Bet she'd been happy sat at home in front of the coal fire watching Rainbow. The dig in my ribs suggested it was time to move.

"Right come on then. Make sure you keep your hats and scarves on."

"And your gloves." Annie added.

Forcing the door open I felt the first sharp biting wind. It was bloody cold. Once out I reached across to open the back door for Lizzie. She very nearly fell out. Still leaning against the door. I moved forward quickly to grab her. Fortunately, the missus hadn't seen. She was still attempting to open the door for Jamie.

"Don't worry love. Let him get out this side." Jamie eagerly moved across towards me. Once out I closed the door. Lizzie was now sat on her bum, not through choice. I looked at the kids. For the first time they both looked as though they'd rather be somewhere else. Annie arrived on my side. Shouting across to make herself heard.

"I'll take the kids. You get the dog."

I did as instructed. Opening the boot turned out to be a harder job than I thought. Heidi looked up towards me. She had her sorrowful eyes. I could only guess what she was thinking. *Fuck off and leave me in here.*

"Come on girl let's have yer." I reached in and grabbed her collar. She wouldn't budge. I then had to lean in and scoop her up in both arms. "Come on the sooner we do this the sooner we can go." The cold biting wind had now found its way up the back of my jacket. I shivered. "Bloody ell girl. You've put some weight on." I slowly lowered her to the ground. Her first move was to cower behind my legs for protection.

"Mick. Can you grab Lizzie?" Annie shouted as she moved forward with Jamie in tow. Lizzie was sat on the floor once again, unable to stand. I grabbed her and joined the others as they slowly moved forward. I could feel Heidi close behind. Still using me as a shield. We'd been to Formby many times but never in these conditions. The last time I'd been here as a kid, my dad had told me back in the late fifties and early sixties thousands of tonnes of waste tobacco product had been buried in the sand dunes. I wondered if today was the day some of it might be uncovered.

Once we arrived alongside the dunes the wind died down. Protected we began to make our way forward. I turned to see where the dog was. She was following but at a slower pace. Occasionally she stopped to look back at the car. Who could blame her?

"Wow, how exciting was that?" Annie asked. As she turned towards Jamie. I was now alongside. I lowered Lizzie to the ground. Both kids still looked shell shocked. They obviously hadn't expected this. "Perhaps this wasn't the best idea." I thought it best I said nothing.

"Mummy when can we have our picnic?"

"You've only just had your breakfast."

"Daddy, can we go back to the car?" The trip out was beginning to turn out a disaster. Annie looked at me. I think she had come to the same conclusion.

"Tell you what." I hadn't come all the way here to head home just yet. "Why don't we have a look at the sea and then we can go back to the car for a picnic. My mind was on the flask of coffee we'd brought with us.

"Good idea daddy." Annie responded with a smile.

Once free of the dunes we turned into the gap leading down to the sea. Fortunately, it was a high tide not far now. The huge waves came into view each crashing forward carrying a frothy white crown. I could smell the sea. The taste of salt on my lips. It was too much for Jamie he ran forward. Lizzie too began to wriggle in my arms.

"Put me down." I could barely hear Lizzie. The sound of the waves had joined that of the wind. I gently lowered her to the ground. Her little legs began to move. Talk about hitting the ground running. She was off. Annie came up alongside and grabbed my arm.

"Thanks for bringing us Mick." She snuggled in against me. Just for that it had been worth it. I pulled her in tight against my side. Watching the kids run forward. All thoughts of the cold now gone. "We won't stay too long. Don't want them catching their death."

The kids had now stopped. Standing close to where the waves stopped. Jamie turned back towards us. His lips moving. I could barely make out what he was saying.

"Berg…" I turned to Annie.

"What's he saying?"

"I'm sure he said iceberg." Kids didn't you just love'em imaginations to die for. "There is something there. Come on let's see." We ran forward together to join the kids. Sure, enough as we got closer chunks of what I could only describe as polystyrene. Crashing against one another as they were carried towards the shoreline. Not quite reaching their destination before being drawn back out to sea. The fine spray of sea water covering as we stood.

"Wow! I've never seen that before. Unbelievable." We were all smiling. Thoughts of the picnic postponed for now. The dark grey sky seemed to turn lighter. Something was missing though. *Where's the dog?* Momentarily I began to panic. That's all we need now.

"What's up with you?" Annie had sensed my anxiety.

"Heidi. I can't see her." I shouted.

"Oh, stop worrying. She's over there watching us." Sure, enough as I followed Annie's direction. The dog was lying flat between two small tunes, partly obscured by a clump of marram grass. She certainly had no intention to join us. I turned back to watch the kids. Now throwing pebbles at the lumps of ice. *Perhaps we could do New Brighton next Sunday?* I was still not quite ready to break the news of regular nightshift. Assuming it would happen.

☐

"Fuckin ell mucker. Had yed in oven or what?" Bennie greeted me as I walked into the deployment centre."

"Beach fella. There yesterday. Very windy."

"Tell you what Mick tha does talk some shit."

"I kid you not. Anyway, what's the latest?" I changed the subject. I had no intention of Bennie or anyone else spoiling my memory of the time spent with Annie and the kids yesterday.

"Gaffer's asked me to have a looksee at tippler, bin playin up. What bout you?"

"If you don't mind, I'd like to have a wander into S31's return. See the RH22 in action."

"Fine by me mucker. I'll probably end up in 16's"

"Fuckin ell, what about 11's. They'll think something's happened to ye."

"Fuck off!"

I left Bennie at the pit bottom, deciding to walk in. The lads on the loco had some shunting to complete before heading back inbye. I'd been with Bennie nearly six months now. I'd learnt a lot from him particularly his man-management style. He had a way of getting things done without falling out. At times it allowed certain individuals to take the piss which I guess he knew about. Often letting it go. His style I'd call "consensual management." He was very much an extrovert. Sex uppermost on his mind. Always looking forward to his next shag. At some point during the shift, it became the topic of conversation. If he wasn't discussing his sex life it was the previous holiday or the next one planned. Often to Spain with his good mate Brian. If he mentioned the term lido to me once more.

His most impressive attribute, however, was how he handled the Manager. Never seeming to get flustered. Other than the time he'd fucked off early for a rendezvous with the suspender lady. He knew when to speak and when to listen. I'd watched with amusement how others floundered particularly when making the end of shift phone call. Stuttering, breaking out in blotches, cold sweats, unable to speak at all. I'd seen it all but not our Bennie. He had an eye for detail too. A memory to die for. He'd never write anything down.

It was now about to come to an end. According to Mr Keech another month and I'd be taking over the nightshift as Assistant Undermanager. Fancy title with less money, a glorified nightshift Overman if the truth be told. It was, however, a stepping stone to my goal. It would mean me leaving NACODS and once more joining the British Association of Colliery Management, BACM. Twelve years since I'd been kicked off the Student Apprentice Scheme for failing my OND.

"Hello Mick Gibson. Hello Mick." My thoughts suddenly interrupted by a tannoy a little ahead of me. Back to the present I was surprised how far I'd travelled. Now at the top of the Wigan Mines Access Intake. I hadn't noticed the stationary belt.

"Steve, Mick here."

"Hi Mick. You anywhere near the Access Road?"

"Just at the top now."

"Bennie said you'd be there abouts." A vision of Bennie appeared in my head. Holding court in the pit bottom cabin with his groupies supping the extra sweetened tea. "Frank's put a latch on V belt. Checking one of the vulcanised joints. Thinks it'll be okay but wouldn't mind a second opinion."

"I'm on it."

"Thanks Mick."

This was the second joint in as many weeks. I'd heard the rep was back this weekend to redo several of them.

I'd only travelled twenty yards before I spotted Frank. He was leaning over the empty belt. Stanley knife in hand.

"Hi Frank."

"Alreyt Mick cock. It's not too bad should last. Couple of them fingers like have pulled away. Told the lad who was here last, conditions too cowd for glue they use." I took a closer look to where Frank had cut the stragglers off.

"You done then?"

"I. I'll take it off. Where you off to Mick?"

"S31's return. Not seen that new machine they're using."

"Can you tell them fuckers to break the fuckin lumps up. I've had to break two up misen. Think cause they've got a big fancy fuck off machine they can send owt out. Huge lumps of mudstone they was."

"Yeah, I will." I moved across to the tannoy opposite. "Steve, Mick ere. Taking latch off now. Stitching good to go."

"Ta Mick." Steve had barely finished his response when the pre-alarm kicked in. Frank reappeared alongside.

"Where you off to Frank?"

"Hang about here for bit longer cock. Than have wander down to 11's."

"Where's your mate today?"

"Crazy Horse, on rest day." I laughed at his comment. His mate Dave was a huge fucker, not an ounce of fat just muscle. Longish jet-black hair. He certainly looked like a Sioux warrior.

"Right, I'll see you later."

I continued inbye. The belts were still running empty. I hadn't noticed how quiet they ran without the mechanical stitching. Before long I was deep in thought once more.

I'd been in the NUM for seven years and now almost five with NACODS. I had no regrets on the route I'd taken. It was longer, harder even but the one thing about it I'd gained a real understanding of the men. How they thought, what made them tick. The good, bad, and indifferent. Each with their own agenda. Some leaders, some followers. Each had their own role to play. Confrontation I learnt was not something to shy away from. If there was a problem, deal with it. Face to face ideally, man to man. Allowing a problem to fester often led to the union becoming involved. Allowing it to get out of hand. The more people that got involved would often add other people's agenda to the problem. Not that I had anything against the unions. I'd been in them all my working life and they certainly had a part to play. But as an official, junior management, senior management I saw it as "lazy management" leaving everything to fall back in their lap. That's not saying I could sort everything out. It avoided it becoming a game between management and the union "who had the biggest dick" was an expression I often used.

Lights ahead of me, the sound of the auxiliary fan and mineral smashing into the chute alerted me to the proximity of S31's return. Continuing inbye as the noise intensity increased, perspiration running down my chest. I slowed on reaching the warwick just above the entrance. A fine cloud of dust lingered above the chute before disappearing inbye. To my left a bank of panels suspended over the main conveyor. One of the panels attached by a single cable to the suspended fan. I made a mental note to get some ear plugs as I reached up to remove a small piece of discarded stonedust bag stuck to the mesh guard of the fan's silencer. Out of habit I placed my hand on the fan motor.

A steady stream of grey mudstone slid down the chute, small lumps in amongst the grey slurry. Spilling onto the belt it slid inbye momentarily until the arriving mound of the black stuff blocked its route. Reversing its direction in the process. The smell of the mudstone so different than coal. Mixed with water often reminded me of stale vegetables. Water from the heading belt was falling freely onto the track.

Checking outbye once more. The haulage rope hadn't moved but I was taking no chances. I moved away from the junction. Without warning the haulage rope in the return began to move. The points at the entrance suggested a run had been dropped earlier. The return had a separate endless rope haulage. Using a Pikrose engine and captivated bogie. The four-foot Bolton pulley above my head screeching as it turned. Standing there I took the opportunity to looksee at the support arrangements.

Everything about the place was big. Leading off the junction steel a few nineteen-foot Shelton's, at two-foot centres followed by the first seventeen, sixteen arches. Then onto the sixteen by fifteen's, all at metre centres. Continuing inbye the cold smell of steel now replaced by oil as I reached the forty-two inch, one twenty horsepower single motor FSW Tiger drive. It began to slow. I guessed they were setting the steel. Half a dozen five-gallon drums of gear oil were stacked alongside the gearbox. Above the belt thirty- six-inch suspended Flexiduct. Between the gib end and drive various shaped stalagmites loomed up from the floor. In places the dirt laden water continued to increase their size. Most of the top pulleys had little contact with the belting. The formation of hardened sludge eggs had put paid to that. Only the previous day the lads had to break the belt to clean off the tailend and chisel off the solidified dirt to prevent the belt from turning over.

On the opposite side of the road the reflective green and white manhole signs lined up perfectly. The standard of roadway in the Ince Six Feet was better than anything I'd seen, including the pipe ranges slung beneath the ventilation ducting. Each pipe individually colour coded for the pump, compressed air, and water. The Victaulic water range diameter increased to four inch due to the use of high-pressure water. Little wonder there was so much water on the conveyor. The belt pre-alarm kicked in. Obviously cutting again. Whatever contract they'd agreed with the Deputy Manager Services, Mr Smooth, these guys weren't hanging about. Wasting no more time I continued inbye.

The recess to my left indicated I wasn't far from the action now. It housed the seven fifty KVA transformer for the machine. Although the belt had been running for the last ten minutes it was only now a steady stream of mud laden water appeared. Its natural flow inbye halted by a mix of coal and dirt piled high. The sludge soon disappeared beneath the black stuff. I counted five lights ahead. Ever since the fitter and electrician became active participants in the heading bonus scheme everybody played a part.

The machine was smaller than I imagined. Not its length or width but its height, just over six feet. The Anderson Strathclyde RH22 was moving forward its telescopic cutting boom extension slewing from left to right, defining the profile of the road. The noise drowning out any sound from the conveyor.

From a conversation I'd had with Glyn Amp he'd explained the power for the machine was supplied by a double contactor gate end box. One box for powering the water supply and the other for the RH22 itself. This had three motors. Two one twenty horsepower for the cutting head and hydraulics. A third one fifty horsepower motor for the high-pressure water system All three being interlocked.

The operator was controlling the machine by a centrally positioned joystick. This I'd been told operated the cutting boom and track. I'd never seen anything like it. The water spray encapsulating the dust produced. One of the team raised a thumb. I did likewise moving in closer. The three vein cutting head with its tungsten carbide picks cutting through the coal and mudstone with little effort. The high-pressured water played its part too. I watched as the mineral fell to the floor before being collected by the synchronised gathering arms. The heavy-duty loading apron lowering as it moved forward. Scrunching and crunching as the fallen material was guided reluctantly to the centrally located twin strand scraper chain. Towards the two-foot-wide scraper chain bridge conveyor. Finally falling onto the forty-two-inch belt.

It was the first time I'd been alongside a heading machine that gave me the same euphoria as watching the heavy-duty power loader on W11's. My overalls soaking up the mist laden air.

I hadn't noticed the electrician appear alongside. I was totally engrossed in the operation of the machine. It didn't get much better than this.

"Mick. Tannoy, control's bin after tha."

"Cheers fella." Reluctantly I made my way outbye.

"Hello Control. Mick here." I placed my ear up against the tannoy.

"Mick, Franks bin on. Reckons that stitching's gotten worse. Suggesting we do it between shifts."

"Does Bennie know?"

"Can't get hold of him."

"Okay. I'll make my way out." I was a little disappointed not to spend more time with the RH22. Hopefully, I'd get chance again.

□

I hadn't realized it at the time, but Friday had been my last shift with Bennie on noons. The Manager had called me in for a meeting. True to his word I was being promoted to Assistant Undermanager on nightshift. The letter I'd received offering me the position of Assistant Undermanager stating my salary as just under fourteen grand, plus a colliery allowance of twelve hundred per annum and something called a special allowance of a thousand pound per annum. There was also an ex-gratia lump sum of four hundred pounds. I would no longer be a member of NACODS. My first big role and back into BACM. The only downside I'd be starting a week earlier on nights as Colliery Overman. Bill had taken his redundancy and still had a week's holiday to take. I was being drafted in to cover. The week had gone well so far three nights under my belt, two to go. It was Thursday morning I was driving home on the M62 motorway. It still wasn't the position I was looking for. Other than the title I was a glorified Senior Overman. I comforted myself with the knowledge it was a step in the right direction. I wasn't sure how much the missus would be happy with me on regular nightshift. In addition, I hadn't mentioned that although my basic wage would be more, not being paid for overtime and the regular quarter shift I booked each day I was on less money.

□

Last night hadn't been such a bad shift. We'd managed to clear a hundred skips, two shears on L33's, and another four on C16's. W11's only one but in addition move the Pantech in and fill the loop. As far as I was concerned an excellent nights work. As did Mr Keech.

"What the fuck." A red light appeared on the dashboard. I wasn't sure but it looked like the engine light. I pulled over onto the hard shoulder. Retrieving the Driver Manual from the glove compartment. Sure, enough it was the engine. *Fuck I knew we should have gotten rid of it sooner. Fuckin Volkswagen Polo!* I never liked it. It was only two weeks previous we'd been looking for another car. I'd been hoping to put this down as a down payment. Looks as though that plans gone out the fuckin window.

Two hours later the RAC tow truck dropped me back at our house. The conversation with the RAC guy had darkened my mood. The price for a new engine would never cover what I got if I sold the car.

"Where have you been?"

"To see the Queen." I answered my wife sarcastically.

"Aren't you funny."

"Dad you're late. We've had breakfast without you." Jamie asked.

"Sorry all. Bit of car trouble."

"Oh no love you've broken down?"

"Dad does that mean we're getting a new car."

"Dadda."

"Blinkin heck when did our Lizzie learn that?"

"You wouldn't believe it. First thing this morning. We were going to surprise you." I grabbed both the children and lifted then up.

"Dad's home now. I need a big hug and kiss." Momentarily my troubles had gone.

"What are you going to do?"

"Not sure just yet. I'll need to borrow my brother's jeep for tonight and see what I can think of." And that was the end of our conversation. It was late and I was tired.

☐

"Evening Mick, bit early cock?" Chris the control room lad greeted me as I walked in. The new control room was now up and running.
Spacious low-ceilinged, the walls brilliant white. Equipment included eight large screens, two sets either side of the comms board, monitoring all underground operations and the environment. The windows opposite covered in long vertical blinds matching the brown carpet tiles. The old control room had become mine and Bennies temporary office. We were all under strict instruction from the Manager not to enter the place unless in our clean.

"Yeah, it's just the fuckin car engine blew up on me this morning on the way home. Worse thing about it I'd been looking to change it two weeks ago. Borrowed my brother's car."

"Lockout on 11's maingate." Chris shouted into the mic. "Happened to me the other year. No way was I getting a new engine fitted. Had me eye on an Austin Metro."

"Hi Chris, just checking a joint." The beltman responded.

"Never mind the fuckin joint. Get the latch off." An anonymous voice added. Chris turned back towards the console.

"Clear. As I was saying Mick piece of cake really. Just filled the engine with oil, took it to the local Rover garage and put it down as part ex."

"Didn't they check the vehicle?"

"Nah, never do… latch back on. They're just happy to get the sale… clear!"

"Interesting." I wasn't convinced though. "Right, I'll see you later. Wouldn't want Bennie moaning. I'm sure someone's missus will be waiting for his services tonight." Leaving Chris, I headed to the old control room.

Throughout the shift my mind kept replaying the conversation I'd had with Chris. Could it work, the garage taking my old fucked up car in part ex? I just couldn't see it happen let alone getting the car to the garage in one piece.
   Once changed I put the thought out of my head. I had a shift to run.

The shift went well. Next morning Mr Keech seemed in a good mood, accepting my shift report without too many questions. I left and headed out to the brother's car. I took a deep breath. It was a cold crisp morning, a light frost covered the cars. The sky was clear blue. Breathing out I left a trail of vapour. It was going to be another bright sunny day. Just as I liked it.
   The sensation coming home off nights before going to bed always seemed surreal. Everything at that time of the morning seemed possible. Once on the motorway my mind began to play out the various scenarios of getting a new car. I had visions of the car sales rep passing me a set of keys and shaking my hand. Mind made up I stopped at the local garage and bought a gallon drum of Castrol engine oil.

"Listen love get the kids up we're going for a ride."
"You've not had any breakfast yet. Lizzie's not feeling too well."
"I'll have something later. Just need to put some oil in the Polo."
"What for…?" I didn't answer. I headed back to the car.
Job done I headed back inside. "Dad where we goin?"
"For a ride darlin. Where's your sister?"
"With mummy. In the toilet. She's been sick."
"Annie you comin or what?" I shouted up the stairs. I was in the moment not wanting to break the spell.
"You've had no breakfast."
"Don't worry. We need to keep movin."
"You haven't told me where were goin yet."
"I will. Let's get in the car first."
"Dadda."
"Good morning, Lizzie. You better now darlin?"
"Dadda."
"I just hope her Dadda knows what he's doin." Annie added.

She watched in horror as I walked passed my brother's jeep opening the doors to the Polo.
"What the hell are you doing?"

"Don't worry just get in. Everything's goin to be fine."
 I emptied the last of the engine oil. Climbing into the car no one said anything. It started first time. *Thank fuck for that. It's got to be a sign!*
"Mick I'm warning you." No more was said. We were on our way. Annie in the front, the kids in the back.

"For goodness sake you're going to kill us all."
"Don't be daft it's only a bit of smoke."
"The engine could blow up." Annie certainly had a point. The smell of burning oil wafted through my partly opened window. We'd just entered Woolton Village, not far now. My plan was to visit the Ford garage at the bottom of Speke Hall Road. I just hoped we didn't all end up in Allerton Cemetery.
 By now we were attracting the attention of every passer bye. Some pointing towards us and waving. I'm guessing they thought we couldn't see the smoke. Seeing it wasn't the problem, I was struggling seeing through it. It had gone from a grey colour to black. Up to now the smell in the car hadn't been too bad.

Annie had her eyes closed. She'd already instructed Jamie to grab his sister and get behind her seat. I had no alternative. At the top of Speke Hall Road, I switched the engine off, freewheeling down towards the garage. Fortunately, turning the engine off and a change in wind direction the black plumes of smoke diluted. The momentum of the car and steep gradient allowed sufficient speed to take a left and climb the short ramp into the Ford garage car park. We came to a complete stop. I applied the handbrake. *Thank fuck.* No one said anything at first. We sat in silence. Reality returning as our daughter threw up over the back seat.
 My wife began to give me her view on the situation. As best she could with the kids listening. I wasn't taking much in. I was too busy thinking of our return journey home. Something up until this point I'd given no thought to.
"And how the hell are we supposed to get home? Cause if you think your taking me and the kids back in this. You've got another thing coming."

"Dad there's a man looking at us from the shop window." I looked across. A sales rep. Obviously enjoying the spectacle of our little domestic.
"Come on we can worry about that later. For now, let's go and sort a car."
We headed straight towards a new silver Ford Escort Bravo.
"Dad it's got a window in the roof."
"Sun roof son. It's called a sun roof not a window."
"Okay Dad. It just looks like a window."
"It certainly does." The fact we were now in the car show room with the gentle hum of the *Real Thing's* latest record in the background. Added to the calmness that now descended around us. I was amazed I still didn't feel tired.

"Good morning, sir how can I help you?"

The next hour passed so quickly with the sales rep accompanying us all on a test drive towards Speke Hall and back. Annie and the kids said very little. My mind made up we headed back to the car showroom. "We'll take it." I commented as I parked the car. I avoided looking at Annie.

Once back inside the sales rep held out his hand. "If you let me have your keys. I'll get our engineer to check your car." *What the fuck! This wasn't supposed to happen.* I looked across to Annie. She was holding Lizzie. Jamie was playing with one of his matchbox cars he'd brought with him. If looks could kill – I was a dead man walking. I passed him the keys, convincing myself it would just be a cursory glance.

Whilst we completed the hire purchase paperwork the sales rep provided the kids with a colouring book a piece and some wax crayons.

I was on cloud nine. Paperwork signed; deal done. We were now the proud owners of a brand-new Ford Escort Bravo. My next problem was how the fuck were we going to get home. I watched as another gentlemen walked across to our sales rep. He looked ever so important. They had a brief conversation. After which our man came back towards me.

"Excuse me sir." Oh fuck. A problem. He's about to cancel the deal. I looked towards Annie she was shaking her head. She wouldn't look at me. I guess we both knew what was coming next.

"Is there a problem. Thought we'd done the deal."

"We have sir. It's just my manager thinks it might be best if you didn't drive your car home. He's suggesting we provide you with a courtesy car. Just for the week until yours is ready. Only if that's okay with you?"

☐

14.   *Finally*

One of the great advantages being the Assistant Undermanager was the freedom the role afforded. Unless instructed by the Manager or Deputy Manager to visit a certain area I had the ability to go where I wanted. Provided I gave myself sufficient time to get outbye and ensure the number one shaft was released in sufficient time to empty the bunkers.

Leaving the pit bottom I'd travelled the main tunnel leaving the loco lads to continue shunting. Walking alongside the track I picked up speed to warm myself up. The air was clear. The smell of whitewash fainter now as I travelled inbye. Bennie had advised we were running short of steel in S31's developments. That had to be the priority. All three coal faces, L33's, C16's and

W11's were manned up. This would be the last time the pit operated three faces at once. Last year we'd had the best annual production since I'd arrived. Eight hundred and twenty-six thousand tonnes with an OMS of nearly three tonnes. The number of men on books was now thirteen hundred, a reduction of three hundred. The conversation with Mr Keech before leaving Cronton was now becoming a reality.

S31's coal face was to be the second heavy duty face at the mine. Two hundred metres long and nearly two metres high. I'd seen the new set of six-leg powered supports in the surface compound. The new white supports with huge pushover rams front legs still wrapped in black plastic covers. The inch and half hydraulic hoses neatly suspended and held together by steel springs.

Although work was going well, I couldn't say the same back home. All me and the missus seemed to do was argue. She continued to make the same point about her being a single parent. Regular noons had been bad enough. Leaving the house before mid-day and then not arriving home till after ten, sometimes later. Regular nights, however, brought a separate set of problems. The biggest being I was always falling asleep. It didn't help during the day, the kids kept sneaking into the bedroom with their mates and waking dad up. I laughed at the thought of it. My only and usual response had been it'll all work out in the long run.

"Hello Mick. Hello Mick Gibson."
"Hi Steve."
"Shaftsmen have been on. Finished maintenance handing the skips back over." I smiled.
"Well, there's a first."
"Just as well, bunker's about three quarters full. With all three faces coaling."
"Best be getting fuckin decent bonus then." An anonymous voice shouted over the tannoy.
"Excellent, thanks Steve. I'll give you a call when I get to a phone."
"Fuckin hate scousers." I chose to ignore the anonymous gentlemen. Wouldn't want to give him the satisfaction. I was still getting to know the lads on regular nights.
"Righto."

I continued inbye. I'd pop into S31's intake first and make sure there was a clear run in for the steel which I guess by now was on its way in. The outbye roads were as black as fuck, not that we were short of stonedust. I passed numerous stacks of it on the way in. I stopped to make a note, taking the opportunity for a quick pinch of snuff. I'd mention to the Undermanager to get some spread. Not that he'd take any notice.

For the first time I could hear the rhythmic sound of the conveyor. The click, click, click as the stitching's passed over the top rollers. I assumed the lads were setting steel. That would be the third ring for the shift, leaving two. *Need to check where the haulage lads where.* Replacing the tin of snuff, I continued forward.

Reaching the cross-cut airdoors I pulled on the belt strip handle. Pressure released the door opened. Walking forward the floor dust rose in the static air. Hanging there like a dark rain cloud. The tiny particles entering my mouth causing me to hawk up. Tapping my pocket out of habit, I realised I'd left my pack of Gallaher's Brown Pigtail in the old control room. *Fuck!* I moved quickly forward letting the door close behind me. The narrow-gauge steel rope attached to a few fishplates suspended over a small pulley caused the door to slam close. Creating more airborne dust. In the distance the sound of the auxiliary fan. Exiting the last door, I spotted the phone on the corner of the junction.

"Hi Steve, it's me. Can you give the haulage lads a shout? See where those arches are. You're kidding me. Hundred skips, fifteen hundred tonne. Best we've done for some time. I agree. The way the faces are producing tonight we'll be leaving the bunkers full. Check with the pit bottom Deputy. Ask him to keep some lads over. Create some room." I waited as Steve shouted on the outbye tannoy. I heard the response from the haulage team. "Yeah, got that. Reckon another hour they'll be here. Anything else? No. Okay catch you later."

Approaching the heading, the noise was deafening I reached up towards the fan. Out of habit I placed my hand against the motor. Satisfied I continued forward. The sound of the auxiliary fan now replaced as the black stuff was thrown forward onto the front plate of the chute to suddenly change direction. The noise was intense at the large lumps of coal smashed against the chute. The dust produced was not evidenced, enclosed within the metal box. The dust suppression sprays doing what they do best. The lads were cutting again. The black stuff was piled high along the centre of the forty-two-inch belt. I continued inbye the sound of the Tiger drive adding to that of the chute. I could feel the heat as I passed the double motors.

Continuing along the maingate. The smell of new forty-two-inch belting filled the air. The whiteness of the new belt structure lit up the roadway. Everything about the place was big, This would be our second heavy duty face. The shearer an all-electric, 230 KW, AM500 costing upwards of a million quid. Another set of lemniscate linkage shield powered supports. Heavy duty AFC and stageloader. Total investment another six million quid.

"Hello Mick. Hello Mick Gibson." My thoughts interrupted by the tannoy alongside.

"Hi Steve."

"Mick, you near a phone?" *Fuck what's wrong now?*

"No, what's up?"

"Lost power to Strata Bunker."

"Who's on it?"

"Deputies there now. Just put a call through to Assistant Engineer, your mate Alan."

"And?"

"Answered phone immediately. Reckons problem is the surface, one of the trannies acting up."

"Any idea how long."

"Not sure. Problem is though bunkers nearly full again."

"Okay, I'll make my way back out." It was so annoying. Last time I'd visited S31's return to see the RH22 we'd had a problem with the belts. I was taking no chances if we had a problem I needed to be there.

□

Before I knew it summer had arrived. In June, the Conservatives had won their third consecutive election, this time with a majority of a hundred and four seats. We had hoped Labour under Kinnoch would have done better, knowing full well it could have repercussions for the industry.

□

I could feel the weight on me. I wasn't exactly sure what had happened. Then the sensation of tiny hands on my face. The gentle sound of children's voices. My mouth being forced open. My tongue now extracted. I felt helpless. Then a voice I recognised.

"This is my Dad." It was our Jamie. I began slowly to regain consciousness from my deep slumber, at that point where you're neither asleep nor awake.

"Oi you lot, get down the stairs. Leave your Dad alone, I've told you not to wake him." The sound of my wife's voice.

"Mum we were only showing our friends." The movement of bodies above the bed clothes as they climbed off. I counted four. Then a tender kiss on the side of my face. I just caught sight of her as she left. It was our Lizzie. Then silence once more. I began to drift back to whence I had come. Darkness.

□

I'd booked a rest day for the Friday, we were off on holiday early Saturday morning. My head was in that place where it goes when you're about to go away for a couple of weeks. I was feeling rather pleased with myself. Driving into work that night the sun was still out. The weather forecast for the next two weeks looked promising. I wasn't going to overdo things tonight. I planned to visit the last of the Lower Florida faces L33's. Production from here would cease whilst I was away. It's replacement S31's was in the final throes of installation. For the first time Parkside was operating with only two coalfaces. C16's had finished production back in May.

Having completed shift handover with Bennie. I popped into control.
"Last shift tonight, Mick?"
"Yeah, looking forward to the break."
"Where tha off to?"
"South Wales. Place called Penally."
"Nice. Where you off neet?"
"L33's and if time pop into S31's. See how the installation is going."
"See your mates back."
"Who would that be?"
"Alan Volt." I smiled.
"Right Steve, I'll catch you later." He never answered as the tannoy burst into life. It was the Overman on L33's.
"Hello Steve. Hello Control."
"Hi Tommy."
"Shearer not quite in tailend. Machine cut out. Sparkie looking at it now."
"Okay, let me know when you're running again."

I continued to Deployment. Most of the lads had passed through other than a couple of officials, including Keith the Face Overman.
"You heard about 33's Mick."
"Yeah, Tommy's been in touch with Control."
"Still no joy. Might be worthwhile giving your mate a shout." To both our surprise, Alan the Assistant Engineer appeared. He was changed ready to go down. Picking up his tallies he turned to me.
"Heard bout shearer Mick?"
"Yep."
"I'm going there now."
"Oh, right." And with that he'd gone. I guess the threat of being put back on the tools had given him a new perspective on life.
"Now that was a first."
"Never expected to see that." I responded.
"Guess you'll be coming in to see us then Mick?"
"Yeah, that was my plan, Keith."
"See you in there."

Having checked the boards, it seemed we were fully manned. I headed back out to check with Alan's equivalent on the mechanical side Gary Gear. To my surprise he too was changed. I liked Gary. Always smiling and keeping himself busy.

"Bloody ell Gaz. You and Alan know summut I don't?" He laughed.

"Nobody more surprised than me to see Alan changed at this time cock. No, I'm off to do a recce on V and W belt drives for Frankie. Plan to replace both gear boxes in couple of weeks. RCM lad from Area reported couple of bad samples from last visit."

"What the fuck's RCM?"

"Fuckin ell Mick tha best be reading up on these things. Routine Condition Monitoring supposed to be future of things to come. Remember our old boss, Mick Hobbit? Sits with him now as the Area's Maintenance and Reliability Engineer."

"I'll take your word for it." An image of Mick appeared; I'd seen him recently coming out of the Top Shunt. "Catch you later."

I headed straight to the baths. I hadn't planned on hanging about. Straight down and hopefully up a little earlier, I'd promised the missus.

The cage was waiting for me when I arrived at the pit top.

"Alreyt Mick."

"All good thanks Stevie." He patted me down. "Control's bin on. 33's running again. Asked me to pass on the message."

"Thanks fella." I continued into the cage, my hand reaching for the top rail. I turned as the mesh gate hit the bottom of the cage. Satisfied with my footing. I released the rail and extracted my tin of snuff. Signalling complete, the cage dropped effortlessly. Then total darkness. The swirling ventilation causing me to shiver, passing the first inset, I closed my eyes. The speed at which I travelled for a moment caused me to panic. Reaching up once more for the rail. I clenched it tightly. Breathing in through my nose, the unmistakable smell of shaft. A mixture of concrete, steel, oil, and cold air. The cage began to slow. Panic over as we came into pit bottom. The sound of the recently completed sixteen-inch compressed air pipe range adding to the background noise.

"Early tonight, Mick. On a promise?" The Onsetter greeted me as he lifted the gate."

"I wish. Loco still inside?"

"Yeah, shunting far end. After a ride?"

"No, I'll be fine. Can you make sure we clear all the empties. Freddie's complaining he's got nothin to load onto."

"Will do."

I kept up a good pace. Within forty-five minutes I'd reached the far end. I'd built up a sweat. Deciding to travel in via the maingate I reached L30's intake, from which L33's gates had been driven. The black stuff was piled high, the sound of the coal hitting the chute getting noisier as I continued inbye. The junction lights ahead appeared. Frankie's curved chute that had first been installed in W11's had proven to be such a success. The Manager had instructed the new Mechanical Engineer Bill Maskill, to install them on all the gate conveyors. It stood out in the distance. The white paint providing evidence of its newness. What I hadn't expected to see was the pile of coal building up near the tailend. It was running back on the bottom belt dropping to the floor via the plough. I spotted the problem immediately. A little tracking was required. Moving a couple of top pulleys outbye of their saddles completed the job, but why was the belt running on one side in the first place? I moved to the back of the tailend. Sure, enough a pile of fines had built up on the blind side. My mouth now coated with the fine dust dropping from the back of the gib roller. Hawking up, I spat out.

Moving back out into the junction I spotted what I was looking for. It was leaning against the inbye junction stanchion. I got myself into a kneeling position behind the tailend of the conveyor. The fines and water continued to fall to the floor. The neoprene on the wiper was almost worn out. There was little appetite to replace anything in the district. I watched as the return belt began to move across the tailend roller. Now running central I returned to see how the top belt was running whilst at the same time returning the two top rollers to their original position. Job done I replaced the shovel.

Moving across to the Meeting Station I removed my helmet and belt allowing me to remove the top of my overalls. Once I'd cleared the shit and small pieces of coal from under my vest, I replaced my gear. I sat down and removed each boot to clear the muck from them too. There was nothing worse than walking on tiny pieces of coal. The pockmarks on the soles of my feet were testament to that. Satisfied, I had a quick pinch and pooped a small chew in. I was ready for the off. One last thing to do. The phone was to my left.

"Hiya Steve. How's things? W11's? Good. Yeah, just at the outbye end. How many skips have we wound? Excellent. Oh, one other thing can you let the Deputy know I'm about to enter his district. Speak later."

I began to walk inbye. The road profile was still reasonable. The floor however was a different matter. Good quality coal but trying to maintain the gate roads required huge effort. All supplies for the face were now sent via the return road. Running anything required down the panzer.

A light approached from inbye. I knew who it would be. I wasn't disappointed.

"Ah, Mr Volt. All sorted I, see?" I sensed the trepidation with Alan. He kept his distance. Half expecting, me to grab him. It was quite amusing to watch.

"Aye Mick, solenoid valve. Electrician fettled it before I got there." *No surprises there then?* It's not that I didn't like Alan, not that I knew him that well. It was just he was lazy. I suppose it was the same in any industry. Majority of lads were hard working. Putting in a full shift. I remember a fitter at Cronton. He was covering one of the developments. I was a young lad at the time on back up. Dragging steel into the headings. The guy as soon as he arrived in the heading curled up on the side of the road and went to sleep. He seemed quite put out when I asked him what he was doing. Told me his job started when there was a breakdown. I could never understand that approach. There's was always something we could all do. We weren't paid for getting our head down. The incident I remember vividly, something I wasn't going to allow to happen, hence my approach with Alan.

Standing there reflecting Alan became a little uncomfortable. "Well, if there's nowt else Mick, I best bidooin plenty paperwork to be catchin up on."

"I bet there is?"

"What's mean by that Mick?"

"Oh nothin. I'll see you later. If I need anything, I'll give you a shout. Suppose you'll be in the office?" Alan shook his head.

"Alsithy." And with that he was gone.

I spat what remained of my bacca onto the belt. The black stuff piled high. It always amazed me, how on some coalfaces as they came to the end of their life the coal simply gave itself up. The one exception for me was L32's. That place had been hard work.

Standing there had caused the perspiration to dry. A shiver went down my spine. I began heading inbye once more. Picking up speed to generate some bodily heat. It wasn't that easy with the reduction in height. I was half expecting to see the Hausher, then remembered it had been salvaged and moved to the return. Two of them were now operating in there. No means of transporting the dirt out the lads piled it either side of the track. Far from ideal at times giving us problems with gas. It looked as though they'd given up on the stonedust barriers. There were more shelves lying on the floor then suspended.

I guessed the machine was well on its way down from the return. The satisfaction of seeing the continuous flow of coal. Must have been the same for all of us. I wasn't far now from the maingate end. The lights from the stageloader clearly visible. There seemed to be more activity around the pantech than normal. Amongst the group I spotted the gate end Deputy. He saw me approach.

"Bout fire rip." I nodded in acknowledgement. Minutes later the dull thud of the explosion. The team waited a little longer than they would normally have done. Probably cause I was there. Then as I reached the stage loader, they headed inbye to clean up.

I didn't recognise the young lad on the stageloader. "Evening fella." I shouted above the noise of the coal free falling against the sides of the chute onto the conveyor.

"Artawreet Mick?"

"I certainly am. Any idea where Keith is?"

"Mick if you don't mind me saying that's a bit of a daft fuckin question. He be with the shearer. Where he always is." I laughed.

"Fair point. Who's Chargeman tonight?" The lad pointed inbye. I turned. Walking towards me was the huge figure of Tommy Beddows. His face as black as an ouzel. The whites of his eyes accentuated. He was smiling, I wouldn't have expected anything less.

"Alreyt Mick. Looking for Ged?"

"No, I was lookin for you actually." Tommy grabbed a blackened water bottle from between the panels. Raising it to his mouth he let it flow freely. Most of it missing, falling either side of his mouth onto his chest. He paid no attention to where it fell.

"Bet you miss im?" He responded wiping his mouth.

"Like a fuckin hole in the head."

"Nay Mick. You can't kid a kidder." Tommy did have a point. I did miss the banter with Ged. I hadn't seen him for a while. "He's bin on sick. Banged his yed." Tommy laughing at his own comment.

"Bet the other guy's off sick too."

"Three of im Mick, I'm told. Won't be drinkin in St Helens for a while."

"Anyway, enough about my old sparring partner. You lads stopping over?"

"Aye Keith's already arranged." The stageloader began to slow. We both turned towards the maingate belt. It was stationary.

"Who's got maingate belt locked out?" The stageloader operator immediately shouted. Soon followed by the unmistakable sound of Keith.

"Who's got the fuckin belt locked out panels? Bout come in on bi-di."

"On it now Keith." I watched as the lad picked up the phone.

"Seems they've putting an injured mon on conveyor." He responded almost immediately. I moved forward and grabbed the handset.

"Steve? Yeah, right got that. I'll make my way there now." As I finished my conversation the maingate belt kicked in.

"What's for do….?" Tommy's voiced drowned out by the sound of the stageloader pre-alarm.

"One of the haulage lads has gone over on his ankle. Could be broken. Taking him out on a stretcher. More serious problem in S31's. One of the lads on installation got his hand caught above canopy. Accidently set the thing on it. May have lost his hand. Tell Keith I'll catch up with him later." I didn't wait for an answer I turned and headed outbye. Fuck I thought the shift was going well.

Forty minutes later I got to the outbye end of S31's. Several lights approaching. I counted five in total. I didn't recognise any of the lads other than the Deputy. Gerry Cook. The injured lad had a man either side each holding onto his side. His right hand raised in the air. The bandage heavily stained. Another guy at the rear was carrying the stretcher. Momentarily the injured man stumbled. Kicking up a cloud of dust in the process.

"Come on lad av a minute." The group stopped as I approached. Gerry walked towards me. Considering the circumstances, he looked calm. He whispered, "Thought old lad had lost his hand. He's been quite fortunate, not that I think he'll see it that way. Lost three fingers including thumb." To prove it Gerry extracted a small see-through plastic bag. Directing the beam of light of his cap lamp towards it. It was a mass of flesh and bone covered in blood with the odd finger nail. The thumb looked intact. "He's ad morphine. May av to give im another shot in a lot of pain."

"Why isn't he on the stretcher?"

"Fuckin ell Mick don't you think we've tried…" The comment couldn't have been more appropriate as the guy collapsed. "Reet lads get im on stretcher."

"I'll let you get on. Is Billy still in there?"

"Yeah, completing a sketch and taking statements. My lads av gone to fetch manrider. Before you ask, we got the journey of timber to bottom of brow."

"Well done." We said no more, they continued outbye.

I'd decided to have a looksee at the accident site. Before heading inbye I allowed myself a quick pinch. Stood there against the conveyor my moment of reflection was interrupted.

"Hello Mick. Hello Mick Gibson." Steve shouted from a tannoy, ahead of me. I moved towards it. In the distance more lights appeared. A total of four. Within minutes I could make out Billy Britain, the Deputy. Three lads followed him. As before two of them were escorting the third. He too looked as though he'd been involved in an accident. A bandage wrapped around the side of his face covering one eye. *For fucks sake what now?*

"Hello Mick. Hello Mick Gibson." I guessed Steve wanted to update on the latest incident. I watched as Billy moved across to the tannoy.

"Steve, Billy ere. Mick's just arrived. I'll update him. Do me a favour and let Gerry know we're right behind im. Don't go without us."

"Will do Bill. Any lads left in there?"

268

"Yeah. Three with the sparkie. I'll be back once fitter's on way out."

"Got that."

By now the lads had reached me. The lad who'd been bandaged spoke first.

"Nah Mick. Never rains but it pours." I nodded. He seemed in good spirits. I couldn't help but notice the bulk of padding behind the bandage. The lads continued outbye.

"Fuckin ell Bill. What's appened now?" Billy as was his want moved closer towards me. Not one to respect another person's personal space. It didn't help him speaking at pace with the added dimension of saliva flying freely from his mouth. I moved back slightly ready for the onslaught.

"I'll tell tha what Mick, never known shift like it!" Perspiration was flowing freely from his forehead. "If it's not one thing it's summut else." He seemed out of breath. I offered him my opened tin of snuff.

"Billy, calm down. Just av a minute lad."

"Calm down tha says. Calm fuckin down. I've never known owt like it."

"Come on what's happened?"

"Two of im working together. Fitter and yon mon. Fitter leaves adjustables on top of canopy. Fitter couples up bagging and sets chock on yon mons hand as he's attempting to remove the fuckin spanner. Yon mon fucks off with arf is hand missing then fitter goes and uncouples a bagging that's still under pressure. Fluid straight in eye. Whole thing pops out. Hanging by a thread. Try as I might, couldn't get it back in socket. Just secured it best I could. Av ad reportables before but not two in one fuckin shift." I moved my head back a little further.

"Okay fella, it appens."

"Not two in one shift Mick."

"Never mind. You following the lads out?"

"Yeah, just make sure they get on ride."

"Go on then."

"See tha shortly Mick." I waited until Billy had moved on before using the sleeve of my overalls to wipe my face.

By the time I got back up pit. The nightshift had gone for a bath. Mr Keech was waiting for me in the old control room. My desk was littered with the nightshift reports including sketches of the accident sites. One of which was covered in blood-stained finger prints.

"Fuckin ell Mick, any other casualties from the war zone?" He was laughing as he said it. "Ambulance just leavin as I arrived."

"Only one?"

269

"I lad. Saving on petrol. Took im both together."

"What about haulage lad?"

"Medical checked him out. Nothing broken. Told him get some frozen peas on it when he gets home. How did we end up in 31's?"

"Leckie got power on to shearer and managed to haul it up and down a few times. Lookin good."

"Excellent. Other than a couple of chocks behind, still on schedule. Right, you go get a bath. That's your last shift for a couple of weeks. Where you off to?"

"South Wales caravan."

"Enjoy marra."

☐

Arriving back at work after the holiday I felt more fucked than usual. I'd spent most of the day filling out an internal application form in response to an advert for Undermanager positions in the Western Area. There were a number of posts up for grabs.

Tonight, I'd plan to ease myself in gently with a trip to W11'S. I was traveling at speed down the Wigan Mines Access Intake, now alongside V belt.

"Mick, come and get tha sat down lad. You're goin to meet thisen coming back." I hadn't spotted the guy sat in the intakes main substation, just below W5's maingate.

"Steve you're back. How did it go?" I asked ducking into the sub-station. The warmth of the place inviting against the intake air outside. The gentle hum of the tranformers in the background. As per my usual routine I checked behind the three transformers. As expected, several sand bags were laid out. The electricians had got a little savvier. No longer leaving them on top of the transformers.

Steve Chubb was out regular nightshift beltman. We sat and had a chat most nights. He'd been away the previous week to a caravan in Cleethorpes. He was one of the nicest characters I'd met at the pit. Since being on regular nights I'd gotten to know him quite well. Round chubby face, tash and most nights a permanent smile.

"Fuckin ell Mick, what's with all the dust? Come and have a minute." He had a point, the cloud of dust I'd created was everywhere. I did as he suggested and sat down. He passed me a cup of his sweet, milky lukewarm tea. "I'll tell tha what. It ain't half cold on theast coast. Plenty sunshine but that sea breeze. Freeze the balls off a brass monkey."

"It is November."

"I it is but same in summer. I'll tell tha that for nowt."

"It's a break though."

"I that it is. You ever had fish and chips with skin still on the fish?"

"Can't say I have." Steve was staring straight ahead at the conveyor. His tea was sweeter than normal. I managed to empty the contents beside me without him noticing.

"Missus was getting a little bored. Littlun scriking most of the time. Took her out for the day up coast. Place called Bridlington. That's where we had the fish with skin on. It war bostin." Steve turned towards me. Nodding towards my now empty plastic cup. "Nother?"

"No thanks mate. Need to keep moving. Where you off to tonight?"

"Stopping ere. Noon shift reported a bad stitching. Asked to keep an eye on it. Hoping to see it through to weekend. Planning to change a hundred metres too directly behind the stitching."

"That explains the roll back of the loop."

"Fuckin ell Mick. Nothin gets passed you." Steve began to laugh.

"Fuck off ye cheeky cunt. I'll see you later. Oh, what about manriding?"

"You don't honestly think if we suspend riding it'll make any difference? Lads walking up a one in four!"

"True but…."

"I'll keep an eye on it. Gets any worse, you'll be first to know."

"Good lad see you later."

The cold intake air hit me as soon as I left the sub-station. Pleased I had my Donkey jacket on. Stepping over the now moving haulage rope, I began walking inbye alongside the conveyor. Piled high with the black stuff. The subdued sound of the belt stitching clearly heard as they passed over each top roller. Shining my lamp ahead the ever-present haze of fine dust particles caught in the beam. I wasn't planning to go too far tonight. Mr Keech had insisted we get at least a hundred skips up. I'd need to be out handy to put some pressure on the shaftsmen. Before I knew it, I'd reached W11's. Coal was pouring off the maingate conveyor. The sound of coal smashing into the chute. I went across to have a look. I'd heard Frankie Glow had made some alterations. The new chute designed to allow the flow of coal to sweep around onto the Access conveyor. There was a big push to provide "lump" coal for the domestic market. Shining my lamp up towards the roof beams. The steel RSJ's looking as new as they day we'd positioned them. The corrugated steel sheets too. No movement at all. Pleased I'd insisted we'd completed the roof bolting as was required and the packing.

Allowing myself a moment to reminisce. It only seemed like yesterday I'd arrived at Parkside. This had been my first job as a Shotfirer. That was over three years ago, I'd become restless. Applying for positions all over the country. The last one in Nottinghamshire. I was convinced I'd get an interview for one of the Undermanager's jobs in the Western Area end of the month.

I moved across into the gateroad. Extracting my tin of snuff. While partaking I decided I would go onto the face. We'd been asked to get two shears off. Then extend the Pantechnicon. After last month's fuck up, I wanted to be there this time. Snuff taken I continued inbye. For a gate road it too was standing well. The Dosco SL120 had done a great job, carving out the profile for 16 x 17 steel arches, showing no signs of weight. The mesh panels holding back the dirt above the crowns. Smatterings of stonedust lay in the wells of the arch. More pronounced on the legs. The crowns always difficult, no matter how tall you were.

JW had ensured the place looked immaculate. It had been the show piece for the pit being its first heavy duty installation. I felt the change in temperature as I reached the drive. I knelt. Peering under the base. I wasn't disappointed, spotless. The neoprene wipers looking as new as the day they were installed The loop too, running true. The place had been operational now for almost twelve months. The second of the heavy duty faces S31 had kicked in during the summer. Parkside was finally down to two coal faces and just over one thousand men. As Mr Keech had predicted when I first joined.

I continued inbye against the forty-two-inch conveyor. Occasionally shining my lamp along its line. Straight as a die. The black stuff piled high. There wasn't a more pleasing sight. This was the standard I'd need to aim for when I became an Undermanager. I knew I would. It had been my ambition the first time I'd seen the guy at Bold Colliery in his white Donkey jacket.

Switching my gaze to the left. Manholes with the reflective labels clear to see along the length. Each perfectly constructed. The haulage track, level as the day it was laid. No problems with floor lift in the Wigan Four Feet unlike that in the Lower Florida. Ahead I spotted the change in height of the road. The outline of transparent plastic containers across the width of the road. It was the first place they'd decided the try out the latest development for containing the flammability of coal dust. The water barrier. I was yet to be convinced. They may have been quicker to install, however the stonedust barrier ensured the constant supply of stonedust into the district. Avoiding the usual panic when a visit was announced.

I was distracted as the haulage rope began to move outbye. Bennie had mentioned to me at shift changeover. The armoured three point three KV cable was on a run in first thing along with a half cut mine car of emulsifying oil.

In the distance I spotted a light walking towards me. It was the engine driver. The Pikrose currently being operated by one of the lads off the Access haulage. He must have followed me down the Access road.

"Alright Mick cock."

"Hiya fella. All good?"

"Yeah, finished off loading. Assisted sparkie hangin it too. Just watch yourself. We'll be on our way back in with belt structure for the move in."

"Will do."

It wasn't long before I saw two stationary lights heading towards me.

"Mick's on his way in." A voiced shouted out from the tannoy just ahead of me. Warning given I watched in amusement as the lights ahead jumped off the empty vehicles. I guessed they'd been sat on the cable carrier. The embarrassed smiling faces confirmed my suspicion's.

"Alreyt Mick."

"Yeah, I am thanks lads. You two must be fucked with all the walking up and down you're having to do."

"Get used to it Mick cock. You do." The smaller of the two responded still smiling.

"Mind how you go." I'd decided to let it go. They'd done well in getting the armoured cable offloaded and hung in the time. The smell of the intake air changed as I continued inbye. Looking to my left I could see why. The grey, white fabric packing bags now replacing the coal sides. I must have passed the face start line. The aroma of Tekpak now added to that of the extracted coal. The sound of the conveyor belt and the stitching's passing over the top rollers causing me to now direct my attention to the belt. The mound of black stuff had reduced. I guess the machine had reached the tailgate. The plan was to complete the bi-di and put the machine in cut ready for the dayshift. I'd agreed that with Charles, the Face Overman.

I'd almost reached the Pantechnicon. The maingate belt was still running, stageloader now silent. "Hello Mick. Hello Mick Gibson." I thought things were going too well. I reached across to the tannoy.

"Hiya Chris. Mick ere."

"Steve's, just bin on. That stitching he's been keeping an eye on has gotten worse. He's wants you to have a look. Thinks it should be done." I didn't respond immediately. If we'd finished cutting in here and S31's continued into the bunker it seemed the correct course of action.

"Chris let me just check with Charles position ere. Any idea situation in S31's?"

"Yeah. Completed two, waiting for pack to go off at tailend before goin in again."

"Okay, tell Steve I'll take his word for it. Prep for doing it. I'll be with him shortly. Tell him to get the haulage lads to assist. Make sure we clear the belts of coal."

"Will do." Things weren't too bad. Change to the plan but heh these things happen.

I continued down to the stageloader. The temperature had increased once more. I could feel the first sign of perspiration running down my chest. The distinct smell of emulsifying oil adding to the surrounding odour of my body. I didn't recognise the operator.

"Any idea where Charles is?"

"Last time we spoke he was with the shearer." No surprises there. One of Charles's many positives was to keep pushing the cutter men. I reached towards the face DAC. Before I had chance to utter a word.

"Hello Mick. Hello Mick Gibson." I turned back towards the outbye tannoy.

"Chris, Mick ere."

"Mick you're not going to believe this." I shook my head waiting for the follow up. "V belt is broke."

"For fucks sake." I shouted out to no one in particular. I had my head down against the tannoy. At the same time slamming my fist against the control panel. The poor bastard operator shit himself jumping back at my profanity. Don't think he'd ever seen me before. Collecting my thoughts together, giving myself a moment to think. I reached back towards the tannoy.

"Chris anyone injured?"

"No, first thing I asked, Steve's checked."

"Tell him I'm on my way out. I'll bring some of the face lads with me. I'm guessing the belts were still full of coal."

"I'll check but think you're right."

"Can you let 31's know. I'll update Charles. Also, can you ask Steve to get the role of new belt ready. May as well change that whilst we're stopped."

"Should I let JW know?" This was something the Manager insisted on. Any stoppage I was to let the Undermanager and Deputy Manager know. I checked my watch. Just turned half four. It was probably a waste of time anyway. JW very rarely answered his phone out of hours. If he did, his stock answer was "You're in charge, get it sorted." Which in hindsight always seemed a fair answer. Not sure how he managed the Manager though. Don't think John Meriden would have got away with it. Mr Keech was normally in for six anyway.

"Nah leave it for now let me weigh the situation up first. Any update on the shaftsmen?"

"Yeah, cleared the shaft half an hour ago. Twenty skips so far." Well at least that was something.

Having updated Charles, I grabbed my jacket and headed outbye the facemen would follow. As we suspected the trunk conveyor was fully loaded with coal. I began to head up the one in four brew. The cold intake air causing me to shiver, my chest still wet from earlier. If I hadn't been informed, other than the belt being stopped everything looked normal. About half way up however the concertinaed belt told me otherwise. Piles of coal lying either side of the conveyor. I spotted a light ahead coming towards me. It was Steve.

"How many men have you got coming out Mick?"

"Six facemen. More if required."

"Make sure they've all got shovels. I'll need the whole belt cleaning off."

"Why not just clear the concertinaed area."

"That'll need doing too. Going to have to use the haulage rope to pull the top belt as we feed the new belt in. Too much weight if we leave coal on"

"You doing that back of the loop?"

"I wish. Going to have fetch the hundred metre role." He pointed towards the conveyor. "Probably about here. Suspend it over the conveyor and use the drive to feed it in. Whilst at the same time use haulage rope to pull the belt up brew trying to keep the tension on. Once the new belt is in, need to clamp the existing. Make off either end and couple up."

"Sounds a piece of cake."

"I wish."

"You know what I'm going to ask next?"

"Sure. How long?"

"Yep."

"If you stop askin me questions with a fair wind I reckon a couple of hours."

"What if we don't put the hundred metres in? Just couple back up."

Steve walked across to the conveyor, placing his hand on the top belt. "See for yourself Mick. It's worse than I thought. Like tissue paper. I couldn't guarantee how long a new stitching would last." I followed him over. I could see the numerous patches of exposed weaving where the top skin had worn away. It was a simple decision to take.

"Okay fella. All yours." Pit beltmen were something different. Most days they spent their time just keeping an eye on things. I know some management questioned why we needed them. It was occasions like this were they came into their own. These were the guys you'd need alongside you when such a calamity arose. I could never get my head round where and when they trained for such incidents. Learning form the "old hands" or as some well-paid fuckin consultant had come up with "on the job training."

I left Steve to his own devices. He'd shout me if anything were required. My job now was to ensure he had the assistance required to complete the job. I contacted the control room to confirm the various activities in the other districts. S31's would add additional belt to the loop. On the coalface, picks required changing on the shearer. In both gates extending the water and compressed air.

The developments too various bits of back up work they could do too. I cancelled all overtime other than those working on the belt repair.

As Charles and his team were the nearest, I arranged two additional men to fetch out two sets of pull-lifts to assist with the roll of belt and confirmed those men already on the way out were carrying shovels. Charles had the forethought to send the Chargeman with those coming out to clear the belt. He was an ex-beltman. I watched as several lights appeared inbye climbing onto the belt. The Access haulage rope too began to move inbye. There was nothing else for me to do other than grab a shovel and start clearing the belt.

I'd already decided to stay on the job. Little point heading out and facing a series of questions when I could give more accurate answers being there. Checking my watch, it was now almost six. The belt was now cleaned off. A lashing chain secured around several chockwood pieces on the top belt the other end attached to the haulage rope. We'd have to reposition the lashing chain each time we reached a rope pulley. The new role of belt had been stitched one end, having used the belt clamp to square it off. We'd have to arrange vulcanising for another day. The smell of new belt filled the air.

Steve had left one of the haulage lads to manually start and stop the belt. Having given him clear instruction to watch the fluid coupling. The last thing we need was to blow that. A fitter was on hand in case. The whole exercise went like clockwork.

"Hello Mick. Hello Mick Gibson."

"Hiya Sidney, Mick here." Chris was now off shift. Dayshift were on their way in.

"I've got Mr Keech here. Can you give him a call?"

"Sorry Sidney. I'm nowhere near a phone at the moment." The Deputy Manager was in the control room as I heard his voice.

"Aye up Mick. What's latest?"

"Most of the new belt is in. Reckon another half hour we'll be coupling up." I turned to Steve he was busy completing the last stitch. He turned to me and nodded. Mouthing the words *probably less.*

"So, you'll be ready for dayshift."

"Yeah." I looked inbye at the piles of coal that now littered the area either side of the belt. "Could do with some men to clear the coal where we've cleaned off."

"Cayle's already arranged to send some of his lads in from Mid- Area. You on your way out now?"

"Yeah, shouldn't be long." There was no way I was going anywhere until we were up and running. I don't think Mr Keech would have expected anything less.

276

☐ I wasn't sure what it was that woke me. I lay there for a few minutes listening to the noises from outside the house. I usually slept with the windows open. I'd always been a bit of a fresh air fiend. Summer was almost at an end. We'd had some decent weather the last few weeks, Nothing unusual there. Something still didn't seem right. The house was quiet enough. I couldn't remember what the missus had said she was doing today. That's if she did tell me. There it was again. Like a whimper. Was it the dog? Then again, a little louder this time. I slipped out of bed as quiet as I could, walking onto the landing. I put my head over the banister. I could hear crying. I grabbed my dressing gown and continued downstairs.

"Annie you, okay?" She was sat in the back room on the couch. She turned towards me as I entered the room. The television was on. The sound turned down. Thomas The Tank Engine was talking to Edward.

"Sorry Mick, have I woken you?"

"No, you didn't. Where are the kids?"

"Next door. With Auntie Ann." Auntie Ann was the next-door neighbour.

"What's up?"

"Oh nothing." I continued into the room and sat alongside her. I placed my arm around her.

"There's got to be something up. Why are you crying?"

"Oh, nothing. You've got enough going on without me moaning."

"Darlin don't keep saying nothing. What is it?" My question came out a little louder than I would have wanted.

She turned towards me whilst at the same time removing my arm from around her shoulders. Tears flowing freely now.

"Mick I can't take anymore. I haven't got a life. It's like being a single mother all you do is work. If you're not working, you're sleeping. The kids miss their dad. I spend all day trying to keep them quiet. They can't have friends around in case they wake you. I'm a young mother I need a life." So much for there being nothing wrong. I'd opened the floodgates now. "I spend most of my time at mum's. I know I'm doing my dad's head in being there all the time."

"You can always go to mine."

"Mick, I've told you before. Your mum and dad are a waste of time. They've always got something else on."

"It won't be for much longer."

"You said that when you were on noons. Then this. I mean what comes next?"

"I get to become an Undermanager on regular days."

"Yippee doo. What does that mean? Normal hours like my friends husbands. Will it be nine till five?"

Well, she certainly had a point there. Pretty certain that would never be the case. I best save that discussion for another day. "It may not be nine to five, but it certainly won't be the unsocial hours I'm doing now. You'll see."

"You promise?"

"Yeah, I promise."

"When?" *How the fuck do I know!* "We won't have to move, will we? We've only just had the new windows put in." Good job I hadn't mentioned my previous applications. One in Yorkshire, the other in Nottingham.

"No, I'm sure it will be fine. There's at least six other local pits. In fact, the Western Area has something like sixteen pits still working." I thought it best to leave out that included North Wales, and Staffordshire. "You wait and see. Everything will turn out just right." Maybe I should have left it at that. "Have I ever let you down?"

"You don't really want me to answer that do you?" She replied laughing. The tears had now stopped.

"It's only another two nights and it's the weekend."

"Yes, not long now, can't wait. Anyway, forget that. You best get back to bed, the kids will be back shortly. I'm sorry for waking you."

"You've got nothing to be sorry for." I made a mental note to pick up some flowers from the garage on the way home tomorrow.

☐

"Hello. Yeah, what now?" It wasn't the answer I needed. "The Manager? Yeah, understood. On my way." I replaced the handset. *This is goin to go down a treat.*

"Who was it Mick?" Seven o'clock Sunday evening. Me and the missus had just sat down, having finally got the kids to sleep. Sunday night was Dallas night.

"Pit."

"On a Sunday. What did they want?" I was only half listening heading to the cupboard for my shoes.

"I'll need to go in." Mr Keech had pre-warned me some weeks previous. The annual Emergency Exercise was to take place on a weekend. I was to take part.

"You what?"

"Sorry love it's something we all have to do."

"But it's Sunday. We're supposed to be going out tomorrow."

"I'll be given Friday off instead." I wasn't sure that was true, but it sounded good. My wife came into the hallway. She had her angry face on.

"You're working five nights a week and now the weekend. What about us? Your family. All it seems to be lately is pit, pit, pit. I'm getting sick and tired of it."

"It'll be worth it in the long run."

"Who for? You?" She turned and went back into the room. The door slammed behind. Our dog had already retreated to her basket looking at me. I returned her stare. *Sorry old girl. No late night walk tonight.*

Shoes on, I grabbed my jacket and car keys. One last thing. I walked into the kitchen to grab the last pink grapefruit in the bowl. I then realised Monday's was also shopping day. Little wonder missus Gibson was so unhappy.

Opening the door to the living room gently I popped my head in. "I'll make it up to you." She was staring at the telly. "I reckon Bobby will survive. There's no way they'd kill off a Ewing." It was perhaps not the best thing to say as a slipper came hurtling towards me. Time to go.

The motorway had been empty. Although now dark I could see the outline of the new Ikea store almost complete. There seemed to be some activity on the airbase too. A large articulated wagon was heading towards one of the hangers. Within fifteen minutes I was driving into the car park. Fairly empty and not unexpected. I headed straight to the control room.

Both Steve and Chris were on shift. The biggest surprise was seeing Don Gold sat there. "Evening all." I didn't receive an answer immediately everyone seemed a little subdued.

"Evening Mick. All the men are on their way out. Should be at pit bottom by now. We lost most of the underground power at seven o'clock. Main fan is still off but the Boosters are running." Steve responded. Don hadn't said a word. All three were now looking towards me. *Wow, this is for real then. A real-life emergency exercise. Don must be the observer.* Time for me to play my part.

"Has the Manager been informed?"

"Can't get hold of him."

"Deputy Manager?"

"Away on holiday."

"Undermanager's?" The phone nearest Steve began to ring.

"Hello. Yeah, got that." He covered the mouth piece. "It's Gerry Cook. He and Jackie Flatt are at pit bottom."

"How many lads underground?

"Eight plus two electricians, two fitters, and two Deps."

"All men accounted for?"

"Think there's an electrician missing." *Fuck and I thought this was going to be easy.*

"We've got two per cent in the main return." Chris added. My first decision was whether to bring everyone up the pit. How would I do that if we had no power? One question I hadn't asked.

"Are the backup generators operational?"

"No diesel." *Fuck.* Then it dawned on me. Five minutes into the exercise and I hadn't called Boothstown. Then everything began to fall into place.

"Have we called Manweb for an update?"

"Yeah, Power should be back with us in ten minutes."

"Good. Put a call through to the Rescue Station." Out of the corner of my eye I could see Don scribbling notes. Steve grabbed the red phone. "I never got an answer to the Undermanager's being informed." The next thirty minutes passed over quickly.

"We've spoken to JW. He'll make his way in but doesn't know how long he'll be due to the roadworks on his route in." *no fuckin surprises there then"*

I turned towards Chris. "Do us a favour. Coffee, black no sugar." I grabbed the mic. "Gerry, Jackie power will be back on shortly. Rescue are on the way in." Again, I turned to Steve. He nodded to confirm. "Once power is on, we'll get your lads out. Where was the leckie last seen?"

"11's."

"The rescue lads will search for him."

"Got that Mick."

"Okay. You'll need to keep with you one man and an electrician. Once I've confirmed okay to go back in, we'll need to start a programme of degassing all the developments. Starting with W15's." I thought it a safe bet that all auxiliary ventilation would need a manual restart. Another phone began to ring.

"Mick power is back." Without warning the door to the control room opened. It was Alan the lamproom man.

"Thought you should know rescue lads have just arrived."

"Thanks Al. I'll be through shortly." I was now in the moment. To my mind this was no longer an exercise. It was for real. "You lads okay for a mo." Steve and Chris both nodded. Don was still writing. I grabbed a rescue plan from the shelf.

I headed out to the lamproom. The rescue team were waiting in the crush hall. The guy walking towards me I took to be the Captain.

"I suppose you'll be going underground regardless of this being an exercise."

"Too right son. Not come all this way for fuck all." I led him into the fitters office making use of the large desk to spread the plan. Within five minutes they were making their way to the pit top. I headed back to the control room.

Unsurprisingly the atmosphere was somewhat more relaxed. Don had stopped writing he was on the phone. I knew who he was talking too. Confirmation received when he replaced the receiver and nodded towards me.

I hung around until the rescue lads had returned to the surface. Making sure a hot drink and bacon butty was waiting for them in the canteen. Don hadn't provided any feedback. I was sure I would get that in the week ahead. By four o'clock I was heading back home. The motorway a lot busier than the previous night. Articulated wagons of various shapes and sizes heading into or out of Liverpool. I'd decided to smooth things at home by just havin a couple of hours kip and get the wife and kids over to Calderstones Park. Anything for a quiet life!

☐

The interviews for Undermanager were taking place at Staffordshire House on a Thursday. I didn't plan on wasting any rest days, so I'd worked the night before. Once parked up I headed for reception.

On entering a large sign displaying *Undermanager Interviews* directed us to a side room. There were several lads already in there. I recognised a few from college. We acknowledged one another avoiding any small talk. We were all feeling a little nervous.

We hadn't had to wait long as a guy from Industrial Relations Tom Brian entered the room. I recognised the face from Old Boston. He told us we'd shortly be called into a series of adjoining rooms to be interviewed by various Manager's. Some accompanied by a Director. There were a series of jobs on offer in the Western Area. From what I'd gleaned before the interview these included Parkside, which I assumed I'd be in with a shout. Agecroft, Bickershaw, Sutton Manor, Hem Heath, Florence, Holditch, Point of Ayr, Lea Hall, and Silverdale. Each of us attending four interview sessions a piece.

Moving into the open plan area we got the chance to see the various Manager's. Although I didn't know them personally, I recognised the faces. Alan Slant, Ron Collins, Joe Medding, Barry Chadwell, and a number of others I couldn't put a name to. Stood talking to the previous Deputy Director Evan Jacks, now Area Director was Ron Groves and Mr Creed. Off to the right stood the Areas two Assistant Directors Gordon Hillatt and Gordon Bird. I'd last met Mr Hillatt when I'd been at Cronton. He saw me and smiled.

My first interview was with the Holditch Manager Mr Collins and Mr Slant from Florence Colliery. I say interview it was more of a chat. Next up was Henry Donkinson from Silverdale, accompanied by Assistant Director Gordon Bird. Henry looked as though he hadn't changed his suit since the last time, I'd seen him. A gang of us from Poly had been to Point of Ayr to see the start of the new drift excavation. Surprisingly no interview with Mr Creed, the final interview was with Ron Groves now at Point of Ayr. Gordon Hillatt accompanied him.

"What are you planning on doing for the rest of the day?" Mr Groves asked.

"Back home to bed, I'm fucked. I was on night's last night and back in tonight." The answer seemed to go down well. Mr Groves in return giving a me a secretive wink.

Back in work that night, my mind kept playing back what I'd been asked and what I'd said in response. I guess each Manager already knew who they wanted. It was the wink I'd received from Ron Groves that had caused the greatest excitement.

Six days after the interviews I still hadn't received any feedback. I kicked myself for not asking when we would find out if we'd been successful. A note on my lamp maybe? I headed home not in the best of moods. Perhaps I'd read into it more than there was.

"Mick it's for you…The Manager!" My wife shouted. I'd just sat down for breakfast.

"Who?" *Why is the Manager phoning me at home? Both faces were coaling when I'd left. I'd made sure of that.*

"The Manager." My wife repeated as she walked into the room. She was smiling she knew when I was agitated. "The Manager for little old you."

"Boss." I listened. "Hmm sorry boss yeah." I couldn't believe what he was telling me. "Thanks Boss." The line went dead. He'd hung up.

"What did he want?"

"The interviews I attended back end of last month for an Undermanager's job seems I've been successful."

"Where?"

"Point of Ayr."

"Scotland?"

"No, North Wales."

☐

My final week had arrived. During one of my conversations with Mr Keech it seemed the Manager was taking early retirement in the not-too-distant future. I had heard from colleagues in Staffordshire something similar was happening to the Manager's at Hem Heath, Florence, and Holditch. It was the result of the Coal Board, now British Coal retiring those at Area level. They in turn bringing in their own people, many a lot younger than the existing incumbents. I sensed another reason too. From my dealings with Mr Creed, he saw Parkside as his pit. Those working there as his people. No matter how much he shouted and dished out bollockings he cared. He cared for his men. I recalled one of my earlier conversations with him. His comment about responsibility for the men's families too. Making sure fathers, sons and brothers returned home safely at the end of each shift. If I were a sceptic, I'd say he was being forced out. Not without a healthy handshake. The old school were on their way. It was time for the younger generation of Manager's. I just hoped Ron Groves at Point of Ayr hung around for a few more years.

After my final shift I went for a bath. Spending longer than usual under the steaming hot water. Standing there reminiscing. I had so many memories. Giving myself a quick dry down I headed towards the lockers.
"Now you fat Scouse bastard. Thought you'd fuck off without saying goodbye?" To my absolute delight and surprise Ged Shalla appeared.
"Well fuck me. Don Gold told me you were on the club." To confirm my statement, he held up his heavily bandaged left hand.
"Should see the other cunt." I smiled. I wouldn't have expected any other response.

Once Ged had gone, I collected my pit gear and loaded the car. My old Donkey jacket I left hanging in the locker. It was time to get my white Donkey jacket. I popped in to say my farewell's to a few colleagues including the Undermanager's. Heading up towards the Top Shunt Mr Keech was walking towards me. Already changed and in his pit gear. He and JW were off to W15's. The new coal face had been running for a matter of weeks, yet to realise its potential.
"Ay up Mick. What you after?" He asked as he exhaled his Players No 6. I wondered how many he'd smoked since I'd provided my last shift report. He seemed relaxed. *Manager must be in a good mood.*
"Just come to say goodbye to the Manager."
"Best be quick. He's got a meeting with Crosfield's shortly."
"I won't be long."
"Bit of advice Mick. Gaffer doesn't do sentiment." *No fuckin kiddin.* "Good luck." And with that he was off. His walking stick clicking on the tile floor as he headed towards the lamproom. I wondered whether I'd see him again. He'd be Mr Creed's replacement.

I knocked on the door not waiting for a response, I walked in. Mr Creed was in the process of taking a tablet. He was holding a glass of water. He turned towards me.
"What the fuck do you want?"
"Just come to say goodbye and good luck."
"You got no manners? Did I ask you to come in?"
"Oops I'm terribly sorry." I turned to walk out.

283

"Where the fuck are you going? You may as well come in." I walked towards the meeting room table and pulled out the nearest chair to his desk. "Why you wishing me good luck?" I reached inside my jacket pocket and extracted a packet of St Bruno. Placing it on his desk. He snatched it and placed it into one of the drawers.

"To what the future holds."

"Think you're the one that's going to need the luck. I've had my chance. Had a good career from it." I was a little taken aback, he was staring into space. They'd gone from angry to something else. I detected a sadness. "You lads have an uncertain future ahead. You're the ones going to need the luck." He stopped suddenly. Conscious maybe he'd said too much. "Right, time you fucked off I've got things to do."

I held my hand out. We shook. "Thank you." He didn't reply just looked me in the eye. I was sure I detected a smile. I turned and left. Almost three and a half years. I'd learnt so much in the short period of time I'd been at Parkside Colliery. So many interesting characters. I was pleased I'd made the decision to come here. It was still a relatively young pit. I might up back at some point in the future. I found it difficult to believe the Manager's comments. Yeah, sure the number of pits would reduce, the country wouldn't be so reliant on coal. I guessed the future would consist predominately of coal, gas, some nuclear and oil. For now, however, my goal had been achieved. I was to become Undermanager at North Wales last deep coal mine, Point of Ayr Colliery.

≈ The End ≈

15. Appendices

Wives and Relatives

Annie Gibson
Jamie Gibson
Lizzie Gibson
Heidi – Families pet dog

The Characters -Parkside

Manager
Patrick Creed
Deputy Manager
Len Keech
Assistant Manager
Godfrey Smooth
Secretary
Susan Worth
Nurse
Sister Chipp
Undermanager's
North - Jack Walters (JW)
Mid Area - Howard Davies / Geoff Hoffman
South – John Meriden
Assistant Undermanager
Tony Ramsbottom
Mick Gibson
Personnel Manager
Don Gold
Manager's Clerk
Frank
Electricians
Electrical Engineer – Alan Fielding
Stan Boris
Glyn Amp
Kenny
Dai Bando
Alan Volt
Mechanics
Mechanical Engineers – Mick Hobbit / Bill Maskill
Jeff Runner
Bob Black
Eric Greenland

Frankie Glow
Brian Token
Gary Gear
Overmen
Lenny Dunliffe
Little Billy
Derek Moore
Bennie Lead
Keith Williams (Wilco)
Colin Keys
Tommy Aldridge
Cayle Shelley
Stuart Bones
Sidney Large
Pete Mint
George Peters
Charles Henry
Mark Worth
Mark Bones
Mick Gibson
Deputies
Harry Roach – North West Area President, NACODS
George Thomas
Freddy Clough (The Poet)
Rob Flannagan (Bobby Bang Bang)
Alan Colley
Gerry Cook
Dan Jacks
Mick Gibson
Jackie Flatt
Billy Britain
Norman Moore
Dave Moore
Joe Kitchen
Billy Pete
Conna Michaels
Vinny
Randy Shakespeare (trainee)
Surface Foreman
Freddie Costa
Control Room
Steve

Chris
Sidney Large
L32's Face Team
Face Chargehand - Ged Shalla
Cliff Johns
Les Peat
Colin Peach
Alf Cherry
Jack Cherry
Johnny Bastard (JB)
Phil Hale
David Butt
Terry
Graham
Arthur Fanny
Bobby Lunt
Hausherr dint
Bryn
Howard
Face Chargehands
Tommy Beddows
Tommy Millett
Teddy
Beltmen
Frank
Dave (Crazy Horse)
Steve Chubb
Haulage Lads
Ronnie and Reggie
Arthur
Terry
Billy
Punchy
Shaft Onsetter / Banksmen
Karl
Billy
Stevie
Colin
Shaftsman
Randy
Baz Cutless
NUM

Frank Prince
ATC
Foreman - Nick Arnold
Cornelius
Jack
Tommy
Safety
Frank Newton
Coal Prep
Simon John
HMI
Mr Gray
Mr Van Gogh
Western Area Staff
Deputy Director – Evan Jacks
Assistant Director – Gordon Hillatt / Gordon Bird
Production Manager – Mr Derek Tuffman
Secretaries – Gladys / Penelope
Western Area Colliery Managers
Bickershaw Colliery – Barry Chadwell
Florence Colliery – Alan Slant
Holditch Colliery – Ron Collins
Lea Hall Colliery – Joe Medding
Point of Ayr Colliery – Ron Groves
Silverdale Colliery – Henry Donkinson
Staff Training
Malcolm Hughes
Mike Penny

The Characters - Cronton Colliery

Manager
Ron Groves
Undermanager
Dennis Hale
Deputies
Harry
NACODS Union Reps
Harry Roach
Shaun Galway– Branch President
Norman Thomas– Branch Treasurer
Keith
Frank

Platty
NUM
Johnny Helsby
Brian
Alan
Tommy Hanley

Miners
Tony Ivor
Tommy Harris
Pete Digby
Tommy Oldcroft
Johnny Bucket
Manager's Clerk
Tommy

Lancashire / Cannock Dialect

Alreyt / Awlreet – okay / correct
Alsithy – see you later
Assthagorttegivies
Ast - have
Beltin – great
Bloawke – bloke / person
Caunt – can't
Clammin / Clemt - hungry
Cewd / Cowd – cold
Cum on willyer
Cut – canal
Dayna – don't want to
Dowya – don't you
Do you want owt or nowt
Dyowannacupataye – do you want a cup of tea
Ey up cocker
Feart – feared
Gonna – going to
Jackbit / Snap - lunch
Lether / Lobby gobbler – person from Leigh
Mon – man / person
Moidered - pester
Nowt - nothing
O-reet – okay

Owsi goein me ole shoe – how's it goin fella?
Owzthisel – how are you.
Ow-zee-no – how does he know?
Rayow – are you
Reet - right
Skin full – belly full (ale)
Skriking – crying
Spayke - speak
Speyk - speak
Suppin – drink
Tharis – that is
Tharaye – that ain't
Tow - too
Up yonder – over there
Wheramya – where are you
Woolly back – person outside of Liverpool
Yo aurite – you, okay?
Yode – you would
Yoe – you
Yon – there/that

Glossary

Advance Coal Face – The long face of the seam extracting all of the coal, accessed through an intake and return. The roads servicing the face are maintained.
AFC – Armoured Face Conveyor.
Airlock – Area between a set of airdoors separating intake from return air.
Alighting Station – Platform to allow riders to disembark from a manriding conveyor or locomotive carriage.
Armoured Face Conveyor (AFC) – Means of transporting coal off the coal face.
Anderson Shearer Loader (ASL) – Coal cutting machine used on the coal face.
Arch – Free standing steel support (arched or square work).
Aspirator Bulb – Used to take samples of methane
ATC – Associated Tunnelling Company
Auxiliary Fan – Ventilation fan. Used to force air into a heading or exhaust air out.
BACM – British Association of Colliery Management.
Bagging – Ventilation duct. Flat or ribbed (used for exhaust fans)
Banjack – Holman percussive drill on extendable leg.

Banksman- Competent person for the purpose of receiving and transmitting signals at the top of the shaft.

Baths – Showers.

BC – British Coal.

Beethoven 100 Shot – Type of exploder.

Belt Structure – top rollers / bottom rollers / stand / side irons.

Bi Di – Bidirectional – reference to shearer cutting in both directions

Blackdamp – Mixture of excess carbon dioxide and nitrogen

Boarding Station – Area used to access a manrider (loco, conveyor etc.)

Booster Fan – as the name implies used to boost the existing air current provided by the main fan.

Bretby – Cable handler running in spill plate on the coal face.

Buttress Chock – Face support between line chocks and packhole

Canary - Bird

Caunch / Kench – Extracted strata above a coal seam to create a roadway.

Cage – Lift / Means of travelling the shaft. Covered in completely at the top, closed in at the two sides to prevent persons or things projecting beyond the sides. Suitable gates at each end with a rigid steel bar easily reached by all persons in it.

Calcium Chloride crystals – used for consolidating floor dust.

Capex – Capital Expenditure.

1st Class (Manager's) Certificate of Competency – a certificate issued by the Health and Safety Executive on behalf of the Mining Qualifications Board. Under subsection (1) of section 147 of the Mines and Quarries Act 1954. Valid with respect to mines of coal, stratified ironstone, shale, or fireclay.

Cap lamp – Battery operated lamp attached to helmet.

Carlton – Make of pipe, typically 6" used for supplying compressed air and/or 3" for pumping out mine water.

CEGB – Central Electricity Generating Board

Chew – tobacco.

Chock – Powered Support

Chock Fitter – Fitter on coal face providing maintenance on powered supports.

Chock Stack – means of support using chock wood.

Chock Wood – Timber – generally 6" x 6" x 2 or 3 feet long.

Cleat – the natural jointing in a coal seam. The direction in which it is very pronounced is known as the **Face Cleat**. Joints at right angles to this are known as the **End Cleat**.

Clevis – Attachment fitted to the pushover ram on a powered support. Used to connect to the spill plate

Clobber – pit gear / workwear

Club - sick

Cock/Cocker – person (typical Lancashire expression).

Colzalene – Relighter fluid for oil lamps

Cost/GJ – Cost of producing coal.

Collier – Faceworker.

Contraband – Any cigar or cigarette, any pipe or other contrivance for smoking or any match or mechanical lighter.

Cowl – Semi-circular metal guard surrounding the cutting disc of a shearer.

Crombouke – coal seam.

Crosscut – Connecting road between an intake and return road.

Cross Measure Drift – any drift driven otherwise than in coal or for the purpose of getting coal.

CRP – Colliery Review Procedure – consisted of three stages, Pit Review / Area Review / National Review.

Crush Hall – Area where men gather to fill water bottles before entering the lamproom.

Crust -Wage.

Crut – Cross Measures Drift / Tunnel

Cunt – Term of endearment.

DAC – Tannoy / means of underground communication on coal face.

DERDS – Double Ended Ranger Drum Shearer.

Detaching Gear – Attached to the shaft cage. Allows the cage to be detached during an overwind.

Development – Tunnel / Roadway.

Deputy Official of the mine, appointed by the Manager to be in charge of a district. To have charge of all workmen in that district and all operations carried out by them therein. To secure the safety and health of those said workmen.

District – underground area of the mine delineated on a plan.

Donkey jacket – Workwear warm jacket.

Downbank - Downhill

Dowty Prop – single hydraulic support.

Dripper – water

FAB – Fresh Air Base not to be confused with Fully Acknowledged Broadcast FAB as used in Thunderbirds.

Face conveyor – AFC.

Face Sprag – Hydraulic ram attached to a chock's canopy.

Fall Up / Fell Up – roof fall.

Family Pit – generally employing smaller workforce than the larger pits where most men working there are related.

Firedamp – Methane.

Fishplates – Mean of connecting steel rails.

Flame Safety Lamp (Oil Lamp) – Originally designed to provide a safe means of underground illumination. Thereafter replaced by electric cap lamps. Primarily used for testing the general body of the mine air. Officials and

Workmen's Inspectors lamps have a self-contained relighter device. This allows the injection, for gas testing purposes, of samples of mine air collected by means of a bulb.

Floor Lift (Heave) -

Free Standing Support – Steel support arch / square work.

Gaffer – Manager / Boss.

Gate End – End of the coal face.

Gate Conveyor – conveyor leading to/from the coal face

GB – General Body

GJ – Gigajoule – measurement of energy consumption.

Gnat's cock – short distance.

Goaf (Waste / Gob) – Area behind coal face after coal extracted.

Gobbin – Spit.

Greenline – signalling cable

Hardstop – plaster.

Haulage Chain - Heavy duty chain running the full length of the coal face to allow the shearer to haul itself along.

Heavy-Duty Coal Face Equipment - term applied to powered supports (fitted with lemniscate linkage)/AFC (minimum design life of three million tonnes, increase size of pans, motors and gearbox)/ shearer (rated power in excess of 230 Kw)

HMI – Her Majesty's Inspector – Mine's inspector appointed by HSE.

Hessian Bag – Sandbag – generally used for packing/support of roof at gate ends.

Holman – Percussive drilling machine. Generally attached to an extendable leg support.

Horseheads – RSJ used to support roof beams.

Huck bolts – Replacement for nut and bolt used to attached lengths of face chain / stageloader.

Inbye – Tunnels / roads leading away from pit bottom.

Ince Six Feet – coal seam.

Intrinsically Safe – Equipment and wiring incapable of releasing sufficient electrical or thermal energy to cause ignition of hazardous atmosphere (methane) in its most easily ignited concentration (5% to 15%)

Job and Knock – Used to describe a set task. Once complete team return to surface.

Jolly – Holiday.

Junction – Landing – place where two or more roads meet.

Keps – Means of supporting cage when at rest.

Kibble – Small manriding cage attached to a steel rope.

Lagging Board – means of cover between roadway supports (arches and square work)

Landing - Junction

Lashing chain – metal chain with hook. Used for pulling vehicles underground by attaching to a steel rope.

Leckie – Electrician

Leyther – Person from Leigh (Lancashire)

Lid – small piece of timber used to secure wooden prop / chock stack

Lifting Station – Area identified for use of lifting gear.

Loadbinder – Means of securing a load to a vehicle.

Locomotive – Train (usually diesel operated).

Longwall Mining – Using the advance or retreat method as against Room and Pillar (Pillar and Stall).

Lower Florida – coal seam.

Maingate – Intake road to the coal face.

Manhole (Refuge Hole) – Provided along lengths of haulage road to protect persons from moving vehicles.

Manriding Station- point at which men would board manriding carriages for transport.

Meeting Station – Area identified at the entrance to a Deputy's District.

Mesh – Welded wire mesh panel.

Methane – Explosive Gas see also known as Firedamp.

Methanometer – instrument to measure % of methane

ME12 -Type of exploder (up to 12 shots).

Mine – A place for the purpose of extracting mineral carried out by the employment of persons below ground. Includes surface land, buildings, structures and works surrounding or adjacent to the shaft or outlet in connection with the working of the mine.

MINOS -Mine Operating System.

Mini Hydrack – Methane boring machine.

Miss-fire – After firing a round of shots and during the examination shots are found failed to explode.

Mudstone - fine grained sedimentary rock

NACODS - National Association of Colliery Overmen and Deputies.

NCB – National Coal Board.

NUM – National Union of Mineworkers.

Onsetter – Competent person in attendance at the entrance of a shaft to receive and transmit signals when any person is raised.

Outbye – Area away from the coal face towards pit bottom.

Overman – Person superior to a Deputy but inferior to an Undermanager.

P1 – Type of explosive typically used in stone / cross measure drifts.

P4/5 – Type of explosive typically used in coal.

Pack – Used to support the area adjacent to the main gate of a coal face. Typically using paper or hessian sacks filled with waste material. In more recent times man made bag filled with concrete type material.

Packhole Chock – Coal face support alongside pack area.

Pantechnicon – A series of rail mounted vehicles typically carrying electrical panels, cables, hydraulic tank, and pump for powering face supports.

Pantograph – Means by which current is collected from contact wires.

Panel Train – Electrical panels on rails as above.

Panels – Used to provide electrical power for underground equipment.

PHB – Pit Head Baths (soap)

Pigtails – Means of connecting wooden or metal sleepers to rails/means of suspending signalling cable

Pikrose hauler – Winch equipped with a steel rope for transporting equipment/material underground.

Pinch – An amount taken as in snuff.

Pit Bottom – Area at the bottom of the shaft.

Pit Top – Area at the top of the shaft.

PLA – Power Loader Agreement.

£/GJ – Cost measure to produce a unit of energy.

Powered Support – Hydraulic prop mechanism to support the coal face.

PPE – Personal Protective Equipment.

PPM – Parts per million.

Pull Lifts – Lifting Device.

Pushover – Term used to describe the movement of the AFC on a coal face, generally after the shearer has extracted coal.

Ramming stick – Wooden rod used to position sticks of explosive and ramming material into a drilled shot hole.

RCM – Routine Condition Monitoring

Rest Day – Days leave / Holiday

Retreat Coal Face - Driving parallel roadways to the proposed extent of working, thereafter the coal face was driven between them. Coal was then worked coming outbye, as opposed to going inbye which was normal (advance coal face). While this system involved major expenditure in driving the gates before any coal was removed, it had the advantage of identifying unexpected faults, seam thinning etc. It also removed the need for ripping, and left the goaf behind, reducing the risk of heatings.

Return gate – A tunnel typically leading from the coal face towards the outbye district.

Ribside – opposite to faceside.

Rip – Extracted strata above a roadway. Usually where the free-standing support has been distorted.

Roof Bolt – Steel or wood of various lengths. Used to provide additional support to unstable ground.

Ropeman – Person employed to splice steel rope on haulage system.

RSJ – Rolled Steel Joist.

Rowhurst – Coal Seam

Scorrick – Small portion.

Scour – Drivage through the waste

SERD – Single Ended Ranger Drum Shearer.

Shaft – Link between pit top and pit bottom.

Shear – Length of coal cut on a longwall face.

Shearing – Cutting on a coal face.

Shunt – Length of rail used for storing vehicles for storing supplies.

Side Ranters – RSJ used to support legs whilst being secured to cross beam.

Sleeper – Support for rails. Usually spaced one metre apart.

Seam – Band of coal.

Self-Rescuer – Respirator to protect against carbon monoxide.

Schaeffler – Type of Exploder.

Shift – seven and quarter hours

Snap – Lunch, Bait. Grapefruit.

Snicket – Small tunnel at the return end of a retreat coal face.

Snurcher / Snurch – inhalation of snuff up nostrils

Spalling – Falling mineral (typically coal).

Sparkie (Leckie) – Electrician.

Spill Plate – Attached to a pan (typically AFC) main use for carrying cables.

Stable – Accommodation for horses / An area at maingate end of a coal face. Created by drill and fire technique in place of a Bi Di.

Stemming rod – Wooden pole used to place explosive to the back of a drilled hole. Followed by packing material.

Shearer – Type of cutting machine used on coal face to extract coal.

Siltstone - sedimentary rock

Square work – Free standing steel support.

Stageloader – Chain conveyor positioned perpendicular to AFC. Used to transport coal onto maingate conveyor.

Stint – work area on a hand filled coal face. An amount of work carried out.

Stitching machine – device used for applying fasteners to lengths of conveyor belt

Stonedust – Limestone dust.

Stonedust Barrier – classed as either heavy or light. In the event of a methane explosion the discharged dust mixes with coal dust to avoid its ignition. Coal dust explosion is more violent than methane explosion.

Strut – metal bar (flat or tubular) to attach adjacent free standing steel supports to one another.

Tailgate – Return end of the coal face.

Tekpack – combinations of Tekcem and Tekbent used a packing material at maingate end of coal face.

Tekbent – Bentonite

Tekcem – Cement

The Boat – Tuxedo Princess (nightclub on the River Tyne)

The Searcher – Person appointed to search for contraband.

Tie Bar – See strut.

Tins – corrugated steel sheets used for cover between the free-standing support.

Tirfor – lifting / pulling device.

Top Shunt – Manager's office.

Transfer Point – point at which one belt conveyor loads on to another.

Transformer / Trannie – electrical device taking high voltage electricity with a small current and changing it to low voltage electricity with a large current or vice versa.

Traveller – person accompanying a Deputy usually on overtime.

Trunk Conveyor – Coal carrying conveyors outbye of the coal face.

Tunnel (Roadway) – Extracted area of ground used to access coal seams.

Twat – Term of endearment.

Undermanager – Person appointed by the Owner of the Mine and providing daily supervision of persons working in the mine. Every part of the mine worked must be under the jurisdiction of an Undermanager and supervise all operations.

Upbank – Uphill

Uplift – Often used in relation to floor heave

Victaulic – make of pipe, typically 3" used for supplying water (firefighting range)

Vulcanise – means of joining lengths of conveyor belt. As against using mechanical stitching. Two ends fused together.

Waste (Goaf / Gob) – Area behind the coal face after coal has been extracted.

Wanker – Term of Endearment.

Wet Note – A chit of paper issued by the Deputy allowing a person to ride the shaft fifteen minutes before the end of shift.

Wigan Four Feet – coal seam.

Winder - Person operating the engine transporting the men up and down the shaft in the cage.

Wint Hole – Short tunnel driven in coal to access retreat face to improve ventilation over top motor.

Workwear – underground clothing provided by the NCB. Generally consisting of overalls (boiler suit), underpants and vest.

Parkside Colliery Coal Faces 1984-1987*

Face	Start Date	Finish Date
L30	February 1981	November 1985
W6	July 1983	September 1985
L31	September 1983	October 1985
C15	October 1983	February 1986
L32	May 1985	November 1986
W8	October 1985	September 1986
V24	October 1985	April 1986
L33	March 1986	July 1987
C16	September 1986	May 1987
W11	October 1986	January 1988
S31	July 1987	September 1989
W15	December 1987	January 1989

*Parkside Colliery- *The Birth, Life and Death of the last pit in the old Lancashire Coalfield* - Geoff Simm 1994

Parkside Colliery Saleable Tonnes 1984-1987*

Year	Tonnes	Output per Manshift (OMS)	Men On Books (MOB)
1984/5	265,868	1.49	1653
1985/6	754,781	2.3	1631
1986/7	826,058	2.82	1335
1987/8	860,014	3.62	1045

*Parkside Colliery- *The Birth, Life and Death of the last pit in the old Lancashire Coalfield* - Geoff Simm 1994

Lower Florida – including L32's*

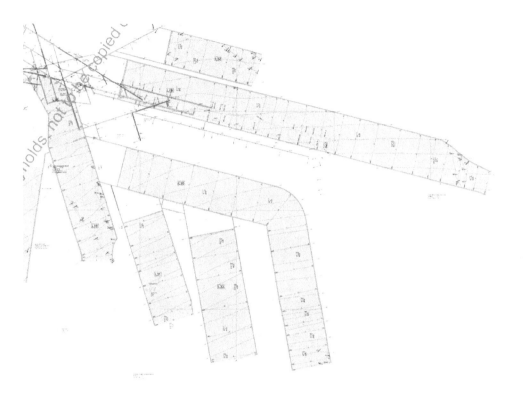

Permission to print kindly provided by Lee Reynolds

Wigan 4ft – including W11'S*

*Permission to print kindly provided by Lee Reynolds

Wigan 5' – V24's

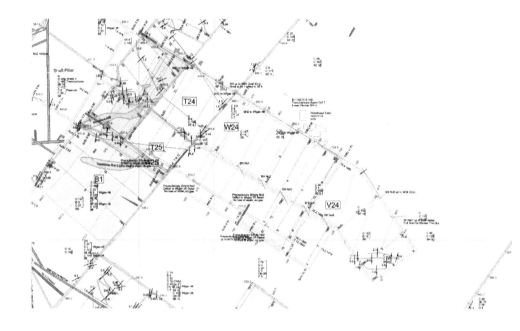

*Permission to print kindly provided by Lee Reynolds

Crombouke C15's and C16's*

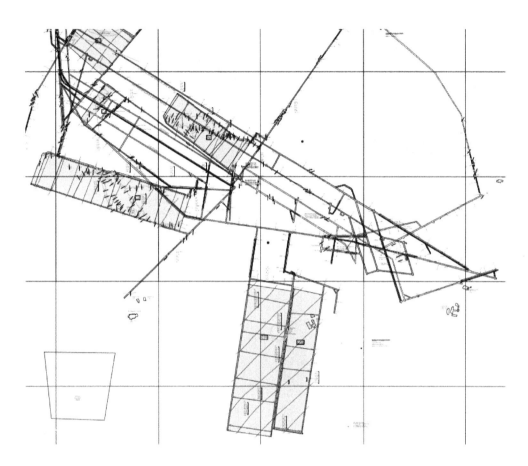

*Permission to print kindly provided by Lee Reynolds

Typical Seam Sections*

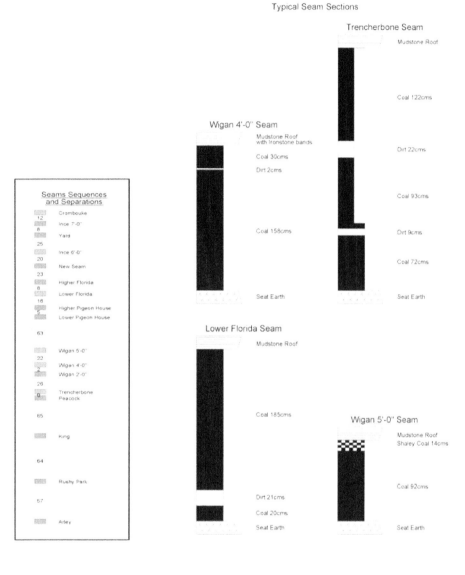

Typical Seam Sections

Trencherbone Seam
- Mudstone Roof
- Coal 122cms
- Dirt 22cms
- Coal 93cms
- Dirt 9cms
- Coal 72cms
- Seat Earth

Wigan 4'-0'' Seam
- Mudstone Roof with Ironstone bands
- Coal 30cms
- Dirt 2cms
- Coal 158cms
- Seat Earth

Seams Sequences and Separations
- Crombouke
- 12
- Ince 7'-0'
- 8
- Yard
- 25
- Ince 6'-0'
- 20
- New Seam
- 23
- Higher Florida
- 8
- Lower Florida
- 16
- Higher Pigeon House
- Lower Pigeon House
- 63
- Wigan 5'-0'
- 22
- Wigan 4'-0'
- Wigan 2'-0'
- 26
- Trencherbone
- Peacock
- 65
- King
- 64
- Rushy Park
- 57
- Arley

Lower Florida Seam
- Mudstone Roof
- Coal 185cms
- Dirt 21cms
- Coal 20cms
- Seat Earth

Wigan 5'-0'' Seam
- Mudstone Roof
- Shaley Coal 14cms
- Coal 92cms
- Seat Earth

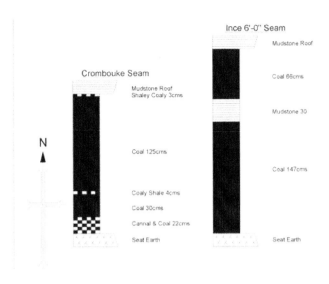

*Permission to print kindly provided by Lee Reynolds

Printed in Great Britain
by Amazon

13209630R00173